The Surrogate Proposal

A.P Harriet

ISBN: 9798335356244
Imprint: Independently published

Cover design by: Art Painter
Library of Congress Control Number: 2018675309
Printed in the United States of America

Dedicated to my beloved family and friends.

CHAPTER ONE

They all sat quietly in the soundproof room, eagerly awaiting the golden moment. The lawyer checked his watch and announced the time, but they couldn't start without him. They had been waiting for 40 minutes, but there was still no sign of him.

"Can we start already?" Theresa said, and Montserrat tapped her. "Why must everyone be here for the will to be read? I mean, we are not in the 18th century," she said.

"Why are we the only ones here?" Faith said, and Theresa gave her a scornful eye.

"We can't start without everybody present; it's what your mother requested," the lawyer said. "Only her children," he added, looking at Faith.

Ten minutes more, the door opened, and Seth walked in boldly, ignoring everybody. Tricia looked at him to register their annoyance, but he didn't spare anyone a glance.

His grandmother had died and left a will.

Mrs. Gloria Rose McGregor was a wealthy woman from a rich family who married into another affluent family. Her fortune was vast, bolstered by her ownership of a five-star rated company with branches spanning the globe. The McGregor family had a legacy of unwavering success, a tradition Gloria was determined to uphold. She loved her family and made concerted efforts to maintain its unity, but somehow it wasn't what she had hoped for. She would agree that it was partly her fault.

Gloria longed for a home filled with people, where children's laughter echoed through the hallways. It was a dream she held dear, but reality fell short. She remarried with hopes of creating this lively family atmosphere, but it wasn't the solution she had envisioned.

From her first marriage, Gloria had three children. Tragically, two of them passed away, each leaving behind one child. The third child from her first marriage never married. Her second marriage brought her two daughters. One married into a wealthy family but couldn't have children, so she adopted a child. The other daughter, a writer, married a fellow writer, and they led a quiet life together.

In summary, Gloria had five children, two of whom had passed away. She had three grandchildren, one of whom was adopted.

They were all present in the room, waiting for the will to be read. After waiting so long, the day had finally come. But Mrs. Gloria had a plan she hoped would work to bring her family together.

They sat quietly as the lawyer opened his briefcase and brought out some documents. Wetting his fingers with saliva, he flipped through the pages.

To the right of the lawyer, who sat at the head of the table, was Seth McGregor, an arrogant, willful, and business-minded billionaire— the first grandchild and only grandson. Beside him was Tricia McGregor, a top-class model and actress, and the second grandchild.

Next was Faith McKinley, the writer and youngest of Mrs. Gloria's children from her second marriage, sitting beside her husband. Maria McGregor, a former plastic surgeon and the third child, sat alone, still single.

Theresa Diego, an event planner and designer, was the fourth child. Beside her was Montserrat Diego, the adopted granddaughter and third grandchild.

The lawyer began.

They braced themselves as the lawyer began mentioning their names and relationships to Mrs. McGregor. He then listed Mrs. Gloria's shares and properties. After hours of intense listening, they finally arrived at the moment everyone had been waiting for. Some sat up, while others gripped the edges of their seats in excitement and nervousness.

"According to the late Mrs. Gloria Rose McGregor, God rest her soul," the lawyer said for the hundredth time. "She states here in her will..." He adjusted his eyeglasses to see clearly. "...that her properties and shares will go to her great-grandchildren—" He paused, expecting the reactions that immediately followed as they all shifted in surprise.

"wait...",

"what?! What do you mean?" Tricia asked.

Theresa sat up and grabbed the will from the lawyer, scanning through it furiously. She couldn't speak when she saw her mother's handwriting and her red seal on the document.

"She wrote this?" she asked, still looking at the papers.

"Sorry, ma'am," the lawyer said, gently taking the document back from her.

"So..." the lawyer continued, "her properties and shares will go to her great-grandchildren, and if by the time I die—that is, she dies," he cleared his throat and continued, "and I have no great-grandchildren, after eighteen months, let my shares and properties be given to orphanages, schools, and care homes. I only wanted my dreams to come true, even in death; I just wanted a full home. Seth," the lawyer said, looking at them.

"Seth," the lawyer said, meeting Seth's eyes and continuing. "Seth, you're a bright young man, filled with vigour and business acumen. But, my dear, work is not everything. Maybe you should consider getting yourself a wife and building a happy family. It would truly make me and your father happy, too.

Maria, my dear, you have your father's heart; you never open up to anyone, not even to your own mother. Why not try opening up to someone who's willing to listen, dear?

Tricia, dear Tricia, money isn't everything. You're nothing like your late mother, who turned your arrogant father, my son, into someone I was proud of. Look around you and welcome the people in your life. Fame shouldn't be your everything. Family is everything.

Theresa, strong like a man, I'm proud of you, but not of what you've become. Maybe it's time you mend your ways and live with the truth.

And my darling Faith, dear, I hold no grudges against you. I know you're still young, but there might be someone out there waiting for you. You have a wonderful husband; why not settle down and create a wonderful home? I expect a grandchild from you soon.

My children and grandchildren—there's nothing I want more than a happy family. If I couldn't have it while I was alive, I want to make it happen in death. Don't resent me too much. I made my mistakes, including my inability to be a mother to my children, but I don't want my children to make the same mistakes. Tell my great-grandchildren that I love them so much. Stay happy. Farewell, my dear family." He stopped.

"Is that all?" Tricia asked, looking around the room, unable to believe how the long-awaited moment had turned into a nightmare.

"For now, yes. Until the next eighteen months."

"She has always been a wicked woman," Theresa swore.

"How are we supposed to trust that our mother actually wrote this?" Maria spoke for the first time.

"This must be a joke! I am not accepting this!" Tricia stood up. "He could have forged it. Who sits in a room and reads a will? Grandmother would not do this to me!"

"Maybe you don't know her very well. The document has her handwriting and seal," Faith said.

"Maybe you planned this with your other siblings," Theresa accused.

"What? Our siblings, you mean?" Faith said, paused for a second, and looked at Maria, who looked away. "None of you were there when Mother was sick, and now all of you have gathered here for her will and..."

"Spare me. She barely cared for me, so why would I? She didn't even mention my daughter; she never saw her as her grandchild. I

7

came for what is rightfully mine, and it is just right that you planned this—the good Faith that everyone loves. Perhaps you planned this with your lovely other relatives. I see you. I watch you."

"Sit down," Maria said to Theresa. The room went quiet for just a second.

"Am I supposed to listen to you and sit, like an obedient younger sister?"

"Just sit down, Tessa," Maria repeated.

"You still know my name. That's quite surprising."

"You are not saying anything?!" Tricia said, looking at Seth,

"I believe this shouldn't be what you're doing now," the lawyer interjected, and the room fell silent. "Your mother," he said, looking at the grandchildren, "and grandmother meant every word she said, and believe me, if you can, everything is set."

They all sat there, staring at each other, their minds racing. They had expected so much, and they had made plans. The room was awkwardly silent until Faith suddenly started sobbing on her husband's shoulder.

Seth stood up and left first, followed by Theresa and her daughter, then Tricia and Maria. Faith left last with her husband and the lawyer.

They all felt disappointed. Most had spent their lives trying to impress Mrs. Gloria, but now they felt betrayed. They couldn't make any claims that the will had been tampered with because they knew their mother, and it was something she would do. Not getting what they expected wasn't their only problem, though.

Could she have known?

Their secrets?

It's not possible? She wouldn't have known.

8

Maria sat quietly in her car. She wondered if her mom knew anything. She watched Tricia walk angrily to her car and drive off. She took deep breaths, steadied herself, and took off.

Tricia felt it was the end of the line. She's been modelling all her life; she never believed she'd outgrow it at age thirty-four. She's been saving her face with the inheritance, but she received a slap across the face. How the hell is she going to make a baby in 18 months?!

Does it even make sense?

She drove to the roadside and held her trembling hands together, trying to catch her breath. She inhaled and exhaled until her hands stopped trembling.

"I'm not giving up, not yet," she said and drove off.

Theresa and her daughter felt they had it worse. She had lost her company due to her gambling husband, the black sheep of his family. Despite him being the eldest son, they were excluded from the family's inheritance after his death. Their last hope of starting over was her mother's inheritance.

Seth's situation was different. He sat in his office, gazing out from his skyscraper. A man of singular focus, he set his priorities and followed them meticulously. Wealthy enough, he admired his grandmother, who was his role model for power and financial control. If he could secure her inheritance, it would elevate his standing in the financial world and expand his influence globally. Taking over his grandmother's companies in other countries could help him realise his dreams.

But what now? Great-grandchildren?

He crossed his legs, pondering.

Inheriting all of it, or at least half of it, would make him one of the richest men in the world. As the only grandson, he felt entitled to it. The thrill of the potential power surge excited him for a few seconds.

What the hell was she thinking?

He fumed, trying to recall the last time he saw his grandmother. Even at 90, she had been strong and clear-minded. She had raised him, and he had been with her until her last moments. Why make things so complicated? He had proved himself worthy. He had expected her to leave him more.

He stood up, staring out through his skyscraper window. Tricia couldn't manage it, Maria was unmarried, Montserrat was adopted, and Faith wouldn't be interested. This leaves him very eligible to inherit it all.

But how?

He rubbed his head, trying to gather his thoughts. He needed a plan—something, anything. Adopting a child might make him seem weak; he couldn't afford to be seen as equivalent to the adopted Montserrat. He needed a strategy to ensure he wasn't pushed out.

He left the office and headed to the bar to meet his friend. Liam had been his friend since childhood and was now his business partner. Liam inherited five-star hotels across the globe, had a rich background, and is also a lawyer.

Seth told him what had happened, desperately needing a quick solution.

"Well, your grandma is something else. What are you gonna do now?" Liam asked.

"Does it look like I fucking know?" Seth snapped.

"So, the inheritance is made for your children. Man, that's funny," Liam said, chuckling. "How are you gonna make a baby in... or do you want to have a baby mama?" he added, frowning.

"Do you think I have time for your jokes, Liam?" Seth said, giving him a serious look.

"Then what? I mean, what's done is done. You can't change a dead woman's will, and she made it clear what will happen if you don't meet her demand."

Seth took a deep breath, rubbing his forehead. "I don't know, man. I need this. I don't know why she made this so complicated."

"Well, I believe we know why. She knew you barely hung out or had fun. Your life is tight, and she's just trying to make it easy for you. She knew you would do anything to get the inheritance."

"What are you trying to say?"

"Okay, see, I have possible solutions for you. One, you get a wife, get her pregnant, and done. Very legit. Or you get a baby mama, still legit. Or you adopt a child—not very good. Or you get a surrogate mother—good and legit. You decide."

Seth shook his tumbler while he stared at his friend. "I can't get married," he said.

"Obviously, but why not? That's what most people do. Marry their business partners," he shrugged.

"Man, you know that's not my thing. I don't need it," he said, not liking how he sounded. Liam laughed.

"Well, see who needs it now." They chatted about it, but Seth got nothing from it.

When he got home, he thought about the options Liam had given him. He couldn't get married; he'd never had anything to do with a woman. Well, he had once, back in the day, but that was then. He'd never been interested in women, who they are, or what they do. He didn't even get to know his mom. Women shouldn't exist at all unless they had a part of his grandmother he liked.

He shoved the thought away and considered the next option. He couldn't possibly have a baby mama—what's the difference? Then it would be all over the news and papers. No way.

Adoption is not even an option.

Surrogacy? Whatever that is, to hell with it. He isn't doing it. He threw the glass of wine he was holding at the wall and stared at the shattered pieces on the floor. That's exactly how his brain feels.

Why would his grandmother do this to him?

He sat on his bed, lost in thought, for the hundredth time. He took his laptop and searched for what surrogacy means and the processes involved.

Three things caught his interest: first, he wouldn't have to stress himself over it; second, the child would have his own DNA; and third, he would only have to pay the surrogate and take his child.

How easy could it be?

That same night, he texted Liam to help him find a surrogate.

CHAPTER TWO

Regina couldn't believe the words coming out of her mother's mouth.

A recent college graduate, living with her mother while job hunting had been pure hell. Her mother's constant nagging about marriage and insignificant issues had worn her down completely. She was fed up, and her mother seemed equally weary of her.

Regina's childhood had been marred by a father who was a drunk, constantly battering their mother. After enduring this, their mother spent all they had on his operation, but he succumbed to liver disease, leaving them in debt. When they almost recovered from it, her mother brought another man into their lives—a fraudster—who plunged them into further vulnerability. Her mother had believed that having a man meant having a complete family, but it only tore them apart, and she realised that when it was already too late.

Regina's older sister, Stephanie, married into a wealthy family of lawyers while she was still a college student. They thought their family issues were behind them, but Stephanie ended up in a troubled marriage, likely due to her own greediness, Regina guessed. Stephanie had always desired the high life. She rarely visited home, seldom called, and never sent money. She had become the married girl who left home.

Then Nora, the youngest, whatever she does in college, nobody knows, because she is the favourite and the best amongst them, according to their mother.

However, when it comes to Regina, she can't really tell what her mother thinks about her, and she's done thinking her opinion matters in her life. She's been through a lot; she wasn't there when they all needed her, and she took most of the problems on her shoulders.

She regretted not listening to her friend and sticking with her part-time jobs after college. Perhaps she could have found a better opportunity by now. She felt she had never been lucky in any aspect of her life—job hunting, family background, or relationships.

Her first and only relationship with Toby had been a disaster. While he seemed genuine, he was no different from other men. He took advantage of her and left. She felt foolish for allowing it to happen, and she vowed never to get married. She wouldn't tolerate a cheating, drunken, or abusive husband like her father or stepfather.

She still doesn't get it when her mom, who's been through the first misery, gets married again to their step-father.

No matter what her mom says—no, she's not even going to allow herself to pay attention to her at all; she's never going to get married, at least not until she can stand on her own without any influence or excuses. She can't let herself become a mother like hers.

Despite everything happening in different, separate years, the experiences were enough to keep her focused and strong in her convictions, and her mother's nagging wouldn't change that.

Regina drained the last of the milk from her cup, trudged up the stairs to her room, and slammed the door to shut out her mother's voice. She collapsed into her chair, staring at the ceiling. As she turned her head, it made a cracking sound. Ignoring it, she mulled over ways to escape her home and avoid her mother for good. She had no money and nowhere to go, which was the worst part.

She'd been job hunting but faced constant rejections, either due to a lack of qualifications, the position being filled, or receiving no response at all. The thought of giving up crossed her mind, but finding a job was her only hope of leaving. Giving up meant staying with her mother forever in the tiny community, doing groceries, crocheting, attending church daily, and visiting the congregation. The idea of celebrating Christmas with the entire community horrified her.

Determined, she pulled out her job file and reviewed the list of potential employers. She crossed off several options before focusing on the last one: a bar. Her mom just won't allow any of her children to work in a bar; she said she's against it and that's all. Unless you want to leave the house, she would say. That's what you get when you have a black Christian mother. She has had experience working in a bar, but it was not pleasant.

Her phone beeped, and she lazily picked it up. Nicki had texted, inviting her out. She thanked God, got dressed, and headed downstairs.

Her mother, engrossed in her crocheting, watched her through her glasses as she walked down.

"Where are you going, Regina Rachel?" her mother asked.

"To see a friend," Regina replied, reaching for the door.

"I'm talking to you, young lady," her mother insisted. Regina stopped and faced her.

"I told you that friend of yours was no good. What will people think when they see you two together? Have you ever asked yourself that? Birds of a feather... And I didn't raise you to flock with that kind of bird," her mother lectured, glasses perched on her nose.

"Mom, I'll be back soon."

"Since you don't listen to me anymore because you're a grown lady, at least do it for yourself. No man wants a lady who keeps bad friends or works in a bar," her mother warned, returning to her crocheting.

Says someone perfect.

Regina thought and rolled her eyes. "I'll be back soon," she repeated.

"Be back early for the church programme," her mother said, not taking her eyes off the hook.

Usually, she would turn and walk back to her room; however, she slammed the door and walked down the street.

Her mother had despised Nicki ever since she was found high on drugs and alcohol, naked, with street guys one morning. She had gotten arrested and Gina had to beg her mom to help release her.

15

She, however, valued Nicki's friendship. Nicki never finished secondary school; her mother was always sick. So, she started with all kinds of jobs to buy her medications, but she succumbed to her illness. Nicki left town after her death without even saying goodbye. Gina could recall that she was in her third year at the university when Nicki came back, looking different. She had helped her with her tuition fees for the rest of the year at the university. Her mother forgot that.

Regina hailed a taxi, texting Nicki that she was on her way.

At the restaurant, Nicki waved her over, and they hugged before sitting down.

"What's up? Your facee..." Nicki said, touching Regina's cheek.

"Well, my mom, as usual," Regina said, signalling for a waitress.

"Marriage stuff?"

"Yep, and more. She's getting more annoying by the day," Regina replied as the waitress took their orders.

"So, what's up with you?" Regina asked.

"As usual, you know, leading the pack," Nicki said, and gisted her about what has been going on in the bar she now manages and how tough it has been.

"Well, enough about me; I have something for you," Nicki said with wide eyes.

"What?" Regina asked, intrigued.

"You're still looking for a job, right?"

"Yeah, of course."

"Well, I have two jobs for you," Nicki announced, but Gina paused for a second, already guessing it could be to work in her bar.

"Chill, I know what you're thinking but this is way better."

"Spill it then."

"Okay, listen," she said, lifting her two index fingers, "one job will pay you enough to stop asking your mom for money. The other can get you enough money to live your whole life in luxury and maybe even shut your mom's mouth for good," Nicki said, watching Regina's reaction.

Regina chuckled at the thought of silencing her mother. "So, what are they?"

"First, you could work as an accountant at our bar. It pays well, I'm the boss now, and you won't have to speak to any of those mofos. However, you'll make connections and friends, get bigger tips from the big guys, you know," Nicki said.

"Nicki—"

"Hold on, I'm not done. The second job is surrogacy. Hmhm, you heard me right," Nicki said, nodding.

Regina paused, then took a long sip from her cola, feeling disappointed.

"So?" Nicki asked,

"Nicks, you know I can't do either of those," she shrugged.

"Why not?" Nicki asked, annoyed. "Girl, life isn't easy; you have to give it back what it gives you to survive."

"Nicks, it's not that. I need a job badly, but I can't work at.your.bar. It's no different from staying home all day with Mom and working nights with guys ogling me. Mom won't accept that."

"Fine, but what about the other job?" Nicki asked, trying to stay calm. She sometimes wondered why she remained friends with Regina, given their different lives. Maybe it was to remind herself of her old self, or maybe she just liked Regina despite her frustrating adherence to her mother's rules. She hates her mother the most.

"I can't do it."

"Why not?"

"Nicks!"

"What? For goodness' sake, Gina, I'm not telling you to commit a crime. It's an easy job: get pregnant, have the baby, and get paid millions! Billions! Do you know who's involved?" she whispered.

"What's wrong with you?" She continued, "You won't even have sex with him. Just get pregnant. Christ! What are you afraid of? We've been through this your mom shit and all. He's a dang billionaire, Riri! Any woman would die for this chance. I thought of you the moment I got the job details." She couldn't control herself; she wasn't asking her to be like her; she just wanted her to grow up.

"I don't know. It's risky and dangerous. What do I tell my mom?"

"What's risky? What's dangerous? And the hell with your mom!" Nicki said, holding Regina's hand.

"Girl, you need to grow up. I could have taken this job or given it to one of my girls, but I chose you because you're my friend. This is your chance to leave your mom and those sh*tholes behind. You need the money; I need the money too. I always need money, but I have a friend who needs it more. Get a life, girl. Travel, do something fun, something different. Get.a.life. Not under your mom. Think it over. Tell your mom you got a job far away and do the shit; that's just it. Simple," Nicki said, her phone beeping. "See, girl, I have to go. Think about it, think so hard about it, and let me know, okay?" She pecked Regina's cheek and left.

Regina sat there, conflicted. Nicki always comes up with silly ideas, but this might as well be the silliest.

Surrogacy? Me? No way!

She wandered down the street, her mind racing. Nicki was right, but it's hard to accept. She couldn't work in that bar and wasn't desperate enough to be a surrogate for a stranger. She needs to do something about her condition but perhaps she is too scared to try anything.

I need to get a life, she thought, sighing.

Sometimes she hated that she wasn't like others, but she couldn't change that.

What's in it? Grab the chance, do the job, and live normally for once.

But she laughed, dismissing surrogacy as normal.

When was life ever normal? Is Stephanie's life normal?

Married for wealth and trapped in chaos, she distanced herself from the family. For Stephanie, they all knew she would do anything to deny she came from their family and she's the only one their mother listens to or rather, the only one that calms their mother when she starts her nagging. While she handled the hard stuff, because she is the hardworking one who takes shit and doesn't complain, Nora was the favourite, the sharp girl whom people like, the popular one who was sent to college and ended up in prostitution and drugs, though their mother doesn't know yet, but they know their secrets well enough. Though not all of it.

To their mom, Nora is her perfect, best child. If only she knew what she'd been up to.

Regina entered their street, shaking off her thoughts. She grabbed the cold iron handle and opened the door.

She froze when she saw her mother eating with Nora beside her. She stood there for a while, staring at them. She hadn't known Nora was coming home. Slowly, she approached the table and greeted her mother.

"Well, where have you been?" her mother asked without looking up from her plate.

"I told you—" Regina began to explain.

"Yes, you told me you were going to meet that godforsaken child and I told you not to attend the church programme. What now? Did she introduce you to one of her men? Melissa was at the programme. Christy is pregnant with her third child, and she came to the programme with her family, and you are out late wandering the streets with lost souls. Did you check the time, young lady? I was calling your cell, but you ignored my call," her mother said, dropping her spoon.

"I didn't ignore your call. I turned the volume down and forgot to turn it back up," Regina replied calmly, trying hard not to provoke an argument. Her mother waved her hand dismissively and continued eating.

Regina stood there, biting her lip and squeezing her hands, holding back the anger bubbling up inside her. "Nora, why are you here?" she managed to ask.

Nora got up and moved to the sink, ignoring her for a minute. Regina watched her sit back down at the dining table.

"You should've made dinner for Mom if you were going to stay out late," Nora said without looking at Gina.

Gina chuckled bitterly. "What did you say? Stay out late."

"Ain't she right? You want me to die so you can have the house to yourself, invite your friend, and turn this place into a bar," her mother said, standing up from the table.

It's only 6:25 PM! How is that late? I'm 26, for goodness' sake! Gina thought, her mouth half-open in disbelief and her hands trembling with anger.

"Nora, can you repeat that? I dare you," Gina said, turning towards Nora.

"What? You're the only one at home. You should take care of Mom, get married, or something. It's not like you're doing anything," Nora retorted.

"You slut!" Gina shouted, and before she could reach Nora, her mother walked up and slapped her across the face.

"Don't you dare say that word in my house!" her mother screamed.

20

Gina held her cheek as tears rolled down her face. She stood there for a few seconds in shock. The slap still echoed in her ears as her mother continued yelling, and Nora tried to calm her down. Unable to bear it, Gina ran upstairs to her room and burst into tears.

Nora had the nerve to tell her she didn't take care of their mother. Where were they when their father died, and she had to work part-time and attend evening school so they could all eat? She had personally raised Nora, and this was the thanks she got? And their mother supported Nora just because she sent some money?

Wiping her tears, Gina lay on the bed, staring at the ceiling. Their lives had never been normal, and they never would be. To hell with her family. Maybe it was time to live her own life without putting anyone else in it.

Surrogacy? What harm could it do?

She fell asleep with a change of heart. She had made her decision. Maybe being a surrogate was the best choice she had ever made. It was her life, and the choices were hers to make. She curled up, imagining what it would be like to be someone's surrogate, until she drifted off to sleep.

CHAPTER THREE

It was a Wednesday morning. Gina had texted Nicki the night before, after the argument with her mother and Nora, about accepting the deal, but she hadn't replied yet. After breakfast, while doing the dishes, her phone beeped—it was Nicki. A church member had visited her mom that morning, and Gina knew they would talk for hours. She took the opportunity to meet with Nicki, telling her mom she was going to buy groceries.

When she pushed the restaurant door open, she saw Nicki sitting in the corner, busy with her phone.

"Hey," Gina said as they greeted each other. She couldn't wait to get everything started.

"So, you've decided, huh? What made you change your mind?" Nicki asked, dropping her phone on the table.

"Well, I was overly motivated to leave that house," Gina said, spreading her fingers wide in the air to emphasise her point.

"Why? Did something happen?"

"Just Nora and her attitude," Gina said, "and Mom slapped me because of her."

"Wait…Nora's back? Oh girl."

"Yeah."

"Well, I'm glad you changed your mind because we almost lost the deal. I called the guy who gave me the deal this morning, and he sounded like he was no longer interested. But I told him that I'd already found someone for him, and he insisted on speaking with you," Nicki said, and Gina nodded.

Nicki wrote down his number and address on the food receipt and gave them to Gina.

"There, listen, this," she said, drawing a circle on the table with her hand, "is just a simple task. All you have to do is... nothing. He will take care of everything. Meet the guy, listen to him, get the stuff in, and in nine months, you'll be free and a millionaire."

Gina smiled as she looked at the address and number. "Thank you, Nicki."

"No, thank me later; I need to go," Nicki said, picking up her bag. "So, when are you leaving? What are you going to tell your mom?"

"That won't be a problem; I'll figure it out."

"Listen, this is the time. I'm glad you changed your mind, and you know I'm here for you."

"Yeah, sure," Gina said as Nicki stood up.

"Inform me about everything and anything, okay? I'll talk to you later," Nicki said, pecking her on the cheek before leaving.

Gina sat there, thinking about what to do next. She had to come up with a plan—a lie—to tell her mom. She looked at the time and hurried to the grocery store.

By the time she got back, her mom was on her usual sofa, crocheting. She looked at Gina through her eyeglasses.

"Was there traffic at the grocery store?" she asked.

"No, Mom," Gina said as she unloaded the groceries.

After placing the groceries in the refrigerator, she went and sat beside her mom. Her mom stopped what she was doing and stared at her.

"What happened?" she asked, studying Gina's face.

"Well, Mom, while I was buying groceries, I met an old friend's sister. That's why I took so long to get home."

"So?" her mom said, looking at her suspiciously.

"Well, we started talking, and... I told her that I was looking for a job. So...she offered me a job at her cousin's company," Gina finished, and her mom nodded.

"What's the job?" she asked.

"Well, she said it's a marketing company, a sort of import-export company. If I pass the interview, then I'll have to work as an accountant. She said I'm lucky, and the interview is on Monday next week, so I have to leave by the weekend to make it." Gina finished her lie and waited in silence.

After a few seconds, her mom asked, "Where?"

"Where what?" Gina asked, confused.

"Where is the job or company located?"

"Oh…" She hadn't thought of that. "New York," she said, and her mom dropped what she was doing.

"That's far from here!"

That's what I want. Though it's not too far, mom.

"Yes, I know, Mom, but it's worth the effort," Gina said, followed by another silence.

"Well, I don't know. You've got to talk to your sisters; see what they say."

"Mom, I don't have to tell them everything. Stephanie is busy as it is with her family. She doesn't need to think about me getting a job. It's just an official job where I have to deal with papers and such," Gina finished with a shrug.

"What are you saying? We are family. We need to know every detail about each other," her mom said before going on and on about family, God, togetherness, love, and Bible quotes.

"Alright, Mom, I'll tell them, but I need to leave by the weekend and I need to prepare for it," Gina said, getting up.

"But you've never gone that far before," her mom said, looking up at her.

That's what living in a tiny community does to you. It makes you afraid of the bigger world.

"Mom, I see this as an opportunity. I need to go out and travel and stuff in order to get married."

"Well," her mom said, curling her lips. Gina knew she had her. Her mom couldn't let herself be blamed for Gina not getting the job, and the fact that she mentioned marriage had even surprised her mom.

"Maybe you should ask Stephanie to help you out. How are you going to deal with transport, feeding, and housing?"

"I can deal with that, Mom. Somehow. So, don't worry about it. If I get the job, they might provide these things. Just pray for me to get this job."

"Yes, yes, of course, you will. For God says in Psalm 30:5 that every one of His words is flawless. He is a shield for those who take refuge in him. People will fail you, but God will never fail you. So, you will get the job."

"Amen, thanks, Mom," Gina said, surprised, and jogged up to her room, happy she had told a good enough lie.

Finally, she was going to have a breakthrough, just a few days away.

She just wished that the lie was true instead of surrogacy.

While she went through the motions of packing and preparing for her trip, Nora couldn't believe Gina was really leaving—and by the weekend, no less. That meant she would be left at home with their mom, alone. On Friday night, she went to Gina's room, where Gina was packing the last of her things.

"So, you're really leaving?" Nora asked, leaning against the wall.

"Yes, tomorrow," Gina replied.

"What did you say the job was all about again?"

"An accountant position in a marketing company, Nora," Gina said, still busy packing her box.

25

"What's the name of the company? Are you sure it's real? I've heard of people being tricked into these kinds of things. I have friends in New York who can ask around." Gina stopped packing and looked at her, annoyed.

"Well, Nora, I am sure it's legit. Thanks for caring," she said, controlling her frustration and resuming her packing.

"Then ask your friend's sister to help me get a job there too."

Gina dropped her clothes, really annoyed this time. "See, Nora, don't spoil this mood I'm in. As you can see, I'm kind of busy. Freda is my friend's sister; she's trying to help me out. I can't ask for more; she's done enough, and I've not even gotten the job yet. So, can you let me breathe?"

"All you have to say is that you don't want to. You don't need to explain."

"What?"

"Why are you getting worked up over a job you've not even gotten— if it's really an accountant job like you said?" Nora said and left.

Gina felt anger rush through her. She imagined rushing over and yanking Nora's hair, dragging her across the room. But she told herself it was just a matter of hours until she left. Nora had suddenly come back that week, claiming she was done with college, with photos of graduation and all. Their mom never doubted her; Stephanie doesn't care. Gina knew Nora was lying, but nobody would listen to her, even if she tried to prove it.

She shoved the thought away as her phone beeped—a text from the deal man. She had sent him a message explaining that she was the girl who took the deal. He sent her instructions on how and where to meet. She screenshotted the message, deleted it, and went downstairs. She joined her mom and sister at the dining table. At first, they ate quietly, but Nora decided to break the silence.

"Mom, what do you say about Regina and the job she's talking about?" Gina slowly looked at her, trying to figure out her new scheme.

"I mean, this friend's sister, out of nowhere, just decided to give you a job in this faraway place. It doesn't really make sense to me," she continued. Their mom didn't say anything; she just continued eating. Nora shrugged and continued, "I'm just saying, I've seen those kinds of things before. Fraud is everywhere. Just be careful," she said, pouring herself some water. The table went quiet again.

After dinner, their mom called them for a quick conversation.

"Well, you see," she started, "I've lived life and seen a lot, as y'all know. I might have made mistakes, but I still know where I stand, and I stand with the Lord. Y'all are grown-ups and know what's right and wrong. I married at a young age. When I met your father, I knew nothing. That's why things turned out like this, unlike the world we live in now. I'm not trying to make a long speech; I just want to say that whatever you do is upon you. The path you choose, you shall walk. When you leave tomorrow, you're taking a new path. My job now is to wish you well and pray for you. I've done my part," she concluded with stories of people who had lived good lives and so on.

Gina lay on her bed, thinking about what her mom had said. They had all been through a lot, especially their mom. Her main goal once was to make her mother happy, but things never worked out the way she wanted. Sometimes her mom could be a pain in the ass, but before that, she was her mom, and nothing would change that. She turned to the other side of the bed, trying to get enough sleep before setting out for the next day.

CHAPTER FOUR

La Luna Hotel and Suites.

Gina read the sign as the car dropped her off. From the moment she arrived at the airport to this point, she had been treated like a princess. It felt both unreal and suspicious. As soon as she got out of the car, someone came and took her luggage, and a lady ushered her inside.

Entering the hotel, she couldn't believe where she was; it felt surreal. As she was escorted to her room, she gaped at the grandeur of the place, trying to hold back her astonishment, but it was obvious. Once they entered the room and dropped off her luggage, the staff left, and she slowly pinched herself. She picked up her phone and called Nicki, but her line was busy. She hung up and walked to the window, her mouth dropping open at the sight of the beautiful city. Everything was different—the fragrance, the grandeur—it was all too much.

She bit her lip and smiled, walking around the room. She sat on the bed, running her hands over the luxurious sheets. Checking the time, she remembered that Liam had said 4 o'clock, but it was already past five in the evening. She considered texting him but decided against it. Instead, she lay down on the bed, staring up at the ceiling.

Gina heard a sound and opened her eyes. She had fallen asleep. Seeing a man standing by the bed, she jumped up immediately.

"Hi, you were asleep when I came in, so I decided to let you rest. Sorry, I'm late; I had something important to take care of," Liam said, checking his watch as he moved towards the couch.

"It's fine," she said, wiping the drool from her lips, wondering how deeply she had slept not to notice him entering the room.

Reginaa! And he came in without knocking? Did he? How did he come in? Oh, yeah, he booked the room.

She thought for a second and tried to make herself look presentable as she walked towards him.

"Thanks for the transportation and all," she said, trying to be humble. Liam looked at her, short of words for a second.

"It was nothing," he said, standing up. "I am Liam, by the way," he said, extending his hand. She took it.

"Regina," they both smiled.

"I guess you must be really hungry and stressed. I'll have them get you something," he said, pointing at her face.

"Thank you."

"Mm," he said, nodding. There was an awkward silence as he pressed his phone.

"Fine," he said, closing his phone. "I will... have someone pick you up tomorrow morning, by 10 am, okay? Feel relaxed and rest up," he said, and Gina nodded.

"Right," he said, heading for the door. He left the room, and as soon as the door closed behind him, he turned and stared at it.

He thought Gina looked too ordinary, which was kind of good, but her hair.

God!

Gina sat on the bed for a while after he left, trying to collect herself. Her head was pounding, and her stomach felt tight. She squeezed it.

"Ouch," she muttered, suddenly feeling embarrassed. She should've said something else to Liam before he left. She had a lot to ask him.

She heard a knock and went to get the door. While eating, she realised that she didn't actually know much about surrogacy. She took her time to research it. She had never thought about it before; she had seen the posters at the hospital whenever she went with her mom for checkups. She never thought something like this could be possible. It was so unbelievable. Her mom would say this was against the Lord, or messing with what God had ordained. She would call it adultery or something else, but she would be totally against it. Gina laughed a little at the thought. It sounds a bit easy but very scary. She reminded herself why she had to do it, and it all made sense again.

Early in the morning, someone came and picked her up. She was taken to a place where she boarded a private jet heading to an unknown destination. The jet landed on top of a building, and she was helped down. She was amazed but tried not to appear weird and awkward.

She was escorted to an office with a huge door. They passed through a smaller door before entering a large office, the kind she had only seen in movies. When she entered, the lady escorting her left and closed the door behind her. Two men were sitting facing each other and were too engaged in their discussion to notice her at first.

"Good morning," she greeted, breaking their conversation. She recognised one of the men; he was the one she saw at the hotel. Liam.

"Morning, Miss Regina. Sorry, come on in; have a seat," Liam said, standing up and shifting one of the seats for her to sit down in.

"Thank you," she said, sitting down. She looked at the other man sitting there. His eyes bore into her, making her feel nervous. She tried to hide her discomfort, but his gaze almost made her cry. She looked away immediately, her heart suddenly beating out of rhythm.

"Well... Regina, I hope you don't mind." Liam asked politely, waiting for Seth to introduce himself, but he didn't.

"Just call me Gina," she said, trying to maintain a smile. She pressed her hands together, trying to focus on the pain.

"Alright, Gina, this is Seth McGregor," Liam said, as if expecting her to show some sort of reaction, but she just looked at him for a second and nodded.

"Do you...know him?" he asked, looking into her face almost too comfortably.

"N-no, I don't," she answered, wondering if she had made any mistake or if perhaps Nicki was supposed to give her a heads-up but forgot to.

Liam looked at Seth and nodded. "Do you even… know where you are?" Liam asked, trying not to sound intimidating.

"New... York?" she said, and the room fell silent for a deep second.

"Uhmm, yeah. So… we all know why you're here, right?" He asked, and she nodded.

"Okay. Have you done surrogacy before?"

"No."

"Have you ever gotten pregnant before?"

Is this a job interview? I didn't prepare for this.

"No."

"Are you in any relationships?"

"No," she answered, not smiling anymore. Her stomach had already started bubbling.

Liam nodded and continued. "Virgin?"

"Sorry?" she said before she could process the question.

"Are you still...a virgin?" Liam asked, as if he were sorry to ask the question.

She looked at Seth, who sat with his hand on his lips. She shook her head, "No," she said, feeling embarrassed. Her mother thought she was still a virgin. She would pray to God to give her children good husbands because they kept their bodies sacred. Gina would feel guilty whenever she heard that, but the new world didn't care about those things anymore.

"Sorry for my questions, but they are necessary."

"It's fine," she said, trying to maintain eye contact, but her eyes kept flicking away in embarrassment.

"Does your family know you're doing this?" She looked again at Seth, who was still staring at her.

"No," she said, feeling guiltier.

"Good. So apart from you, who else knows you're here?"

For a moment, she got scared. "My friend knows, Nicki."

"Alright. Here's how this is going to work," he said, bringing out a file. "This contains our deal, our contract," he said, handing her the file. "All you have to do is go through it, sign it, play your part well, and you will get paid handsomely. I don't know why you chose to do this, but..." he shrugged.

"When you're done reading this, we'll sign it tomorrow. So you have from now until tomorrow to make up your mind whether to stay or leave. All you need to do is get pregnant, give birth, and give us the child, and you'll be paid well. Easy peasy."

She took the file. "I'll read it."

"Okay, take your time. I'll have the pilot take you back. We'll meet again tomorrow."

She nodded and stood up. She looked at Seth again before turning towards the door. Seth shifted in his seat when she left.

"What do you think?" Liam asked.

"What do I think? Seriously?" Seth said, and Liam laughed.

"I think she's okay."

"I think she is weak. I suggest you get someone else," Seth said, standing up.

"I don't think so. She looks good. She is a bit weird, but at least she doesn't look like trouble."

"No, she looks like trouble."

"You want me to change her? I don't think we can find a better candidate. Time is not on your side," Liam said, and Seth turned and looked at him.

"Fine," Seth said. As long as she gets pregnant and produces a great-grandchild for his grandmother, that's fine.

"Dinner?" Liam suggested, and they left the office together.

Gina sat on the bed, drying her hair with a towel. She grabbed the contract with one hand and walked to the couch. After a mini feast, her belly felt heavy. She opened the contract; it was only three pages long. She twisted her lips and nodded, skimming through the first sentences about the surrogacy process and the numbered items outlining her dos and don'ts.

First, she would stay in the contractor's house throughout the pregnancy, follow his instructions, and keep the pregnancy a secret among the four of them. She wondered who the fourth person was.

Nicki?

No contact with family or social media, she scoffed. She would give them the baby and walk away with the money, all ties with the baby severed. Her heart skipped a beat at the thought. No relationship with the baby whatsoever, no legal responsibilities. She stared at the sentence for a while, skimming down the page for more threatening rules. She looked for the payment amount, but it wasn't listed, only that she would be paid handsomely.

She closed the contract and dropped it on the couch. She jumped on her bed, thoughts of home crossing her mind. Why was she suddenly missing home? She picked up her phone and called her mom.

"Hello?" her sister Nora answered.

"She's alive," Nora said.

"Where's Mom?" Gina asked.

"Church."

"Oh... how is she doing?"

"Where are you? Did you get the job?" Nora asked, waiting for Gina to respond.

"Yes, I'll start work soon, though I have yet to sign the contract," she said, feeling caught when the line suddenly went quiet.

"Hello?"

"Okay," Nora said.

"Tell Mom," Gina said, but the line beeped; Nora had cut the call. Gina rolled her eyes and tried to call Nicki, but her line was busy. If it weren't for Nicki, Gina might have thought she had been sold off, but Nicki wouldn't do that. She sighed and curled up on the bed.

Seth sat in a bar, waiting for Tricia, who had called to meet up. After another ten minutes, he got up to leave, but then he spotted her walking in and sat back down.

"Sorry, something came up," she said, ordering a glass of vodka.

"What do you want?" Seth asked, and she smiled.

"Is that the first thing you have to say to a sister you haven't seen in a while?" He ignored her, sitting impatiently. Tricia smiled again, staring at the empty shot Seth had drunk from.

"It seems like you got ahead of me. You can handle yourself now," she said, taking a sip of her vodka. "You usually get drunk by the third sip. How many times have you been here without me?"

Seth stood up in annoyance and tried to leave.

"Alright, chill. Just calm down. I'll go straight to the point!" Tricia said, holding his arm. Seth pushed her hand away and sat down.

"I just wanted to know what you're going to do about Grandma's will. Do you think the lawyer manipulated it or something? Should we do something about it?" she said, sounding like she was thinking aloud. Seth looked at her and sensed her desperation, which gave him an advantage.

"I don't know what to do, and God knows how much I need that money," she scoffed, taking another sip of her vodka. Seth didn't say anything, deep in thought.

"What was the old lady thinking? Did she tell you anything, like secrets or anything...?"

"Why am I here?" Seth asked.

"What are you going to do about the will? Getting the old lady a great-grandchild? Isn't very funny?"

"Why do I have to tell you that?" Tricia stared at him. "You do your thing; I do mine, so butt off my case and try to get a life," he said, taking his jacket to leave.

"Cold-blooded bastard!" Tricia said, not caring if he heard. He turned and looked at her for a second before leaving. Tricia sat there for a few minutes, feeling frustrated with her life. No, she was already frustrated. The only person she thought cared a little about her was dead, leaving her in deep misery. Nothing was going well, and she was alone. She stared at herself in the silverware in front of her for a while. She used to be so beautiful; she still was, but they wanted younger people now, so they discarded her when they didn't need her. Where did all that money go? She wondered.

_____

Seth removed his watch, dropped it on his desk, and walked into the bathroom, staring at himself in the mirror. Back in the day, he and Tricia had been so close. You would think she was his everything.

He loved her. Like a big sister? Like a mother? For a while, he thought he was doing it all wrong. Why did his heart race whenever he saw her? She is his sister; he wasn't supposed to feel that way. Was it affection or just stupidity? He was a fat, dumb bastard then. Yeah, that's why! Or was it excitement that he felt?

He blinks, bringing himself back to his senses. He shouldn't be remembering those days; they were the most hated days of his life. He was the child who longed to be loved, but not anymore. He was

35

the billionaire everybody wanted to be like, everybody wanted to please.

His phone beeped; it was a text from Liam.

"Have you called the doctor?"

"Not yet," he texted back.

"Okay, I'll call her. What about the lady?"

"What about her?"

"You should call her and see how she's doing."

"Why?"

"Because she's now your responsibility."

"Not yet."

"What?"

"She hasn't signed the contract yet."

"Fine, I'll do that too. But what if she changes her mind?"

"I don't care."

"You should care; she might spread rumours."

"Then we'll shut her mouth for good."

"Well, check your email tomorrow. I'll send you all her details." Seth read the last text and dropped his phone to take a shower.

Liam texted again, "That's her number, in case you change your mind." Seth knew he wouldn't, but he saved her number anyway.

CHAPTER FIVE

Regina woke up to the sound of the doorbell. She lazily pushed herself off the bed and walked to the door, her eyes still heavy with sleep. She opened the door and rubbed her eyes to see clearly. It was Liam and the other man who just stared at her the other day.

"Good morning, Gina." Liam greeted her with a smile and a wave.

"Hi, good morning," she replied, stepping aside to let them in. She touched her dress and wiped her face, trying to look presentable.

She followed them into the living room, trying to discreetly rub off the drool on her lips and breathing into her hands to check her breath, which smelled awful. She had been sleeping more comfortably and deeply since she arrived.

Liam sat down and picked up the contract from the floor, flipping through it. "I guess you read it, right?" he said with a smile.

"Uh, yeah, I did," she lied. She hadn't actually finished reading it, but it was just a contract, she thought.

"You didn't sign it," he pointed out, looking at her.

"Oh, right... I was just curious," she said, feeling nervous.

"Go ahead," Liam encouraged her.

"I... didn't see the amount I'd be paid," she said shyly, feeling embarrassed.

Liam glanced at Seth, who almost scoffed. "You'll be paid handsomely before, in the middle, and after the period. It's the last thing here," he said, pointing at the contract.

"Oh, yes, okay," she said, biting her lip and rushing to her bag to find a pen. She caught a glimpse of herself in the mirror and saw how messy her hair looked, feeling even more embarrassed.

She walked back to them with a pen, and Liam patted the couch, signaling her to sit beside him. She signed the contract, and Liam exhaled, closing the file.

"So, everything will start tomorrow. First, you'll have a medical screening," Liam explained.

"Medical screening?" she asked.

"Yes, to ensure you have the potential to carry the pregnancy," he replied.

"Oh," she said, trying to tame her unruly hair with her hand.

"After that, everything else will follow," Liam said, signaling Seth to speak, but he remained silent.

"So, are you ready for this?" Liam asked.

"Yes, I am," she replied, smiling, then glanced at Seth, who seemed eager to leave.

What's wrong with him? she wondered.

Is he his secretary? No, he looks too elegant.

His lawyer? He's probably his lawyer.

"Okay then," Liam said, getting up, and she stood up too. "You're a very lucky girl." He hugged her, while Seth was already heading to the door.

"Would it hurt to at least say hello to her?" Liam asked Seth in the elevator.

"It wouldn't," Seth replied, adjusting his jacket.

"She's your child's mother-to-be," Liam reminded him.

"She's just a surrogate, that's all," Seth said indifferently.

"She's human too," Liam argued.

"Is she? Didn't you see her hair? She looks more like an animal than a human to me," Seth retorted, stepping out of the elevator. Liam sighed and followed him.

38

"You're the animal, Seth. You are," Liam muttered.

Gina entered the doctor's office, taking in the pleasant smell that filled the air—a stark contrast to the hospital hallway. She hated hospitals, having had too many bad experiences with them. She closed the door behind her and looked around the office, which reminded her of her own room but was more sophisticated and filled with medical equipment.

A middle-aged woman with a warm smile motioned for her to sit. "Okay, Doc, I'll have Sandy send it over when I'm done. Coffee is on me today," she said, ending the call with a smile.

"Miss Regina Rachel Johnson?" the woman asked.

"Yes," Gina replied.

"You look beautiful," the woman complimented.

Gina chuckled. "Thank you."

"Nice to meet you. I'm Cate, a surrogate expert, and I've been expecting you," she said, extending her hand.

"Oh, nice to meet you too," Gina said, shaking her hand.

"Alright, come with me," Cate said, her big doe eyes almost bulging out. Gina followed her into a larger room with a bed and various medical equipment. Gina felt a wave of fear, wondering if they were going to plug her into something or draw her blood.

"Sit down; don't be scared. Be comfortable. You're with an expert here," Cate reassured her with a smile, as if speaking to a child. Gina sat on the bed, still looking around nervously.

"Have you done this before? Surrogacy, I mean?" Cate asked, gathering some equipment.

"No," Gina replied.

"In a relationship?"

"No."

"Why did you decide to do it?" Cate asked, stopping to look at her when she didn't respond. "Money"

Gina smiled.

"It's fine; who doesn't need money? You can trust me. Surrogacy is not a hard thing to do. It's just like getting pregnant normally, except you won't have to work for it, if you know what I mean," she winked, and they both laughed. "Bringing a baby into this world is not a small task but its a beautiful thing."

"Don't worry, you're in good hands. " Cate reassured her. Gina's heart skipped a beat when Cate turned on a machine.

"I'm just going to do some medical screening and a wellness check, which won't take much time. I'll check your body system for any infections and other stuff you don't need to know about. It'll be done before you know it," Cate said, positioning Gina for the screening.

Cate talked non-stop about surrogacy and successful cases, making Gina feel more comfortable. Gina nodded and smiled, the guilt she had been feeling slowly dissipating.

"Why does he want this?" Gina asked Cate.

Cate smiled and shook her head.

"Will I be related to the baby by blood?" Gina asked again.

Cate looked at her for a while and stood up. "See, I'll give you a piece of advice. I believe you signed a contract, met with a lawyer, or something like that. I don't know the reason or purpose," she shrugged, "but this shouldn't be your concern. Just focus on why you decided to do it in the first place and..." she shrugged again and touched Gina's nose before returning to her work.

After nearly an hour, they were done and back in Cate's office.

"I'll see you tomorrow. By then, some of the results will be out. If they're all good, we can carry on with the next level," Cate said, clicking and typing into her computer. "After the important part, you won't need to come to the hospital. The rest will be done at home.

Just relax, okay? Everything will be fine. Like I said, you're in safe hands."

"Thanks," Gina said, leaving the office. She texted Liam that she was done and waited for him in the cafe near the hospital.

While waiting, she started noticing pregnant women and mothers with their babies. She had never paid much attention to such things before. She accepted this deal, but she hadn't thought it through— the consequences, the end result. Remembering Cate's advice, she sighed.

Her phone beeped with a message from the driver who was picking her up.

As the driver drove through the expansive compound, Gina's mouth hung open. Liam had told her she would be moving into a house, but she never expected something like this. They passed the first gate, then the second and the third.

She sees this kind of thing in a movie, but this is real life. She laughed into her hands and asked the driver to wind down the glass.

"Wow!" she exclaimed as they passed tall, well-shaped trees and gardens. The car stopped in front of a large mansion and she got out.

"Oh my god," she whispered, covering her mouth and laughing as she moved closer to the fountain in front of the house, touching the sculpted mermaid.

"Miss Regina?" someone called.

"Yes?" she replied, stepping away from the fountain. A woman walked towards her, her expression unreadable.

"I'm Rosa, the head housekeeper. I was informed you'd be coming today," she said.

"Yes, call me Gina," Gina said, and the woman smiled, making her age hard to determine.

"Come on in," Rosa said.

Gina followed her inside, her mouth still open in amazement. She marvelled at the huge chandelier, grand staircases, and elegant decor.

"I was informed just yesterday that you'd be coming. There's still a lot to do in your room, so for now, you'll stay in the guest room. By the weekend, it will be ready," Rosa said, opening the door to the guest room.

"Oh my god," Gina said, standing there in awe.

"Miss?" Rosa called, still holding the door.

"Ma? Oh," Gina nodded and walked into the room, biting her lips to hold back her laughter.

I am going to sleep in this gigantic bed? Oh my goooood!

"Feel at home. I'll come for you when dinner is served," Rosa said.

"Yes, ma'am," Gina replied, trying to contain her excitement.

"Call me Rosa," she said, and Gina nodded before she closed the door and left her alone in the room.

"Oh my god!" Gina screamed into her hand, then went around, carefully touching everything. She looked out the window at the beautiful garden stretching into an empty field. "wooow."

Gina jumped up from the bed, her heart pounding. Someone had pushed the door open and was staring at her.

"Christ!" she exclaimed, holding her heart and breathing hard. "You forgot to knock."

"It's my house," Seth replied, his hands behind him.

He talks...

"Wait, what? Your...your house?" she asked, surprised. She jumped down from the bed immediately and felt a little dizzy.

"You heard me," he said, as if forcing himself to talk, yet nonchalantly.

"Sorry, but why... am I in your house?" She asked, trying to understand his point with her eyes squinted a bit due to the headache from the little siesta.

Seth looked at her with pure exasperation. "You mean to tell me you were driven from the hospital to this house, walked into this room, and you don't know where you are? And you're asking me why you're here?", Gina stood there looking at him, confused. She rubbed the back of her head, trying to understand the situation. "What should I call that? Uhmm... ignorance or just absolute stupidity?" Seth said, putting his hands inside his pocket and not taking his eyes off her.

Gina eyed him, still not fully understanding.

Why would this guy, who only stared and barely spoke, be here, spouting nonsense? Why is he claiming she is in his house? And where is Mr. Liam?! She glanced behind Seth, but there was no sign of Liam.

"I want to talk to Mr. Liam right now," she demanded.

"Why would you want to talk to him?" Seth asked, folding his arms and leaning against the door, looking both amazed and annoyed by her ignorance.

Gina searched her pockets, then the bed and drawers, looking for her phone. "Where is my phone?" she muttered, more to herself.

"You won't find it," Seth said calmly.

"What?" she snapped, frustration evident in her voice. "your phone",

"a-and why is that?", she asked, annoyed.

"you signed a contract you didn't read? Well, I guessed as much," he said, leaning off the door, unfolding his hands.

"I read the contract!", she claimed, but even she could hear the uncertainty in her voice.

"Then why are you looking for your phone?" he asked, his tone both mocking and incredulous. "Why wouldn't I? It's my phone!" she retorted, her voice rising. What's going on! Seth stood there, dumfounded.

"The contract clearly stated that all personal belongings would be confiscated until the end of the contract," he explained and Gina was gaping.

It might be the little siesta she had, because she can't seem to understand a word the man standing in front of her is saying and her head is banging.

"Excuse me," she said and she walked past him down the stairs. The woman who welcomed her said she was going to prepare a room for her; she took her luggages, so it will probably be there. She needs to talk with Mr. Liam.

Wait! She thought.

Is this a scam?

She stopped walking and thought about it.

It can't be! No

She shook her head in disbelief and gave out a little laugh.

No

The first thing that came to her mind was Nora laughing at her for being so stupid. She turned back and saw Seth walking out of the room. "Excuse me, sir," she said, walking fast towards him.

Seth didn't stop; he kept walking. He knew the first time he set his eyes on her that she's just a dumb girl, but not to this level.

Does she not even know him?

She never acted like she does. He thought.

He was going to call Liam to cancel the deal, but he can't keep on letting him deal with his problems; he's got a life too. He just has to manage. He walked into his office, ignoring Gina.

She followed him inside his office; it was so huge that it caught her attention for a few seconds.

"Sir, sorry to disturb you but I don't really get what's happening," Gina said, standing there all confused, her face furrowed in what seemed like anger and confusion.

Seth ignored her, sat on his desk and took his tab.

"Sir?!", Gina called again, yet he ignored her; she was starting to get really annoyed.

"Mr. Seth", she called and Seth raised his eyes to look at her.

"I get it that you don't want to talk to me, me neither," she said, pointing to herself.

"I just want to talk with Mr. Liam-",

"why?",

"Why? Because he's the reason why I came all the way to New York!", she she exclaimed, and Seth almost laughed. He sat up, his back on his chair, nodding his head. He almost laughed in annoyance.

"you thought Mr. Liam", he said, mimicking her, "is the donor?", he asked, his voice dripping with sarcasm.

"Thought?" she sniffed.

This is a scam, oh god

"Mr. Liam is the donor," she stated, but her confidence was wavering.

Seth just stared at her, saying nothing.

"He's not?" she asked, confusion turning to shock. "Then... who is?"

The answer hit her like a tonne of bricks. She looked Seth up and down, a realisation dawning. "You're the donor?" she asked but the answer came to her immediately.

Wait a minute; this is his house.

It can't be!

Then Mr. Liam... Mr. Liam is the lawyer and he's the boss

Lord!

Seth dropped his tablet on the desk, clearly regretting ever listening to Liam. But he had started this, and he would see it through. He just has to deal with a dumb idiot for awhile and get the inheritance and everything will go back to normal.

"You said you read the contract. I don't care whether you did or not; you've signed it. Now do your part perfectly well," he said, walking past her.

Gina stood there, her mind reeling. The middle-aged housekeeper, Rosa, walked by and saw her. "What are you doing in there?" Rosa asked, making Gina jump.

"Nothing. Actually, I was looking for you," Gina replied, walking towards her.

"Do you need anything?" Rosa asked.

"Yes, my stuff. You had them taken when I arrived hours ago," Gina said.

"It's no longer in my possession," Rosa replied, closing the door.

Gina nodded and followed Rosa down to the guest room. "Dinner will be ready soon. Just stay in your room and don't wander about," Rosa instructed before leaving.

Gina walked into the room and sat on the bed, regretting not reading the contract thoroughly. She thought about Mr. Liam—*was he Seth's lawyer? That would explain why he did all the talking.* She sighed in relief, thinking it wasn't a scam, but her heart still pounded with anxiety.

She held her heart with one hand and opened the window with the other. She looked out through it to the beautiful garden. The moon is out and the light made it look so magical.

She thought of her mom. They must be expecting a call from her, and she wondered if Nora told her she called. She exhaled and sat on the bed.

She touched her stomach, thinking about the journey ahead. Tomorrow, everything will start. She laughed at the thought of getting pregnant so soon. Is it tomorrow? She laughed at the thought. The door opened, and Rosa appeared, announcing that dinner was ready.

Gina followed Rosa to the dining room, her mind still racing with unanswered questions and a growing sense of trepidation.

CHAPTER SIX

Montserrat sat on her room window, smoking, when her mother pushed the door open.

"What are you doing sitting there early in the morning?" her mother asked.

"What else am I supposed to do, Mama?" Montserrat replied.

"There are a lot of things you can do; one of them is getting pregnant. You get that?" her mother snapped.

"What?" Montserrat asked, not expecting that response.

"We need to get our hands on that money, no matter what," her mother said, rubbing her forehead and pacing the room. "She didn't even mention me in the will", "I believe you heard when that stupid lawyer mentioned that mother's will be going to her great-grandchildren"

"How are we going to get a great-grandchild?" Montserrat asked, bewildered.

Theresa stared at her daughter, frustration evident in her eyes. "Why are you so dumb? Am I the only one doing the thinking? Our business has fallen under, and you're still clueless!" She approached Montserrat and laid a hand on her lap. "If we can get you married and pregnant, then that's it. Isn't it simple?"

"Get me married?" Montserrat repeated, still in shock.

"That's what the letter said," Theresa said, throwing the letter she was holding onto the floor and walking to the door. "Let's make it happen. You can even marry that... Hector. I don't care. We don't have time, and we need to survive," she said, walking away. Monsterrat jumped down from the window, picked up the letter and read through it. "legitimate child?" she said and continued reading, "through marriage."

Rosa knocked and entered the study. Seth was at his desk, typing into his computer.

"Sir, letters from last week," she said, dropping them on the table. She turned to leave but stopped. "The woman doctor is here. She's with the lady in the guest room. She requested your presence," she added, but Seth didn't respond. "And the lady's room is ready for her to move into," she finished and she left without waiting for a reply.

Seth paused his work and went through the letters. He was expecting one from Forbes but was disappointed not to find it. He tapped his finger on the desk. He can wait for a little while until he gets his hands on the inheritance. One letter, however, caught his eye. He picked it up.

From Gloria McGregor?

Grandma?

He tore it open and read through it quickly. Then, in a fit of rage, he crumpled it and threw it at the door. "F*ck!" he shouted, filled with anger.

He loved his grandmother; she had completely raised him. But because of that, he believed he should be special, not lumped in with the rest of the family. He got up to meet with the doctor, eager for all of this to be over.

Opening the door, he found Gina and the doctor laughing. They stopped when he walked in.

"Oh... Mr. Seth, it's nice to finally meet you. I'm the surrogate expert, Cate," the doctor said, standing up and extending her hand for a shake.

"How long will this take?" Seth asked, ignoring her gesture.

"Uhm, the results came out good. The next step is to fertilise the egg and then implant it in Gina," Cate explained, switching to a professional tone. "Since you want to do this secretly, I personally suggest traditional surrogacy, which is simpler and faster—"

49

"Then start," Seth interrupted.

"We can't do it without your... contribution," Cate said, pointing towards him. For a moment, he didn't understand, then it clicked. Embarrassed, he left the room.

He sat down for a while, thinking of what to do, and then called Liam.

"So you're asking me how to get your own sperm out?" Liam asked, laughing.

"I'm damn serious, man. The doctor is waiting," Seth replied, frustrated. "Damn men, you are a shame to us men," "Liam."

"Alright, all you have to do is masturbate; its that simple," Liam suggested.

"I... I can't do that," Seth said, shaking his head.

"what? Man, you never touched yourself? Damn, I sound gay."

"Any other way?"

"I can call someone for you," Liam offered.

"Forget it," Seth said, cutting off the call as Liam burst out laughing. He sighed and headed to the bathroom, determined to get it over with. A message came in from Liam with a video link.

"So why do you prefer being called Regina to Rachel? I prefer Rachel, but Regina is nice too and not common," Cate asked Gina.

"I don't know; that's what everybody in our neighbourhood has called me since I was little. Some called me little Gina, and some called me Reg. It sounds like Rej with a J, but my best friends call me Riri or simply Gina. I liked it," Gina said, chuckling.

"I like it. Maybe I should name my baby Regina," Cate said, touching her stomach.

"You're pregnant?" Gina whispered, and Cate nodded.

"Surrogacy?"

50

"No."

"Wow, how many months?"

"Just—"

"Here," Seth said from the door. Cate walked over and took the glass from him.

"When will it be done?" he asked.

"It depends. I'll let you know through mail." He left without a word.

"Why is he sweating?" Gina whispered.

"I don't know," Cate whispered back.

....

Gina followed Rosa to her new room. The guest room was bigger than her new room, which looked like it was underground. She looked around; it was simple. Just a bed, a wardrobe, a television, a table, a fridge, and a chair. She opened her wardrobe; there were only nightwears of the same kind in different colours. She turned to ask Rosa why, but she was already gone. None of her luggage was there.

She sat on the bed, then touched her stomach. Cate had said they needed to fertilise the egg or whatever it was they were going to do first. Whatever it was, she just wanted to get it done and over with. She lay on the bed, thinking about home.

Two weeks later...

"Well," Cate said, removing her glasses, "everything went well. We have to wait for about two to three weeks, then I'll check up on her again. If we're successful, then she should be pregnant. She should be more careful with whatever she does from now on, and she'll need rest once you get back." She reached for her drawer. "These are the medications she'll continue to take. She should eat healthily. I'll be checking up on her often, though." She handed the medications to Seth.

51

"Are we done?" he asked.

"Yes," Cate replied.

"Do I have to bring her here myself next time?"

"Obviously, yes. You're the surrogate father. I'm sorry, but after the pregnancy test, I'll be visiting your home personally. And don't worry, we'll have someone escort the two of you through the emergency elevator," Cate said with a smile. Gina smiled back appreciatively, unlike Seth, whose face was so rigid.

He got up, and Gina followed, waving goodbye to Cate.

"Why do you want a baby?" Gina asked when they were on their way back to the mansion. Seth pretended he didn't hear her and continued tapping on his tablet.

"I just want to know. You just—" she shrugged, "—could've adopted one, married or... Why surrogacy?"

"The contract clearly stated no personal questions or questions related to this, but you were too dumb to even read a few pages," Seth said as if talking to his tablet. Gina stared at him, hating the way he always talked to her.

"Well, you asked me a lot of really personal questions the first day we met, remember?"

"I'd like it if you'd stay quiet and not talk to me. I'm working," he said. Gina didn't say another word and counted the minutes until the engine stopped and she could step out of the car.

She walked in and went straight to her room. She laid down on her bed, not allowing herself to think. She kept staring at the freshly painted lemon-green wall until she fell asleep.

She woke up late into the night, feeling a sharp, twisting pain in her stomach. She slowly got off the bed. Her medication and a tray of fruits were sitting on the table. She slowly opened the mini refrigerator, but it was fully stocked with fruits and water.

She sat in front of the refrigerator for a while, then crawled to the door. She got up and tiptoed to the kitchen, trying not to disturb or wake anyone.

It was 10:45 PM. She thought he might be in his study. She slowly looked around for something to eat. The more time she wasted, the more her stomach tightened.

She finally saw packs of noodles stacked on a corner in the cupboard, probably hidden by Rosa. It took her five minutes to get them ready. She sat on the floor by the kitchen cabinet, ready to satisfy both her twisted stomach and her starving tongue. She didn't care how hot it was; it was all so good and satisfying.

While she enjoyed her quick dinner, she didn't mind getting caught. She might've signed a contract she didn't read, but she sure knew she didn't sign up to die of starvation.

"What are you—?"

She jumped at hearing the voice she hated the most. He turned on the kitchen light, still staring at her and her pot of noodles.

"What are you doing?!" he repeated, snatching the pot of noodles from her. "Are you out of your mind?" he asked.

She chewed on the last noodle in her mouth, ignoring him.

"How did this get here?" he asked, throwing the pot and the remaining noodles into the sink. Rosa walked in just in time.

"What's happening?" Rosa asked.

Gina got up and tried to ignore him.

"I am talking to you!" he screamed, dragging her by her hand.

"Ah!" Gina shouted, holding her stomach. Seth released her, his face mixed with anger and concern.

"Are you alright?" he asked.

Gina stood upright. "I'm fine."

"You're not supposed to eat this kind of stuff," he said, his face back to default.

"Well, you should've provided me with something better. I was starving."

"You were starving?"

"You stocked the fridge with only fruits. I needed something... I needed food," she said. Seth took a deep breath, trying to calm his anger and shock.

"Go get some rest. We'll call the doctor to check on you tomorrow," Seth said.

"I said I'm fine!" Gina protested. She couldn't go to that hospital again; she hated hospitals.

"You heard me," he said, heading for the kitchen door. "Don't ever try this again," he said and left.

Gina stood there for a while, hating how he talked to her like she was nothing, like she was just a piece of equipment he could discard at any time. She took a deep breath and walked back to her room while Rosa cleaned up the mess she had made in the kitchen.

The next day, Gina sat on her bed, feeling restless. She was tired of waking up to nothing and spending her days aimlessly. She needed to figure out how to reach her family. She couldn't imagine what her mother would say, especially after Nora likely added her own embellishments. Her mother would be furious and demand she come home. She needed to find a way to communicate without making any mistakes.

After taking her afternoon medication, she fell asleep. When she woke up, the sun was setting. She took a bath and thought about her plan. She needed to find Rosa, who was usually in the kitchen, but there was no sign of her.

Gina sneaked around the big house, looking for her belongings. After wandering for hours without success, she went back to her room, feeling down and bored. She checked the time; Rosa would probably start dinner soon, and Seth would be back too. Just then, it clicked—she should check Seth's study.

She sneaked into his study but quickly heard Seth talking with someone. She ran and hid behind one of the shelves. When did he come back? He walked in, his phone wedged between his shoulder and ear, loosening his tie. He dropped a suitcase on the table and left the study for his room.

Gina took a deep breath and sneaked out of the study. She followed him to his room and listened. For a while, she heard nothing. As she turned to leave, she heard the shower running. She turned back, slowly opened the door, and walked in. She quickly looked for his phone.

She found it on the bed and hurriedly typed in her mother's number. She couldn't remember the whole number, so she deleted it and typed in Nicki's number instead, sending her a text:

Can u foj a leta to my mom? tell her I gt d job been busy don't ever call or text this line! New york

She sent and deleted the message and ran out of the room, closing the door behind her with her heart pounding in her chest.

She ran to her room and closed the door. She sat with her back on the door, still breathing hard. She heard footsteps coming down the stairs and quickly ran to her room, covering herself. The door opened, and Seth walked in with Rosa.

"Did the doctor come?" Seth asked Rosa.

"She said tomorrow morning. She had an emergency," Rosa replied.

"Did anything happen today?" he asked again.

"No. She was sleeping when I went to the grocery store. She didn't eat her lunch, though."

"Why are you telling me that now?!" Seth snapped.

Gina shook at the harsh sound of his voice.

"I'm sorry, sir," Rosa said.

"Wake her up for dinner and keep a close eye on her unless you don't want your job anymore. This is important to me," he said, leaving the room. Rosa waited until he walked out before following, closing the door behind her.

Gina turned towards the door, feeling sorry for Rosa. She was old enough to be his mother, yet he talked to her like that.

"This is important to me?" Gina scoffed. "Arrogant bastard," she muttered. She thought about dinner but was tired of eating mostly fruits and vegetables. It gave her goosebumps.

....

She sat quietly at the dining table while Rosa filled it with different dishes. Her mouth watered at the sight of it. She hadn't had anything like this since she came. They are still filled with vegetables, but with different, delicious looking recipes. It looks like it was ordered. Gina thought.

She stared at Seth while he ate quietly, his attention focused on his tablet. He didn't even notice her, or maybe he was acting like he didn't see her. Gina wondered why he allowed her to have dinner with him; maybe it was because he caught her the other night.

She shoved the thought away and enjoyed her meal, knowing it could be taken away from her at any time.

CHAPTER SEVEN

Maria McGregor walked into the church quietly, the service was already underway. She knelt down on the last pew, feeling out of place. It had been years since she last attended church or kneeled to pray. Her life had always been about work. She felt ashamed for being there just because she was in need, and not just ashamed for coming to church but also for thinking of an old friend and...

She sighed and stood up for the Lord's Prayer.

After the service, she waited outside while the priest greeted the congregation. He saw her and was surprised but smiled and continued his greetings. When he was done, he walked over to her, still smiling broadly. Maria smiled too and they hugged.

"Father Raymond," Maria said as they embraced.

"What do I owe this visit to?" Father Ray asked, still surprised. Maria just smiled.

"Has it been thirty years or more?" he laughed. "You haven't changed at all. Come on," he said, holding her shoulder as they walked through the bricked street to his office, stepping on the fallen leaves.

"You've gotten old," Maria said, and they laughed again.

"Well, the years are catching up," he replied as they entered his office. He brewed some coffee for both of them. He held his hips as he sat down.

"When did you get so old?" Maria asked, making a funny face. She hadn't expected him to look so different; the Raymond in her mind was still young and vibrant.

"I've been growing older since you left. Did you think I'd stay young Ray forever?" He laughed, his voice cracking. He hit his chest to clear his throat.

Maria stared at his face, trying to reconcile the man in front of her with the Raymond she left over thirty years ago. Leaving had been one of the hardest decisions she'd ever made. One of the many.

"How have you been?" Father Ray asked, shifting her cup of coffee towards her.

"Good. You?" she asked, bringing the cup to her mouth and sipping noisily. Father Ray laughed, and Maria stared at him, her mouth still on the cup.

"You still do that," he said. Maria set the coffee down and wiped her mouth, suddenly feeling nauseous again.

"What brought you here?" he asked. Maria took her coffee with shaking hands and drank it all. He stared at her, leaning back on the sofa and clasping his fingers together.

"Is this about the inheritance?" he asked. Maria stared at him, surprised and more nauseous. He knew after all.

"Where is she now?" she asked, clutching her bag tightly. He shook his head, sitting up.

"I can't tell you, Maria," Father Ray said, standing up. Maria followed him.

"Why not?"

He turned to her. "She doesn't want us to."

"What?" She walked up to him, taking his hand. "Ray, you have to help me."

"Why? Because of an inheritance? I know you, Maria, but this isn't right," he said, holding her hand, which was on his.

"I would've tried if you came with good intentions. I'm sorry, but it's for the best. Thirty years is a long time for anyone to grow a conscience," he said, removing her hand from his, revealing a deep scar. Maria stared at it, blinking several times, trying to push the memory back where it belonged—in the past. She then walked out of the office.

Father Ray stood there, staring at nothing, remembering what happened years ago. He touched the scar on his hand, and the memory flashed again. Then a knock came on the door, startling him.

Seth reached for his phone on the bed. He answered the call and dropped it on the desk.

"What's good?" he asked, looking in the mirror, trying to get his tie right.

"Hey man, forget about what's good. Check the net," Liam said and waited.

Seth opened his tablet and frowned in anger for two seconds before dropping it on the bed and his eyes caught Gina standing at the door, which was open. She knew he saw her and wanted to knock anyway, but seeing his expression, she withdrew her hand.

"Have you seen it?" Liam asked.

"Yeah," Seth said, still struggling with his tie.

"Wow! Your sister is something else. In fact, your whole family. How could she fake her own marriage, then try to hide the groom's identity? Does she think anyone is going to buy that? Is she crazy? I mean.."

"She can do whatever she wants. I don't care," Seth said, glancing at the door to find Gina still standing there.

Can't she see that I'm busy? What does she want now?

"Well, you're in for a fight. Don't you want to know what the others are doing? Since Tricia got married out of the blue, what about the others? They might start claiming they have children somewhere or something," Liam said, but Seth didn't reply. "Well, it's up to you. When are you making the trip?"

"Now," Seth said, finally done with the tie. He checked it, not entirely satisfied, and saw Gina still standing there. "Okay, drop by

Simon's when you're back. Let's hang out," Liam said and Seth ended the call.

He closed his briefcase and looked at the door again. Gina was still standing there.

"What do you want?" he asked.

Gina shuffled in and saw his briefcase. "Are you going somewhere?" she asked, pointing at the case.

"Why are you here?" he asked again. Gina smiled at the thought of him leaving.

"Oh, uhm... I just wanted to tell you that the test is tomorrow, the pregnancy test," she said. He nodded and picked up his briefcase to leave.

"When are you coming back?" she asked.

He stopped and looked at her. "You shouldn't be asking me personal questions, remember? It's not what you'll be paid for," he said, leaving the room. Gina stood there, embarrassed and ashamed. He walked back in.

"Get ready by twelve tomorrow. I'll pick you up," he said and left again.

Gina rolled her eyes and sat on his bed. She lay on it, feeling how good it was. She got up and started walking around the room. First to his drawers, nothing interesting until she opened the last one. There were pictures. She took them out, one by one. The first picture showed him as a baby, carried on someone's shoulders, with a woman beside them. She guessed they were his parents.

She saw a few more: a fat boy and a lady, then another with their friends, but it was defaced with a pen.

"What are you doing there?"

"Oh my god!" Gina shouted in surprise as the pictures fell from her hand, scattering all over the floor. "I'm sorry, I didn't mean to—"

Before she could finish her sentence, Seth dragged her out of the room. "Don't ever come near my room again," he said and slammed the door.

Gina stood there for a few seconds, her heart racing. She walked to her room and curled up in her bed, tears threatening to fall, but she blinked them away. She thought of the text she had sent to Nicki. Could she have replied? She bit her nails, wondering what could be going on at home. Maybe her mom had already filed a missing person report? And Nora wasn't the type to sit quietly and not try to do something hateful. Nicki must be worried too, or maybe she had heard from Liam.

Of course, Liam. She had forgotten about him.

She got up from the bed and went to the kitchen, where Rosa was often busy. She saw her scraping potatoes. Gina didn't say anything; she just leaned against the wall, watching Rosa slice each potato into cubes. Rosa glanced at her but didn't stop cutting. After a few moments, she paused.

"Do you want anything, young lady?"

Gina looked at her. She liked the woman, but her stern face always scared her. "No, nothing," Gina said, turning to leave.

"Do you read books?" Rosa asked. Gina nodded.

"I can get you some books to pass the time," Rosa said, continuing to peel and cut.

"Thank you, ma'am."

"Call me Rosa," she said with a wink and a smile.

"Okay," Gina said, chuckling.

"Come and sit down," Rosa said, and Gina obeyed. She scooped some meat soup with a bowl of rice, fresh corn, and green peas and placed it in front of Gina.

"Thank you," Gina said, excited.

"Go on and eat fast. He could come back any minute."

"I thought he went on a trip."

"Guess it was cancelled. He left his suitcase," Rosa said. Gina nodded, enjoying the hearty food. When she finished, she wiped her mouth and thanked Rosa. She took the plate from her and started washing. Gina watched her back, which reminded her of her mom.

"Have you sent a message back home?" Rosa asked.

"No," Gina answered, wondering how she knew her thoughts.

"Do you want to?" Rosa asked, cleaning the sink. Gina stood up and walked to her.

"Are you going to help me?"

"I'm not going to help you," she said, walking out of the kitchen. Gina followed.

"What?"

"I can get you to a place where you can send a message, but I have nothing to do with it. You get me?"

"I promise," Gina said, all excited.

"Change into something else and follow me."

Gina rushed to her room, changed into another of her big night dresses, and ran out to meet Rosa standing by the door.

"We'll use the back door."

"But..." Gina tried to say.

"What is it?"

"Can't I do it with your phone?"

"What phone?"

"Your phone."

"I don't have a phone. Now, if you're having a change of mind, you'll do me good by staying back."

"I'm so sorry."

Gina followed her to a tiny game shop filled with people, all wearing headphones and eyes glued on their systems. Rosa took her to the shop owner, who requested a special service. Gina was taken to a smaller room with one computer on a desk; it looked like an office. The shop owner powered the computer, and Gina logged in.

"Do whatever you want, but be fast. I'll be outside," Rosa said and left.

Gina exhaled and typed into the computer. She texted Nicki first. It didn't take a minute before Nicki texted back.

"Girl, what the hell!" she texted and called. Gina took the video call. The screen showed Nicki in her car with a worried look.

"Girl, what happened? You left me worried—so worried. What the hell happened? Where have you been? Why haven't you called? Your line has been switched the fuck off!"

"Calm down, Nicki! I'm sorry, it's not my fault."

"What?!"

"Listen, I don't have enough time. Did you receive my message?"

"Yeah, I did. What's going on, Ri?"

"Did you send the message to my mom?"

"No, the hell I didn't. I thought you were kidnapped, trafficked, or something. I couldn't reach the deal guy or you, so I didn't. I had to verify first. But really, I even thought of telling her the truth so we'd start looking for you. Now tell me, what's happening?"

"Nothing much. I've done it. Nicki, my mom must be worried."

"Yeah, she so damn is. Your snitch of a sister has been on my tail. So why... what is happening? Talk to me."

"Well, I've done the surrogacy, though we are yet to confirm the pregnancy. I signed a contract before that, and I didn't get to read all of it, so my stuff was confiscated. I can't make any calls, leave the house, or do anything at all without telling him. I just sneaked out, thanks to Rosa."

"Who's Rosa?"

"Nicki, there's no time. I just want to know how everything is at home."

"Where are you first?"

"New York!"

"Where in New York? I mean, the deal guy... he didn't fill me in."

"Seriously, you gave me away without any information."

"I was busy, you know, and everything happened so fast."

"Fine, I just need my mom to know that I'm fine."

"Well, tell them you got the job; you've been too busy to call. She'll hype, of course, but she'll cool down. She's been giving me the eye every time I see her, though."

"Alright, I'll see if I can get to them."

"First, where in New York are you?"

"Nicki, I don't know. I'll try to talk with you again. Bye."

"Wait—" Gina cut the call before Nicki could say anything else. She called Nora next. She called twice before she answered.

"Gina?"

"Nora."

"Gina!" she screamed.

"Shhh, why are you screaming?!" Gina tried to calm her so their mom wouldn't hear.

"Where the hell have you been?" Nora sounded like their mom back in the day.

"How's mom?"

"Oh... You still remember you have a mother, really?"

"Don't give me an attitude, Nora. I've been busy."

"You've been busy? Busy enough not to even call in to know how your own mom is doing, for how many weeks and why are you whispering?!"

"Shh, I know, okay? I got the job and have been busy ever since. I just had this little spare time so—"

"Is that your office?" she asked, but Gina ignored her. "How's mom?"

Rosa opened the door. "We have to leave," she whispered.

"Who's that?" Nora asked.

"Nothing," Gina replied.

"Now," Rosa said again, and Gina nodded.

"Gina, where are you and what are you doing there?"

"Okay, Nora, send my greetings to Mom. I need to get back to work. I'll call in soon. Take care of Mom."

"Gina, where the hell—"

"Is that Regina?!" Gina heard her mom's voice and cut the call, logging off immediately.

She followed Rosa out of the office, through the small room now filled with more people, and out into the street. It was already getting dark, which surprised Gina.

Seth walked into the bar and spotted Liam waving him over. He walked towards him, removing his loose tie completely. Taking a seat beside Liam, Seth ordered a drink.

"How did it go?" Liam asked.

"As it should," Seth replied, sounding weary.

"As it should?" Liam raised an eyebrow. "Man, you look exhausted."

"Who wouldn't be in my situation?" Seth muttered. Liam ordered another glass of whisky for himself.

"So, what are you going to do about Tricia?" Liam asked, swirling his drink.

"What am I supposed to do?" Seth said, sounding indifferent.

"It's clear she got married for the inheritance," Liam remarked.

"She didn't get married," Seth countered, but Liam raised his eyebrows in scepticism.

"How do you know? You'll be surprised on that day. Plus, I guess she's going to get pregnant too, if she hasn't already," Liam scoffed.

"At least you're getting somewhere, ahead of them all, I guess," Liam said, taking another sip of his whisky. "What about your first aunt? She never married. Is she going to get married too?" Liam laughed loudly. Seth smiled faintly and finished his drink. "Grandma wouldn't have mentioned her if there's no possibility of that," he said, standing up.

"I'm leaving,"

"What, already?" Liam asked, surprised.

"What about the get-together? You going?"

"No," Seth replied firmly and walked away.

Rosa and Gina were in a taxi, the sky darkening outside. Rosa tapped her feet anxiously, thinking about the risk she had taken and how she might lose her job. Gina sat quietly, twisting her hands, feeling guilty for putting Rosa in this position. The thought of facing Seth made her heart sink.

As the taxi turned towards the house, they saw Seth's car driving through the gate. Rosa grabbed Gina's hand, and they hurried inside through the garden gate. Rosa quickly set out plates, setting for dinner, while Gina sat at the dining table, breathing hard and her hands trembling.

Seth walked in.

"Good evening, sir," Rosa greeted him as usual.

He walked to the fridge, grabbed a can of water, and drank half of it. Lowering the can, he noticed Gina sitting quietly at the table. He looked at her for a moment, then closed the fridge.

"We'll go to the hospital tomorrow afternoon," Seth said, finding her calm demeanour a little strange. Gina just nodded. Without probing further, Seth walked away. Gina exhaled deeply, then went over to Rosa and hugged her.

"Thank you so much," she whispered. "I'll never do that again."

Rosa smiled, and Gina walked to her room. She lay on her bed, trying to recall her mom's voice. She never thought she would miss it so much.

CHAPTER EIGHT

The next day, after confirming her pregnancy at the hospital, Gina walked straight to her room. She felt moody, unexpectedly. She had thought she'd be happy knowing she was carrying a baby, but instead, she was overcome with anger and melancholy. Curling up on her bed, she closed her eyes. Rosa walked in and told her that Seth wanted to see her. Slowly, Gina got up and made her way to his study. Liam was there too, but she didn't spare him a glance. He just disappeared from her.

Seth pushed a bank book towards her. It included her name and bank details and showed a balance of a million dollars. She took the book and stared at it in disbelief.

"I'll pay in more as we progress," Seth said, but Gina was lost in her thoughts, overwhelmed by the amount. She had never dreamed of having such a sum. It seems unbelievable and unreal because she is not feeling excited, just...

"Thank you," she finally said, then got up and walked out.

"What's wrong with her?" Liam asked.

"How so?"

"Didn't you see her face? She looks troubled."

"Am I supposed to be worried about that?"

"She's carrying your baby."

"And I'm giving her everything she needs."

"and what is that?", he asked and Seth poured himself a drink.

"Well, she just got paid; I think she is happy."

"That look is not how 'happy' looks," Liam said and Seth just looked at him to explain himself. "Look, you need to do more. Your baby is in her belly. Everything matters—the environment, her mood, everything."

"Did you bring the file?" Seth asked, dismissing the topic. Liam sighed, wondering why he even bothered to give advice.

Fr. Ray walked into his office to meet his visitor. He paused by the door upon seeing Maria. Dropping his Bible on the desk, he went to the coffee jug.

"Want coffee?"

"Yes, please."

"Cold or hot?"

"Cold."

He handed her a cup of cold coffee and sat down with his.

Maria took a sip and went straight to the point. "I need to see her."

"I told you already that you can't see her."

"She's my daughter!"

"Whom you abandoned thirty years ago, Maria."

"Raymond, you know what happened better than anyone."

"Of course, I even helped during her birth!" he said, taking a deep breath. "You had a choice."

Maria's tears flowed. "I had no choice."

"You had many choices, Maria, but you chose to run away and lie, for the same reason you're here today," Fr. Ray said, sipping his coffee.

Maria dried her tears with a handkerchief. "At least let me see her. My mother knows about her," she said and paused, not looking at Ray. "She knew all along," she said, wiping tears rolling down her cheeks. Ray shifted and dropped his cup on the old wooden table.

"I'll tell her everything myself and explain why it all happened."

"Why not let this go, Maria? You'll only hurt people all over again."

"Nothing like that will happen. I never hurt anybody; I just did what I could," Maria said, standing to leave.

"She's living near the convent, teaching children from the orphanage," Fr. Ray said without looking at her.

"Thank you," Maria said, walking out of the office.

Fr. Ray regretted it the moment he told her. He knew it might be a bad idea. He looked at the wound marks on his hands, a reminder of the past he carried in his heart. Maria.

Seth sat in his car, watching people enter and exit the building. He never wanted to attend the reunion but he couldn't be a coward. Liam tapped on the car window, signalling him to come out. They greeted each other and walked into the hall, where people were busy reconnecting. Liam greeted those he knew while they walked around, but Seth avoided eye contact.

The programme began, and everyone settled down. While the current principal gave a speech, Seth felt someone staring at him. He glanced to his left and saw Tricia waving at him, attracting attention.

"F*ck," he muttered, looking away.

"What?" Liam asked, then realised. "Relax, man."

"I'm relaxed," Seth replied through clenched teeth.

After the prize-giving and reminiscing, everyone mingled, catching up with old friends. Seth and Liam were with a group when Liam noticed Tricia approaching.

"She's coming," he whispered to Seth.

"Hey,!" Tricia said, hugging Liam and the others. The women with her did the same.

"Hey, brother," Tricia greeted Seth.

"Is that Seth?" Mandy, one of the girls asked. "OMG, Seth,"

"I see you on TV, but you look better in person," another said seductively.

"Well, he's got some muscles," Mandy remarked, and they laughed.

"Tricia," Seth interrupted.

"You remember Mandy, right? Our last summer night in school." Tricia asked, trying to provoke him.

"How could anyone forget her? Her name is all over for her affairs, trending on every porn site. I didn't expect to see you here," Liam mocked. Mandy's face turned red with anger, and she walked away.

"Butt off, boy," Tricia snapped.

"Sure, but I'm disappointed. I mean, you didn't even invite your brother to your wedding. I bet we all want to know the lucky guy who will share the McGregor inheritance with you." Tricia felt a surge of anger as people around her started gossiping. She looked at Seth, who stood with his hands in his pockets, doing nothing, and stormed off.

Seth felt relieved. Seeing Tricia angry or annoyed always made him extremely happy. Years ago, during their last summer night, Tricia had scarred him. Seeing the familiar faces takes him back to that night and he feels like they are talking about him again.

That night, Tricia acted kind and invited him to their party, introducing him to her friends. They forced drinks on him, making him sleep with a girl while they took videos and pictures. He later found out it was all planned by Tricia, and the girl was Mandy. Perhaps that's when he started hating girls, seeing them as manipulative and destructive. He felt betrayed and isolated. His grandmother got him a therapist, but that wasn't what he needed. He felt alone and lost. His parents were gone, the sister he adored betrayed him, and his grandmother barely had time for him. It might have been childish, but he always felt alone. His grandmother thought providing for him meant she cared, but it wasn't enough. Everyone around him wanted something, always taking and never giving, making it hard to know who was genuine. He grew up teaching himself that nobody was real, living without love or affection, and he learned to accept that.

———

Faith McKinley, Mrs. Gloria's last daughter from her second marriage, sat before the mirror, applying her mask. Her husband lay on the bed.

"I saw this letter among the bills. It says it's from your mother."

"What?" she asked, turning to face him. "Let me see." She sat beside him, opened the letter, and read it quietly. Her face turned red with shock.

"What does it say?" her husband asked.

"Nothing."

"Nothing?"

"I said nothing!" she snapped, surprising him. "Sorry, it's just the same thing she said in the will. I'm just stressed out," she added, going to the bathroom to wash her face. She looked at herself in the mirror and wondered how her mother found out she had a daughter. How did she find out?

———

"Cut!" the director said for the sixth time, clearly annoyed. "Let's take five." Everyone took a break, and he walked over to Tricia.

"Let's talk."

"I'm listening," she said, looking in the mirror.

"Look, if you can't get this right, we're calling in a younger artist. Your name is all over the news, creating a bad image for us. So act right! We're trying to help you here," the director said, leaving her staring at herself.

After shooting a scene, they wrapped up for the day. Tricia got into her car and opened her tablet. The headlines read:

Daily News: *Actress Tricia McGregor Suspected to Be Pregnant!*

Alarm: *Actress and Model Tricia McGregor Could've Faked Her Own Wedding!*

CBS News: *Tricia McGregor After the Inheritance...*

She threw the tablet and hit the steering wheel furiously, screaming.

Seth! she thought.

It's all his fault! She adjusted her hair, thought of what to do, and drove off with a smile.

Seth sat in his office, reviewing papers, when his secretary walked in with a large envelope.

"This came in for you." She dropped it and left.

He opened it, and pictures fell out. He picked them up one by one, each revealing Gina and Rosa leaving the house, entering a taxi, and walking across the road. In anger, he crumpled a picture showing Gina's face closer. The envelope was labelled *From Tricia!*

"F*ck!" he shouted, kicking his chair backwards. He grabbed the pictures and stormed out. Gina and Rosa were in the kitchen. Gina was telling Rosa about her family while Rosa prepared lunch. "I think he's back," Rosa said and it amazed Gina how she always knows.

"He came back early," Gina said, surprised.

Seth stormed in, startling them. His muscles twitched as he threw the pictures on the table. "When the f*ck did this happen?" he demanded, sounding dangerous. Gina got off her seat to see the pictures, feeling her skin crawl. She looked at Rosa, whose face had turned rigid.

"I asked a damn f*cking question!" he screamed.

"It's all my fault!" Gina screamed back.

Seth smirked dangerously. "What?"

"I'm sorry, sir. I dragged her into it," Rosa said, stepping in front of Gina.

"What?" he asked again, almost losing it.

"Rosa, no. It's my fault," Gina insisted. "I had to call my family and tell them I'm fine, but you cut off all communication. What else was I supposed to do?" she yelled.

"What did you say?" Seth asked, walking towards Gina. She hid behind Rosa.

"You're... fired," he said to Rosa.

"No!" Gina cried, stepping forward.

"To your room," Seth commanded, kicking down a chair before leaving. Gina tried to follow him, but Rosa held her back.

"Let him be."

"I'm so sorry," Gina said, tears streaming down her face.

"It's not your fault," Rosa reassured her and she left the kitchen. Gina stood there, blaming herself.

Left alone, Gina wandered the big house, thinking of ways to bring Rosa back. She decided to wait for Seth and try to convince him to rehire Rosa.

Seth walked into the bar and saw Tricia sitting alone in her usual spot. He walked over and sat down.

"Hi, brother."

"What's your point?" he asked.

"Whisky or vodka?"

Seth slammed the picture on the table, trying to stay calm. "What does this mean?"

"Oh," Tricia said, picking up the pictures. "Are you asking because you don't know or pretending not to?" She scoffed. "Maybe the media will tell you—they're good at making stories like this," she said, gulping her whisky.

"Do whatever you want," Seth replied.

"What?" she exclaimed, not expecting his calmness. He was supposed to flare up, like she did. Or was it nothing?

"Get your life together before prying into others," he said, leaving the bar.

Tricia gripped her glass, trying to break it, then threw it at the wall, screaming. "Get my life together? Who the f*ck is he to tell me that? F*ck you!"

Gina woke up early. She had fallen asleep, waiting for Seth. She tried to open the door, but it was locked. Realising he must have locked her in, she knocked and pushed until she was tired, then sat back on her bed. A few minutes later, she heard a key turn and stood up. Seth walked in with a tray of milk and toast. Gina watched him place the tray on the desk.

"What do you think you're doing?" she asked.

"Eat," he said, turning to leave.

"It's not her fault; I asked her to help me," she said but he ignored her, walking to the door.

"What am I to you?" she asked, stopping him.

"What?"

"What am I to you? First, you took my luggage and blocked all communication. What am I to you that you're treating me like a prisoner? Bring Rosa back. It's not her fault. I forced her to help me. Bring her back, and I'll never leave this room. I'll do everything you order," Gina said, tears streaming down her face. Seth stared at her for a moment.

75

"Eat," he repeated, and he left, locking the door behind him. Gina stood there, staring at the door, biting her lips and clenching her fists. She looked at the milk and toast, her mind telling her to go on a hunger strike, but she was too hungry. She lay on her bed, facing the wall.

"I still think this is a bad idea," Liam said to Seth in the kitchen.

"What is?"

"Locking her up! She's pregnant and can get depressed in there."

"She called for it."

"So, you're going to cook and do everything for her?"

"If I have to."

"Well, you have to. What if she decides to do something stupid?"

"She already did."

"Man, I'm regretting ever suggesting this to you," Liam said, frustrated.

"Sorry, bro. I'll deal with this. Now, can we get down to business?"

"I want to see her."

"No."

"No what?"

"No, you can't see her."

"Why?"

"You just can't."

"Man, you're pissing me off."

"What's gotten into you? I told you Tricia is not going to let this go just like that,"

"and so what? Her finding out doesn't mean anything. They are still going to find out about the baby in the end. You're getting on my

76

nerves. She doesn't deserve how you're treating her; that's it," Liam said, taking the last toast and leaving the kitchen. Seth sighed, feeling the weight of the situation.

Montserrat and Hector posed for wedding pictures while Theresa watched from the corridor. She handed an envelope to a reporter beside her.

"Do it well," she instructed. The reporter nodded, taking the letter.

Theresa's plans were going well. She had decided to give Hector and her daughter a chance, given the situation. Once everything was settled, she would ensure they divorced. She threw her cigarette away and walked off while Montserrat and Hector continued taking pictures.

CHAPTER NINE

Faith drove for hours, her mind racing. She couldn't stop wondering how her mother had found out about the daughter she had hidden away.

How?

Eighteen years ago, she travelled abroad for her master's degree. There, she met Damien and fell in love. But their dreams for the future didn't align. After all these years, the past was resurfacing, and she couldn't hold back her anger. She pounded the steering wheel repeatedly, trying to release her frustration.

I've been the good girl for too long for this. I gave my daughter up for this?! I gave up everything for this?!!

She screamed and pulled over by the roadside, struggling to catch her breath. Taking a deep breath, she started the engine again. She had to get through this. After fifty more minutes of driving, feeling nauseous, she arrived at his house. She got out of her car, her heart pounding. She didn't know how to face Damien again. And their daughter.

She stared at the house that could have been her home. Their home. Hearing laughter, she tried to hide behind her car, but it was too late. They stopped when they saw her. She gripped the car handle, trying to stop herself from shaking.

For a few seconds, Damien couldn't believe who he was seeing. He told his daughter, Violet, and his wife, Ruth, to go inside. They continued their conversation as they walked in. Faith stared at the girl as she disappeared. She smiled as Damien approached her. He hadn't changed at all, she thought.

"Faith?" he called.

"Damien," she replied, releasing her grip on the car door, but her hands still trembled, so she clasped them together against her belly.

"How have you been?" he asked.

"I've been good... How have you been?"

"As you can see, we're good," he said, glancing back at the house. The main question hung in the air between them. "What are you doing here, Faith?"

"Damien, I..." She paused, choosing her words carefully. "I just want to talk with my daughter."

"Your daughter? I'm sorry, but I don't get you. What daughter?"

"Damien—"

"Faith, don't do this. I'm sorry, but I don't have anything that belongs to you. You made sure of that years ago."

"I—"

"Please leave. Please, please," Damien said, walking away from her. "Is that her?" she asked, but Damien looked at her for a few seconds, nodded, and walked away.

She didn't blame him. It was her fault, her decision.

Gina woke up to find a package on the table and a pile of books beside it. She thought of Rosa and ran to the kitchen, finding Seth breaking eggs into a bowl. Only then did she realise she was outside her room. Her door was open.

She stood at the kitchen door, looking around but seeing no sign of Rosa.

"Good timing. Sit," Seth ordered.

"I'm not hungry, thanks," she replied, turning to leave.

"Sit," he repeated harshly. Gina turned back, suppressing her hatred for his arrogant behaviour. She walked to the table and sat, staring at the burnt egg on her plate. Seth sat down for his own breakfast, engrossed in his tablet.

Realising Gina wasn't eating, he said, "You should eat."

"Must I do everything you order?" she murmured and Seth looked up at her.

"I don't like eggs," she said, pushing the plate away. Seth put down his tablet.

"You ate eggs yesterday."

"Yes, I was hungry."

"So, you're not hungry now?" he asked. Gina remained silent, staring at the table. Seth sighed, took her plate, toast, and tea, and dumped them in the waste bin.

"what are you doing?", Gina asked.

"You said you weren't hungry," Seth said, sitting back down.

"I never said that!" Gina protested, but Seth ignored her, picking up his tablet again.

"Where's Rosa?"

"She'll be gone for a while," he replied immediately, still not looking at her.

"It wasn't her fault. Bring her back," she said, trying to sound strong.

"You sound like you're commanding me," he said, looking at her through his long lashes.

"I... just… bring her back."

"Go back to your room. I'll call you for lunch," he ordered, standing up.

As Gina stood to leave, Liam walked in.

"Good morning!" he said, dropping the bags he was carrying.

"Thank God I came on time." He began unpacking the bags. "Hello, Gina. Are you ready for a majestic breakfast?"

Gina didn't reply; she just stood there as he unloaded the bags.

"What are you doing?" Seth asked.

"What do you think I'm doing?" Liam replied, placing the food on the table. He separated the chicken and fresh salads from the cookies and other treats. "These are for you," he said to Gina, spreading his arms wide. Her mouth watered.

"Wow," she said, trying to fake a smile, She is still angry at him but it's fine. "All these for me?"

Liam walked around and pulled out a chair for her.

"Yes, ma'am," She sat down, and he served her.

"You're eating for two, remember?" he reminded her. Gina nodded and dug in, ignoring Seth. It's true that she was mad at Liam for leaving her in Seth's hands, but now she has decided to let it go. He was a good man. She thought as she enjoyed her meal.

After breakfast, she took the goodies to her room and stocked her fridge. Feeling tired, she lay down, thinking of nothing in particular.

She got up and walked to the mirror, rubbing her stomach. It still looked normal, but she wondered if a baby was really inside. It had been five weeks already. She sighed and picked up one of the books from the table, climbing back into bed.

Seth and Liam were in the library. Seth was feeling angry about what Liam had done. Gina was his responsibility, not Liam's.
"She's not supposed to be taking those," Seth said.
"Why?" Liam asked.
"Because she's pregnant."
"What I gave her was food, not poison. And she was starving. You were going to starve her this morning. A pregnant woman, Seth."
"She said she doesn't eat eggs, which she ate just yesterday. She was giving me attitude."
"Not attitude! She's pregnant. That's bound to happen. Her moods will change. She'll crave weird things."
"What do you mean?" Seth asked.
Liam rubbed his head. "Why do I feel so responsible for this shit? Ugh!" He slumped onto a sofa. "Look, man, I read about this pregnancy stuff. A lot comes with it. You should look it up yourself. I can't tell you all of it, okay? This is important to you, not me. I'm just helping you out. Set aside your ego and hatred for women and deal with this. It's just advice. Take it or leave it. I'm leaving." He got up and left.

Seth sat at his desk, closed the tab, and googled pregnancy, surrogate pregnancy, and what to expect. He skimmed the information, picking out points, but suddenly stopped and closed the tab. He leaned back, thinking of what his family might be doing. He had been handling the company since his grandma got sick. The others used to kiss up to the old woman's ass, but now that she was dead and with the conditions she left them in, everybody was just calm. Too calm. It gets on his nerves.

He received a letter. Did they receive one too? Why would his grandma expect great-grandchildren from them? It almost seemed impossible for some of them. Montserrat wasn't married; she didn't even mention her in the will.

Faith was her daughter. Even if she miraculously got pregnant, she would be giving birth to a grandchild. And Maria wasn't married either. Could she actually go so far as to have a child? Unless she adopted one, even so...

"Oh, fuck," he muttered, rubbing his head and taking a deep breath.

Maria sat in the moulded chair at the orphanage, waiting for the Rev. Sister, who had welcomed her. After a few minutes, the Sister returned and took her to a small office. An older woman sat there with a smile, and Maria smiled back.

"Welcome, dear," the woman said.

"Maria, this is our reverend mother, Sister Philomena," the Rev. Sister introduced.

"Good morning, Sister," Maria greeted and sat down while the other Sister left. They stared at each other for a long, awkward second.

"Sister, I... I was directed here by Rev. Fr. Raymond."

"Oh, Fr. Raymond. A great priest, he is."

"Yes."

"Is everything fine, dear?"

"Well... yes... just that..." Maria twisted her fingers, staring at the old red carpet, wrinkled against the cement floor. Sister Philomena held her hands.

"Go on, dear."

"I heard my daughter is a teacher here. So, I came to see her."

"Your daughter?" Sister Philomena said, and Maria read her face, wrinkled but still showing emotions.

"Yes, Fr. Ray told me she's here, teaching the children." Maria placed her hands on the Sister's wrinkled hands. "Sister, I... I've not seen her for so long. I want to apologise for leaving her. I really want to be with her now, but I don't know how to do it."

Sister Philomena smiled, her wrinkled cheeks almost blocking her eyes. "You know, Maria is a very bright girl. Yes, her name is Maria. I named her Maryglory, but people preferred calling her Maria. I raised her myself," she said. "Although Fr. Raymond didn't give me the whole story when he handed me baby Maria, I figured I had to take good care of her. While she grew up, she asked a lot of questions. She was brilliant, very. I used to tell her that one day you'd come looking for her, but she outgrew that." Sister Philomena looked at Maria.

"She looks a lot like you," she said, taking a deep breath. "She's teaching the children now. She got married five years ago and is living happily, but I don't know if she'll be happy to see you."

"She's married," Maria said, not asking, and the Sister nodded. A tear fell from Maria's eye. "But don't worry. She's your daughter, after all. There's always a connection between mother and daughter. She'll be done with the children soon," Sister Philomena said with a weak smile, and Maria nodded.

Maria listened carefully as Sister Philomena filled her in with stories about her daughter, showing her pictures of when she was little, as a teen, and when she got married.

"I think they're done. Come," Sister Philomena said, slowly getting up. Maria held her arm as they walked outside to the field.

Under the sun, children were running around.

"Do you see her?"

Maria shielded her eyes from the sun to see better. She saw a young woman stepping into the sunlight. Her heart skipped a beat. She looked like her mother more than Maria herself did.

A little boy ran to the woman, and she touched his hair with a smile.

"She has a son, Peter."

"She has a child?" Maria asked.

"I told you she got married five years ago, didn't I?" Sister Philomena said. Maria stood there in surprise.

I have a grandchild?

Seth and Liam sat at the bar, discussing business. When they were done, they ordered a drink.

"Have you heard from Katy? Katy Moore?" Liam asked.

"Who?" Seth replied, not paying much attention.

"Don't shock me! Katy, your first and last date ever!" Liam said, drawing Seth into the conversation.

"We didn't date. What about her?" Seth asked, taking a sip.

"The world wouldn't say the same. Well, I saw her last week. I forgot to tell you. She was looking charming as always. We talked for a bit, and she'll be staying here for a while. What do you think?"

"I don't care."

"Well, you should. You need to see her. She's still single, and she asked about you."

"I still don't care."

"You know, when I saw her, I thought the two of you could be a super couple. Imagine marrying her. She has a child for you, and you inherit your grandmother's properties. Add Katy's wealth, and damn, man, there'd be nothing else you'd need in this world," Liam said, but Seth wasn't paying attention. He was stressed out and hadn't had a good sleep in a long time. He yawned.

"I know I'm boring you, but you should think it through. And before I forget," Liam said, pouring himself another drink, "she didn't only ask about you. She is interested in your company."

Seth looked at him, turning the ice in his glass.

"Advice, my man: loosen up. If not for anyone, Katy is a nice catch. She would make a perfect partner." Liam raised his glass at Seth and downed the drink.

"What about Gina, the pregnant girl?" Liam asked.

"What about her?" Seth replied, gulping his drink down.

"Is she good?"

"Of course she is," Seth said, trying to avoid another quarrel.

"She's a good reader. The last time, she told me she needed new books," Liam said. Seth kept quiet.

"Did you do the transfer to her family?"

"Yeah."

Liam nodded. "How many months now?"

"Just two months."

"Wow." They stayed for another hour before deciding to go home.

Seth walked into the kitchen for water and found Gina there. He stood by the door, trying to figure out what she was doing. "What are you doing?"

"Oh, you're back," she said, turning to find him standing by the door. "I am making dinner," she said with a wide smile, hoping he'd be amazed, or at least pretend to be.

"Sit down," she told him, pointing at a chair.

"I'm not hungry and you shouldn't—"

"I'm fine," she said, touching her stomach. "Just sit," she commanded. "Please," she added.

Seth closed the fridge, dropped his jacket and bag on one of the chairs, and sat down. She hurried and set the table. She served him and sat beside him, unlike before, when she used to sit at the end of the table.

"So, there were ingredients, so I decided to make dinner. Enjoy," she said, trying not to be too comfortable. She wore a smile throughout the dinner to maintain positive energy before her question.

Seth couldn't believe he enjoyed it. After dinner, he told her to just sit.

"I'll handle the rest," he said. Gina watched him while he washed the dishes. She wanted to know if he had gotten the piece of paper she dropped in front of his study. He had warned her not to cross his room or study, and she thought it would be better that way because she couldn't face him and make the request. So she wrote it down on a piece of paper she tore out of one of her novels and dropped it in front of his study.

"You can go to bed."

"Oh... okay," she said, standing up sluggishly, her heart beating out of her chest. She turned towards the door but turned back again.

"Uhmm... I wanted to know if you sent the money," she said, biting her lips.

Seth stopped washing the plates and looked at her for a while. She was biting her lips with her hands behind her. Her belly was still not showing.

That's why she's acting all nice, he thought. *To know if he sent the money?*

"Yes," he said, continuing to wash.

85

Gina almost asked him, "Really?" just to be sure she heard him right, but knew that would be a mistake.

"Can I call them?" she asked. Seth turned sharply.

"It's fine if—"

"No," he said simply and turned back.

"Alright, good night," she said, going to her room.

Seth finished with the dishes and walked to his room. He thought about her request. Liam was the one who actually saw it. He wouldn't have done it if Liam wasn't there, but he couldn't take another blame from him again. It wasn't in the contract that he would take care of her family. For a second, he thought she was behaving herself, but just like everybody else, she wanted something from him.

Early in the morning, Seth woke up to make breakfast but found Gina already on it.

"Good morning!" she said with a smile.

"I told you not to cook again."

"No, you didn't," she said with a smile.

"I'm telling you now."

"I have nothing else to do. This is the only fun thing I am doing, and you're asking me to stop. Can't you show a little appreciation, you demon!" Gina snapped. She bit her lips immediately after finishing the sentence. It's not like her to talk without thinking, but she just did.

"What?" Seth said, surprised. First, look at the tone of her voice. Secondly, she just called him a demon.

Unbelievable!

Who is this?

Gina held her mouth. "I'm... I'm so sorry. I-I didn't mean to say that, I swear," she said. Seth stared at her for a few seconds and stormed out.

"Fuck!" she said, hitting the table.

"She called you a demon." Liam asked, bursting out laughing.

"I knew she was putting on an act. Can you believe she raised her voice at me, as if she's my grandma? Even Grandma never did that," Seth complained.

"Her audacity is awesome. I mean, I don't blame her."

"Seriously? What do you mean?"

"Yeah, but don't take it to heart. She's pregnant."

"So?"

The door opened, and Seth's secretary walked in with a bunch of flowers and an invitation.

"It came in just now," she said, dropping it and leaving.

"Wow," Liam said, opening the invitation. He nodded and turned it for Seth to see.

"It's from Katy. She's inviting you to her annual celebration."

Seth took the invitation.

"Tell me you're going."

"Do I have to?" he said, not really asking.

"Yeah, bro. This is a golden opportunity, and you need to grab it. You know that. Katy Moore is a golden opportunity, both in your business and private life," Liam said as Seth kept staring at the invitation but thinking of something else.

CHAPTER TEN

Maria walked into the convent at the same time she had been doing for the past two weeks since she saw her daughter. She couldn't gather the strength to talk to her. She just wanted to watch her from afar for now.

She sat on the moulded chair, waiting to see the children push open the door like they usually did. She sat quietly, the weather cool and the sun starting to set, casting its orange light on her. She didn't block it and suddenly found herself back in school with Raymond and Frank. They were her friends—her only friends. They hung out together like siblings, playing in the field after school and watching the sunset every evening before going home. She had fallen in love with Frank long before he found out, but Raymond knew all along. He had told her when he confessed his own feelings to her.

She and Frank finally got together after school, and they were crazy in love. Despite his ruggedness and lack of princely charm, she couldn't help but love him. He was mature for his age, unlike calm Raymond, and he didn't come from a humble background like hers. She dove in without thinking. Things went too far, and she got pregnant. At first, it didn't bother her; they were going to get married. But things went wrong. Her father had died years ago, and her mother remarried and had other children, whom she cared about so much. She gave them the best of everything, unlike her. She gave them her full attention and didn't care if Maria came home late or why her clothes were dirty and rumpled like she used to.

Maria planned to marry Frank, move to a quiet place with a pool and a garden, have children, and live freely.

But what about her family? What about her mother?

Her mother had always said she took after her, until she remarried and had other daughters. Since then, Maria has fought to get her mother's attention. When she told her mother about marrying Frank immediately after summer, her mother said she was too young for marriage. She advised her to study more and explore life more before thinking about marriage, and Maria believed her because she adored her. But it was hard to do.

Maria lied to her mother that she had gone to study but stayed with Raymond, trying to think it through. Would her mother say the same thing if she knew she was pregnant? She couldn't imagine how much she adored her mother and that she was able to let Frank and everything they had go. It still hurt her. She broke up with Frank, the hardest thing she had ever done, but what about the baby? She never told her mother about the baby.

During the months she stayed with Raymond, it was the hardest. She was young and pregnant, feeling alone throughout the cramps, pains, aches, and hunger. She watched the news and her own family through it. The pain increased when she learned that her elder siblings had died in an accident. Now, she was all alone. That night, she walked into the woods, lost and unable to face her mother or take it anymore.

Raymond came home early that evening after hearing the news of her siblings' deaths but couldn't find her. He searched everywhere until he heard a scream. He found her hanging off a shallow cliff. She had slipped and went into labour. Raymond held her hand and tried to drag her up, gripping a root beside him to help. He felt the root tearing his skin but held on strong until he was able to drag her up. He couldn't ask for help or leave her alone to find help. He watched and held her as she screamed and pushed, and he was the first to hold the baby when it came out.

When Maria woke up the next day, she found herself in a local hospital near Raymond's. The first thing she thought of was to go home. And that's what she did. That's all she did.

She felt a small hand on her face and saw a little boy standing before her.

"You're crying," he said. Maria touched her face. She was lost in her memory, not noticing when the children ran out.

"You're sad," the little boy said. "Here, Mommy said candies make people happy."

Maria took the candy from the boy with a smile. "Thank you, dear," she said to him, and he smiled.

"What's your name?" she asked him.

"Peter! I'm so sorry; he's always running off," her daughter said, grabbing her grandson by the hand.

"It's fine; he's a good boy," Maria said nervously, staring at her daughter.

"Yes, he is. Should we go see Daddy?"

"Yes!" little Peter said. They waved at Maria and walked away. She felt her heart hurting, shrinking.

She looked to her left and saw Fr. Raymond standing there with Sister Philomena. He walked to her and sat beside her.

"How long are you going to wait to tell her?"

"Just a while," Maria said as tears rolled down her face. Then she burst out crying. He held her to his chest. Things went so wrong, he thought.

Seth kept checking himself out in the mirror, taking out different shirts and trying them on.

"Going somewhere?" He turned to see Gina standing by the door.

"Sorry, the door was open," she apologised immediately.

Seth stared at her stomach. He hadn't paid attention to her lately, and her stomach was suddenly bulging out a bit. He was beginning to think she might not be pregnant. He dropped the shirt he was holding, finally choosing one to wear. Gina walked in slowly and stood by the wall with her back against it, watching him put on his shirt and shoes.

"Wow, you shaved too. Is it a party, a date?" she tried to start a conversation.

Seth stopped and stared at her. "What do you want?" he asked, turning to get his tie.

"Hmm... nothing," she said. Seth watched her through the mirror. She was staring at her feet, playing with them. He shook his head and tried to get the tie right.

"Let me help you," she said. He turned to see her right behind him. She slowly raised her hands to help, and he allowed her.

"I used to watch my dad do it, just once or twice. He's not actually a suit man. I'm not sure I'm getting it right, though." It was weird that she was touching him and even weirder that he allowed her. When she was done, she patted it softly.

"Okay," she said, and he turned to see himself in the mirror. It wasn't so good; it looked a bit bumpy.

"Uhmm, but if you're trying to impress a girl, you don't have to look so official and all. You can do without the tie, like this." She walked to him, loosened the tie, and tried to unbutton his shirt.

"What are you doing?" he asked, pushing her hand away.

She stared at him, and anger rushed through her for two seconds. "Chill," she said to him, then loosened two buttons, exposing his chest. "There," she said, smiling.

She gave him a once-over. "I think this will do. Good luck," she said, leaving the room.

Seth stared at the door for a while, then at himself in the mirror. He looked at his half-open chest. She actually touched him, he thought, looking at the door again. He buttoned up, picked up his tie, and left.

Seth walked into the crowded hall. He didn't expect to be there at Katy's party. They almost had something in the past, but it didn't work out. It was not his fault. She claimed it was love, but he knew women like her and what they were capable of. His grandmother, for example, married two powerful men. He clearly saw how it all ended.

He saw Katy talking with her guests. Their eyes met for just a few seconds. He wouldn't deny that Katy was beautiful and a financial icon that could really boost him, but she always smelled like danger.

"Hey, man," Liam said, and they greeted each other. "you look fly, what's with the buttons?" he said, laughing.

"what?",

"Nothing," Liam said, shrugging. They looked towards Kate as some men surrounded her,

"Told you she's an amazing woman. Still dashing. You're about to make a score, man," he said, nudging Seth. "I knew you'd make it. You even dressed for it. I mean, who won't fall for Katy?" he said, and Seth almost rolled his eyes.

"So, how's Gina?"

"Fine."

"And lonely, I guess," Liam said. Seth looked at his friend, but Liam didn't spare him a glance and went ahead to greet people he knew.

Seth stood there, thinking about what Gina could've wanted to ask him. She obviously wanted something. Then he thought about her previous request and her hand on his chest. He blinked and looked around him to bring himself back to the moment. His eyes caught Katy staring at him across the hall. She raised a glass at him and winked. Liam watched from across the hall.

Gina walked to the garden and sat there, marvelling at the tranquilly that always enveloped the mansion grounds. Despite expecting a flurry of activity from maids and workers, everything remained impeccably maintained and serene. She stood up and strolled around, admiring the flowers, but soon found their scent irritating. Lately, she has been feeling weak and nauseous. She went inside, turned on the TV, and quickly fell asleep.

When she woke up, her whole body ached, and the room was dark. She stood up carefully, feeling a slight pull in her abdomen. She steadied herself and made her way to the fridge for a glass of water. As she drank, she glanced at the calendar on the wall, ticking off the days until she entered her second trimester. She was currently in her seventh week. Cate had recently visited for a prenatal checkup, using a Doppler ultrasound scanner to check the baby's heartbeat. Despite the surreal feeling, she still found it hard to believe she was actually pregnant. She sighed, took her vitamins, and continued wandering through the house, but there was no sign of Seth. Feeling increasingly lonely, she returned to her room and slipped under the duvet, trying to ignore the slight headache and body ache.

Seth finally found a private moment with Katy.

They walked slowly through the lighted garden, holding wine glasses, and talked about business before switching to personal matters, with Katy doing most of the talking. She inquired about his inheritance, and he assured her he was working on it.

They eventually sat by the pool, their backs to the water. Katy became flirty, slipping her hand inside Seth's open shirt and kissing him. When he didn't respond, she tried to kiss him again, but Seth gently pushed her away. They sat in silence. Katy was slightly annoyed, but she knows Seth and this time she's prepared for him; she's not ready to let him go, not again. Seth knew it was the cue to create something between the two of them but he just can't do it. While he was still thinking, Katy pushed him into the pool and joined him, laughing.

"What the fuck was that?" Seth said, stepping out of the pool. Katy stepped out too. "Loosen up," she said with a smile and took his hand. "Come on, let's get you dried up." Annoyed but resigned, Seth followed her to her room to change.

"Are you leaving?" she asked as he finished dressing.

"Yes, I have to go," he replied.

"Even if I ask you not to?" she said, standing naked before him. She walked over and wrapped her arms around him, kissing him passionately. "I can give you a baby," she whispered, and Seth took her lips. He grabbed her tiny waist and carried her to the soft bed.

Seth returned home in the morning and checked the kitchen, expecting to see Gina, but she wasn't there. He went to his study and then to her room, knocking twice before entering. He found her lying on the bed with broken glass on the floor. He rushed to her side, feeling her forehead; she was burning with fever. He quickly called Cate.

A few minutes later, Cate arrived and examined Gina.

"How is she?" Seth asked anxiously.

"She's fine, just a normal pregnancy fever. She'll be okay soon. How's her diet?" Cate inquired.

"Good," Seth responded.

"I'll be checking up on her regularly, but since I'm almost due, I'll assign another doctor. Don't worry, she's one of the best. Gina looks unwell overall—she's pregnant and depressed, which is bad for the baby. She needs companionship, exercise, a good diet, and comfort," Cate advised, patting Seth's shoulder before leaving.

Liam walked in after Cate left. "Is she good?" he asked.

"Yeah, she's fine," Seth replied. They went to his study.

"What happened?" Liam asked.

"I came back and saw her—" Seth began.

"You spent the night with Katy?" Liam interrupted, smiling.

"It's nothing," Seth said. They heard the doorbell.

"You expecting anyone?" Liam asked.

"No," Seth replied, surprised.

"I'll get it," Liam said, returning moments later with Katy.

"Hey," Katy greeted. Seth stood there, surprised.

"Okay, man, uhmm... see ya later," Liam said, winking and pecking Katy goodbye. "This place looks different; where's everyone?" she asked, dropping her handbag.

"How did you get in?" Seth asked as Katy sat down.

"I still have the pass," she said, dropping the card on his table. "You should at least welcome me first."

"I just left your house," Seth said, pouring himself a drink.

"Without saying goodbye. I miss you already," she said, hugging him from behind. He removed her hands.

"Wine?" he offered.

"Yeah," she said, following him to the mini bar. Seth brought out a bottle of red wine and two glasses.

"Oh... you still remember my favourite," she smiled, taking the glass from him. "How's Tricia? I haven't seen her in a long time; she rejected my invitation too."

"I don't know," he replied.

Katy looked at him for a while. "Marry me," she said, causing Seth to choke on his drink. She laughed as he hit his chest.

"You're all so rigid and strong, but I know your weaknesses," she said, wrapping her hands around him and kissing him. He untangled her arms and almost pushed her away. They heard a sound.

"Did you hear that?" Katy asked.

"What?" Seth pretended not to hear it.

"It's like it's coming from that...way," she said, trying to follow the sound. Seth held her back.

"Sit here; I'll check it out," he said, walking to the kitchen. Gina was wiping up spilled water.

"What the hell are you doing up here? I have a visitor!" he hissed.

"I was thirsty," she said, taking a can of water and leaving the kitchen.

"Anything?" Katy called out.

"I told you to sit down!" Seth dragged her to the door. "You have to leave."

"You're kicking me out?" she asked.

"Something came up," he said. She looked at him for a moment and nodded.

"Tonight then, dinner, 8:30pm," She pecked him and left. Seth watched her drive off and then walked to Gina's room. She was sitting on her bed, holding the can of water, half-empty.

"Sorry, I was really thirsty," she said, lying down and turning her back to him. She felt something drop on the bed.

"If you need anything, just call me. Don't ever leave this room without my order!" he commanded, then left. She turned after he left and found a small mobile phone on the bed. She grabbed it and scrolled through, finding only one number saved—his. Ignoring it, she dialled Nicki's number, but it didn't go through. She tried Nora's number, but it did the same thing.

"Fixed dialling?" she muttered.

CHAPTER ELEVEN

Tricia sat before the mirror in the makeup room, scrolling through her tablet for any news about Seth, but found nothing. Frustrated, she bit her lips and kept searching. A photo of Montserrat and her new husband caught her eye, and she scoffed, "What do they think they're doing?" She threw the tablet onto the desk, still glaring at it. She knew she had made a fool of herself by paying a journalist to spread rumours about her marriage, but she couldn't think of a better option.

She tapped her nails on the desk, staring at herself in the mirror, feeling increasingly despondent. Noticing two young models behind her giggling about something, she ignored them and applied her usual red lipstick. The girls laughed and she felt it ring in her ear, almost driving her crazy. She squeezed the lipstick in her hand, trying not to embarrass herself.

"Right! Have you seen the new director?" one model asked the other.

"He's here already?" the other replied.

"Yes, this morning. There's a lot of stories about him, but he's crazy handsome." she whispered,

"I want to see him already."

"Shall we?" They left, leaving Tricia's hand shaking as she brought the lipstick back to her lips again, but her hands were terribly shaking. In anger, she threw it at the waal. She had opposed bringing in the new director and had clearly asked for a different choice, but they brought him in anyway.

Why?

She was no longer valuable to them. Her words and choices no longer mattered. He's going to see her horrible position; she's no longer the queen of the light. She touched her cheeks, fighting back tears.

A knock came on the door, making Gina frown, thinking it was Seth. Instead, a lady walked in with a smile, dressed like a doctor.

"Hi," the lady said. Gina thought she looked familiar but was more surprised to see someone new. She hadn't seen many people since arriving—only Seth, Liam, Rosa, and Cate.

"Hi," Gina replied, glancing behind the lady to see if Seth was with her.

"Oh, he's busy upstairs," the lady said, noticing Gina's glance.

"Oh," Gina said as the lady dropped her kit and smiled, revealing a deep dimple on her left cheek.

"Don't worry. I'm your new doctor, Dr. Lucy Reigns."

"New doctor? What about Cate?" Gina asked.

"Cate? Oh, Dr. Lewis. She's almost due," Lucy said, unlocking the kit and taking out her equipment.

"How's she doing?" Gina asked.

"Good, I guess. I didn't say she's sick," Lucy replied, smiling as she put on her gloves. "You don't have to worry about her. She's a doctor and in good hands. You should focus on yourself," she paused while Gina just stared at her, "just joking. I'll be your doctor until childbirth. You're in my care, so you don't have to worry about anything. I received a report on your progress from your former doctor. You're safe with me," she assured Gina as she looked through her file.

"It's been long since I saw her, I mean Cate. The last time I was sick, we didn't get to talk," Gina said.

"I see. Open your mouth," Lucy instructed, and Gina complied. "How have you been feeling recently?"

"More energised in the evening; morning sickness; my stomach is rising."

"Yeah, I can see that. No quickening yet?"

"No what?"

"Do you feel any movement in your belly?"

"Hmm... no."

"Any other issues or complications?"

"I just have trouble sleeping nowadays."

"Alright," Lucy said, writing it down. "Is your diet balanced?"

"I think so."

Lucy checked the fridge, scanned its contents, and nodded. "Is that all you take?"

"Almost, but he makes breakfast, lunch, and dinner."

Lucy smiled. "Alright, I'll talk to him about the rest. You need exercise and more ventilation, okay?"

Gina nodded. As Lucy packed her equipment, Gina asked, "Have we seen each other before?"

"Sorry?"

"You look so familiar, so I thought... never mind," she said, and Lucy nodded.

"Alright, see you next checkup," Lucy said and left. Gina thought for a while, her instinct telling her they had met before. She prayed they hadn't.

She turned to the mirror, noticing her stomach bulging out slowly every day. Liam had promised to visit today; she remembered and checked the time. She picked up the phone Seth had given her, but she couldn't make any other calls apart from his. She had dialled her mom's number and other numbers she could remember, but they always beeped off. Only one number worked. She dialled his number, and it rang for a while before he answered.

"What do you want?" She scoffed and cut the call. She lay down, opened the book she was reading, and unfolded the page where she had left off. The door opened, and she turned to see Seth standing there.

"You called?"

"What? Oh! No... yeah, sorry, I just..." She struggled to find a reason.

"I just wanted to know if Liam was there. He said he'd come."

"What?" he said, looking a bit confused.

"I'm sorry, it's nothing; I'm good," she said, but he turned.

"Come up," he said, leaving. Gina got up and followed him to the kitchen.

She sat down while he prepared lunch.

"It seems like you were busy. I can do lunch," she offered, but got no response.

"You got a new doctor," she said, wanting to discuss Lucy.

"She said Cate is almost due. I wish I could see her. She's a good woman. I wonder if it's a boy or a girl. Did you see her? By the way, the new doctor looks familiar," she paused, thinking again. "But don't worry, I don't think we've met before," she chuckled. "Did she talk to you? She said she'd talk to you about other things. She said I need more exercise and ventilation; she also—"

Seth turned sharply, and she stopped talking. He dropped a bowl of fresh tomatoes in front of her. "Pick out the heads."

"Aww, they look so cute. This is from the garden, right?" She got no response.

"Wow, I always wanted to make a garden out of the small space in the backyard, but Mom never agreed to it. She said it would bring insects and stuff," she said, lost in her thoughts. Seth clenched his jaw as he cut the carrots, wondering why she was talking to him.

"She just didn't know how healthy it is to eat fresh vegetables. She never liked vegetables. Do you like vegetables?" she asked, standing up.

"I'm done. Wow," she said, admiring Seth's neat julienne cuts. "Where did you learn to cut so neatly? My mother is the only one that can—" Seth stared at her again.

"Sit.down," he said, pointing to the chair. Gina felt a little angry. She was trying to be friendly and she's tired of talking to herself. He might as well just bring Rosa back.

"Sorry," she said, sitting down. Seth watched her through the glass cabinet as she bit her nails. His hand slipped, and the knife slit his finger.

"Fuck!"

"What?!" Gina rushed to him, took his bleeding hand, and shoved it into the sink, washing off the blood. Then she sprinkled salt on the cut.

"Ouch! Fuck!" Seth exclaimed, taking his hand back.

"Don't be a baby. It'll stop the bleeding," she said, taking his hand and blowing on it. Seth watched her for a while and then pulled his hand away.

"I'm fine," he said, moving her aside. His hand brushed against her stomach, and she felt a movement.

"Did you feel that?!"

"What?" he asked.

"I felt my stomach move. I think that's what the doctor called quickening."

"What?" he asked again with a face Gina couldn't read.

"Never mind," she said, sitting down. she almost hissed. Sometimes, it's just better to sit in that prison room than to see him.

They heard the door open, and Liam walked in. "Ha! I'm always on time."

"Liam" Gina stood up and hugged him.

"Easy there, pregnant woman," Liam said, and Gina released him, sitting back down. "And how is the little guy doing?"

"He's fine. Wait... little guy? What if she's a girl?" she asked, pretending to frown.

"Well then... howdy, little angel?" Gina laughed.

"You look happy today. I like that," Liam said, pointing at her.

"Well," she shrugged, "did you get it?"

"Yes! All of them."

"Aww, you're a darling," she said, blowing air kisses and grabbing the bags.

Liam went to Seth. "Hey, man."

"Hey," Seth said, watching them through the glassware, wondering when they had become so close and chatty. "Have you finalised the contract?"

"Almost," Liam replied.

"You know it's tomorrow."

"Yeah."

"The interview. Katy's going to be there. Are you ready?"

"Ever."

"How's she, Katy?"

"She asked me to marry her."

"W-what?" Liam asked, trying to hold back laughter. "Man, she's head over heels for ya. So what did you say?"

"What do you expect me to say? Nothing."

"Nothing?"

"Should I have said yes to a lady proposing to me?"

"Well, but it's a good thing."

"Hey, Liam, you didn't get the orange colour. It's my second favourite!" Gina said, still going through the bag.

"Next time, baby."

"Baby?" Seth asked before he could think.

"What? She's sweet."

"Since when?" Seth asked, confused and annoyed.

Tricia returned to the makeup room after the shooting. She had been avoiding eye contact with the new director. Playing a supporting role among younger models was already disappointing and disgraceful. She wanted to change and leave immediately but he was there in the room. Seeing him, she turned to leave.

"Patricia," he called, and she turned with a forced smile.

"Noah," she greeted and walked in, closing the door behind her.

"What are you doing here?" she asked, feeling sheepish.

"You've changed," he said, with that wild smile she once loved. Still love.

"That's what everyone's saying," she replied, and they hugged briefly.

"Want to grab a coffee?" he asked, and she nodded.

At a nearby café, they settled on hot coffees.

"So, how's life?" he asked.

"Don't even ask," she smiled, taking a sip.

"I heard you got married," he said. She looked at him, embarrassed.

"Not..." she paused. "What about you, married?" she deflected.

"Engaged," he replied, showing her his ring. Tricia smiled, biting her lip.

They sat in silence for a moment.

"It could've been us," Tricia said sadly.

"You told me to leave."

"And you left?" She looked around, blinking back tears. "You know what I was going through."

"You weren't going through anything, Tricia. You were so focused on your career that you barely gave anyone a chance. I hung in there until you pushed me away."

"Yeah, and I don't want to ever see you again," she snapped, then left abruptly.

Faith sat in her car, waiting to see her daughter or Damien. A tap on her window startled her. A woman stood there.

"Let's talk. I am Damien's wife," she said. Faith hesitated but got out and followed her inside.

"Who are you?" the woman asked after Faith declined a drink.

"I'm Faith, a writer—"

"To Damien, I mean."

"We were... course mates."

"Then you must be the woman who abandoned Violet," the woman deduced. Faith nodded.

"So, what do you want?"

"I just want to take my daughter home," Faith said.

"Home? Your daughter?" The woman chuckled. "Do you think I am going to let that happen?"

"Look, I'm not here to pick a fight or deprive you of her."

"Then why are you here suddenly? For the inheritance?"

"What? No... I just..."

"Then why now?" the woman demanded.

"My mother... knew, and soon my husband will find out."

"So? What difference will it make?"

"I'm sorry I let her go. I had to."

"I'm not giving her to you," the woman said, standing up.

"I'm not asking you to," Faith said, following her to the door.

"Don't ever come back," the woman warned, locking the gate behind Faith.

Montserrat hugged her mom and sat beside her.

"Hi, mother."

"Pregnant yet?"

"No."

"What are you waiting for? We have fourteen more months. We're running out of time."

"I'm trying, mother."

"Don't try! Just get to bed with Hector."

"I know your plans, mother, but I love Hector. That's why I married him—not for some inheritance or to make babies!" Montserrat protested. Theresa stood up and slapped her.

"Get your mind together. I'm doing this for both of us. Your father's family won't give you a dime. You know that!" She sat down and held her hand.

"Stick with me, and let's do this together," she whispered harshly before leaving.

Montserrat touched her red cheek as tears rolled down.

Maria sat on the moulded chair, her new hobby. She dreamed of her daughter and grandson every night. She checked the time repeatedly.

"Why are you here again?" she heard someone ask and turn. Her daughter was standing behind her. Maria stood up with a smile.

"Oh... Hi."

"I know who you are. What do you want?"

Maria stood there, tears welling up.

"You... how... how did you find out?" she whispered.

The door opened, and the children ran out.

"Let's go somewhere quiet," Maryglory said.

They walked slowly through the field path.

"When did you find out?" Maria finally asked.

"A long time ago. When I was still young."

"How?" Maria asked, her heart beating hard against her chest and her eyes filled with love, sadness, and disgrace.

"When I found out that orphanages are for children without parents, I asked Sister Philomena and Father Raymond who my real parents were. They couldn't give me a straight answer for a while," Maryglory smiled. "Until one day, your mother came. She was supporting our orphanage at the time. I became her favourite. When I was eighteen, I saw you for the first time. You came with her to the orphanage."

Maria stopped walking. She couldn't remember that.

"Somehow, I knew I had a connection to your mother. It was obvious that I looked like her. My suspicion rose when I saw you with Father Raymond that day and later heard him tell Sister Philomena about you." Maryglory stopped walking. Maria didn't move.

"I followed you for a year and tried to like you, but I kept asking myself why you left me. You couldn't even recognise me."

"I'm so sorry," Maria said, sobbing.

"What are you doing here?" Maryglory asked, folding her arms.

"I... I just..." Maria stammered, guilt shutting her mouth.

"If you're here for my baby, leave. We have nothing to do with you. I just wanted to make that clear," Maryglory said, walking away.

Maria felt her knees wobble. She kneeled there, her heart aching and tears streaming down. She wondered what she had done to herself and what her life had become.

CHAPTER TWELVE

Seth was in his study, deeply engrossed in his work, when Gina knocked on the door. Without looking up, he asked, "What do you want?"

"Can I come in?" she asked softly. Receiving no reply, she slowly walked in and settled on one of the two sofas, pulling out her crocheting equipment. Thanks to sweet Liam, she was no longer bored.

Seth was so absorbed in his work that he didn't notice Gina's presence. Hours passed, and at 6:47 PM, he finally realised his back was aching and his throat was dry. He decided to finish the last set of documents before calling it a day. Just then, he remembered he hadn't made dinner. As he stood up, he saw a ball of wool at the foot of his chair. Frowning, he picked it up and noticed Gina asleep on the sofa. For a moment, he was surprised. What if someone, obviously Katy, had come?

He gathered her crocheting materials and stared at her for a second. It annoyed him that she was sleeping peacefully on his sofa. He tried to call her and realised he hadn't called her by her name before. Unsure of how to address her, he awkwardly called out, "Hey!" But Gina was deeply asleep. He tried again, more annoyed, and then bent over her, hitting the sofa. Gina jolted awake, her face just inches from his. They stared at each other, both startled. Gina, confused and disoriented, panicked and instinctively slapped Seth, making him fall backwards onto the floor.

Realising what she had done, Gina covered her mouth in shock.

What have I done? What was I thinking? Oh my god! she thought.

Seth quickly stood up, trying to maintain his composure despite the humiliation and anger boiling inside him. "I'm so sorry," Gina whispered, but Seth ignored her, walking out of the study with his face burning from the slap.

How could she?! He fumed as he looked at his reflection in the bathroom mirror, his face still burning. Why is she so stupid? What was she thinking? He was disgusted. She disgusts him. She's a dumb girl and she's getting to annoy him badly. He knew she was the wrong person for this. Her face flashed in front of him.

"f*ck!" He splashed cold water on his face, cursing her in his mind.

Gina left the study, leaving her equipment behind, and tiptoed to her room, her mind racing with regret and disbelief at her action.

What have I done, What was I thinking? Anyway, it wasn't my fault; he woke me up like I was some slave or something!

She kept thinking about it, and it became funny to her, but how is she going to face him?

My head

Her stomach twisted. They haven't had dinner yet; they didn't even have lunch. She picked up her phone to call him about dinner but she knows that it's totally a bad idea. They are obviously not going to have dinner. The phone beeped, startling her. She opened the message to find, "*Come up.*"

She dropped the phone and hurried to the kitchen, peeking in to see Seth already eating. He had ordered food online.

She sighed and quietly sat down, eating slowly despite her hunger. She was contemplating how to apologise when she began,

"I'm sorry ab—," but Seth cut her off by standing up and clearing the table, ignoring her unfinished apology. He took the vegetables first, then the mashed potatoes. Gina watched him in surprise. She stared at her plate; she hadn't touched anything.

Reaching for the chicken, Gina accidentally stabbed Seth's hand with her fork.

"Jesus!" they both screamed as blood started dripping from Seth's hand. Gina stood up and the fork fell to the floor. She felt cold sweat running down her spine all of a sudden, her heart beating hard against her chest.

What has she done again?!

She stood there frozen while Seth turned on the sink faucet, letting the water run over his wound until it turned pink. He turned off the tap, opened one of the kitchen drawers and grabbed a kit. She rushed to his side to help.

"let me help", Before she could touch his hand, Seth withdrew it and, by accident, knocked down the antiseptic, and the whole of it poured on the floor, Seth snapped, "Get out!"

"I just want—"

"Get the fuck out! And don't ever touch me or let me see you again!" he yelled, making Gina run out of the room in tears.

The next day, after an interview, Katy insisted on following Seth home. She talked non-stop on the way, but Seth remained silent. Katy announced their relationship during the interview, expecting Seth to react, but he remained calm, much to her surprise. Maybe he's starting to like her after all, she thought and smirked.

At the mansion, Katy followed Seth to his study and settled on his desk.

"what happened to your hand?" she asked but he ignored her.

"Want anything?" he asked.

"Something creamy or hot," she replied and Seth left. She stood up, walked to the sofa and sat down, relaxing on it. She saw a bag sitting on the table. She opened it and found wool. She was surprised. She heard footsteps, kept them back, and pretended she was doing nothing. Seth returned with a glass of champagne.

"I asked for something hot or creamy. This is neither," she complained.

"You should drink up and go home," Seth said, scrolling through his tablet. Annoyed, Katy bit her lips and got up. She walked to him and sat on his lap, taking the tab from him. She kept it on the desk and wrapped her hands around him.

"What kind of girls do you like?" Seth tried to lift her off his body but she pressed it against him, her chest on his.

"Girls that crochet?" She teased him, attempting to kiss him.

"Are you drunk?" he asked and Katy gave out a crooked laugh.

"It doesn't suit you," she said and she tried to kiss him. Seth lifted her off and placed her on the desk. "You need to go home."

Katy, masking her anger, gulped down the champagne and grabbed her bag. Seth is not good with girls, she knows; its probably nothing serious. "Remember, we're dating. We should make more public appearances. What about tomorrow, lunch?"

"I have things I need to do," Seth replied.

"I'll see you at Monte Cristo's. We'll go together from there," she said, pecking him before leaving. Seth tried to follow her,

"don't worry, my driver's here", she said and walked out.

Seth walked into the kitchen, noticing the dripping tap and guessing Gina had just been there. *Careless.* He thought.

After the previous day's incident, Gina stayed away from Seth, avoiding him at all costs. She only came up for lunch and dinner, which she ate quickly before retreating to her room. He doesn't cook anymore; he orders food and stocks it in the fridge every day, so all she has to do is microwave it and eat. She takes breakfast in her room. She no longer read the books Liam brought, feeling increasingly isolated and frustrated.

She had heard a girl's voice from his study the other night when she went to get her equipment. Not that she cared; she just wondered who would like such a man. Her baby bump was getting bigger, and she felt more alone every day. The doctor has checked up on her more often, but she's not as chatty as Cate. She heard Cate had put to bed a baby girl; she wanted to see her. She sat alone on her bed, legs crossed, her baby bump touching her legs. She kept staring at the TV, but her mind was somewhere else.

A knock came from the door, startling her. Liam walked in.

"Helloo," he said, and sat beside her. They hugged.

"how are you doing?", Gina paused her lips and shrugged.

"I know, come on," he said, standing up.

"did you get anything for me?", 'Wait for it", he grabbed her hand and they walked up the stairs to the kitchen. Seth was with his tab again, scrolling. Liam started with the books and then the fruits; he got alot of them.

"Guess what? My mom visited his bachelor son and decided to get a lot of things," Gina laughed. She wasn't excited; she just wanted to do something that would pause the boredom for awhile.

They ate and chatted, and Gina ate like she'd never eaten until she couldn't take anymore. Liam made some juice and brought it to the table. "thank you",

"to the baby", Liam said,

"To the baby," they clicked their mug together and continued their chat. Gina talked about her family, how her mother can be, how she cried when it got to her father, and then talked about how crazy Nicki can be. Liam talked about his high school days and the girls he had dated.

Seth, pretending to be engrossed in his tablet, listened to their conversation. He felt disgusted at first, annoyed, almost laughed, and felt it was silly to listen to them. Back to his tab and back to listening to them.

Around 9 pm, Gina felt tired and needed to sleep.

"the doctor will be coming tomorrow for a checkup; I need to get to bed", Liam followed her back to her room and pecked her good night. He walked back to the kitchen, yawning. He picked up the mugs and kept them in the sink.

"Men, I think am going to sleep over; I am hell over tired",

"no",

"what", he said, yawning again.

"never mind",

"good night, man", he said, leaving the kitchen.

Seth walked to the sink. He clenched his teeth at how dirty it was. He walked down to her room after cleaning the kitchen. He slowly opened the door; she was soundly sleeping. He looked at the calendar where she marked the date; she didn't marked today yet.

He had been checking up on her every night, unless he felt so stressed out. He felt guilty for shouting at her, but he just wanted to teach her some manners. He closed the door and went back to his room. He found Liam soundly sleeping and snoring. He hissed and left the room to go to the guest room.

The next day, the doctor arrived for a check-up. During the examination, she surprised Gina by asking, "Why did you choose surrogacy?" They've never had a personal conversation. Lucy looked at her, not backing out; she wanted to know why.

"money? You love him?" She asked with a smile, then she checked her temperature.

Gina was taken aback. "I needed a job," she replied.

"Does your mother know?" the doctor pressed.

"Why are you asking?" Gina asked, her heart pounding.

"Because I know she'd never agree to this," the doctor said, trying to insert a syringe into Gina's hand.

Gina pulled back. "Do you know me?" Lucy smiled, "relax", she said, taking her hand again but Gina took it.

"do you... really... know me?", Lucy stood up and closed the syringe.

"You don't remember me?" the doctor asked, smiling. Gina felt her hand shaking all of a sudden but she kept her eyes on her. "Summer, 2014, camp party?"

112

Gina's mind raced. She had invited Nicki over, so she was with Nicki and Toby.

Omg Toby!

She remembered, "You're Toby's girlfriend!"

"Ex," the doctor corrected. "What a coincidence, right?"

She saw that Gina's face has changed. "Don't worry. Your secret's safe with me," the doctor assured her. "I'll see you again next week", She said but Gina kept staring at her till she left the room.

Gina was left disturbed. Could she trust her? She decided not to tell Seth, fearing he might cancel the deal.

Only God knows what he can do. She thought, shaking her head.

A knock came from the door. She looked up and Seth was standing by the door.

"Are you alright?" he asked but there was no sign of real concern in his tone. She nodded and laid down, facing the wall.

Seth stood there for awhile and shut the door. He hasn't seen her like that before.

....

Seth woke up when he heard something scratching on the door. He turned on the light, went and opened the door and found Gina lying on the floor. He hurriedly bent over and picked her up, He dropped her on his bed, and that's when he noticed the blood running down her legs.

"What the f*ck!" He picked up his phone and called Liam first; he couldn't make out what he was saying, so he cut the call and called the doctor next. Gina lay on the bed, She kept moaning slowly and couldn't open her eyes.

"hey, look at me", Seth said, placing her head on his laps, The doctor called back.

"hello, how's she now?",

"her eyes are damn closed!",

"Calm down, Mr Seth; I'll be there soon; just give me a short description of her current state." Seth took a deep breath.

"I think the bleeding has stopped; she's breathing but she is not f*cking responding to me!",

"alright, listen to me, help her sit up a little and rub her stomach slightly; I'm almost there", "what?", he asked but the line has tripped off. He placed double pillows and laid her on it, Gina moaned again. He slightly started to rub her stomach; it felt strong on his hands, He rubbed his temple with his other hands.

Could it be that the baby's gone? he thought.

Oh, fuck no

Few minutes later, the doctor arrived. She rushed to her and opened her eyes, then started the basic treatment.

"Did she complain about any disturbances or aches?"

"No, she didn't," Seth answered.

Lucy requested that he leave the room. He obeyed and went to his study, but he kept pacing up and down.

About thirty minutes later, Lucy walked into the study and he rushed her, "how's she?",

"she's fine, she just suffered a little shock, it often happens on first pregnancies, she's fine, the baby is fine, she just needs to rest", she said, Seth nodded and exhaled.

"the baby is okay too", she said and there was two seconds silence.

"okay", he replied.

"alright, I'll come back tomorrow to check upon her again",

"what if she starts bleeding again?"

"she won't; I'll do another check up on her tomorrow, and then we'll see if she's having any complications", "alright, thanks for coming". After the doctor left, he walked to his room. Gina was sleeping quietly. Her body's neat but there's still tiny droplets of blood on the floor. He took his time and cleaned it up. He checked up on her again before sitting down on the sofa.

Gina woke up in the morning, and she was a bit confused on what had happened. She tried to get down the bed, and just then Seth walked in with her breakfast.

"what happened?", she asked.

"stay in bed", Gina said, taking back her legs as he placed the breakfast on his desk.

"How did I get here?" Seth set the table and placed the breakfast before her.

"eat up; the doctor will be here soon",

"wait, I was bleeding!", she remembered and raised the sheets but there's no blood.

"omg! Is the baby okay?" she asked with eyes wide open.

"yes, the doctor said you're both fine; now eat", She exhaled and remembered their last conversation.

"the doctor came last night? Did she say anything?", Seth was walking to the door when she asked the question, He turned and stared at her for two seconds.

"I just told you what the doctor said", he said, turning and leaving the kitchen. While he boiled the hot water, he wondered whether she got dumber after what happened.

When he came back, she was done. He took the table, empty mug and plate, "thank you", she said, Seth ignored her and walked out of the room. He came back with the doctor. Gina's heart skipped at seeing her with Seth.

"hello, how are you feeling?", she asked, touching her forehead.

"I think am okay",

115

"do you feel any aches or discomfort anywhere?", Gina flew her head,

"can you remember what happened last night?",

"I just felt like I wanted to pee, then I saw blood, then I felt dizzy and tired, Is my baby alright?",

"Yes," she said, looking at Seth, then back at her. Gina felt her heart jump again.

"Mr Seth, can you give us a minute?", Seth looked at both of them, then nodded, He left and closed the door behind him.

Gina stared at lucy,

"I think you're carrying a twin",

"What?" Gina gasped.

"It's just a guess, but I've handled many pregnancies. Yours feels the same," the doctor explained. "What are you going to do?"

"what do you mean?",

"you signed a contract, right?",

"yes ", "so, you're going to give him the baby?", For the first time, the thought crossed her mind, She stared at her for awhile.

"Yes," she answered, almost whispering,

"do you even know why he's doing this?" the doctor pressed, but their conversation was cut short as Seth entered with Liam.

"wh-", Gina said but stopped. Seth and Liam walked in as Liam rushed to her side. "are you alright?", Gina smiled nervously and nodded, Lucy got up to leave.

"she's okay now; we'll start our normal checkups. Just make sure she does some exercise, gets some light, eats healthy, and needs a lot of rest too", she told Seth, smiling at Gina before leaving.

Gina was disturbed; she kept nodding and smiling at everything Liam was saying.

What does she mean? She thought,

She couldn't shake off the doctor's words. She had signed a contract without fully understanding it. What were they going to do with her baby?

Her mind raced with worry, her hand instinctively rubbing her growing belly.

CHAPTER THIRTEEN

Tricia stared at her phone again; the calls had stopped. Nobody cares for her, she thought, picking up the wine bottle. She tried to drink from it, but nothing came out. She chuckled as a tear fell, then threw the bottle against the wall, shattering it.

She hadn't gone to a photoshoot in four weeks. She couldn't handle not being the lead model. She couldn't stand the embarrassment of Noah's presence or the mocking laughter of the younger models. It rang in her ears, making her feel so inferior.

She had fought with one of them, and everyone took her side. It was humiliating; they all looked at her as if she didn't belong anymore. The stage was no longer hers; the spotlight had moved on.

Tears rolled down her cheeks as she remembered how Noah looked at her and left after the altercation, probably disappointed. He couldn't even take her side. She wiped her tears as her phone beeped again. Her hand shook as she picked it up and tapped on the newest notification.

Headline: McGregor's Inheritance in Line:**
*Another big news from the city heads, as the granddaughter announces she's a month pregnant. This is no rumour, as she's seen walking out of the hospital with her mother and husband.

They went ahead to give an interview, where they showed proof of the pregnancy.

Tricia stared at the picture of Montserrat with her mother. She clenched her teeth, her hand shaking terribly. Another notification came in. She wasn't going to open it, but she saw Noah's picture on it, so she clicked.

Noah had set a wedding date with his fiancée. His fiancée looked familiar, so she looked her up and found out she had won a modelling competition once and had been taking international ads. *She's a model?*

She threw the phone at the wall and screamed. She cried for a few minutes and then felt numb. She just sat there, her eyes locked on the picture of her grandmother hanging on the wall. Then she let out a crooked laugh.

"Smile," Theresa told Montserrat as the reporters flashed their cameras.

They had the reporters interview them for thirty minutes while Theresa answered all the questions. Montserrat sat there, feeling uncomfortable. They had seven more interviews lined up for the week. Some cameramen even came to the house. She felt so tired and frustrated.

As they stood up for more pictures, Montserrat hurried to the car where Hector was waiting.

"Are you okay?" Hector asked.

"I'm just tired," she said, resting her head on his hand. Theresa joined them.

"We should go shopping for baby stuff. I bet people will take pictures. Where's the most popular mall in the area?"

"Ma!" Montserrat called.

"What?" Theresa snapped.

"I'm tired. I'm just four weeks pregnant," Montserrat said, trying not to stress herself more.

"Don't act like I'm doing this for myself!"

"Oh yes, you are! You are!"

"We need to create more publicity!"

"We've created enough, Mother! I'm pregnant!" Montserrat said and left the car.

"You better go get your wife and make sure she gets her attitude together," she told Hector.

"I think this is enough for a day," he said, looking at her.

"It's not like I'm doing this for myself alone," she said, and he went after Montserrat.

Maria waited after the service as Fr. Ray did his usual greetings. He made two cups of coffee and sat beside her, handing her a cup. They sat quietly, watching the dead leaves move with the wind.

"Have you seen Frank since then?" Fr. Ray asked. Maria hesitated, feeling caught in the act.

"No," she said, wrapping her hands around the mug to let the warmth overwhelm her.

"He came when you left," he said, taking a sip. "He knows about her."

"What?!" she said, turning to face him.

"I couldn't hide her from him," he said, touching the tip of his mug while remembering that day years ago.

"Why are you telling me this now?" she asked.

"I don't know."

"Does she know?" she asked, and he nodded.

"He comes once in a while, but after she had a baby, he comes more often," he said. Maria's hand trembled. She imagined what it would feel like to see him again.

"He should be coming soon. Peter's birthday is on Tuesday," he said, standing up. Maria sat there, wondering what to do. He looked at her, pitying her. He almost wished he could turn back the clock, but he knew he shouldn't. He had his own share of that pain, and all this would only open the healing wound.

Nora walked down the stairs. Her mother was in her usual chair, crocheting. Nora went to the kitchen to make dinner.

"Have you heard anything from your sister yet?"

"Not a thing, since the video call and the money," she said, continuing to make dinner. While she was cooking, a knock came at the door. Nora opened it, and Stephanie walked in.

"Stephie?" Nora called, surprised. Their mom turned, equally surprised.

"Evening, Mama," Stephie said, hugging her.

"What's wrong?"

"Must something be wrong before I visit my own home?"

"Young lady, this is not your home anymore."

"Well, Mama, I'm not young anymore. What have you got cooking, Nora?" Nora rushed to the kitchen to finish making dinner.

They sat around the table, having dinner. Stephie avoided questions about herself.

"What job did you say Gina is doing again?" she asked as their mom's phone vibrated.

"Talk of the devil," Nora said, picking up the phone. She tapped on the notification and gasped.

"What is it?" Stephie asked, reaching to grab the phone from her. Nora extended her hand to view the message again.

"Oh my God!" she said, turning the phone to show them.

"Regina Rachel just sent another five hundred thousand dollars!"

"Another what?!" Stephie asked.

"She sent us half a million dollars months ago," Nora explained, giving her the phone. "She just sent another one!"

"Oh my God!" Stephie screamed in excitement.

"Send it back!" their mom said, hitting her hand on the table and startling them.

"What?!" they both asked.

"I said send it back," their mother commanded.

"Why?" Stephanie asked.

"We can't accept it."

"But why?" Nora asked.

"She left months ago, called us once, but sent tonnes of money? We don't even know exactly where she's working. We haven't seen your sister in a long time, and the two of you are happy over the money she sent." She threw her plate into the sink.

"But Mom, sending money means she's fine, right?" Stephanie said, and Nora nodded.

"Send it back, woman!" she said, going back to her chair to continue crocheting.

"Explain this to me," Stephie said, already feeling excitement rush to her head.

"She sent half a million dollars at first, and now..." Nora said, staring at the phone.

"Wait, she sent half a million to only you and Mom. What about me?"

121

"To Mom's account."

"What's the job again? How was she... Where exactly is she?" Nora ignored her.

"I can go and look for her if you two are worried," Nora suggested. "I mean, instead of sending the money back, we can find out what she's exactly doing."

"You're not going anywhere," her mother said.

"We should know if she's okay or not and why she's sending such money home, right?"

"What are you two talking about? She's not lost or kidnapped! Someone who sends money to her family is fine and okay with me," Stephanie said.

"I'm not changing my mind," Geraldine concluded.

"I have a business trip to New York on Monday. I'll see what I can do then," Stephanie said.

"I'll go with you," Nora said.

"Sis, I said a business trip. What job is she doing again?"

"She said an accountant works at a... company. I don't know, something like that."

"You should leave her alone. She left on her own. Probably that girl she called her friend introduced her to one of her evil ways. God knows I taught y'all the good ways."

"Mom," Stephie called.

"You never know," Nora supported.

"She's not a kid; she's a grown woman," Stephanie said, leaving them in her room.

Gina sat on Seth's bed, crocheting. Liam walked in with a smile.

"How are you doing, sweetie?" he asked, pecking her cheek.

"I feel okay."

"Yeah?" Gina nodded. Seth walked in with a tray of fruits.

"Your belly is getting big," Liam said.

"Yeah, you want to feel it?" She moved the yarn to the side so Liam could touch her stomach.

"Wow, it's so strong."

"Yeah, the baby moved once. I was so sure I felt it."

"Really?" Seth cleared his throat, and Liam sat up. As Seth was about to set the tray down, Liam took it from him and gently placed it by Gina's side.

"It's time to eat. The doctor said you need to eat more fresh foods, vegetables, and fruits," he said, picking up a slice of fruit with a fork. "Here." Gina took it.

"Thank you," she said. Seth ignored them and moved to the other side of the bed, touching her forehead for the tenth time. Gina rolled her eyes.

"I'm fine," she insisted, but he said nothing and went to his desk, gathering some files before heading to the door.

"If you need anything, text me," he said and left. Liam pecked her cheek and followed Seth.

Gina stared at the door for a while, thinking about what Lucy had told her. She didn't want it to bother her, but she couldn't help it. She wondered whether she could ask Liam why they wanted the baby. She rubbed her stomach and felt her eyes sting at the thought of giving her baby away.

What are you doing? Don't nag me; it's too late to start regretting. Lucy had mentioned she might be carrying twins. Is that even possible? Cate never said anything like that could happen. On second thought, it was Lucy Reigns who said it.

She sat on the bed for a while, lacking the appetite to eat and unable to shake the thoughts from her mind. She looked around for water. It was on the far side of the desk. She reached for the cup first, then tried to grab the jug, but her hand slipped, and the glass jug fell and shattered on the floor.

Her heart skipped a beat as she looked at the door, expecting it to fly open and reveal an angry Seth. Slowly, she climbed down the bed and began picking up the glass pieces as best she could.

The door swung open, and Gina flinched at the sight of Seth rushing to her side. He clenched his teeth, picking up the broken glass.

"What the hell happened?"

"I just wanted—"

"I told you to text me if you needed anything, didn't I?" Gina stayed silent, fearing she might regret speaking. She tried to pick up another piece of glass but cut her finger.

"Ouch!"

"Don't f*cking touch anything!" he screamed. Gina immediately stood to leave but stepped on the water and slipped. She screamed, but Seth caught her just in time, his arms wrapped around her, one hand behind her head and shoulders, the other around her belly. She felt the warmth of his body and the strong scent of his cologne overpowering her senses. His body is actually touching hers.

"Are you okay?" he asked, his heart pounding. Something terrible could have happened, and he could have lost the baby and his inheritance.

Why can't this woman ever be careful?!

"Ouch!" Gina felt pain in her hand, which she had hit on the bed frame, and her leg was bleeding. He slowly helped her stand and sit on the bed.

"Don't do anything," he told her and he went to get the first aid kit. Gina's cheeks were hot, and her heart was racing. She kept taking deep breaths until Seth returned with the kit. He cleaned and bandaged her finger first, then massaged the other hand she had hit on the bed frame. Gina kept quiet, only saying, "Ouch," occasionally.

She didn't know why, but her heart kept racing, her eyes were acting weird, and her cheeks were hot. Seth slowly lifted her leg onto the bed and began cleaning it. Gina giggled.

"You think it's funny?"

"Sorry," Gina said, clearing her throat.

He applied some balm and tried to bandage her leg, but Gina started giggling again. He looked at her.

"Sorry, I can't help it. It tickles," she said, bursting out laughing. Seth almost smiled but kept his composure. When he was done, Gina wiggled her legs.

"Thank you," she said. He closed the kit, cleaned the area, and ordered lunch. Afterward, he moved his work files to his room. Gina thought he would ask her to move back to her room, but he didn't. Instead, he decided to work in his room to keep an eye on her, though he didn't say so. Somehow, Gina found that both attractive and uncomfortable at the same time.

When she woke up in the morning, Seth was standing before his mirror. She closed her eyes and opened them again. Seth was only wearing a towel around his waist, and she stared at his chest. She felt the same feelings again. Her heart suddenly changed rhythm, pumping hard against her chest, her cheeks burning. He turned to look at her, and she pretended to be asleep.

Seth had intentionally missed Katy's calls, so she sent a message. Seth decided to meet with her; he didn't want her to visit since Gina was staying in his room.

He slept on the single couch in his room, waking up occasionally to check on Gina. Each time he did, she was soundly sleeping. He had covered her leg, which was outside the duvet. He touched her head to feel her temperature, which was normal. Unconsciously, he stared at her for a while, then she mumbled something and threw her leg out of the duvet again.

In the morning, he saw one of her legs outside the duvet. He remembered covering it again last night, sighed, and went to the shower.

When he was done, he took out the clothes he would wear and placed them on his chair. He walked to the mirror to apply some cream.

He could see Gina in the mirror, her legs still outside. He took a step back to see her face and noticed her eyes were open. He looked at her on the bed, but her eyes were shut. He looked back at the mirror with her eyes still shut. He walked back to the bathroom, sure he had seen her eyes open. He looked at his chest and touched it, smirking.

During breakfast, Gina felt so uncomfortable, like she had done something wrong.

"I sent money to your family," he said, and Gina raised her face immediately. Their eyes locked for a second before she looked away.

"You did?" He didn't reply.

"It was sent through your account, so they thought you sent it."

"Oh." Gina nodded, avoiding his eyes. She wanted badly to know what was going on at home.

"Thanks," she said, losing her appetite.

Gina completed the sweater she was crocheting. She had initially planned to make it for herself but changed her mind halfway. Seth walked out of his wardrobe, all dressed up.

"You're going out?"

"Yeah, I might be a little late. There's dinner in the fridge." Gina nodded.

"Seth," Gina called, and he turned. It was the second time she had called him by name; it felt foreign in her mouth and weird in his ears.

"Yes," he answered, surprised that he did.

"The weather is cold outside, so I decided to make this for you," she said, handing him the sweater. He took it, appreciating its softness. Wrong timing, but she couldn't wait to see his reaction.

"Thanks," he said and he walked out.

Just thanks? She stared at the door for a while.

"What was I expecting?" She muttered, picking up another ball of yarn and thinking about what to crochet next. One idea came to mind.

Baby clothes.

She thought about Seth for a few minutes, then shook her head and started a new crochet project for her baby.

Seth came back earlier than expected. He found Gina sleeping with yarn all over the bed. He packed the yarn and tried to help her into a comfortable sleeping position, but she woke up. Seth took his hands away and stood up straight.

They had dinner, and Gina went to take a bath. When she came out, she found a box on the pillow. She opened it, her mouth falling open at the sight of a beautiful necklace. She dropped it back on the pillow when she heard Seth walking in. He moved to his desk and got busy. Gina wanted to ask about the necklace, wondering if it was meant for his girlfriend.

"The doctor didn't come today," she said.

"Tomorrow," he replied. She bit her lip.

"For your girlfriend?" she asked. Seth looked at her, and she pointed at the necklace. He went back to his work.

126

"For you," he muttered.

"Oh?" Gina said it in surprise. She grabbed the necklace and opened it. She stood before the mirror, trying to put it on but struggling with the clasp. Seth watched from the corner of his eye as she struggled, feeling the urge to help her but unable to.

"Oh my God," Gina muttered, turning to Seth. "Did you see that?" She walked to him, grabbed his hand off the desk and placed it on her stomach. He withdrew it immediately.

"The baby moved! Oh my God, he moved again." She took his hand and placed it back on her stomach. He felt the movement.

"What the—" he said, taking his hand away again.

"You felt it, right?" She laughed, watching her belly move. Seth watched in surprise.

CHAPTER FOURTEEN

Faith watched from afar, waiting. She couldn't give up, not yet. She never knew the mistakes of her past could hurt her so much. Her mother had sent her a private letter, revealing that she had known all along about her daughter's existence.

How shameful! Faith thought, rubbing her hands over her face, trying to calm herself. She had been playing the perfect daughter, not realising her mother knew the truth. She had told lies, not knowing they were seen through. She wiped away a tear that threatened to fall.

"You're my real mother?" came a voice behind her. Faith turned to see her daughter standing there. She nodded slowly.

They walked to the beach and sat down to talk. Faith told her daughter what had happened between her and her father. She explained how, as a young woman, she had been crazy in love with Damien. He was every girl's dream at school, and when he singled her out, she felt like a queen. Damien, a country guy, was adorable, innocent, and sexy, but he didn't fit into her mother's plans. She had step-siblings and cousins and felt like she had to compete for her mother's love. Before she could let go of Damien, she found herself pregnant. She could have aborted it, but it was the only thing that could prove her love for Damon—a gift.

They spent hours talking, with Faith sharing stories about her mother and the inheritance. Faith was happy that her daughter was willing to talk to her and didn't blame or get mad at her.

"Why aren't you angry at me?" Faith asked.

"Because Father always talked about you—not in front of Mother, though. He's always telling me stories about his youth," her daughter replied.

"But he hates me," Faith said.

"No, he doesn't. He's just doing it for me."

"Can I hug you?"

"Of course," her daughter said, and they embraced.

"Good morning. How are you feeling today?" Lucy asked Gina.

"Good," Gina replied.

"Are you sure?" Lucy asked, looking at her bandaged hand.
"You didn't come yesterday."

"Yeah, I had an emergency."

"What were you telling me the last time you came?" Gina asked, but Lucy ignored her.

"Open your mouth," Lucy said, giving Gina an oily, nice-scented multivitamin E capsule.

"What's this?"

"It's for oxidative stress," Lucy explained, and Gina nodded, although she didn't understand what that meant.

"You said I might have twins."

"I said that?"

"Yes, you did!" Gina exclaimed, suspecting Lucy's usual sneakiness.

"Well, this is a surrogacy baby; it's not possible at this stage," Lucy said with a smile. Gina imagined herself jumping off the bed but felt too heavy.

"Does that mean all you told me last time was a lie?"

"What exactly?" Lucy replied, making Gina feel her nerves stretch.

"You mentioned my contract and why Seth chose to do this!"

"Seth," Lucy said, raising an eyebrow.

"Well, that's his name."

"About the twin, I was just being cautious in case he was listening. He was listening," she said, sitting beside Gina. "You signed a contract to carry and birth his baby, then walk away without it, right?" Gina swallowed hard and nodded.

"And you don't even know why he only wants a baby, not the mother?"

"Why?"

"I can't tell you; my job is at risk." she said with a smile,

"What?! So, what do you want me to do? Why are you even telling me this?"

129

"Because I know you, and by the way, you've already started the journey. I won't lie; I was surprised to find you in this state, given your background," she smiled. Gina clenched her teeth.

"Oh, and I'll be getting married soon," Lucy said, flashing her ring. "Wish me luck," she winked. "Nice necklace, though," she added, walking to the door and stopping. "Oh, and don't worry, your secret's safe with me. My job is on the line," she said and left. Gina rubbed her hair with her two hands.

Should she even listen to her? She said her job is at risk? Is it that serious?

Regina. she thought.

Seth walked in, his phone to his ear and shuffling papers. He was wearing the sweater she made for him. She watched as he dropped the phone, opened his laptop, and got busy. She sat on the bed, thinking. She tried to go to sleep but couldn't. She got up and went to his desk, sitting before him for a while, but he didn't spare her a glance.

"Can I help with anything?" she asked, and he looked at her for three seconds.

"No," he said, returning to his work. Gina bit her lip, tapping her finger softly on the desk.

He looked at her again and threw a file in front of her. Gina took it.

"Sort it out in chronological order," he said, and Gina nodded with a smile.

They worked in silence. When she was done, she watched him, unsure of what else to do or say. She picked up a framed picture that was face down on the desk—it was a picture of Seth, Liam, and Tricia.

"Is this you?" Gina asked. "Oh my God, you were so fat! You were fat?" She said it softly and laughed lightly.

"What's so funny about it?" he asked, feeling ashamed.

"Nothing, just that... Oh my God, and this is Liam, right?" She burst out laughing again.

"Alright, give it back."

"Why?"

"Just give it," he said, extending his hand to take it.

"No, this is funny. I love it." Seth stood up and walked around the table to take it from her, and she stood up too, walking backward. "What are you doing?"

"I'm not done looking at it."

"You're done."

"Uh-uh," she said, shaking her head, still moving backward as Seth walked towards her.

"Give it to me."

"I won't," she said, laughing. "You all look great here." Seth took a big step towards her. She tried to move backward but missed a step and fell. Seth quickly stepped forward, grabbing her by the waist. The picture fell from her hand and shattered on the floor.

Gina felt her heart beating against her chest. They were face to face, and she felt her face flush. Her little baby bump touched him, and his strong cologne filled her nose again. She almost gagged.

Just then, the doorbell rang.

"I think someone's—" Before she could finish, Seth helped her up and walked to the door.

"Stay here and don't move," he said, and Gina nodded.

Katy walked in and tried to peck Seth, but he withdrew.

"What are you doing here?" Katy walked past him and sat down. "Can I at least have a drink?"

"What do you want?" he asked. Katy exhaled and walked to the mini bar to fix herself a drink. She poured a glass of whisky and downed it at once. She looked at him and noticed the sweater he was wearing.

"Did she make that for you?" she asked, pointing the empty glass at Seth. She dropped it and walked towards him. "You have been ignoring me. I thought we were dating," she said, sounding angry. "I went to your office several times. They told me you're working from home, Seth McGregor," she said, wrapping her hands around him. "That got me thinking."

He tried to remove her hands, but she pressed her body against his.

"Is she richer than me? More beautiful?" Seth pushed her away.

"You need to leave," he said and she chuckled.

"What are you hiding?" He picked up her bag.

"Leave." She bit her lip and took her bag from him.

"And we have nothing together," he said.

"Are you sure you want to do this?" she asked, her eyes teary, but he didn't respond. She walked out in anger.

Seth walked back into the room. The shattered glass was still on the floor, and the picture lay on his desk. Gina was already asleep.

Maria stopped by the bakery shop and picked up the cake she had ordered earlier. Her heart was pounding in her chest, and she almost changed her mind. She couldn't bear the thought of seeing Frank again after so many years. She stopped at the church to pick up Fr. Raymond. When they arrived at the front yard, there were balloons everywhere, and they could hear singing and chattering. Maria hesitated, but Fr. Ray nodded at her encouragingly. He knocked, and MaryGlory opened the door. She hugged him, but when she saw her mother, her face changed. She looked at Fr. Ray, who smiled warmly at her. He had talked to her about forgiving her mother, but it was quite hard to do. She didn't expect her mother to have the guts to come to the birthday party. She gave her a weak smile and walked back to the table.

Before dinner, it was only Frank who hadn't arrived. Maria met her grandson, whom she saw as intelligent and bright, just like his grandfather. The door opened, and her heart jumped again, just as it had every time the door opened. This time, her heart burst into flames, and she almost cried. Frank was standing at the door, just a few seconds away from her. He hugged MaryGlory, then Peter ran to him happily. Fr. Ray hugged him, and everyone else welcomed him, but Maria just stood there, ashamed, different, odd, and frozen.

Frank stared at her for a few seconds, surprised. The room was quiet and intense. MaryGlory called Peter to blow out the candles and make a wish. They had a wonderful night, but not for Maria, Frank, and Fr. Ray.

After the party, everyone decided to call it a night. Maria stepped out first, followed by Frank and the others. They all said goodnight. Fr.

Ray stayed inside to help MaryGlory pack the remaining food. Frank and Maria stood uncomfortably, staring at the starless night.

"Hi," Frank said, breaking the silence.

"Hi," Maria said, chuckling.

"How are you?"

"I'm okay, and you?" He nodded, thinking about whether he was okay or not.

"Good," he finally said, and another awkward silence followed.

"He's a good boy," Maria said, referring to Peter.

"Yes, he is. He's growing faster than we did in our time."

"Yes."

"I'm sorry about your mother," Frank said after another long silence. Maria looked at him fully for the first time since he had walked into the room. She had avoided looking at him, even when he passed her a plate during dinner. He hadn't changed at all—not one bit. Same height, same colour, same eyes, same body—not even a little change.

They heard the door close, and Fr. Ray walked out.

"What are you both doing out in the cold?"

"Want to grab a beer or two?" Frank asked.

"Are you kidding me? I've had enough for today."

"For old times' sake."

"Oh, don't 'for old times' sake' me. My body is growing weak, unlike yours. Why don't you take Maria home? We have plenty of time for old times," Fr. Ray said, walking past them.

"How are you going to get back home?" Maria asked.

"It's not that far."

"No, it's late already. I'll drop you off and then get home."

"No—"

"Why don't you two go ahead? I can get to the hotel on my own," Frank said. Before Maria could argue, he had pecked her on the cheek and waved them goodnight.

"You should've gone with him," Fr. Ray said. Maria smiled at him. "Don't do that."

133

"What?" He said that, and Maria laughed as they drove off. MaryGlory, who had been watching from her window, closed the curtain and climbed into bed.

Tricia watched as Katy stepped out of Seth's house. She walked quickly to her car and slammed the door. Tricia watched from her car as Katy slammed her hands on the wheel before driving off. She wondered what could be happening. She had thought something was going on between Katy and Seth—that they would marry or were planning to marry soon. She looked at the mansion and thought something must be going on. She had sent someone to monitor him and had received pictures of his movements. She thought Seth was hiding something. It was unlike him to not be doing something, especially concerning their grandmother's inheritance.
What could he be planning? she thought.
If it's not Katy, then who is it? Who was the lady caught on camera with the maid? He didn't even flinch when I showed him the picture. What is going on? She folded her arms, thinking hard. She picked up the envelope beside her and took out the pictures. Three women now, she thought, staring at the picture of Gina and Rosa. She understood that the girl with Rosa could be a new servant since Rosa had been their head servant since they were teenagers. But then there was Katy, whom she believed Seth was dating and could marry, and she had just stormed out of his house. And there was this other lady who came often.
What is happening? Another clue: Seth had started working from home. Seth is working from home. What is he hiding? She ducked as another car parked in front of his house. She watched as Liam walked out with bags and a bouquet.
Why would Liam give Seth a bouquet?

Montserrat sat on a couch as a doctor checked on her. She sat there for a few minutes while the doctor repeated his routine. When he was done, Montserrat got up, walked to her room, and locked the door. She entered the tub and reached for her drink, sitting beside it.

It slipped and fell onto the marble floor, shattering. She stared at it for a while, then picked up a piece and slit her hand.

CHAPTER FIFTEEN

Tricia barged into Noah's office, drunk.

"What are you doing?" he asked, surprised.

She removed her shoes and climbed onto his desk.

"What the heck are you doing, Tricia?" he asked again.

"Remember when you said you liked my crazy side? When you remind me every second how much you love me?"

"Tricia, you're drunk. You need to go home."

She laughed. "My home is a mess, and my life is a mess. I don't care anymore," she said, climbing on top of Noah. He shifted his head to avoid her bad breath, but she took his face in her hands and placed her lips on his. Noah pushed her away, and just then, the door opened, revealing his fiancée. He pushed Tricia down, and she hit her ankle on the desk.

"Honey, it's not what you think—" Before he could finish, she had already run out of the door. Noah left Tricia there and went after his fiancée.

Seth threw the paper dish into the bin and helped Gina to the bathroom. She could have gone on her own, but recently her body felt too heavy to carry. She was starting to feel uncomfortable almost all the time. It was even difficult to breathe.

She stared at herself in the mirror while she waited for Seth to get her towel. He came back with a dry towel, took her hand, and tried to help her into the tub.

"Can you help me wash my hair? I haven't washed it in two weeks," she asked, not really expecting him to agree.

He took her shampoo, which Liam had gotten for her, and started applying it to her hair. Gina found it surprising and funny; no one had washed her hair apart from her mother, and that was years ago. He really washed it like a pro.

"Have you done this before?" she asked while he washed.

136

"My grandmother."

"Really? She must be sweet."

"Yes, she was." Gina waited a while before she whispered, "I'm so sorry." He didn't say anything but continued washing. "What was she like, if you don't mind?"

There was silence for about a minute. Gina thought he wouldn't answer.

"She was a good woman. She raised me after my parents died when I was little." He went on to tell her about his grandmother, his high school days, and his incident with Tricia, though not in detail. He continued as Gina took her bath. She laughed, nodded, smiled, felt bad for him, and yet was proud of him.

When she was done, she wrapped the towel around herself and asked Seth to help her out of the tub. They hadn't talked much about personal stuff before, and he had never talked this long, not to her. He held her wet hand and helped her out of the tub. She missed a step, and Seth had to wrap his arm around her shoulder to steady her. It was an intense moment; his body was touching her bare skin, and the room's temperature made it even harder to break the trance. She didn't look away, and neither did he. They stared at each other as if they were seeing themselves for the first time.

A heavy bang brought them back to reality. Seth released his hands and left the bathroom immediately. He heard another bang, turned off the lights, and went straight to the door. He opened it, and Katy was standing there, looking elegant and classy as always.

She pushed herself towards Seth, wrapped her arms tightly around his neck, and smashed her lips against his. She wanted him at that moment—all of him. Seth held her tiny waist and pulled her off him. "The f*ck?"

"I want you," Katy said and she grabbed Seth by the neck for another kiss, but he pushed her off again.

"Have you gone crazy?"

"Yes. For you."

Seth rubbed his forehead. Women disgusted him, especially her kind—desperate women. He thought she was better.

"Do you want money? I have loads of it. I can give you more than half of my shares," she said, walking close to him and undressing. "I can make you the richest man on earth. Just be mine and mine alone," she said seductively, placing her hand on his chest.

Gina wanted to know who could be at such an odd hour. As she walked to the door, she heard someone talking. She peeked and saw a nearly naked woman running her hands all over Seth. She felt her heart shrink. Without a second thought, she turned and left.

Seth removed Katy's hand from his body and zipped up her dress. He picked up her bag and tried to drag her to her car, but she insisted. Her once seductive play turned to anger, jealousy, and hatred. She felt ashamed.

She took her bag from Seth and laughed sadly.

"Why?" she asked. "Why don't you want me?"

Seth ignored her, hoping the drama would end soon so he could get over it without overreacting.

"Just answer me, and I'll leave," she said, her face turning red. "Am I not beautiful enough? You don't like girls with too much money? Am I not your type?" He still kept quiet, which annoyed her more.

"Is there someone else?" she asked, struggling to keep her voice steady. "Does she like crocheting? Does she like lavender shampoos?"

He looked at her. "What are you saying?"

"Is she here?" she said, throwing her bag.

"You need to leave now. I don't want to hurt you."

"You already have," she said, walking past him to the door leading to the rooms.

"F*ck!" he said and ran after her.

She kept screaming and pushing open doors.

"Where the f*ck is she?!"

She pushed open Seth's bedroom door, and Gina was standing there in her baby bump dress, shocked. Seth came in and couldn't do anything to help the situation.

Katy stood there, her mouth hanging open for a few seconds, trying to process the shock of her life. Not only did he have someone already, but she was also carrying his child.

"Katy—" he said, trying to take her hand and drag her out, but she pulled away immediately. She looked at Seth with a new mindset and a broken heart.

"You're the worst! And remember today—you hurt me real bad, and I'm going to pay you back for it," she said, glancing at Gina again before storming out.

Gina felt like she had done something wrong. She watched Seth go after her. She stood there, confused about what was happening.

She sat on the bed, waiting for Seth. When he walked in, Gina knew immediately that he was back to his old self and that things had become complicated because of her. But she had to know what was happening.

She wanted to ask if he was fine and if everything was fine, but all the questions felt wrong. She opened her mouth to say something, but he spoke first.

"I'll see you in the morning," he said, walking out of the room.

Seth couldn't rest his mind. He knew women could be dangerous. Katy could easily talk to the media, and she was manipulative. He needed to act fast, he thought. He didn't want to satisfy the press by revealing Gina's identity. They didn't need to know who the baby's mother was.

He kept thinking of what to do and ended up calling Liam.

Theresa sat beside Montserrat in the hospital while the doctor attended to her. Her phone kept vibrating in her purse.

"The baby is safe, and so is she," the doctor announced. Theresa exhaled in relief. She had rushed upstairs to Montserrat's room to find water snaking out from the bathroom. She had to call Hector, who broke down the door. They found Montserrat in the tub, blood dripping from her hand, and rushed her to the hospital.

Theresa took another deep breath before leaving the room to take her calls. Every day was getting harder. She owed more money and still had old debts to pay. The inheritance was her last hope, and she would do anything—anything at all—to get her hands on it.

Gina woke up in the morning but couldn't find Seth. The big house was dead quiet. She walked around but couldn't find him. She took the opportunity to step out of the mansion.

Apart from the guest room, her own room, Seth's room, and the kitchen, she had never actually looked at the house properly. It always felt like a prison. But it was quite beautiful. She walked to the fountain and sat beside it for a while. The sun falling on her skin made her shiver. She wandered to the garden at the back of the mansion.

She sat on the rock bench and thought about herself. She never imagined her life would take this turn. She was pregnant with a rich man's child and paid to have his baby. She wondered what happened to her dreams. Romantically, she never wanted anything to do with men because they all seemed like her father. On the other hand, she wanted a family. She wanted a simple, happy family—people she could make breakfast for, take to school, water her garden, and do all those homely things. Not forgetting a decent job.

But here she was. She thought about her life after this. In a few months, the contract would be over, and she would have to decide what to do next. Should she go back home to her mama? Only God knew what would happen then. She wondered how long she could hide this secret from her family or, worse, how to tell them about it. She took a deep breath and felt her baby kick. She smiled, feeling a sting behind her eyes. She had avoided thinking about all this, but the time was near. Could she ever leave a baby she carried for months? Somehow, she regretted ever making that decision.

She heard the doorbell ring and jumped out of her thoughts, her heart beating against her chest. She slowly got up and went back inside through the kitchen's back door.

Someone answered the door. Gina was surprised; she thought Seth wasn't around. She went upstairs and peeked through a window. She saw a lady but couldn't make out her face. She was sure it wasn't the one she saw yesterday. She stood there for a while, watching the lady. She tried to see Seth but couldn't. The lady looked up, and Gina stepped back, leaving the curtain open. She felt their eyes lock. Scared, she walked back to her room and sat down.

Seth had heard Gina leave the room. He wondered where she was going but didn't pay much attention. After a while, she didn't come back, so he went out to look for her. She could miss a step or slip again; she shouldn't walk around on her own, he thought. He looked around until he saw her through the window, sitting quietly in the garden, rubbing her stomach, sometimes smiling, sometimes nothing. He watched her for a while, then heard the doorbell ring. He watched her slowly get up and walk towards the back door before he went to get it.

When he opened it, Tricia was standing there. She smirked. "Hello, brother."

"Tricia?"

"Surprised?"

"What are you doing here?" he asked, rubbing his forehead.

She rolled her eyes. "Excuse me?" she scoffed. "I might have stayed calm all this while, but this mansion? This mansion is not yours yet."

"What are you here for?"

She took a step towards him. "You know, it's so unlike you to be so calm. It's suspicious. What are you hiding, Seth McGregor?" she said, narrowing her eyes in suspicion.

"If you're done, please leave." She smirked.

"Have you seen the news today? You're making headlines again." She swiped up on her phone and showed it to Seth. "What do you have to say about it? Is it true you have a girlfriend? A pregnant girlfriend?"

"You need to leave."

Tricia nodded and looked up, seeing a lady standing there. She backed away, looked at Seth, and smiled. "I heard there'll be a shareholders' dinner party soon."

"You're not invited."

"I don't need to be invited. See you soon, brother." She turned to leave, then saw Liam walking in. She smiled at Seth again and walked away.

"Hey, man," they both greeted.

"What's going on?" Liam asked, pointing at Tricia.

"Man, I... I don't know," Seth said, and they walked to his study.

"So, Katy came here drunk, made a pass at you, you rejected her, and she went crazy and found out about Gina?"

Seth nodded.

"Alright, then today there's a headline: 'Seth McGregor and His Hidden Girlfriend, Supposedly Pregnant; Seth McGregor Breaks Up with Business Icon Katy Moore,' and lots more."

"Yeah?"

"Yeah."

"So, what's your point?" Seth asked.

"I don't even know what my point is. All I know is that you're in deep sh*t."

"So, what do you want me to do?"

"First of all, we need to take Gina somewhere safe."

"Why?"

Liam exhaled and walked closer to Seth. "Whoever leaked this information is probably out for you. It could be Katy; it could be Tricia. The most important thing is that your baby is safe."

Seth nodded.

"I don't know much about relationships, but Katy Moore never lets go of anything she bites, and your sister is just as crazy. She looks like she can do anything to get the inheritance. The baby is almost due; there are only a few months left, and everything will be over. We just need to be careful."

"What inheritance?" Gina asked from the door.

Both of them turned and stared at her, not saying another word. Gina walked in. She had wanted to see Liam, then saw both of them whispering, so she decided to eavesdrop.

"If I understood correctly, this—everything—is just because of an inheritance, right?" She started losing breath again, breathing through her mouth. "Is it?"

"Yes," Seth answered.

She took a deep breath. "Gina, uhmm... this is getting a little complicated. We'll sort it out, just—"

"You'll sort it out?" she said, placing her hand on her waist while she struggled for breath. "You'll sort it out? What is..." she chuckled. "Are you alright?" Seth asked.

She kept struggling for breath, feeling pain below her abdomen. She closed her eyes to take in the pain slowly, but it was getting severe. She bit her lip and made a sound. They both rushed to help her sit. "Don't touch me!" she snapped, surprising them both. She slowly turned, using the wall for support, and walked back to her room. She stood for a while until the pain subsided. A sharp sting at the back of her eyes made her regret ever taking the offer. She had always thought maybe Seth wanted a baby or maybe he was gay and they both wanted a baby. But an inheritance? How? What was going to happen to her baby? What had she gotten herself into?
STOP

CHAPTER SIXTEEN

They sat around the table, chatting and reliving their past. Fr. Ray sat up to leave.

"You're leaving already?" Maria asked.

"Yeah, I have to say mass tomorrow morning."

"Do you need me to drop you off?" Frank offered.

"Nah, you two need to catch up."

They smiled at each other as he left.

"So," Frank said.

"So," Maria echoed, smiling as she took another sip from her drink.

"You know, you need to give her some time," he said, running his finger around the tip of his shot glass. Maria found it attractive. "I mean our daughter."

Maria stared at him as tears welled up in her eyes. It dawned on her that they actually had something together—a daughter. Frank moved to sit beside her and hold her face.

"Oh, Frank," she whispered as he wiped her tears with his thumb. He kissed her forehead, then her cheeks.

"I'm so sorry," she whispered again as Frank kissed her lips.

"I've missed you so much," she said, kissing him back.

Father Ray, who was watching from afar, smiled and started his way down the lonely road.

"I have a daughter," Faith said while sitting before her mirror. She had been fighting to tell her husband but couldn't bring herself to do it. She felt pain in her palm and stopped twisting her hands.

"I have a daughter," she said again, looking at her husband through the mirror, her heart beating against her chest.

Her husband dropped the newspaper he was holding and looked at her. After a while, he replied, "I know."

Faith turned around on her stool to face her husband. He knew?

"Your mother told me years ago."

Faith covered her mouth with her tiny hands and sobbed. She felt ashamed and disappointed in herself. Her husband went to her and tried to touch her, but she stood up and walked to the window, still crying. He held her from behind and tried to console her.

"I'm so sorry. Oh, John, I'm so sorry," she said, burying her face in his chest and crying more.

Stephanie opened the window to welcome in the air of New York. She stared at the busy streets while her mind wandered off.

She had gone home after a long while but couldn't bring herself to tell them why she came.

She was in deep trouble. Real trouble.

She had been tricked.

She was told she could earn seventy percent from a business introduced to her by two men who claimed to be business developers. She earned once and then foolishly, out of greed, took her family's shares into the business. She had called, texted, and even visited the business centre, but it was all fraud! Cold sweat ran down her spine.

She had kept it a secret, knowing it wouldn't be long before they found out. They would burn her alive. Not only were the shares at stake, but her mother's house was too. She bit her thumb, thinking about how foolish she had been.

But then she went home, and God answered her prayers through Regina.

Regina told her she got a job, but the money she was sending home over that short period of time was extremely much. She was a blessing from God. Whatever she was doing, she better keep doing it. But first, Stephanie needed to find her.

A knock on the door brought her back to reality, and she went to answer it.

Gina opened her eyes and saw someone looking at her. It was Lucy. She tried to sit up.

"Slowly there," Lucy said, helping her sit up. "Oh, look who's almost due." She said, and Gina looked at her, wondering why she's being so chatty and happy. Not that she cared; she had her own problems to deal with.

"You need to be careful now with everything you do. The baby is fine and healthy," Lucy said, closing her file, "but you don't look so good."

Gina stared at her for a while. "What do you know about this family?"

Lucy opened her mouth to say something, but they saw Seth standing by the door.

"Don't fail to call me, even if it's the slightest discomfort," Lucy said, packing her stuff and leaving.

They didn't say a word to each other for a while.

"My grandmother was a rich woman," Seth said, rubbing his palms. "She died a few months ago. She left a will. She wanted her inheritance to go to her great-grandchildren. That's why..." he finished, pointing at Gina.

Gina felt her red, flushed face start to cool. She still had many questions, but at least he cared to explain. She ignored him and tried to get out of bed. Seth watched her struggle, then walked over and picked her up.

Gina didn't get a chance to tell him not to touch her, but it all felt weird. Her cheeks flushed, but this time it wasn't with anger, and her heart was beating strong against her chest. Why?

"Where do you want to go?" he asked a second time.

"Hmm?" She could smell him. "I need to take a bath," she said, pointing towards it.

He took her there and laid her in the bathtub. He tried to remove his hand from under her shoulder but found himself face-to-face with her. She could feel his breath on her lips; his eyes were locked on hers. They were too close. Before they could break away, their lips tangled. It felt like fire running through their veins, like a spark. Their bodies ached to bond, to drown in each other, but then lightning struck. He released her lips and couldn't bring himself to look at her.

What had he done?

146

"Call me if you need anything," he said, leaving. He walked straight to his grandmother's room. He hadn't been there in a while and didn't know why he chose to go there of all places.

He sat on the bed and rubbed his head. He stood up and looked in the mirror. He was looking at himself but not thinking of anything at all. He couldn't get his mind together. He just kissed her. He just kissed her! And he liked it. He rubbed his face again.

Gina kept splashing water in the tub, reliving the kiss for the tenth time.

He kissed her, and she kissed him back.

Why did he kiss her?

Why did she kiss back?!

It's just a kiss, she told herself, feeling her face flush.

But it's a kiss from Seth! From Seth!

She found herself smiling sheepishly and biting her lips. She stopped splashing the water when she felt a tingle below her abdomen, and then she felt like something hooked her. She slowed her breath, trying to take it in. Then it felt like the hook tightened.

She emptied the water in the tub and slowly took her towel. She slowly climbed out of the tub and felt a sharp pain that made her kneel on the floor, then she cried out in pain. The hook turned into a feeling like her belly was about to burst; it loosened for a second and then came back stronger.

She screamed, holding her belly. Seth couldn't hear her. She crawled to the bathroom door and screamed Seth's name.

Seth shut his grandmother's door just as he heard the scream. He waited to make sure he heard something, then heard her scream again.

He rushed in to see her crawling on the floor. He picked her up and laid her in his arms, fumbling to get his phone from his pocket.

"The f*ck!" he shouted as his hand trembled.

"I... I... think the baby... the baby..." Gina tried to say between sobs and screams, unable to keep it together as the pain strangled her.

Lucy picked up on the second ring.

"Get here now!" Seth's voice rang out.

"What happened? Is she okay?" Lucy asked, hearing Gina's screams in the background.

"No, she's f*cking not! I think she's in labour or something."

"Labor? Did her water break?"

"What?"

"I'm on my way," Lucy said, changing her route.

"Ouch!" Seth exclaimed as Gina dug her fingers into his skin. He felt helpless; she was in pain, and all he could do was hold her.

Lucy arrived fifteen minutes later. The pain had subsided. Gina's face was streaked with dried tears; her breaths were short and fast. Seth picked her up and placed her on the bed. Lucy had him bring water to clean her up. She changed Gina from the towel into her gown.

After making sure Gina was peacefully resting, they left the room and went to Seth's study.

"What happened?"

"It's false labor. It happens to a few women. We need to be vigilant; the day is near. She needs more strength and energy. Do you still plan on a home delivery?" Seth nodded. "Then we'll need a few nurses with me. As you know, I can't do it alone, but I'd prefer you think about it. I won't say a word about this, but for the other nurses..." She shook her head. "In a hospital, if there are any complications, we can easily handle them. But everything is fine. You decide," she said, picking up her bag. "Oh, and..." Lucy tried to talk about Gina's family but remembered it was meant to be a secret. "Never mind," she said and she left.

Seth went and sat beside Gina, removing the hair hanging on her face. His eyes lingered on her lips for a while. His phone beeped; it was Liam. He walked to his study and called him.

"Is she alright now?" Liam asked.

"Of course."

Liam nodded. They went ahead to discuss the upcoming dinner party.

Seth couldn't get his mind together. He kept feeling Gina's soft lips and the sensation they gave him.

"I kissed her," he whispered.

"What?"

"I kissed her," he repeated.

"Who?" Liam asked, thinking of who it could be. Katy? Gina?

"OMG! You kissed who?! Damn! Man!"

"I don't know. I don't know what got over me."

"Oh, I'll tell you what got over you. Your eyes finally opened, your mind finally loosened up, and your heart popped open. You're in love, man!"

"What are you... I'm not in love! Her lips were just... there."

"The sh*t you're spitting, man. Her lips were there, and then what? You took it! I'm proud of you, man."

"Let's not talk about it."

"Oh, how the hell am I going to get this outta my head?"

"The dinner party!" Seth said,

"F*ck you, man," Liam said, and they went back to planning the dinner party.

"I have a plan. I want to move her to the game house."

"Because of Tricia? That's a great idea, but how are you going to do it? The reporters have been lurking around your house recently. They've got their eyes on you."

"I know. That's why we're going to do it during the dinner party."

"You think that will work?"

"That's the best I've got."

Liam nodded, and they moved on to the rest of the details.

Seth stopped working and went to the room to check up on Gina. She was awake. He walked to her and felt her forehead.

"How are you feeling?"

She nodded slightly. "What happened?"

"The doctor said it's false labour."

"False?" Fear rose in her. If that was false labour, how would real labour feel?

"I'll fix dinner."

After dinner, Gina felt she was back to normal. Seth was busy the rest of the day, so she let him be. She wanted to talk about the kiss. The next day, she heard noises and people talking.

Later in the night, after bathing, Seth was still busy. She felt that the longer she waited to ask him about it, the more insignificant it might seem.

149

"Is there something going on in the house?"

"Hmm?" he answered, still focused on his laptop.

Gina flipped her fingernails, trying to gather the strength to ask the question.

"Can I ask you something?"

"Hmm?"

It took her another minute.

"The other day... in the bathroom..."

Seth stopped typing.

"We kissed. You kissed me," she said, staring at him. "Why?" She prayed in her heart for an answer, a response.

Seth swallowed hard, trying to compose himself. "I forgot about dinner," he said, standing up. Gina followed him and held his hand. He stopped and turned to look at her.

"Do you have any feelings for me?" She stared into his eyes, and he stared back, falling deep into them.

"I'll make dinner. I'll call you when I'm done," he said, leaving the room.

Gina felt a sting at the back of her eyes. She sounded desperate. She was in love. With a rude man. She knew she never had better luck, especially when it came to men, whom she hated so much.

But her heart betrayed her. She had denied it, but the evidence was everywhere. She stole glances at him, loved his scent, and loved being around him. Her heart beat faster whenever their skin touched. She never knew she could feel like this. She had read about it in books but she never thought her life would have a chapter like this. Why did it have to be him?

———————————————

Tricia sat in her car, listening to Liam and Seth talk about the dinner party and Gina. That's her name. And Seth is in love. Ain't it funny?! Well, of course, everybody is in love, everybody is doing fine, and nobody cares about Patricia! Well, then, it's my turn!

"Tie her up and send her to the farmhouse," she commanded.

"Yes, ma'am," replied two huge men in the backseat.

Lucy squeaked and kicked as they dragged her out of the car and into a van.

CHAPTER SEVENTEEN

Gina chose a tie for Seth as he told her about their plan.

"Why am I leaving? Is it because of the party?"

"No," Seth replied. He wanted to tell her everything but couldn't. "You'll just stay there from now on, until you're due."

Gina nodded.

"Here, let me," she said, taking the tie from him and tying it for him. "There," she said as his scent caught her nose again. She was going to miss him. For a few seconds, they stared at each other, then the door pushed open, and Liam walked in.

"It's time," he said to Seth. "Hey, baby," he said, kissing Gina's cheek. "You ready?" Seth nodded, and they turned to leave.

"Stay here. I'll come back for you," Seth said, leaving the room. Gina sat on her bed, thinking of many things. She kept hearing classical music playing in the background. She'd never been to a grand party before. She lay on her bed as the music lulled her to sleep.

Seth kept his eyes wide open as the guests kept arriving. He saw his aunts come; he wasn't expecting them. This only proved they were all interested in the inheritance, which started to worry him.

Theresa arrived first with Montserrat and Hector. He wondered if she was really pregnant; her stomach was still flat. Then Maria came with a man he didn't recognise. Faith arrived last with her husband.

They were all waiting for Tricia.

Not long after, Tricia arrived, dressed in a long, shiny black dress. Seth looked at Liam, who nodded.

They had planned to keep their eyes on Tricia while they transferred Gina through the backyard without anyone noticing.

Seth checked his watch after making his speech. It was 8:45 p.m. He decided to wait for an hour more. His mind couldn't focus on the party. It was filled with thoughts of Gina and why? Probably because... Well, of course, they had to transfer her to a new place and everything, enough to fill his mind with thoughts of her.

He blinks hard, trying to focus on his surroundings. His eyes were on all his family members; he didn't know what they had up their sleeves. All he knew was that he had to protect his own.

He didn't want them to know his plan or how he got to have a baby. What mattered was that the baby had his DNA, and that was the goal.

The baby. The inheritance. And Gina. *F*ck!*

"Hello, brother," he heard behind him. "You look charming, as always," Tricia said, kissing his cheeks.

"I am busy."

"I noticed," she said, and Seth stared at her for a few seconds. "I've missed home."

"I believe there's more to drink and eat than to be walking around trying to create trouble," he said, turning to get away from her.

"Well, I was expecting to see her. You can't hide her forever, you know." Seth gave her a stare and whispered into her ear, "What about your husband? I heard you got married. I was expecting to see the lucky man." He looked at her, and her face had already swollen with anger. Seth smiled as an old couple walked towards them. He took the opportunity to dismiss Tricia.

Despite the inheritance, Seth believed that when it came to their company, he had the upper hand. Nobody in his family could compete with him on that front, but the inheritance will give him legitimacy.

Liam met him while he was still greeting some guests. He whispered, saying that everything was ready. Seth nodded and went back to the greetings. Ten minutes later, he left the party.

He opened the door, and Gina got up. She had been sleeping peacefully.

"Are we leaving now?" she asked.

"Yes, everything's ready. Come on," he said, helping her off the bed. They opened the door, and Liam signaled them to keep moving. They went down through the kitchen and out into the garden. Gina felt the cold air hit her body and gripped Seth's shoulder.

"Are you alright?" he asked, and she nodded.

"Are we going far?"

"No."

"Will you visit?" She asked and it took him some seconds to answer.
"Yes."

They reached the small gate, climbed down a few steps, and then he pushed it open. A car was waiting outside on the street with three men standing by it. One of them opened the door, and Seth helped Gina in.

"I'll be there as soon as I can," he said, kissing her cheek, something he did without thinking. He closed the door and watched as the car drove off. He stood there for a few seconds, wondering why he kissed her cheek. He was beginning to surprise himself.

He walked back inside and joined the party as if nothing had happened. Tricia and the rest of the family were still present.
A relief.

Faith hadn't received any invitations to the party, but she thought she didn't need one to attend. She wasn't going to join the fight for the inheritance, but she wanted it. She felt comfortable immediately upon walking into the grand hall. She saw Theresa and her daughter. They were never close, even as kids. She had never been close with any of them. Everyone thought she was their mother's favourite, and she knows their mother loved her unconditionally. Her eyes stung at remembering that she was no longer with them.

Her husband hadn't wanted them to go, but she felt it was right to attend.

She wanted to bond with them, to be part of them, but she knew it would never be possible.

Theresa had always been about the money, the same reason she married into the family she did, the same reason she adopted a daughter. But she was also someone who didn't know how to use an opportunity. She was also very predictable. Faith saw Maria with a man; she was shining. She noticed they were holding hands throughout the party. Maybe she was going to marry after all. Faith felt that Maria hated her for reasons she'd never know. But she had always admired her. Apart from Steven, the firstborn, and his wife

Rachel, Maria had been a friend and sister when they were little. But then she suddenly changed, left home, and returned. They had never spoken since.

Seth and Tricia had been carried by her when they were little babies. She was just a few years older than them. Now they were all grown, each with their own life.

Seth was a successful young man who was brilliant. She was there when it all happened. When the little boy grew up, he used to be so chubby, and now just look at him.

One thing that changed about him as he grew was that he lost his genuine smile when his parents died. *Poor child.*

But thanks to her mother, he received love in abundance. Tricia had always been a girl who believed she was strong enough to stand on her own. She had always been sassy and too proud, and recently, the news about her was so unlike her. She had known all about them from their mother, who seemed to know all of them like the back of her hand. She used to worry a lot. Sometimes she thought she might not have raised them perfectly. She used to pray so hard and try to get them together but she always failed.

She felt the warmth of her husband's hand on her shoulder and turned to smile at him. She had been blessed with a wonderful man. Damien would've been wonderful too, but she gave up on him. Thank God they had a daughter, but what about it? Sometimes she wondered which she regretted more: leaving Damien or disappointing her mother.

A sharp movement caught her eye. It was Montserrat storming out of the hall. A charming young woman walked in after that. Faith scanned her through; she looked elegant and familiar.

She dropped her glass of champagne and excused herself to the restroom.

《《《《》》》》

Seth hadn't kept his eyes on Tricia yet, but she was wandering around with a wide smile—nothing suspicious. He saw Katy walk into the hall, a surprise since he hadn't expected her to come. She is one of the company's important shareholders and carries the aura of her grandmother, yet she is a desperate woman. And he hated desperate.

Gina sat quietly in the car. She had no idea what was happening or why she was being moved to another house.
What had she gotten herself into?
She touched her belly.
It's almost over.
Over?
She thought she would be happy that this was going to end soon, but she wasn't.
Why?
Why?
Maybe because she didn't know what to do with her life after this was done. Maybe because she didn't know how to keep the secret from her family or even tell them. Maybe she didn't have the heart to leave her child—
Oh, whatever is going to happen?
She's not your child Regina, you have already sold her. She told herself. You are not even related to her. She fought back the tears that threatened to fall.
She bent her head towards the car window. She hadn't been out for months. She opened the window and breathed in the cold air.
Seth.
Her heart jumped a bit.
It's nothing, she said, closing her eyes.
The car stopped.
"What is it?" she asked the man sitting beside her as the driver wind up her window,
"Looks like a checkpoint," the driver answered.
"Checkpoint?"
Gina watched as a man walked to their car and knocked on the tinted window. The driver rolled down the glass, and the man outside raised a gun and shot him.

Gina screamed as the other men in the car were shot simultaneously. She kept screaming as another man opened her door and dragged her out of the car. His face was covered, unlike that of the first man. "Please just let me go. I'm begging you," she cried in the hands of the man who kept pushing her to another car. She heard another gunshot and got really scared.

Are they going to kill me? OMG! I'm going to die!

She thought and bit the man holding her. At the same time, she felt a lash on her cheeks and fell to the floor. She heard them cursing at her or maybe arguing, but she couldn't see anything; her vision was blurry. She felt them drag her up slowly and into the car.

Stephanie downed her third glass of whisky at the bar. She'd gone to ten bars already and similar places, but no one had heard or seen Gina. She felt disgusted. She noticed a young man, clearly younger than her, giving her the eye. She chose to ignore him and dared him in her mind to walk up to her.

And he did.

"Hello, lovely."

Lovely? Funny.

"Hello."

"Need another glass? It's on me."

Seriously?

"Alright."

"So, what's up?"

Ha! What's up is that I'm older than you, and you're just a f*ck boy.

"Been watching you."

I noticed, f*ck boy!

"Oh, you have?" she said.

"Yeah." He chuckled and breathed into his hands. "You know, this hasn't happened in a while, and the worst part is that I'm bad at it," he said, laughing with his throat.

What's he saying?

"What?"

"I mean, I haven't had this feeling I'm having now in a long time."

Feelings? The boy is talking about feelings.

"You might not get it, but the moment you walked in, my heart felt alive."

Hmm, is this a modern tactic?

"Oh."

"I'm sorry, I'm not good at this."

She raised her eyebrows, and he laughed again.

"I'm sorry. I am Ken, by the way."

He wants my name.

"Call me Nicki," she lied.

"Lovely name."

"Yeah."

Her mind clicked. Nicki!

F*ck!

Why hadn't she thought about it?

"I have to go." She downed the whisky and raised the glass to him.

"Thank you," she said and turned to leave.

"Can we see each other again?" he asked, and she turned.

"Hmm, we'll see each other here again," she said and left.

She got back to her hotel and searched for the bar Nicki was managing and got a number.

Seth threw his tie on the bed as he called for the tenth time. None of the men transporting Gina answered. He turned to leave.

"Where are you going?" Liam asked.

"What does it look like? I'm going to the house."

"You can't leave the party!"

"F*ck the party," he said and left.

CHAPTER EIGHTEEN

Gina felt a throbbing headache. She heard someone calling her name but couldn't piece together who, why, or even where she was. The door opened, and someone was pushed in. Another person walked in behind, closing the door and blocking the sunlight. Then everything went black again.

She heard her name being called again, this time accompanied by sobbing. As her vision cleared, she saw Lucy sitting in front of her. That's when she noticed her hands and legs were tied. Then she remembered the checkpoint.

OMG! She screamed in her mind as she tried to loosen herself.

She started panicking. "OMG, what is happening? Why are my? OMG!"

"You need to calm down," she heard Lucy say. "What is going on?"

"Are they going to kill us? My family doesn't even know where I am. I've not seen them for so long," Gina cried, struggling to breathe. The other lady started crying too.

"The f*ck! Can you two stop?" Lucy shouted. "Gina, breathe. Slowly, yes, slowly." Gina followed her instructions.

After they calmed down, Gina asked again, "What is happening?"

Lucy took a deep breath. "Well, it's kinda my fault. Wait, no, I'm a victim too."

"What are you saying?" "Well, we've been kidnapped; that's what happened." "Why, I don't even know anyone," Gina said and Lucy laughed.

"Simply put, Tricia kidnapped us," Lucy said.

"What? Why would she do that?" Montserrat asked.

"Well, isn't it obvious? Because of the f*cking inheritance."

"Omg, is she crazy? What is she trying to do?" Montserrat said, about to start crying again. Lucy rolled her eyes.

"Wait, I don't get a single thing going on here. Who. Is. She, and why would she kidnap me, you, and who is she?" Gina asked Lucy, referring to Montserrat.

Lucy took a deep breath and started. "I'm going to brief you on the sh*t you're into. Their grandmother died," she said, pointing her face at Montserrat, "leaving a bunch of inheritance, but she wanted it to go to her great-grandchildren. Now, Seth—your darling—has a surrogate, which is you. Tricia secretly got married; we don't know to whom. Then there are the rich daughters who want the inheritance too. This one here," she nodded towards Montserrat, "is the granddaughter too—the adopted grandchild. Tricia kidnapped you because she found out you're pregnant with Seth's baby, and this lady is pregnant too, so she's gone crazy."

"This doesn't make total sense to me," Gina said.

"Yeah, I just wasted my strength," Lucy replied.

Gina thought about the lady who saw her in the room and the one who saw her through the window. Which of them is Tricia?

"This is weird," Gina said.

"Tell me about it. They're all money-crazed."

"So what is she trying to do?" Gina asked, trying to ignore the voice in her head.

"Well, she obviously wants to get rid of the great-grandchildren," Lucy said.

"I won't let her touch my baby," Montserrat said.

"She can have her own baby."

"Well, I think they have a time limit, and I guess her marriage was fake and all," Lucy replied.

"Why would she do that?" Gina asked.

Lucy rolled her eyes. "I've been here the longest. I am exhausted," she said, relaxing her head on the chair.

"By the way, why did she kidnap you too?"

Lucy raised her head and looked at them. "Well, it's because of you."

"Me?" Gina asked.

"Yeah. After I was done checking up on you, I was walking to my car when someone showed me a gun and forced me into a car. I met Tricia there. We made a deal: I'd tell her the truth, plant a device in Seth's office, and I'd live."

"I see how you're living," Gina said sarcastically.

"Well," Lucy said, shrugging.

"I'm not surprised," Gina said.

"What?"

"You'll never change after all. Once a snitch, always a snitch."

"F*ck you."

"Oh yeah, you spilled everything and probably didn't tell us the whole story. There's money involved because you could've chosen not to tell."

"You b*tch! Chosen not to tell when I had a f*cking gun to my head."

"You got any excuse for Toby?" Gina asked.

"Oh!" she chuckled. "Does it still hurt? You know, Toby was just this innocent guy, easy to tame," she said with a smirk.

"B*tch!"

"Have you seen him recently? He's as hot as ever."

"Wh*re!"

"Yes, b*tch!"

"Can you two stop?" Montserrat shouted.

After a few seconds of silence, Gina said, "Well, we'll see how a snitch's wedding goes," with a smirk.

"Don't you dare talk—"

The door opened, and a lady walked in, closing the door behind her.

Gina felt her toes freeze, and her hands felt like they were hooked to the chair.

They all stared as Tricia walked to the middle of the room. Gina was on the left, Lucy on the right, and Montserrat had her back against the wall facing Tricia.

"Isn't this the most perfect dream?" Tricia said, looking at each of them. Her eyes locked with Gina's. She walked to her and lifted her face with one finger. "Whatever he sees in you," she mumbled, looking at Gina. "Seth, I read him wrong, but at least I'm not too wrong," she said, looking down at Gina's stomach.

"Just let us go," Montserrat said.

"Aww, baby cousin," Tricia said, standing up. "I didn't come this far to just let you go so easily."

"This is not what we planned," Lucy said through clenched teeth.

"We?"

"I did exactly as you f*cking told me!"

Tricia removed her gloves and slapped Lucy across the face. "You don't shout at me."

"You should just let us go. This won't prove anything," Gina said.

Tricia turned to her. "Say that again."

"You can't keep us like this. I am pregnant!"

Tricia slapped her. "I have the upper hand here! Proof? Watch me while I prove it, b*tch!" She turned and started walking to the door. "I'll be back soon for y'all, and y'all better build up good manners," she said, slamming the door.

161

Lucy spat out blood. "Yeah, we'll build it up with hands tied to the f*cking chair and a wide tongue, b*tch!"

"Are you okay?" Montserrat asked Gina, who nodded.

Seth loosened his tie and threw it onto his desk, staring at it and recalling how Gina had tied it for him, her soft hands brushing his neck. He could hear Liam describing Gina to the detective. He rubbed his head and exhaled deeply, blaming himself for such carelessness.

He hadn't been himself since last night, when he learned Gina had been kidnapped. They had found the dead escorts. He couldn't believe it had actually happened, though he feared it might. They had called in detectives, despite his reservations, at Liam's insistence.

They had suspected everyone—his aunts, Tricia, and Katy. They had checked their movements during the party, but nothing seemed off. Except Montserrat.

A younger detective came in to report something unusual. They followed him to the parlour, where a fellow detective was reviewing the CCTV footage. Montserrat had been acting strangely throughout the party, almost like she was hiding, and then she stormed out.

"Could it be her then?" Liam asked.

"It could," Seth said, heading back to his study to grab his key. He found it on the desk but dropped it. As he bent down to pick it up, he saw the device.

"What's it?" Liam asked from the door. Seth held up the device, staring at it. Liam walked over, took it from him, and examined it.

"What the—this is—who could—no way!" "Katy? the doctor?"

"Katy wouldn't," Seth said, rubbing his hair.

"If it's the doctor, why would she?"

"I don't know. Someone could have sent her."

"This is getting more complicated."

A bang on the door interrupted them. Seth walked to the parlour, where the detectives had left. Through the window, he saw his aunt Theresa banging on the door with someone behind her.

Seth opened the door.

"Where is my daughter?" Theresa demanded.

"What?" Seth said.

"We came to the party and suddenly we couldn't f*cking find her!"

"Let me get this straight. You're looking for your daughter, and you think I have her?"

"Bring out my daughter, you monster! I know what you're up to. Don't you try me!" She tried to attack Seth, but Hector held her back.

"I'm sorry, man. We haven't seen her since last night. Are you sure you haven't seen her?" Hector asked. Seth looked at him closely, noting his boldness.

"I haven't."

"Alright then."

"Is that all you have to say, you good-for-nothing?" Theresa screamed at Hector.

Seth shut the door on them while they continued their drama.

"Montserrat is missing," Seth told Liam.

"Missing? Then—Tricia?"

Seth nodded. "I can't rely on the detectives," he said, picking up his keys.

"What are we going to do now? We can't do it alone; remember the dead escorts?"

"Then we need to move faster."

"Where are we going?"

Seth ignored him and stormed out.

"What's going on?" Theresa asked as they saw Seth storm out, followed by some detectives. She looked at Hector, who shrugged. She eyed him and walked towards their car.

Maria felt like she was living in the moment forever. Her daughter, her grandson, and her whole family were with her on a picnic—her daughter's idea. She wondered if her daughter had forgiven her, as she hadn't looked her in the eye yet. Or maybe it was her who hadn't looked her in the eye, feeling shy and ashamed.

Yesterday, with her whole family in a huge room, it felt like the oxygen was being sucked away. She hadn't seen them in a long time, apart from on TV. Only her mom was missing.

Peter's laughter brought her back to the present. The boy circled on her lap, was a feeling out of this world. She better enjoy it while it lasts.

"Doesn't this place smell like raw grass?" Lucy asked.

"Shouldn't we be figuring out how to get out of here?" Gina replied.

"I can't feel my hands and I'm pregnant," Montserrat said, sobbing again, but this time with no tears.

"You're pregnant?" Gina asked.

"Yes."

"How many months?"

"Two."

"Oh my god, they shouldn't be doing this to you. How do you feel?"

"Yeah, now you're the doctor," Lucy mocked.

"I feel weak and tired. I feel fed up. I feel like my life is messed up. I feel messed up. I just feel—" She started crying.

"It's fine, I understand. I've been there."

"You have?"

"Yes. Just so you know, I'm a surrogate. I lived with my mom, who always nagged me about getting married, about my job, and every other little thing. I still ask her for money, and none of this should be happening at my age, so I took this job. I couldn't risk letting it go."

"And the funniest part is that her family doesn't know about this. Her mom would flip if she found out what her daughter was doing," Lucy added.

"They don't know?" Montserrat asked.

"Once this is over, I'll figure out what to do next," Gina said with a smile.

"Well... I... I'm not so close with my mom. I've always done what she wanted. Then I lost my dad. I was adopted, though. My dad's family never liked me either. I married Hector because I love him, but things weren't as I imagined. Mother wants the inheritance because of the debts we owe. But I'm tired; I'm tired of everything."

"What do you know about being tired when you've lived a life of luxury all your life?" Lucy said. "You wonder how I became a doctor? I got pregnant. After college," Lucy said, almost forcing herself to talk about it. Gina looked at her, paying close attention. "Don't worry, it's not for Toby. It was for someone else. It was a boy, but he died two years later." She bit her lip. "It wasn't easy. It was a miracle that I survived. Matthew, my husband-to-be, helped me all through, and I'm marrying him soon if we survive this."

"I'm so sorry," they whispered.

"Don't give me that look. You started the talk, so I just decided to summarise mine."

"Congratulations," Gina said.

"So what about you? What are you going to do?" Lucy asked.

"Hmm... Once the baby is born," Gina said, looking at her stomach. "I'll go back home. I might open a restaurant or a fashion school; it has always been my dream."

"What about the baby?" They both stared at Gina, who shrugged.

"I don't know. It's a contract and we are not even related. So," she said, almost whispering it.

"What about Seth?" Lucy asked. "I see the way he looks at you. He cares."

"He cares for the inheritance."

"He cares about you."

"How do you know that?"

"I just know."

"I've known Seth," Montserrat said. "Not very well, but I've seen him with Grandma. He's different around her, so I thought maybe he's not as rocky as people think he is."

"I know, it's ju—"

The door opened, and the sun fell on their eyes. Tricia walked in with some men.

"Get them," she commanded as the men untied their ropes and blindfolded them.

"Where are you taking us?" Gina asked as Tricia walked towards her,

"Let me tell you a little story," Tricia said, lifting Gina's chin with her finger. "There was once a dumb boy, I know; we grew up together and he always loved to tag along like some leech. So, one day, I invited him to a party and introduced him to my friends. That night, he lost his virginity. Since then, he has been dumber, but then, all of a sudden, he's changing and I don't like that. Why? Because it's disgusting, it's annoying. I hate to see him feel like the world is under his feet."

"Well, you're a terrible storyteller," Gina said. Tricia chuckled.

166

"I want to do something terrible. I feel like that's the only thing that can make me happy. But I won't start with you; you should be the last. I want my brother to watch what I'll do to you."

"What do you mean?"

"Oh... he almost caught me this morning. He thought I kidnapped you. Well, he's right. He swore to kill me if anything happened to you. My brother is in love. What an ugly thing to see," she said, walking to the door.

"What will you gain from this?" Gina asked. Tricia stopped and turned to her.

"I don't care about gain anymore. I care about hurting those who hurt me," she said, then left.

The men dragged them out of the room. They felt the hot sun on their bodies and then were pushed into a car that drove off a minute later.

CHAPTER NINETEEN

Seth saw Tricia walking out of her house, watched her get into her car, and followed her. Gina had been kidnapped along with his baby, Montserrat was missing and pregnant, and even the doctor had vanished.

"Damn it!" he thought, hitting his hand on the wheel. This could only be Tricia's doing. He just needed to catch her in the act.

Liam had called him multiple times, so he turned off his phone. Liam didn't support him doing this alone, but Seth had no choice. The inheritance, his baby, even Gina—everything was on the line.

He watched Tricia for a while but saw nothing suspicious. He had searched her house the other day. She had let him in, laughed at him, and denied everything, claiming she was at the party the whole time, which she was. But he knew her better than anyone and knew how manipulative she could be.

He followed her back to her house late at night. It was another wasted day. As Tricia slid the key into the lock, Seth grabbed her, and she screamed.

"What the hell are you doing here?!" she said, realizing it was Seth.

"Where did you hide her?"

"I don't know what you're talking about?" she said, trying to wriggle her wrist out of his strong grip.

"Stop f*cking pretending!" he shouted at her.

"I don't f*cking know what you're talking about. Now let me go!"

"Listen!" he said, drawing her near and twisting her hand more. "If you hurt as much as a hair on her head, I'll kill you myself!" He pushed her against her door. "I'm watching you," he said and left.

Tricia stood there, watching him drive off. She blinked back the tears stinging her eyes and, scared, drove off to Mandy's.

The three women sat in dining chairs, arms and legs still tied, watching as their kidnapper whispered with a lady.

"What are you looking at?" Tricia asked, moving to the corner of the kitchen with Mandy. She was scared after Seth threatened her, so she moved them again. This time, Mandy's apartment felt like the safest place. Seth could never guess.

"Patricia, what the hell do you think you're doing?" Mandy asked.

"See, it's just for some time, okay? Till I figure out what to do next."

"The last thing I want right now is getting twisted in your family war"

"Calm down, okay?"

"Calm down? Do you know what you're placing on me? Your cousin's pregnant woman? Seth? No way."

"Listen, Mandy, help me out here! I'd do the same for you."

"Ha! You?"

"Fine! But I really need your help. I need to get that inheritance. Please."

Mandy looked at her. "What do I gain then?"

"What?"

"What do I gain from this? If I am going to take this risk, I should get some per cent," she said and Tricia paused for a moment,

"Fine, I'll pay you, handsomely."

Mandy exhaled and looked at the three women. "So what are you going to do to them?"

"I don't know yet."

"Fine. Hope they'll comply though. I can't take any headaches." She said and lighted a cigarette,

"I'll make sure of that," Tricia said with a smile and walked back to them.

"Just wait a little bit. The game will be on soon," she said to them.

"You won't get away with this," Montserrat said.

"We'll see then," Tricia said and turned to Mandy. "You can starve them whenever they misbehave, but don't touch them until I say so. However, if any of them tries to escape, shoot them," she said, placing a gun in front of Mandy and then leaving.

Mandy sat with them at the dining table, and she took some puffs while looking at them one by one. "I don't care what's going on, but you all better behave. I'm doing this for the money. If you comply, we'll live peacefully. But if any of you misbehave, I'm going to shoot. You'll sleep in the same room, eat, and wash there. That's your prison until whenever and whatever happens. You get me?" None of them replied. "You f*cking get me?!"

"Yes," Montserrat and Gina answered.

"What are you staring at, b*tch?" she asked Lucy, who rolled her eyes. Mandy slapped her cheek. Montserrat screamed, and Lucy spat out blood.

"No screaming," Mandy commanded, and Montserrat bit her lips. "Now, are we clear?" They all nodded. "Good."

"I told you not to go after her," Liam said.

"Man, I can't."

"Seth, let the police deal with this."

"They aren't even suspecting her at all. They should be watching her!"

"I'll get them to do that. Don't you think you're putting them in more danger by confronting her? We are not even sure, it could be someone else."

"Liam, she's f*cking pregnant."

"Yeah, I know," he said and exhaled. "It's going to leak, you know?"

"I don't care anymore."

"Oh yeah?" Liam said, giving him a look. "When did it start?"

"What?" Seth asked.

"When did you start falling for her?"

"Falling for who?"

"Oh my god, I can't believe I didn't see this happening. When did it start?"

"I don't know what you're talking about."

"Yes, you do. Did you tell her? Oh my god, yes, the kiss, right?"

"I don't know," he said, walking out.

"You—you don't know? Wow... Man, wait up!" Liam said, running after him.

Mandy opened the door and dropped a tray of food for the three women before leaving. Gina couldn't move a finger; she couldn't sleep, not on the bed or the floor—they were all uncomfortable. Lucy grabbed the tray and set it before them.

"We at least need to survive, even if it's just for a little while," she said as none of them reached for their plates. "For your babies."

Montserrat reached for hers and took a bite of the burnt bread and egg. The smell got to Gina, making everything worse.

"Are you alright?" Montserrat asked her.

"I don't eat eggs. The smell—" she said and shut her mouth, trying not to vomit.

"Then eat the bread," Lucy said.

"I can't."

"You're almost due. For the baby, you need to. You need strength."

They watched as she slowly took the bread and took a bite.and

A while after eating, they heard a sound, like moaning, then it became louder. Lucy started laughing first, and they joined her.

"Isn't it too early?" Gina whispered.

"Morning is the best moment," Lucy said pushing down the burnt egg.

"Hector likes it in the morning. We used to shower together."

"Mat likes it any time. I drive him crazy," Lucy said and they laughed.

"What about you?" Lucy asked Gina.

"Me? I don't know."

"Don't tell me—"

"What?"

"Toby was your—"

"No."

"you've never been with anyone else," Lucy said looking at her with amazement. "No"

"Then tell us!"

After some seconds, Gina said, "Well, you're right." Lucy's jaw dropped,

"No way!"

"High school?" Montserrat asked.

"Since f*cking high school!" Lucy said and Gina shrugged.

"This is hard to believe. Then Seth is the second."

"No, nothing happened between us."

"Thats hard to believe. You're lying."

"No."

"Not even a kiss?"

"Well..."

"I knew it!"

"Seth kissed you?" Montserrat asked. "I thought he was gay or something."

"Tell us about it."

"I don't have the strength."

"Just summarise. We're bored." Lucy said looking at Montserrat for agreement,

"Well... it's nothing, he just... he just helped me to the bathroom, and I don't know, our faces were close, our bodies were touching, and... so we kissed."

"That's it?" Lucy asked.

"Yeah. That's all." She said and forced the last bite of the bread down.That's

"So what happened after?"

"Nothing."

"He didn't... say anything?"

"No."

"Ah... you two are boring," Montserrat giggled.

"What was I supposed to do?"

"Okay, listen. He kissed you, which means he's attracted to you. You should've taken the opportunity to have sex with him—hot sex in the bathroom or anywhere."

"Oh my god, really?"

"Yeah, you crave his touch, don't you?"

"Can you hear yourself?"

"Of course. Sex with Seth McGregor would be one in a million. Can't believe someone missed such a chance."

"I'm pregnant."

"So?"

"Wait," Montserrat hushed them. They heard someone shout, then smash something, and slam the door. Soon they heard footsteps approaching their room.

The door opened, and Mandy walked in, looking like a mess, holding a cigarette. She took a chair and sat down. She blew out smoke and turned the chair to face the girls.

"Look at all of you," she blew smoke towards them, and Gina coughed.

"She's pregnant," Lucy said.

"The f*ck I care?" She took a puff from the cigarette. "Y'all are all over the news," she laughed.

"We're over the news?" Gina asked.

"Apart from you. Your face wasn't there. Do you know what y'all are worth?" She laughed with her throat.

"You're bleeding," Gina told her. She touched her face and felt the blood on her hands.

"You know, people treat you the way you treat yourself, but men are scumbags too—except Seth," she smiled, looking at Gina. "I still remember our night together like it was yesterday. It was memorable. He was so innocent."

"It wasn't exciting for him. You hurt him," Gina told her.

"You said what?"

"He despises that night. He despises you!"

Mandy rushed to her and slapped her across the face. Lucy rushed and held Gina.

"Don't make me lose my temper!"

"B*tch" Gina said softly. Mandy tried to slap her again, and Lucy held her and twisted her arm behind her back, pushing her towards the wall. She asked Montserrat to get the door. While Montserrat rushed to open it, someone pushed it open, grabbing Montserrat. Mandy stepped on Lucy's toes and hit her head on her face. Lucy held her broken nose. Gina couldn't help; she just kept crying and shouting. The man who entered tied up Montserrat and Lucy and walked out with Mandy.

"B*tches," Mandy called them before leaving.

Tricia stared at the church as tears welled up in her eyes. Noah was finally getting married, and she wasn't the bride. She removed her seatbelt and got out of the car. She entered the church quietly and sat at the back. There were flowers and ribbons. The bride was wearing a gown with pretty floral designs.

It could've been me and you, not her! We had something together.

She watched them emotionlessly. His smile was genuine. He never smiled at her like that, or did he? He was supposed to be hers! She felt their eyes lock. Her heart started beating. She watched as he kissed her while his eyes still held hers.

Is he doing it intentionally? Why does it hurt so much? I can't bear it! I don't think I can!

She stepped to the middle of the church and pulled out a gun. Nobody noticed, nobody saw her—except Noah. He saw her as she pointed the gun at his wife, she pulled the trigger, and Noah blocked his wife as the bullet pierced through his shoulder. People started screaming and scampering for safety. Tricia watched as the bride bent over Noah with blood already soaking her white dress. When she realised what she had done, she dropped the gun and covered her mouth as tears welled up in her eyes. She got herself together, ran off to her car and drove off. She couldn't hold the wheel strongly because of her trembling hand. Tears kept falling, blurring her vision.

Oh my god! What have I done? What have I done?!

She pulled over and cried for a while. She heard sirens and got scared.

I shot Noah! Oh my god! What have I done? What should I do?!

She started the engine and drove to Mandy's.

Stephanie sat before her laptop, researching Seth McGregor. Nicki had said her sister was involved in a deal.

Surrogacy? Regina?

She kept tapping her feet on the floor while she read about the inheritance, the millionaire, the girlfriend, and the missing ladies.

Oh Regina, what have you gotten yourself into?

She closed the laptop and stood up. She bit her nails as she walked to and fro, contemplating what to do.

Should I go there? No! What am I saying? Gina is kidnapped. What the hell is going on? What should I do? F*ck!!

"How long do you think it's going to take before we find them?" Liam asked forwarding the video they got from the agent on Tricia's movement as Seth drove them back to the mansion.

"I don't know, but I won't let it take long."

"She might hurt them."

"She better not touch her," Seth swore. After a minute of silence, Liam said, "So, you two kissed?"

Seth stepped on the brake. "Man! What the f*ck!"

"What did I do? I just asked you a question!"

Seth sighed and continued driving. "So?"

"So what?"

"Just say it, man."

He sighed again. "I told you before, didn't I?"

"Told me what?"

"Yes, we kissed."

"Oh yeah?!" Liam said, laughing.

"Yes, and that's it."

"And that's it? No, that's not it. I'm seeing something."

"Shut up!"

"you hated her," "Nothing changed" "hm, I hear you"

Liam laughed as a notification caught his attention, "She...she shot someone?" Liam asked, sitting up

"Who?" Seth asked, stepping on his brakes again.

"A wedding was dismissed as the groom was shot by his ex, the famous model and actress Patricia McGregor. Whoa! She has gone crazy?"

"She's finally lost it," Seth said, taking the phone from him. "What about the Gina? She can do something to them."

Before he could finish, Seth reversed the car.

"Where are we going?"

"We need to find her."

"We don't even know where she is!"

Seth ignored him and drove off. He swore to strangle her himself if anything happened to Gina or the baby.

The door opened, and Tricia rushed in with some guys.

"Get them!" she said, breathing fast. "Hurry!"

"Where else are you taking us? If you wanna kill us, just f*cking do it!" Lucy said as one of Tricia's men dragged her up.

"You wanna die? Just wait a little bit!" she spat as her phone rang. It was Seth. She turned it off.

They were dragged into a van. Gina felt miserable. She was weak, and cold sweat ran down her body. She felt extremely uncomfortable. She lay her head on Lucy's shoulder and bit her lips, trying to control herself from whatever was happening to her. She didn't care what was going on. She was extremely tired. She had gotten herself into this, after all. She might as well die in it. Her mother would say she deserved it after committing such an act.

Is surrogacy too bad? I hate this feeling.

She took a deep breath and fell asleep for a while.

Lucy woke her up as the van stopped. The door opened, and they were taken out one by one.

"What's the problem?" Tricia asked as she waited for them to bring Gina out.

"I don't know, ma'am. She's... She's sweating a lot."

"So? Carry her!"

Tricia said and walked out on him.

178

They were taken into an old abandoned factory. Gina couldn't take any steps, although the huge man was almost carrying her whole weight. She felt the baby weighing down her stomach. She just wanted to sit down and open her legs wide; maybe that would loosen the pressure she was feeling. She gave up when she saw the stairs they still had to climb. She heard Tricia command someone to help the man holding her. She felt another hand carry her. She didn't know how many stairs they climbed, but it felt like hours.

"What is happening to her?" Tricia asked, seeing how Gina was sweating with her eyes closed.

"Tie her to the chair!" she said, pointing to the chair with a gun. "Fast!"

"Gina, are you okay?" Lucy asked.

"Shut it!" Tricia commanded.

"She's losing it. Can't you see?!"

Tricia hit her across the face with her gun. "I. Don't. Care." She stepped away from her and turned her phone on. She dialed Seth's number, and he picked up immediately.

"Where the f*ck are you hiding them?!"

"Calm down, brother. I admit I got them. Wanna see?" She set the camera so he could see them: Montserrat, Lucy, then Gina.

"The f*ck did you do to her? Where the hell are you? I swear—"

"I told you to calm down," she said, gritting her teeth. "Their lives depend on you. Don't even try to do anything stupid."

"What the f*ck do you want?!"

"Five hundred million."

"What?!"

"I want it now, and every hour you waste, I will add another five hundred million."

"Are you out of your f*cking mind?!"

"Not yet, but I'll let you know once I've lost it. You have two hours, and Seth McGregor, don't even dare to get the police involved unless you want her dead," she said, pointing her gun at Gina.

"Let—" she cut the call and waited.

_____

"F*ck!" Seth screamed, hitting his hand on the wheel.

"So what do we do? The police need to know."

"You f*cking heard her, Liam. F*ck!"

"Then we're giving her the money?"

"That's our only choice."

"How sure are we that she'll not harm them? You saw the news. She shot her ex at his f*cking wedding!"

"So what are you saying? We have two hours, two f*cking hours!" They waited for a few minutes, thinking of what to do.

"Alright, we get the money first, then we'll figure out what to do next," Liam suggested.

Stopped

CHAPTER TWENTY

Tricia's phone rang, and it was Seth on the line. "I've gotten the money. Now, where do I bring it?"

"Oh, so fast. That's great. I'll text you the directions. Seth, I swear, any wrong move, I'll shoot them all," she said before ending the call.

"Gina?" Lucy called out when she noticed Gina wasn't moving. "Gina, answer me!"

"What's wrong with her? Hey, check on her," Tricia ordered one of the men.

"Her body's cold and sweaty, but she's breathing," he reported.

"She needs a doctor," Lucy said urgently.

"I don't want to hear your voice, again," Tricia commanded.

"If anything happens to her or the baby, your brother won't take it lightly. I'm her doctor; I need to check on her."

Tricia hesitated but then loosened Lucy's restraints. "Don't even think of doing anything silly," she warned.

Her phone rang again, and she grabbed it immediately. "I'm looking at the building," Seth said.

"I changed my mind," she said, stepping away from Lucy and looking out the window.

"What?!"

"I need a helicopter, fast. You have less than an hour to get it, and in half an hour, you're adding another million."

"Are you f*cking joking?!"

"Do I look like I'm joking? Oh, and Seth, I'm losing patience. Drop the money in the theatre room and step out, then get the copter."

"F*ck!" she heard him say as she cut the call.

"Felix, watch them. Don't even take your eyes off them," she instructed, taking the other men with her.

"Gina, can you hear me?" Lucy asked but received no response. She could see Gina's chest rise and fall, but the sweat was alarming.

Lucy looked at the huge guy standing by the wall and a thought came to her head immediately. She looked at Montserrat, trying to communicate silently, but Montserrat couldn't understand her signs.

"Hey," Lucy called to Felix, "Hey, Superman."

"Shut up," he responded.

"If you let us go, you would be paid finely, more than she can ever pay you."

"I told you to shut up!" he said, slowly walking closer to her.

"You can be paid double, triple, even," she said, watching him take another step closer. Then she hit him across the face with her loosened hand, quickly freeing her legs. Before he could get up, Lucy hit him with his chair and ran to Montserrat.

"Once I untie you, run; do you hear me?"

"Watch out!" Montserrat screamed as Felix grabbed Lucy by the hair. He smacked her on the face, and she fell to the floor. Montserrat screamed and launched at him. He turned and pushed her away. Lucy got up and jumped on him, but he threw her at Gina's feet. As Montserrat got up to hit him again, he kicked her, and she hit the wall.

"What the hell is going on?!" Tricia demanded from the door. Lucy rushed to Montserrat.

"Omg, are you okay?" she asked as Montserrat felt something dripping down her legs.

"The f*ck!" Lucy exclaimed as they saw blood dripping on the floor from Montserrat's legs.

"Oh my God! What is happening?!" Montserrat said, almost panicking.

"What the fuck happened here?!" Tricia asked Felix.

"We need to take them to the hospital now!" Lucy shouted.

"I asked a f*cking question."

"She's going to lose her baby if we f*cking don't!" Lucy said, still holding Montserrat.

"F*ck!" Tricia said, pacing up and down and thinking of what to do. She needed to get out of this whole mess. While she was pacing, she heard police sirens approaching.

"The f*ck! I warned him," she said, gritting her teeth.

"What did you do?" Seth asked Liam as he saw him walking out of the police car.

"Man, listen, we can't do this on our own. She killed someone."

"F*ck you, man!"

"Seth, she's dangerous."

"I asked you...f*ck!" he screamed, kicking the air in anger.

"Mr. Seth, I am the officer in charge. We'll take it from here. Don't worry; they'll be fine," the officer assured him.

Seth looked at the officer and walked away with clenched teeth.

The police officer returned to his team, who had scattered around the building.

"Miss Patricia, it would be better if you comply with us. Step out of the building with your hands in the air," he said into the speaker and waited, but there was no response.

Seth's phone rang and he answered immediately, moving away from the police "I warned you, brother."

"Listen, I didn't call them, so don't you dare touch her."

"I'm sorry, but I can't promise you that."

"Patricia!"

"Send the helicopter. If anything happens to me, they'll all die. Your time is running out brother," she said before ending the call.

"What does she want?" Seth heard Liam behind him but ignored him.

"Seth, you have to trust them if you want to save Gina!"

"I heard you."

"You have to."

"Who are they?" Seth asked as he saw some people with the detective.

"Your aunt and the doctor's fiancé."

"You called them?"

"Why not!"

"I'm sending the team in," the police officer said. Liam looked at Seth, but he didn't say a word, so the police proceeded.

Gina started whimpering, and then she began breathing hard, gripping the chair.

"Ma'am," Felix called to Tricia.

"What?!" she snapped, then she saw Gina.

"It's...," Gina muttered.

"What?"

"You need to stop all this, or they're all going to f*cking die. She's going to bleed to death, and she's going into labour, and you? Your life will have to end too."

"Don't you dare talk to me like that."

She heard the helicopter and took a deep breath. "Take them to the rooftop," she commanded.

Gina screamed, but her voice was weak. She gripped the chair harder as the pain shot through her veins and her whole body. Felix helped Montserrat up; she was numb, the bleeding had stopped, and her body was stained and in shock. He carried her up the stairs to the rooftop. Gina screamed as they carried her up the stairs. She grabbed their hands, but the pain was only beginning.

Tricia watched as the helicopter neared the rooftop. She heard her blood pumping in her ears; she couldn't wait for this to end. She looked at Felix and his men, then at Gina, Lucy, and Montserrat, and then she thought of the inheritance. Then she thought of her life after this—she just wanted a quiet life where no one knew her.

One billion is enough to start a new life. F*ck the inheritance F*ck everybody.

She drew her gun and shot the men—all of them.

Then she turned to the three women. "Should I start with you? You wanted to die so badly," she said to Lucy. "you gain nothing from doing this." "No, I gain a lot from doing this. You get to die, they get to die, all of you get to die and I get to live." "And you think you will be happy?" "why not? Nobody cared about my happiness, it has always been me. Maybe, you should send a message to my grandmother. Tell her to f*ck herself!"

"Freeze!"

She heard and turned sharply to see the police. "Drop your weapons and raise your hands in the air."

Tricia slowly dropped her gun and raised her hands.

Seth appeared behind the police, and then he saw Gina on the floor with the other ladies. He felt adrenaline rush through his body. He rushed to her and held her up.

Tricia took a step backwards. "Ma'am, do not take another step."

She took another step and another. The police moved forward, guessing her intention, but before they could act, Tricia jumped off the building.

Seth couldn't care less what else was happening. With the help of Liam and the police officers, Gina and Montserrat were rushed to the hospital. Gina screamed and breathed heavily through her mouth while her eyes were still shut, ignoring everything Lucy was telling her to do. She could hear different voices but she felt like she was transforming. It felt like the baby was tearing her inside.

She kept screaming and crying without tears, her mouth dry.

Lucy, Theresa, Hector, Seth, Liam, Cate, and Lucy's fiancé all waited anxiously. The doctor treating Montserrat came out and announced that she had lost her baby. Theresa dropped to the floor as Hector held her, trying to calm her down. The doctor further announced that Montserrat was in shock and needed rest. "What about Gina?" "still in labour," he said, and walked back to the room.

Seth kept pacing up and down. He hated waiting. What was taking them so long?

A nurse came out, refusing to tell them the situation.

"F*cking tell me what's going on!" Seth screamed at the nurse.

"She's still in labour. She's weak, and the baby turned."

"What do you mean the baby turned?"

"I'm sorry, excuse me," the nurse said, running off.

They waited for another hour, with nurses and doctors running up and down. After hours of waiting, the door slowly opened, and the doctor walked out.

"How is she?" Seth asked, holding the doctor.

"She's fine, the baby too. Congratulations," he said with a smile.

Seth took a deep breath.

"She was weak, and we considered a C-section, but," he shrugged, "everything turned out well. The baby is okay, but she is anaemic, and is currently on blood transfusion."

"I need to see her."

"She needs rest. The nurse will show you the baby. You can see her, but you can't go into the room yet," the doctor said, instructing a nurse to take them to the baby.

"Congratulations, sir," he said and walked away. Seth followed the nurse into a room that smelled foreign to him. The nurse slowly took the baby and placed him in Seth's arms. Seth felt nervous inside. He had never held a baby before. The little human just lay in his hands and it felt unbelievable.

"Omg, isn't he a pretty one?" Cate said, smiling.

"Oh, little man," Liam said, touching his legs.

Seth transferred the baby to Cate as the nurse led him to where Gina was. He watched from outside. She looked different with all the wires connected to her. He wanted to touch her.

"She'll be fine," Liam said behind him. His phone rang, and he left to answer it. He came back a minute later. "Tricia survived the fall."

Seth clenched his teeth and left with Liam to see her.

Stephanie walked into the bar, trying to figure out what to do. How would she approach Gina? Their mom would surely flip out when she finds out.

187

"Hey, beautiful," she heard behind her, and turned to see who it was. No Please!

"Hi.

"Yes, me," he said, chuckling.

"We meet again."

"Yeah," he said, sitting beside her. "I actually waited for you every day," he said with a smile.

"Oh, you did?"

"I knew you'd come again, so I didn't give up." He laughed a little and stared at the table. Steph looked at him, he's just too young.

And why is he always smiling? Is he shy? He's cute.

"Well, here I am." She said,

"Yes, uhmm, drinks on me."

"Nah, it's on me."

"No, it's on me."

"Fine," she said with a smile.

They talked for a while, and she started to like him. It felt good talking with someone—a guy, actually. It had been a long time, and it made her feel weirdly sweet. She is married but to hell with it! She might as well go to the bottom hell since she's going there anyways.

He excused himself to the restroom. It gave her a little time to think about her plans. Her eyes darted to the TV playing by the end of the room. People were interested in what it was saying, so she tried to know what was going on.

That's when she saw the headline at the bottom of the screen. She felt blood rush to her head.

"Are you okay?"

"Hm? Yes."

She heard the bartender talking about what happened—the kidnapping, the girl who fell off the roof. Her heart sank.

"Are you sure you're okay?"

"Yeah, it's just...uhm, excuse me, I have to go."

"I can give you a ride home."

"No, it's f—"

"No, I don't mind."

"Fine."

They walked out of the bar together. Her thoughts were filled with what-ifs. What if Gina got hurt? What about the money? She needed to react fast.

She heard the guy talking but wasn't interested. He walked her to her room, and she had to invite him in. She brought up the McGregor family as a topic.

"Well, the family is actually filled with very, very important people. It's a great family."

"So what's with them? Why are they all over the headlines?"

"Well, they always make the headlines. There's this talk about inheritance."

"Inheritance?" she said, sitting beside him.

"Yes. The McGregors are old money. Grandmother died, leaving inheritance for grandkids, so things are pretty messed up."

"How?"

"I'm not sure, I think they're all into getting the inheritance, so everything is messed up."

"I heard someone fall off the roof."

"Yeah, recently, I think one of them kidnapped some ladies."

"Some ladies?"

He chuckled. "Why are you so interested in them?"

"Hm? Oh, uhm, I'm just curious."

He smiled and touched her hand with his finger. "Why are you curious? Or are you always the curious kind?" He walked his finger up and down her hand, looking her in the eye.

Oh boy.

"No, I'm—just, I just want to know, yeah."

"You're beautiful."

What is happening to me?

She licked her lips as he touched her face. "I couldn't get your face out of my head," he said, kissing her jaw, "I kept thinking of you", he kissed the side of her lips, "day and night," he said and kissed her lips while working his hands down her legs.

CHAPTER TWENTY-ONE

"Where's my baby?" Gina asked as she finally fully recovered. Cate slowly carried the baby from the cradle and placed him in her arms. His eyes were shut. Gina touched his face and then his hand. "He's so cute," she said smiling as tears rolled down her eyes.

He's finally here. I actually gave birth. "He's so beautiful." Is it over? Will I really have to leave this angel?

"Oh boy," Lucy said with a sigh.

"Let her be, I know that feeling," Cate said.

They watched them for a while. "What about the other lady?" Gina asked Lucy.

"Sadly, she lost her baby, but she's fine now."

"Oh, that's so bad. What about her, the one that kidnapped us?"

"I heard she survived the fall."

"Enough. Here, give me the baby and rest," Cate said, taking the baby from her.

"What about Seth?" she wanted to see him badly, to see the look on his face, to see him carry their baby. their baby. (remember that lucy will tell gina that the baby actually has her blood since it's traditionally done and it's her egg that was used and the trad method was used cause Seth wanted to avoid the to and fro to the hospital and keep it a secret.)

"He was here. He left before you woke up."

Gina just nodded.

"Has he seen the baby?" she asked, scared.

"Yes," Cate answered, guessing her fear. She just smiled.

Her eyes were heavy, so she decided to close them for a while. Gina heard people speaking but couldn't make out what they were saying. She tried but fell asleep again.

When she woke up, she saw someone looking at her but couldn't make out who it was. She turned over to the other side and remembered she had a dream about the baby. Her mum was carrying him, and Seth was beside her. They were holding hands. She smiled. But...

191

Where's the cradle?

She turned again and saw someone that looked like her sister. She looked around her and realized she was still in the hospital. She felt a touch.

"Regina, are you okay?"

Oh my God! It's her!

She pushed Steph's hand and stared at her.

Am I still dreaming?

"Regina, can you hear me? Are you okay? Should I get the doctor?"

Oh my God! Oh my God! This is real! What is hap— How did—

"Is she awake?" Nicki asked as she walked into the room. "Oh dear, how are you feeling?"

"She won't talk to me," Steph said.

"Riri? Should I get the doctor?"

"What is happening? How—how?" Gina asked, still in shock.

"She's fine. You need to get better first," Nicki said.

"What? Get better? you-Nicki, what is happening?" "I'm sorry, but everyone was worried, so I told her."

"Oh," Steph said. "Well, you asked. I was worried. Everybody was. And she found out on her own."

"What?!"

"Hey, you need to calm down, okay?"

"Where's my baby?"

"Uhh, Gina, listen, you need to relax and get better first."

"Get better? What the f*ck are you saying? I need my baby now!"

"Gina—"

"the f*ck!" Gina said, trying to get off the bed,

"They've taken the baby. Your contract is done, and you'll be paid fully once you're healed," Steph spat out.

"The f*ck," Nicki said.

"That's what they told me."

"Wait, what? How—wait, how many days have I been here?"

"A week."

"Oh my God. I don't—I don't get this," Gina said, pulling out the drip from her hand.

"What are you doing?" Nicki asked. Gina ignored her and headed for the door. She felt her head spinning like blood was rushing to her head, then her weak legs and the sick smell of the hospital. Then she slumped to the floor.

Gina sat by the hotel window, watching the busy streets of New York. She kept thinking, wiping the tears crawling down her cheeks. It's been over a week since she was released from the hospital and Seth never asked how she is doing. All she got was an email about ending the contract. Just like that...

So, she was discarded just like that... Seth discarded me like that... So this is all over? I thought...

She wiped another tear and stared at her luggage sitting by the couch. it reminded her of when she came to New York and the first day she moved into the mansion. She got off the window and opened the boxes. They were just as she parked them. She thought she and Seth had something, but again, it was Seth.

What had I expected? It's just a contract. Tomorrow everything's going to end. And I'm going to leave my baby.

"Beer?" Steph said, handing her a can. She took it without a word and popped it.

"So, what are you going to do next?" Steph asked.

"Why are you here?"

"Well, everybody is worried about you. Mum is worried. I had a business here, so I decided to look for you as well."

Gina scoffed. "So everybody is worried, then you, Stephanie, decided to save them from worrying. What do you care?"

"Hey, girl, you don't talk to me like that. I'm still your sister, four years older than you."

"Oh really? An older sister who doesn't know responsibility? An older sister who cares more about money than family!"

"You don't talk to me like that Regina?"

"You can't even protect your marriage!" Gina spat.

"Well, at least I'm not some whore who got pregnant and gave out her child!" she spat and Gina felt it pierce right through her heart. She laughed as the tears she's been holding back came streaming down her face "A whore? I agree, fine. But, do you know what it feels like to cater for our family? Have you ever worked so hard for

something you want?! You've always had it the easy way, so you won't f*cking know! Do you know how much mom pressured me in that house? Do you know what I have been through? All of you have had it the easy way. I, Regina, have to work for everything I want and own! I'm a whore? I left my child, yes! And then what?! And then f*cking what!" She threw the beer on the floor startling both Steph and Nicki, who was standing by the door and stormed out.
She stepped into the elevator and dropped down, crying. She wrapped her hands around her knees and wept. She felt someone's hand on her shoulder and jumped up immediately. She hadn't noticed when the elevator stopped and opened.
"It's me."
She wiped her tears to see who it was.
"Toby?" She stared at him, shocked. "What are you—how..?"
"Hi", he said and Gina stood up, wiping the tears on her face.
"How have you been?"

Faith hugged her husband. "Thank you," she said, kissing him, as they settled for dinner with her daughter. She felt grateful for having such a husband. He interacted with her like they've known each other for a long time. She couldn't wish for anything more.
After taking her bath, she sat before the mirror, applying her cream.
"Have you read about your step-cousin, Seth, and Patricia?" her husband asked after dinner while she was setting the clean dishes.
"Yes, very terrible. I read about them in the news yesterday."
"She is horrible."
"She's not. I remember her; she used to be very sweet. She just... lacks love."
"Who knew your cousin had such a plan. I mean, he has always been distant and mean. I know he is like your mothers' shadow and will not sit idly and wait, but, I never saw that coming."
Faith turned to her husband, smiling and exhaling. "I don't know, but Seth is a lovely boy. Both he and Patricia had a rough childhood. That's why mother loved them so much."
"This is all for the inheritance."
"I won't say that I'm totally not interested in the inheritance, but my family matters more." She looked through the window at her

194

daughter cuddling with the dog. "They are family too, but I can't do anything. Montserrat lost her baby, and Patricia jumped off the rooftop—thankfully, she survived. This is not what mother wanted." She said as her husband rubbed her shoulders.

"So, everybody knows about me now," Gina said, downing a glass of whisky.
"Lucy told me. She told me you're here in the city," Toby replied.
"Hmm... I see. So, how have you been?"
"I've been good, I'll say. After college, I did industrial training at a publishing company, and now I own one."
"That's cool"
"Yeah."
"Cheers!" she said and downed another shot.
Toby talked more about himself, trying to renew their bond, but Gina was far away, lost in her thought.
"I heard from Nicki that you graduated with honours." he said after minutes of talking without a response.
"You've seen Nicki?" she asked,
"Yeah, years back when I went home."
"Oh. Well, yeah, I did." her voice was already sounding coarsed.
"So, you're working here in the city?"
"What?"
"You work in the city?"
"Yeah,"
"Where?"
"Hm? Oh, it's just a, um... I don't want to talk about work." she said sitting up, already feeling fed up with the conversation.
"Oh yeah, right." he said staring at his shot, thinking of something else to say.
"Earlier," he said, "at the elevator?"
"Nah... it's nothing, just going through some stuff."
"Oh."
"Yes... you look good. I mean, you changed. Not much, but, you changed," he said chuckling,
"Thank you."

"Nah."

"How's your mum and your sisters?"

"They're all fine."

"It's been a long time."

"Yeah," she said with a smile, looking at him fully for the first time. He changed too, more masculine. But not like Seth.

Gina climbed into the bathtub, closing her eyes and feeling sweet goosebumps from the hot water. She lay there, her eyes shut.

She found herself in his house, her belly bulged out, wearing long gowns and puffy slippers. His scent filled her nose, then his strong body against hers and his soft lips on her lips.

She bit her lip hard and got out of the shower, suddenly feeling disgusted and a sort of rage bubbling inside her.

She wrapped the towel around her and walked back to the room. She saw her box and handbag by her bed. She sat down on the bed and took a deep breath. Everything kept flashing before her; it all felt like yesterday.

She took out her phone from her bag and saw a hard-covered document. She took it out, and it was the copy of the contract. She slowly tore the envelope and brought out the document. Looking at it, all she could see was her baby—his innocent face, his soft hands, his curled hair and Seth.

What is wrong with me?

She looked up at the ceiling, trying to push back the tears that were tempting to fall down her cheeks. She put the document back into the envelope and took out a pair of jeans and a floral top from her box.

Her heart skipped a beat at the thought of seeing Seth again.

I was kidnapped because of him. I almost died! I carried his child! And all he could do was send me to an expensive hotel?! I almost died giving birth to his child! He doesn't care if I die or not. All he cares about is money, his f*cking inheritance! I am sure he doesn't care about the baby too. What will happen to him?

"Gina?" She heard someone call.

"Yes?" she answered quickly wiping the tears on her cheeks.

"What are you thinking?" Nicki said, smiling. "I know, girl, we haven't actually talked," she said, sitting beside her on the bed. "I don't know what the hell happened within this past few month but, it's over and he paid you more than I even thought. I thought you'd be happy, exited and all, but, I don't know, it's the opposite and I want us to talk about it before anything else. Did something happen?"

"Nothing happened."

"It doesn't look like it," "Nothing happened," she said and Nicki just stared at her,

"If you say so, though I don't believe you, get this over with." she said and turned Gina to face her, "I am no kid and I know you, something happened and it's okay that you don't want to talk about it. But I have one advice for you," she said and waited for a response but got a weak smile. "When you go there today, close the contract, get your remaining payment, and get out, okay," she said and Gina stared at her, "what?"

"What about the baby?"

"What?"

"I mean, the baby. Who will take care of him?"

"Wait. You worry about the baby? the sh*t, you talking about, girl? The baby is a billion times richer than you, and you're worried about him."

"No, you don't understand. I know him. He cares about the money, not the baby. He might not even look at him his whole life!" Gina tried to explain.

"I don't know the sh*t you're talking about, but you should not mind the baby, I am warning you." She said as Gina tried to pull away from her but she pulled her back. "Listen, all you have to do is close the f*cking contract, get back here, and we'll have some ladies' time and relax, okay?" She asked but got silence, "Regina, do you hear me?" "I heard you." She said and Nicki stared at her for awhile, sighed and patted her laps before leaving the room. Gina took a big sigh and dressed up.

Seth got off the conference meeting and drove home. He'd been checking his watch throughout the conference, unconsciously. They would be ending their contract today, and he felt nervous and uneasy, for a reason he can't tell.

He got out of his car and jumped up the stairs to his room. He went to the kitchen where Rosa was cutting some vegetables. He expected to see her sitting down by the table, but she wasn't there.

"She is not here, yet." He asked Rosa.

"No, you said twelve. It's still after eleven. She must be on her way." He nodded and left. He had reemployed Rosa after Gina gave birth. Someone needs to take care of the baby.

He took a quick bath and went to his study. He checked his watch, and it was 12:01 pm. The doorbell rang.

Liam walked in seconds later.

"She's not here yet?" he asked Seth.

"Haven't seen her."

"I can't wait to see her." He said looking at Seth to see his reaction, but he just stood on his desk, tapping his leg.

The doorbell rang again, and Rosa went to get it.

Gina looked around the big house. It had changed, or maybe she just missed it. She rang the bell again. When the door opened, she saw Rosa standing there.

"Rosa?" she said as a big smile crossed her face. Rosa smiled back and they hugged.

"I've missed you."

"Same here," she said and released her. "welcome dear," she said looking at her with a lovely smile that Gina read. She has given birth and Seth has thrown her out. Fair? "He's waiting inside," Rosa said and Gina nodded walking in.

Seth sat there, rubbing his hand on his lips. He heard her talking with Rosa, and his heart beat increased.

"And she's here," Liam said as Rosa opened the door, and Gina walked in.

"and you're looking sweet," he said, hugging her. Gina smiled.

"I swear, I've forgotten how you look without your baby bump." Gina smiled again and looked at Seth. He was just staring, as usual.

"Well, sit down, m'lady." Liam said shifting the chair for her to sit down.

Gina sat down, and Liam sat beside her. Seth sat properly and brought out the contract.

No "hello." No "how have you been?" Gina thought.

"We've finally come to the end of the contract, and like I promised, once the contract is sealed, you'll receive your final payment," he said, turning the contract towards her.

Gina chuckled and bit her lip. She took the contract and stared at it for a moment. Then she looked at Liam. "Can you give us a minute?"

"Hm?" Liam asked, not getting it. She looked at Seth. "Oh... alright." He nodded and left the study.

Seth was surprised for a minute, he was feeling abnormal and too conscious.

"Where is the baby?" Gina asked immediately Liam closed the door.

"What?" Seth asked.

"Where's the baby?" she asked again, almost whispering.

"You can't see him."

"Why?"

"It's in the contract."

Gina let out a sigh and clenched her teeth. "Who will take care of him?"

"That is not your business."

Gina nodded. "You left me at the hospital."

"You needed to recover."

"You didn't check up on me."

"I did."

"After I left the hospital, you didn't."

"You weren't my responsibility anymore."

Gina paused, taking in the blow. Then she let out a little laugh trying to push down the temptation to just burst out crying. "We kissed," she said, looking at him, her hands terribly shaking. His face was rigid as ever, showing no emotion. He was just staring.

"We kissed," she said again.

"That was a mistake."

Gina raised her eyebrows, then looked back at her fingers. She clasped her hands together till she felt the pain "I was kidnapped because of you, and I almost died. You don't care?"

"I raised your payment."

Gina nodded, biting her lower lip. "Last question," she said, taking a deep breath. "All those months, you felt nothing?" She shook her head. "Nothing at all?"

They looked at each other for a moment.

"No," he said.

"No?"

"Nothing."

She felt her nail pierce her skin and unclasped her hands. She nodded and took a deep breath. "Fine. I'll be traveling soon. Let me see the baby."

"You can't."

"I just... want to see him before I leave."

"It's clearly written—"

"F*ck you."

"What?"

"F*ck! You!" Gina said as tears rolled down her eyes. She wiped them off. "You know what? You? You are the worst of them all! You are selfish! You are arrogant! You are self-centered and stu-pid! You think you have it all? Well, all you have, let me tell you, is your stupid ego! You only care about yourself and your damn money. You always want to be in command; you feel like you have the whole world under your feet! I'm glad this is all over! I couldn't breathe freely around you; I couldn't talk freely. I kept walking on eggshells! I was kidnapped, and I almost f*cking died, but all you think about is your f*cking self and contract." She stood up, pushing the sit back. "If you felt nothing, you shouldn't have kissed me, you motherfucker." She said and picked up her handbag. "Goodbye, Seth McGregor!" She said and left.

Seth sat there, staring at the door. Liam rushed in. "What the f*ck happened?" Seth sat up and left. "Right."

Gina entered a taxi, wiping tears from her face, then burst out crying. How could he be so mean? How is she going to live her life now?

CHAPTER TWENTY-TWO

Gina couldn't face going home with her messed-up emotions and didn't want to confront her sister and Nicki, so she called Toby instead.

Sitting alone at the bar, she had already finished a bottle of beer by the time Toby arrived.

"Hey, are you alright?" Toby asked, taking a seat beside her. "I came as soon as I saw your text." His concern was evident.

"I'm sorry for calling you out," Gina replied.

"Hey, it's fine," Toby reassured her.

"Thank you," she said with a small smile. Toby ordered another drink.

"You don't look good. Did something happen?"

Gina smiled and raised her beer. "I just want to get drunk."

Toby laughed. "You drank your first beer with me."

"I was underage."

"You said you wanted to have fun."

"And then you took me to a party filled with..." she trailed off.

"You liked it."

"But you cheated." She said, not meaning for it to sound like that. Silence fell between them for a while.

"I still regret it," Toby finally said.

"You don't."

"I do. I wouldn't have lost you."

Gina looked at him, a bit surprised, and then she smiled.

"I wouldn't have lost you," he said again, trying to not drop the conversation. "After that day, it felt like I was punished for cheating on you. I had my worst days," he chuckled. "I needed you. I came to see you several times, but I would always meet your mum or your sister. They wouldn't let me see you." He said and Gina sat up, "You came to the house?"

"Yes, several times."

"I thought you never cared. I didn't you...came"

"You told me to get out of your life."

"I never said that."

"You... I stopped coming when I received a text from you warning me not to come again. So, I didn't, although I should've, but I told myself that I got what I deserved."

"I never texted you," Gina said shaking her head. "In fact, I waited for you, a text or something,"

"You never—"

"Yeah, and then I saw you with Lucy at the mall. So I thought you two were back together."

"You saw us?"

"Yeah, I mean..." Gina said with a mixture of a smile and a confused look. Toby wanted to say something but couldn't get himself to.

"It's all in the past now," she shrugged,

"But it's all my fault, and I'm still sorry."

"It's been a long time."

"I missed you though," Toby said, looking into her eyes.

"Sometimes, some things will happen and it will remind me of you." He said but Gina just stared. She knows what is happening, but he couldn't possibly still have feelings for her? She chuckled as his hand touched her cheeks.

"I missed you, Rej," he said and slowly brought his face towards hers, and took her lips in a passionate kiss. Gina slowly pulled away, "I'm sorry," she said trying to not make him embarrassed, "Yea. No, I'm sorry," he said and an awkward silence followed.

"Want to get pizza?" He asked.

"what? uhmm, no, its... it is getting late," she said with a smile. "I live close by. We can have a glass of wine. or two. for old time's sake." He said and Gina thought about it, then nodded.

They walked into Toby's apartment, where he offered Gina a seat, but she kept looking around. From his room, the view of the streets and skyscrapers was impressive.

"Wow," she said as Toby handed her a glass of wine. "Nice view, neat apartment."

"Yeah, it's nice, but I'm usually busy, so I end up sleeping at the office."

"Oh really?"

"yea," he said and they clinked glass.

"It's my pleasure to have you here" he said, just as the doorbell rang. "Who could that be?" he said and went to get the door. Gina used the moment to look around more. He saw his graduation pictures and what seemed like a group picture with co-workers. "just the neighbor," he said and sat down across Gina,

"So, how's your company going?" she asked.

"Hmm, okay. It's hard sometimes but, you know that thing when you love what you're doing." Gina nodded.

"So what else do you do apart from business?"

"Hmm, I gym."

"You? Gym? Toby?" Gina laughed for the first time.

"Yeah, I know, it's not really my thing, but I have this uncle whose help I need. His free time is usually when he's at the gym, so..."

"Your uncle?"

"Yeah, he's a distant uncle, rich, just inheritance stuff. I want to be on his good side, you know." he said smiling, but Gina felt dragged back to what she's been trying to get off her mind.

"Why is everybody talking about inheritance?" she muttered.

"What?"

"It's just that it's everywhere, even in the news," Gina said. "what is that?" "the inheritance stuff," "Oh, yea, I mean, my uncle don't even have a direct heir, so," he shrugged and Gina nodded.

"Wait," Toby said, reaching for her face. Gina withdrew, "you have something on your face," Toby smiled and wiped her cheeks. He felt his cologne feel her nose with his face seconds away, she felt so uncomfortable.

"Thank you," she said with a smile, and then there was a minute of silence. "welcome."

Gina's phone rang—it was her sister. "I... have to go. Thanks for tonight. I'm really grateful."

"Not at all. I'll take you home."

"No...no, you don't have to."

"I want to, I can't just let you go home on your own." Gina nodded and he grabbed his keys.

"Can I use the restroom?"

"Sure."

Gina took her time in the bathroom, staring at herself in the mirror, wondering what she was doing. Why did she call Toby? Why was she at his house? What does he think he is doing? She rubbed her head as she heard the doorbell ring. She turned off the tap, drying her hands.

She walked out of the bathroom to find a woman sitting where she had been.

"Oh, hello," the woman said giving her a surprised look.

"Hi," Gina replied, glancing at Toby as she picked up her bag to at least introduce them, but the looked a bit lost. "uhmm," she said,

"Uh, Gina—" Toby started.

"I'm Toya, his secretary."

"Hi, nice to meet you. I'm Gina."

"Nice to meet you, Gina."

After an awkward silence, Gina said, "I have to go."

Toby tried to protest, "Are you sure?" He asked and Gina got a little confused but nodded,

"Very," Gina replied, smiling at Toya before heading to the door.

Ignoring texts and calls from Nicki, Steph, and even Liam, Gina scrolled through her messages, hoping for a miracle—a message from Seth, but there was nothing.

She rubbed her shoulders as the cool night air hit her, walking aimlessly as she battled with her thoughts.

Should she close the deal and leave everything that happened in New York behind? Forget about Seth, whom her heart still yearned for, and the baby she had carried for months? She could almost feel the baby's tiny hands wrapped around her finger.

Or should she keep going, take whatever comes her way, and maybe stick with Toby? They had kissed earlier, but was it just nostalgia, or was there something still there? They weren't the same people anymore—he owned a big company, and she was just a surrogate who couldn't move past everything that had happened.

Different thoughts raced through her mind. The urge to return to the bar and get drunk, to reminisce, grew stronger. Her heart pounded at the thought of Seth's lips on hers, then she remembered her kiss with Toby.

What is actually going on? What is wrong with me? she wondered, as confusion overwhelmed her.

Seth walked into his office after a long meeting and sank into his chair, closing his eyes for a moment to catch his breath. The peace was short-lived as his phone beeped with a message. His heart dropped when he read it—Tricia had escaped from the hospital, despite the security in place.

Fury bubbled inside him as he rushed out of the office and headed straight to the hospital, berating himself for ever trusting the police to handle her. The only thing on his mind now was the safety of his baby.

When he arrived home, he found Rosa calmly preparing dinner. Nothing seemed out of the ordinary to her. Seth hurried to the baby's room, where he found his child sleeping peacefully. Relief washed over him. He remembered Gina's face as she begged him to see the baby. He wondered if she had already left the city and tried to push the thought aside, but it lingered.

"So, you didn't get to close the contract?" Nicki asked, her tone incredulous.

"No," Gina replied, her voice heavy with frustration. Nicki took a deep breath out of annoyance.

"what about the last part of the payment?" "I don't know."

"What the hell." "You won't understand." "No. I don't understand, and I don't think I will," Nicki said, clearly exasperated.

"And she met Toby," Steph paused her nail she was filing and added, finally, decided to join the discussion. "Uh-huh, what are you not telling us?" Nicki asked, "There is a lot you are not telling us," Nicki said and sat beside her,

"What happened?"

"I just want to see my baby," Gina said, her voice cracking.

"My baby?" Steph echoed. "I thought..." she wanted to say but stopped.

"Is that all? what about the guy, the Seth?" Nicki pressed.

"What about him?" Gina deflected, irritation creeping into her tone.

"Tell me you're not doing all this because of him," Nicki said.

"I told you why already. Besides, he is arrogant and... so full of himself?"

"You. You like him."

"I don't!" Gina snapped, rolling her eyes.

"I prefer Toby. He's more handsome," Steph chimed in.

"You haven't had a close look at Seth, have you?" Nicki asked.

"I haven't, but Toby is her sweetheart," Steph insisted.

"What are you two doing? And how did you know I met Toby?" Gina asked Steph.

"He sent you a text," Steph said nonchalantly.

"You went through my phone?"

"It kept ringing."

"And then?"

"He's inviting you to a party," Steph added, unfazed.

"Steph?" Gina said, grabbing her phone and checking her messages. "You replied?"

"Well, I just told him you'd go," Steph said, raising her hands in mock surrender.

"How could you do that?" Gina asked, feeling betrayed.

"I thought you'd want to go," Steph explained, sounding defensive.

"You did the same thing years ago, didn't you? You went through my phone and you sent Toby that text, right?"

"I don't know what you're talking about," Steph said,

"I... did," Nicki confessed.

"What?" Gina said, stunned.

"He cheated on you, and I didn't like him for you, which you knew. So, I just thought it was the best thing for you," Nicki admitted.

"Oh my God," Gina groaned, burying her face in her hands as a headache began to pound in her skull.

Steph's phone rang their mum on the other end. Steph updated her on finding Gina and how her work was going fine. Their mum refused to speak with Gina, and Gina didn't mind. Her life felt like a mess already.

"When are you calling Mum?" Steph asked, but Gina ignored her and left the room, fed up with everyone trying to control her life.

Gina answered the door and accepted a box from one of the hotel attendants. She spread the dress on the bed, just staring at it. She hadn't spoken to Nicki or Steph since the day before.

Nicki meant well, Gina understood that, but she wished everyone would just stay out of her life. Stephanie was probably up to something too; she might have gotten divorced and was out looking for someone else to latch onto.

Sighing, Gina rubbed her aching head.

"Need help?" Nicki asked, appearing in the doorway.

"No," Gina said, unbuttoning her shirt, ready to take a shower and get ready.

"Hey, I'm sorry, okay? I just knew something was up between him and Lucy back then."

"And you didn't care to tell me?"

"I... sorry," Nicki mumbled but Gina ignored her. "I'm sorry Riri."

"Fine." She just said.

"Very forgiven," Nicki said with a small smile.

"I'm just tired," Gina admitted, sinking onto the bed.

"You should be. A lot is going on, and you're not talking, like always," Nicki said, sitting beside her.

"I just don't know what to do," Gina confessed, the exhaustion evident in her voice. "I'll be going back tomorrow."

"What? Why?"

"I have a business to handle. They can't do without me. I've been away for too long."

"Oh..."

"So spill everything," Nicki urged, a hint of a smile on her lips.

Gina smiled back, though it was weak. "I don't know. I think I'm in love, but then again, I'm not sure. I keep feeling like I'm not complete. I don't want to end the contract. I'm scared... scared I'll never get to see my baby again, scared that I've left a part of me here, somewhere far from home. I don't know if you'll get it, but I don't want to leave." She confessed, trying not to show all her emotions that felt like weakness. That feels so unlike her.

"I'm regretting ever telling you about this," Nicki sighed.

"I'm sorry."

"I'm not blaming you. I should've known how emotional you can get and how much you wanted a good family."

"I've never been so selfish. I just, I don't know but, I just can't help it. I can't get myself to stop, not yet." she said looking at Nicki,

"Come here," Nicki said, pulling her into a hug.

"So, tell me," Nicki said, pulling back, "Do you think the rich guy loves you back, or is it just a one-sided crush?"

Gina laughed then covered her mouth with her hand in embarrassment. "No, we kissed."

"Whaaat! You!"

"It's not me. He just—we just kissed, and he told me it was a mistake."

"What?"

"Yeah."

"Screw him."

"Nicki"

"What? I think you should go for Toby. What's going on between you two?"

"Hmm... nothing. We kissed, but it's nothing."

"Whaaat! So you're going around kissing all the cute guys?!" They both laughed.

"Did he say anything?" Nicki asked, her curiosity piqued.

"Nope. We just chatted over a drink and nothing else."

"Uh-huh?"

"Yeah."

"Then go for him. That's my advice. I would've gone for the rich guy, but he looks like a lot of trouble to me. End the contract. The baby is going to be fine. You don't need to worry about him."

"What if he grows up and asks for his mom?" Gina asked and Nicki laughed. "what?"

"He won't lack anything, that's a fact, and not to touch your wound, but these rich people have their lives all planned out. he'll be fine. what you should be doing now is setting your own life, having fun without boundaries. Rich people don't know how to have fun, believe me." Nicki said and they laughed.

"I root for Toby. And you should get ready."

"Oh, yeah."

"Look sexy," Nicki winked and left.

Gina sat there for a while and dressed up. Staring at herself in the mirror, she wondered if she had dressed up too much. She wore a red dress that hugged her body, accentuating her figure. She touched her stomach, imagining Seth in one of his tuxedos beside her. She touched her cherry-red lips, lost in thought, until her phone beeped, snapping her out of her daydream.

She grabbed her phone and purse and left the room.

"Uh-huh, you killing someone tonight?" Nicki teased.

"Oh wow," Steph added, impressed.

"I'll see you guys later," Gina said.

"Yeah, slay them all, baby!" Nicki cheered, and Gina smiled before leaving.

Toby was waiting for her in the lobby, his heart skipping a beat when he saw her. "You look amazing."

"Haven't dressed nice in a long time."

"You look beautiful," he said, making her blush.

At the party, Gina felt torn between wanting to escape and enjoying the night. Toby guided her around, pointing out and introducing her to almost everyone there. She felt exhausted within 20 minutes of being at the party. They looked like a couple, but something still felt off. To her, Toby had changed a lot. He was no longer the fragile guy with soft looks; he had become more masculine, and confident. He is someone else, popular, and she couldn't help but notice his secretary staring at them, their eyes kept locking.

Gina grabbed a drink and watched as Toby greeted more people. A voice beside her broke her thoughts.

"Humble," said Toya, Toby's secretary.

"What?" Gina asked, surprised.

"He's a nice guy," Toya said, nodding toward Toby.

"Oh, yeah, he is."

"He's always been too kind and hardworking. Likes to please everyone, feels for everyone. Barely has time for himself."

"You know him so well," Gina said, swirling her wine in her glass.

"Yeah, he's my ex."

Gina stopped and looked at her, stunned.

"We broke up just recently."

"Oh."

"Yeah, he's too honest and kind. That's his flaw." Toya kept staring at Gina. "But I want him back. He's too good to let go." Toya's gaze lingered on Gina for a moment before she laughed lightly. "Don't mind me, I am just joking," she said laughing. "enjoy the party." She raised her glass and walked away.

Gina touched her necklace, her nerves jangling after the encounter.

"Are you okay?" she heard Toby ask behind her.

"Yes," she replied, forcing a smile.

"Wanna dance?"

"Come on," before she could say anything he took her hand as they slowly started dancing. She wrapped her arms around him, inhaling the scent of his cologne, letting it calm her nerves. But then she felt eyes on her. She glanced up and froze.

Seth?

She stopped dancing, "are you okay?" Toby asked,

What is he doing here?!

CHAPTER TWENTY-THREE

Gina unclasped her hands from around Toby, her heart racing. "Are you alright?" Toby asked again, concern etched on his face. "Yes, I just need to use the restroom," she lied, quickly excusing herself and rushing out of the hall.

Once inside the restroom, she leaned against the sink, staring at herself in the mirror, her thoughts spinning.

Why did I run away? Why am I running?

She bit her lip, taking a deep breath to steady herself. A woman walked in and smiled at her in greeting. Gina managed a weak smile back before stepping out of the restroom, only to feel someone grab her hand.

"What—" she started, turning to see Seth staring down at her. Without a word, he dragged her outside the party hall.

Seth had had a terrible day at the office, made worse by the news that there was still no trace of Tricia. Desperate to assert his authority and reassure the shareholders, he had reluctantly decided to attend the party.

But when he saw Gina walking around with another man, a surge of conflicting emotions hit him. Relief that she was still in town was quickly followed by jealousy and anger at seeing her with someone else. When their eyes met across the room, he felt an overwhelming urge to pull her out of the hall from the eyes of everybody. Without thinking, he followed her when she left the hall, grabbing her hand as soon as she stepped out of the restroom.

Gina snatched her hand away when they stepped outside the arena, glaring at him. "What do you think you're doing?" she demanded, rubbing the spot where he'd held her.

Did I hurt her? Seth wondered, a flicker of guilt crossing his mind. They stood in tense silence for a moment, staring at each other.

"What are you doing here?" he finally asked, his voice sharper than intended.

"What do you care?" she shot back.

"You were supposed to leave the city by now"

"Why, am I bothering you?"

"Yes."

Gina scoffed, rolling her eyes. "Well, don't worry. I'll be leaving soon, so you can have the whole city to yourself," she said, turning to leave.

"Tricia escaped," he blurted out, stopping her in her tracks.

"What?" Gina spun around, her eyes wide with shock.

"She escaped two days ago."

"How's the baby?" she asked walking back towards him, her voice trembling.

It took Seth a moment to respond. "He's fine."

Gina closed her eyes, exhaling slowly as she processed the news.

"You should be careful," he warned.

"Why?"

"She knows your face. She can do anything to you to get back at me." "I don't think so. Why would she? I mean nothing to you and I am no longer carrying your child,"

"This is not some joke" Seth said but Gina looked sternly back at him. "Does it sound like a joke to you? You said it too",

"Just be careful and stay put in the hotel. It's more secure there," he advised, stepping closer. Gina instinctively tried to step back, but her feet felt rooted to the ground.

"You know the hotel we're in... ah, right, that's the best thing you could do?" Gina's frustration seeped into her voice.

Seth stared at her, his thoughts a jumble of confusion. Why did he care so much about her safety? Why were they even having this conversation?

His eyes drifted to her red lips, and memories of their past encounters flashed through his mind. He blinked them away, forcing himself to focus.

"Just stay safe and stop going around the city with just anybody," he said, his voice tinged with possessiveness as he turned to walk away.

"It's not like you cared. And Toby is not just anybody," Gina snapped, her voice sharp.

Seth halted, his teeth almost clenched. "He was my ex." She added, regretting it immediately she said it.

"Was?" Seth turned back, his eyes narrowing as he waited for her answer.

Gina hesitated, searching for the right words. She knew lying would be risky. "I don't have to hide because of your sister. I have nothing she wants," she said, turning to leave again.

"You can stay in the mansion," Seth offered, his voice laced with an unfamiliar vulnerability.

"What?" Gina stopped, turning back to face him, confusion and disbelief mixing in her expression. "Why would you care about my safety when I am no longer your responsibility. What use will I be for you? Why? Are you bored because there's no one to boss around? Why would you care about my safety?" "Can you stop being stubborn and just fucking listen," "Mind yourself Mr. Seth, we have nothing together," she said, "yes we do," he said and everywhere fell silent for some seconds as Gina felt her heart beat out of rhythm. She stood there hoping, scared, for the next word that would leave his lips. "We've not signed off the contract. So, you are still my responsibility." He said looking at her. Gina stared at him unbelievably.

"Gina?" Toby's voice called out, and she turned to see him approaching, concern etched on his face. "Is everything alright?" he asked, wrapping an arm around her shoulders protectively. "you're cold. Are you alright?" Then he noticed Seth. "Mr. McGregor?" he said, surprise flickering in his eyes. "Tobias, we met once," he added, extending his hand.

Seth took it, not breaking eye contact with Gina. After an awkward silence, "I'm going home," Gina said, her voice strained.

"Sure," Toby replied, smiling politely at Seth before guiding Gina away.

Seth stood there for a few minutes, his teeth clenched, his heart burning with an emotion he didn't want to acknowledge. The cold air biting at his skin seemed to calm him slightly, but it wasn't enough.

He wanted her, and the realization made him furious. He rubbed his forehead in frustration before heading to his car.

"Screw the party," he muttered, slamming the car door shut.

He drove home, his mind a storm of conflicting emotions. When he arrived, he went straight to the baby's room. Rosa was there, trying to soothe the crying infant with a lullaby. Seth stood at the door for a moment, watching them before stepping inside. Rosa handed the baby to him, and he rocked him gently until the cries subsided and the baby fell asleep.

He placed the baby in the cradle, sitting beside him in the quiet room. Thoughts of Gina with her baby bump, and then how her hands tangled around another man's shoulder, swirled in his mind, stoking his anger. Unable to shake the images, he stood up abruptly and stormed off to his room.

He hated the way he was feeling and the fact that no matter how hard he tried to deny it, it only became stronger.

Gina sat quietly in the car as Toby talked about his past business dealings with Seth, but she wasn't really listening.

"Toya," she interrupted him, her voice cutting through his monologue.

"What?" Toby asked, slightly taken aback.

"Your secretary."

"Toya?"

"Yes. What about her?"

"She's your ex?"

Toby was silent for a few seconds, processing her question. "How did you find out?"

"She told me," Gina said, her voice cool.

Toby nodded, his grip on the steering wheel tightening slightly. "We dated for a few months. I met her through a contract with her father's company. She was fresh out of school, very intelligent and bright. She wanted me to hire her, wanted to get a job without her father's influence."

Gina looked out the window, trying to distance herself from the conversation, but his words kept pulling her back. He seemed to have become quite the storyteller—something she hadn't noticed before.

When Toby finally finished, Gina forced a smile, relieved that they had arrived back at the hotel. She told him there was no need to walk her to her room.

He pecked her on the cheek, and she walked to the elevator. As the doors opened, she noticed a man standing inside, his back turned to her. When he turned to face her, she was startled by how handsome he was, the kind of good looks that belonged in magazines.

Gina stepped inside, managing a polite smile as she tried to calm her racing heart. She prayed he wouldn't talk to her, and to her relief, he didn't.

As she walked to the room, she smiled at herself. Reminding herself of how strong she is, and how beautiful she is, trying to get any thought about her life in the past few months. She sighed swiping the keycard. As the door opened, she froze, her breath catching in her throat at what she saw.

Steph popped the champagne she had requested and downed a glass, her mind racing. Time was running out, and she had found her sister but still had no plan to get the money from her. She lit a cigarette and glanced at her phone. Her husband hadn't called—not even once. A text came in, and she swiped the screen to see it was from Ken, the guy she met at the bar. She replied with her room number. With Nicki out visiting places before her departure tomorrow and Gina off having her own fun, why couldn't she indulge a little? She ordered more champagne, all on Seth's tab. She had met him briefly when Gina was in the hospital and hadn't liked his presence—too strong, too intimidating. He never smiled or even acknowledged her as Gina's sister. Instead, he had his assistant handle all the details, including their free lodging in New York, which had been a blessing. When Ken arrived, she didn't waste time on small talk. They dove straight into a heated encounter on the couch, oblivious to everything around them—so much so that neither noticed when Gina walked in.

"What the heck?!" Gina screamed, causing Steph and Ken to jump apart, breathing heavily.

"Hi, sis," Steph greeted her with a smug smile, pulling back her bra strap.

"Hi," Ken mumbled, embarrassed as he quickly grabbed his shirt, "I'll see you later, babe," he pecked her and headed for the door.

Gina held her breath as the smell of sweat and stale cologne wafted past her.

She stared at Steph, trying to calm the fury bubbling inside her.

"What? A girl's got to do what she's got to do to survive," Steph said nonchalantly. She got up and poured herself a glass of champagne.

"You. Are. Married, Stephanie!" Gina hissed.

"So f*cking what?" Steph retorted, rolling her eyes.

"What? Mom never raised us to be like this!"

"Oh, but she raised us to sell our eggs, didn't she?" Steph shot back.

"How dare you!" Gina snapped, her voice trembling with anger.

"Oh, baby, life isn't fair. You do what you can to survive. I'm not judging you, so stay out of my business and mind your own."

Gina clenched her fists, trying to reign in her emotions. She had planned to take a bath and clear her head, but she couldn't let this slide. "Why are you really here, Stephanie?"

"I told you."

"Did you break up with your husband? Divorce?"

"Not yet."

"Not yet? Then why are you actually here? I know you, Steph. You barely care for anyone else, tell me why you are really here."

"Oh really?"

"Yes!"

"Well, maybe you're right. I need money."

"I expected no less," Gina said dropping her purse on the couch and folding her arms.

"Yes. I got involved in a business deal that went south. I sold some family shares—and mom's house."

"You… you what?!" Gina's voice cracked as she felt a wave of disbelief washed over her.

"I went home and heard about the money you were sending. I thought maybe you could help."

"Stephanie, Jesus!" Gina sat down, closing her eyes as she tried to process the information.

"I was just trying to survive in that family. None of you know how I live there."

"Oh, please, spare me the pity party. You married into a good family, but you were too selfish and greedy to appreciate it."

"Don't talk to me like you know what's going on," Steph spat back.

"Oh, I know. I know all too well. A family that trusted you with their property can't be that bad. You signed up for whatever's coming to you."

"Don't talk to me like that, Regina Rachel."

"Sorry, Stephanie, but I lost all respect for you a long time ago," Gina said, her voice cold as she stood up and walked to her room. She closed the door but she couldn't take it, she needed to let out this steam before it burned her. She opened the door and walked to Steph.

"We are going home this weekend. Get ready, because I'm going to spill it all."

"Go ahead, b*tch!" Steph shouted after her.

"I will, and I promise you—you're not getting a penny from me!"

"To hell with your money, b*tch!" Steph yelled as Gina slammed her door shut.

Gina collapsed onto the bed, screaming into her pillow, releasing all her pent-up frustration. After a few minutes, she lay there, breathing heavily, feeling the anger slowly drain away.

She stood up feeling all tired and exhausted. She unzipped and slid into the bath for a long, hot bath, letting the water soothe her aching muscles. Finally, she slipped under the duvet, her body suddenly heavy with exhaustion. She took a deep breath, willing herself not to think about anything else.

Montserrat sat quietly, staring out at the beach, her eyes blinking slowly as the wind blew through her hair, sending shivers down her spine. Since losing her pregnancy, she had become more withdrawn, speaking less and barely eating.

Theresa had learned to keep her distance, giving Montserrat the space she seemed to need.

After the kidnapping and the loss of her baby, Montserrat had spent weeks in a wheelchair, refusing to leave her room until she heard that Tricia had escaped. The knowledge that Tricia was still out there, alive and free, filled her with a burning desire for revenge. She wanted to make Tricia pay, to make her feel the same pain she had endured. Maybe Seth would help, or maybe she would have to do it on her own.

She blinked again, pulling herself out of her thoughts as she turned to go inside. She noticed her mother watching her from a distance but ignored her, heading straight inside. It was all her fault.

Tricia moaned in pain as the doctor helped her up. She grabbed her walking stick and took a tentative step forward, wincing as the pain shot through her leg. But it was less intense than it had been days ago. With every painful step, she saw Seth's face in her mind, her thoughts consumed with how to get back at him.

She stared at herself in the mirror, her reflection a haunting reminder of what she had become. Half of her face was damaged beyond recognition, and she could barely see out of one eye. The sight filled her with a rage so intense that she screamed, lashing out at the mirror with her fists until it shattered, cutting her hands. The doctor rushed over, pulling her back into the wheelchair as she struggled against him, her fury overwhelming her.

Later, Mandy visited her, updating her on Seth's latest activities. "What about the pregnant woman?" Tricia asked, her voice cold. "I'm not sure, but there's nothing on her—not even on the internet," Mandy replied cautiously.

"Find out everything you can about her," Tricia commanded, her hatred growing with each passing day. She thought about her situation, about Noah, about Seth, and about the inheritance that should have been hers. She needed time to plan her next move, but one thing was certain—she would make them all pay.

CHAPTER TWENTY-FOUR

Gina dropped her phone and sat on the bed, feeling drained. Toby had called but she ignored it. She was fed up with everything happening in her life.

She wanted a job and money. Now she had the money—enough to get anything she wanted—but happiness still eluded her.

What's my next move? she wondered.

Her bags were packed, and she had told her sister they were going back, but she wasn't ready to face her mother just yet. She grabbed her handbag and suitcase, sneaking out of the room quietly while Stephanie slept on the couch. She made her way to the elevator, then to the lobby, where she sat for a while, contemplating her next steps. Eventually, she boarded a taxi, giving the driver a new direction. She wanted to stay at a guest house for a while, somewhere she could think things over and figure out what to do next—somewhere she thought Liam or Seth wouldn't find her.

After checking in, Gina dropped her suitcase and stepped out to have a drink or two. This part of New York seemed quieter, filled with couples holding hands and enjoying the scenic views. The streets were lined with cosy restaurants, coffee houses, salons, and bars. She strolled for a few minutes, taking in the atmosphere, and thought how nice it might have been if she were more of a traveler.

Eventually, she stepped into one of the bars and took a seat on a long stool, ordering a drink.

As she looked around the bar, she noticed everyone seemed busy being happy. Smiling at the bartender, she took the drink from him, her thoughts drifting.

Should I open a business? she mused. What business? She considered her skills and how she could turn them into something profitable. Or should I invest in something?

She rubbed her head and finished her drink just as another bottle was placed in front of her.

"It's on me," the bartender said with a wink.

Gina smiled. "Thanks."

"Welcome. You look new here. First time?" he asked while cleaning a tumbler.

"Mm-hmm," she nodded.

"Welcome to our neighborhood," he said, before moving on to tend to another customer.

Gina found herself staring at him, thinking how bartenders always seemed to be sexy in the movies. Her thoughts were interrupted when someone snatched her phone off the counter.

"Hey!" she screamed, jumping off the stool. But before the thief could escape, someone caught him, slamming him against the wall with a hard punch before retrieving the phone and tossing the thief out of the bar.

Gina stood there, her heart racing—not from the thief, but from recognizing the man who had saved her.

Seth?

He walked towards her, wearing a cap pulled low over his eyes. Gina squinted, trying to make sure of what she was seeing.

"Seth! How—?"

"I told you to stay in the hotel," he cut her off, grabbing her hand.

She snatched her hand away. "Were you following me?"

Seth glanced around, noticing the curious stares from other patrons. He pulled down his cap further and grabbed her arm, dragging her out of the bar.

"Stop dragging me!" Gina protested, pulling back hard and ending up falling to the ground.

"Are you okay?" Seth asked, reaching out to help her up. She got up immediately.

"How did you find me?" she asked, feeling a sting on her elbow. "Were you following me?"

Seth sighed, adjusting his cap. He didn't even know why he was there, just that when his men reported she had left the hotel with her luggage and wasn't heading to the airport, his first instinct was to go after her.

"I told you not to leave the hotel, didn't I?"

"You don't have any right to tell me what to do?"

"We haven't closed the deal yet, so you're still mine."

"What?"

"You heard me."

Gina scoffed, shaking her head. "I'm done with you," she said, turning to leave.

Seth caught her by the elbow, trying to turn her around. "Ouch!" she winced, and he quickly let go.

"You can stay at the mansion," he said, his voice more controlled now.

Gina stopped in her tracks. She had heard him offer that before, but now it felt different.

"Why would I stay at the mansion?"

"Just until we find my sister."

"What do you care?" she snapped.

"It's just for your safety and for the deal, of course."

"Why do you care about my safety?" she asked, her voice softer now, almost curious.

"We need to officially close the deal to avoid—"

"Goodbye, Mr. Seth," Gina interrupted, turning to leave again.

"I thought you wanted to see the baby?" he called after her, making her pause in surprise.

Before she could respond, a man suddenly hit Seth on the head, again and again, until he collapsed. Another man grabbed Gina as she screamed and kicked in a desperate attempt to free herself.

The man who had attacked Seth hoisted his unconscious body over his shoulder as blood dripped down from Seth's head.

"Let go of me, you bastard!" Gina screamed, kicking at the huge man holding her. "Let me go!" she cried, kicking in the air as they whisked her into a bus. Gina saw the car Seth must have come in, but his men were already down, either unconscious or worse.

The men shoved Gina into the bus next to the unconscious Seth and locked the door.

"Oh my God, Seth, can you hear me? Please wake up!" she cried, shaking his body. Blood had run down to his neck and chest, and Gina felt her fear turning to terror.

What if he's dead?

"Oh my God, please! Just let me go!" she pleaded, banging on the vehicle but it started moving making her lose balance.

She heard them call someone, saying they had her. Tricia, oh my God, it has to be Tricia, she thought, tears streaming down her face. Right! Some people saw us! Help!

Gina scrambled up and pounded on the sides of the bus. "Help! Help! Somebody!" she screamed, her fists slamming against the metal.

The bus stopped suddenly, throwing her backwards. Her head hit the iron wall, making her vision blur. The door opened, and she tried to get up but felt dizzy. One of the men yanked her up, tying her hands and feet before covering her mouth with duct tape.

She didn't fight back, feeling the beer she'd had earlier churning in her stomach, making her nauseous. She lay down, closing her eyes, the dizziness overtaking her.

When she woke up, she was slung over a man's shoulder. Her eyes felt heavy, but she could make out the other man carrying Seth. Their footsteps crunched on a gravel path, not leaves. She noted. She heard another voice, but she couldn't understand what it was saying. Her breathing was shallow, her body drenched in sweat, and something was lodged in her throat. She was dropped onto a hard, hot surface, unable to open her eyes as the dizziness and nausea overwhelmed her.

Seth felt a throbbing headache as he slowly opened his eyes. The air was thick with a scent—something like tar, rusted iron, or crude oil. He glanced around, spotting Gina lying on the floor, her hands tied. F*ck!

He crawled over to her and gently slapped her cheeks. "Gina! Wake up! F*ck," he muttered, panic edging his voice. Gina stirred, and he sighed in relief. Quickly, he loosened the ropes around her wrists and ripped the duct tape from her mouth.

"Are you okay?" Seth asked, his voice softening as Gina started to cry. He let her rest her head on his shoulder for a while. When she finally calmed down, Seth stood up.

"We need to figure out where we are," he said, walking towards the door. It looked like they were in a container, and the door was locked tight. "It's your sister"

"F*ck!" he cursed, kicking the door in frustration.

"This is all your fault," Gina whispered.

"What?" Seth asked, turning to face her.

"This is all your fault!" Gina screamed, her voice trembling with anger.

"Is this what we're supposed to be doing now?"

"I don't care!"

"Well, you should, because we're in trouble. Big trouble."

"Which you started!"

Seth tried to contain his anger, knowing it wouldn't help their situation.

"If it hadn't been for your stupid ego, none of this would've happened," Gina continued, her voice rising.

"Can you shut the f*ck up!"

"Don't you dare tell me to shut up!"

"Why are you so stubborn? You realise that If you had stayed where I told you, this wouldn't have happened."

"Don't you dare call me stubborn again!"

"You are so f*cking dumb and stubborn," Seth shot back, his frustration boiling over.

Gina lunged at him, slapping him hard across the face. She hadn't meant to hit him so hard, and now she stood there, scared, watching as Seth moved his jaw. She almost stepped back, afraid of what he might do next.

Seth stared at her, then slowly moved closer. Gina stepped back and he followed until she was pressed against the wall, her heart pounding.

"W-what are you doing?" she stammered, trying to brace herself for whatever was coming. But then she straightened, deciding she wouldn't back down.

He dare not lay his hands on me!

She stared back at him, trying to look bold despite her fear. Seth moved his hand, and she flinched, but then she felt his hand at her

223

back, pulling her close against his body. They stood there for a few seconds, just staring at each other.

"I don't know why I care. I don't know what you're doing to me," he whispered before pressing his lips to hers.

Seth kissed her hungrily, feeling a fire within him that he couldn't quench. He wanted this moment so much, he imagined this moment all night, all day. He wanted to devour her, to feel all of her. When she moaned, it drove him to kiss her even harder, but Gina pushed him away, breathless and ashamed. She had let it happen again. She had even moaned.

F*ck!

She couldn't move, couldn't look at him. She just sat there, consumed by a swirl of emotions.

For hours, they sat on opposite sides of the container, neither one speaking. Seth couldn't bring himself to say anything, but he kept glancing at Gina, noticing how she was shivering and rubbing her arms.

She should've worn better clothes, he thought.

He took off his leather jacket and draped it over her shoulders.

Gina didn't look at him. "No, I'm fine," she tried to protest, handing it back.

"You're shivering," Seth insisted.

"I'm not—"

"Just take it!" he snapped, cutting her off.

She didn't argue further, wrapping the jacket around herself.

After sitting in silence for a while, Seth finally spoke. "Why did you take the offer?"

"What?" Gina murmured, still lost in her thoughts.

"Why did you take the offer?" Seth repeated.

She looked at him, confused for a moment. "What offer?"

"The deal," he clarified.

"Oh," she said, clutching the jacket tighter around her. "I was looking for a job," she began, taking a deep breath. "I graduated from college three years ago, but I've been at home, looking for a good job. Tried part-time gigs, but they didn't work out. I told you about my mom before—she was being a pain in the ass." She

224

scoffed a touch of sadness in her voice. "And I wanted to do something different. I thought I should grab the chance," she added.

"What did you study?" Seth asked, genuinely curious.

"Interpersonal management and public administration."

They fell into silence for a few seconds before Seth spoke again.

"Does your family know about this?"

"Just my sister, the one you saw at the hospital."

"You told her?"

"She found out on her own. She needed money, so she... she cared."

She said and stopped talking. Her heart raced as she processed their situation. Why is he being nice all of a sudden?

He asked me to move to the mansion, said I could see my baby, kissed me again! Does he like me or not. She felt the urge to ask him but kept repressing it. For a moment the silence was deafening, she decided to take the chance.

"Why did you kiss me?" Gina asked, her voice steady as she looked him in the eye. He looked back but didn't say a word.

"Why did you kiss me?" she repeated, determined to get an answer.

Seth felt his face flush. How can she be so bold and stupid at the same time?

"Do I look like a puppet to you?" she continued, her voice rising.

"I'm a human being too, and I have feelings. Do you know that?"

What do I say to her?

"You think because you have some money you can do everything you want," she said, gesturing with her hands. "Well, I don't have money—"

I like her. I don't even know why. She has all the wrongs—she's stubborn, careless, not exactly pretty, not fashionable... but she's bold, strong. F*ck, what am I saying?

"I like you," she confessed, throwing the jacket off. "F*ck, I love you. Damn me! I hate myself for it and I don't even know why!" she cried out. "You're such a—"

Seth cut her off with another kiss.

"Stop kissing me!" she snapped, pulling away just as they heard someone opening the door.

Tricia walked in with two men. "Hey, brother. Oh, did we interrupt something?"

225

"You've gone out of your mind," Seth said, his voice filled with anger.

"I know, bro, I know," Tricia replied with a twisted smile, her eyes shifting to Gina with a frown.

Gina instinctively wanted to hide behind Seth but knew she had to stand her ground.

"Patricia, you need to end this now," Seth said, trying to reason with her.

"That's what I plan to do, brother," Tricia replied, taking a limping step closer to Gina.

"You'll regret this," Seth warned, moving to block Gina from Tricia's approach.

She stopped, looking at Seth with a cold, calculating expression. "Do you remember when we were kids? We used to be so close, but things changed. You were always the favorite—your parents were the favorites too. And they ended up killing my parents. I hated everyone. Nobody cared how I was doing, and again, you stole the spotlight. Take the girl," she commanded, and the two men moved towards Gina.

"No!" Gina cried, trying to hide behind Seth.

"You need to stop this now, Patricia!" Seth shouted.

"Why? This is fun," Tricia sneered, signaling the men to grab Gina. Seth attacked the men, but one of them punched him hard in the face, drawing blood from his nose.

"Oh my God!" Gina screamed, rushing to him, but the men dragged her away.

Seth, despite the blood dripping from his nose, got up and launched himself at the men again. Gina was screaming, and crying, as the fight intensified. Suddenly, they heard police sirens in the distance, getting closer.

"F*ck!" Tricia hissed, realizing her plans were crumbling.

Gina rushed to the door, trying to open it and scream for help, but one of the men lifted her, trying to carry her away. Seth, with a burst of energy, hit the other man and lunged at the one holding Gina. The man dropped Gina and punched Seth several times, causing him to spit out blood.

The sirens grew louder, and Tricia, panicked and desperate, pulled out a gun, pointing it at Gina.

"So bad things didn't work out as planned, bro," Tricia said, her voice laced with bitterness. "I wanted you to watch everything you love die—everything you own, everything you want. I wanted to kill your tiny baby first and then your stupid lover and then you",

"Tricia don't..don't this, you still have your life to live"

"No I don't, you stole my life a long time ago, I don't have any life left in me. Look at my face, look at my f*cking face! Look at me! Do I look like I have a f*cking life?!! Huh!", She cocked the gun, Gina stood there, tears flowing down her cheeks,

"F*ck! What do you want?",

"What I want?", She laughed, " nobody has ever asked me that, nobody",

"I'll give you everything, just let her go!",

"Why? Is she important to you? Do you love her?",

"Yes, yes! I love her, I f*cking love her",

"Why, she's not even your type?",

"More reason why I love her", Gina stood there, crying cause she's about to die, crying cause Seth loves her after all, crying cause her life is so messy.

"I hate this", Tricia said

"What are you doing? Don't", Seth said,

"It's disgusting. You used to love me, despite being your sister, I knew back then, so I used it against you, I liked it that way. You were a dummy then, but you grew up after all and now you got yourself a lover. It's really disgusting", she said and pointed the gun back at Gina,

"No!", Seth screamed and she shot the gun.

The door was pushed open,

"Drop the gun and turn around, with your hand on your head", the police said, Tricia did as was told and they hand cuffed her and took her out.

227

CHAPTER TWENTY-FIVE

Gina opened her eyes, her vision blurry, and the room spinning. She closed her eyes again, trying to steady herself. The smell of antiseptic and the sound of distant beeping filled her senses. When she opened her eyes once more, she saw someone hovering nearby.

"Stephanie?" Gina asked, her voice shaky. "Where's Seth?"

"Just lay back down, Gina. He's fine," Stephanie said firmly, but Gina could hear the tension in her voice.

Gina struggled to recall what had happened. The memory hit her like a wave—Tricia, the gun, the shot. She shot up in bed, heart racing.

"It should've been me," she whispered, her body shuddering with the realization.

"Calm down," Stephanie urged. "He's in surgery, but he's stable."

Gina swung her legs over the side of the bed, pulling off the IV and monitoring equipment.

"For goodness' sake, Gina, that man is dangerous! You've almost died twice because of him. My advice as your sister: let's close this deal and get out of here," Stephanie pleaded.

Gina turned to face her, anger and desperation mingling on her face. "This is my life, Stephanie. I'm going to live it the way I choose, without your advice. If you want to leave, go ahead. I have things to figure out."

Ignoring Stephanie's protests, Gina stormed out of the room, her mind racing. She asked the nurses where Seth was and hurried to his room. Without knocking, she pushed the door open.

Seth was sitting on the edge of the bed, his back to her. He turned when she entered, his arm in a sling, bandaged and bruised. The doctor with him nodded at Gina, said something to Seth, then left the room.

"Hey," Gina said softly.

"Hey," Seth replied, his voice equally quiet.

"It could've killed you," Gina pointed to his injured arm.

"Yeah," Seth admitted.

"Thank you," she whispered, her voice breaking.

"What?"

"I said, thank you."

Seth nodded, and an awkward silence filled the room. He rubbed his bandaged arm, searching for something to say. Gina looked at the well-made bed, "are you being discharged,"

"yes," "What? Why? you've not fully recovered" Gina asked, concern creasing her brow.

"I have things to do," he said, wincing slightly as he adjusted his position.

"You should stay a few more days," she insisted.

"It's not your problem," he said, his tone dismissive.

Liam entered the room, breaking the tension. "Hello," he said, giving Gina a warm hug.

"Hey," she replied, her voice softer now.

"How are you feeling?" Liam asked, his concern genuine.

"I'm okay, just a little sore."

Seth watched their interaction, feeling an unfamiliar pang of jealousy. He should've asked how she was first, but the words hadn't come.

The door opened again, and Toby rushed in, his face pale with worry. "Gina! Are you okay? Where does it hurt?"

"Toby, I'm fine. How did you know I was here?" she asked, surprised.

"Stephanie called me. I came as soon as I heard."

Toby then noticed Seth and Liam. "Mr. McGregor? What happened?"

Liam helped Seth up, and the two men moved toward the door. Seth stopped and looked directly at Gina. "Tomorrow, 9:30 a.m., we'll close the deal."

Toby looked at Gina, confused. "Deal?"

But Gina's focus was on Seth. "What if I don't want to?" she challenged.

"You don't have a choice," Seth replied coolly.

"I have the right to do what I want."

"You signed a contract," he reminded her, his eyes hard.

Gina clenched her fists, anger bubbling up inside her. Liam signaled Toby and they left the room for the two of them. "I hate you with all my heart," she spat out.

Seth didn't flinch. "I'll have someone pick you up soon," he said, turning to leave.

"I don't need your help," Gina shouted after him.

"I'm not asking," he replied over his shoulder. "You'll be under my care until the deal is closed. Your things are already at the mansion."

Gina's mouth fell open in shock. "What?!"

But Seth didn't wait for her response. He walked out, leaving her seething. Gina gritted her teeth in anger.

What had she expected?

Seth being all sweet and kissing her around is just him being a devil! Toby walked in and tried to console her, but Gina's mind was racing. She felt cornered, desperate, and furious. No one had ever made her feel so helpless, so out of control.

Fine, she thought. If this is how it's going to be, I'll give him what he wants. Then I'll figure out how to get my life back.

When the car pulled up to the mansion, Gina's heart was pounding. Memories flooded back, along with a wave of anxiety. She twisted her fingers, feeling a knot in her stomach. The woman who greeted her at the door was unfamiliar, as were the others bustling around the mansion.

Once alone in her room, the same one she had stayed in before, she felt a chill run through her. Her luggage was by the wardrobe, just as Seth had said. She undressed and stepped into the bathroom, sinking into the tub. As the water rushed over her, her phone rang, but she ignored it. She just needed a moment of peace, away from the chaos of her life.

But even in the warm water, she couldn't escape the storm brewing inside her.

Montserrat turned up the volume on the TV when she saw Tricia and Seth. The pain she'd been trying to suppress surged back, overwhelming her. She screamed and began hurling objects around the room.

Theresa, hearing the commotion, rushed in. She tried to calm Montserrat down, but it was no use. Panicked, she called for her husband, but before he could reach them, Montserrat had already bolted out of the house.

She was consumed with a burning need for revenge—Tricia would pay for what she did. Montserrat stopped at the station, forcing herself to calm down enough to gain entry. When she asked to see Tricia and was denied, her rage erupted again.

A week later, Montserrat was found in her home, having stabbed her hand in a fit of despair. She was rushed to the hospital.

Gina stepped out of her room after a long bath. As she walked down the hall, she heard Seth's voice coming from the study. She peeked in, catching only a glimpse of his back before she moved on.

In the kitchen, she found one of the house staff peeling potatoes. "Good evening, ma'am," the woman said. "Dinner will be ready soon."

"Let me help," Gina offered.

"Oh no, ma'am, it will dirty your hands."

"I'm fine," Gina insisted, picking up a potato and a peeler.

After a few minutes of working in silence, Gina hesitated before asking, "What about the baby?"

The woman paused, clearly nervous. Gina noticed the hesitation and pressed gently, "It's okay, I've lived here before."

The woman gave a small smile. "I'm not sure, ma'am. The last time I saw him, a doctor came to check on him. The nanny takes care of him, and we've been told not to talk about the baby."

Gina dropped the potato, her heart sinking. "Is he sick?"

"Shh… I don't know, I just saw the doctor—"

Gina didn't wait for her to finish. She dashed out of the kitchen and headed straight to the study. She burst through the door, and Seth looked up at her, surprised.

"Hold on," he said into the phone before hanging up. "What's this about?"

"I heard the baby is sick," Gina said, her voice trembling as she moved closer to his desk.

Seth studied her for a few seconds before saying, "Have you lost your mind?"

"I need to see the baby, please," Gina pleaded.

Seth stood up and walked toward her, his expression unreadable. "You want to see the baby?" She nodded. "What for?" he asked, his voice cold.

Gina felt her heart breaking. "I gave birth to him"

Seth's face hardened as he stepped closer. "I hate repeating myself, but I hate it even more when I have to do it because of people like you. You signed a contract, Gina, and I paid you handsomely, and in a few days, the contract will be over. You gave birth to the baby, that's all there is to it."

A tear slid down Gina's cheek despite her effort to hold it back. How could she have fallen in love with this man? What had she done? She wiped her tears away, her voice full of venom. "I am biologically related to him," she said and Seth paused for a while, "fine then. I will be fair. Have every dime I paid you ready before we close the deal and I might consider giving you back 'your baby'" "Go to hell and burn there," she said, turning and storming out.

She wandered into the garden and sat for hours, lost in thought. Her phone beeped—a message from Stephanie. She hadn't read the ones from Nicki and Nora, or even Toby's. She slid the phone back into her pocket.

Once she closed the deal tomorrow, she'd go home. It was a hard decision, but it was the right one. Her old life, with all its flaws, was better than this. At least she knew who she was back then. The only thing she regretted was leaving her child behind.

She had wanted a family, a wonderful one, but look at her now.

She heard footsteps and quickly wiped her tears.

"Ma'am, dinner is ready," the woman from the kitchen said.

Gina followed her inside and sat at the table. She had no appetite, but her stomach growled in protest. The room was eerily quiet as she picked up her spoon and began eating.

Seth had watched her from the window for hours, wondering if he had said something to hurt her. He sent the maid out again to call her to dinner. When he saw her wipe away her tears, a pang of guilt tugged at him. Should he have let her see the baby?

The baby had developed a high fever while Rosa was away. He had fired the nanny he'd hired to replace Rosa for letting the baby get sick. Now, as he checked on the sleeping infant, he felt a knot of worry in his chest. He closed the door quietly and headed back to his study.

On his way, he noticed the light in the kitchen was on. He walked in and found Gina making something. She turned, glanced at him for a second, then took her cup of coffee and brushed past him as if he wasn't there.

Seth stood there for a moment, the silence of the kitchen pressing in on him. He turned off the light and returned to his study, trying to focus, but his mind was a whirlwind. Frustrated, he slammed his fist on the desk, immediately regretting it as pain shot through his wounded shoulder.

"F*ck!" he cursed under his breath, struggling to regain his composure.

CHAPTER TWENTY-SIX

Gina woke up early, packed her things, and waited anxiously for the clock to hit ten. But time dragged on, each minute feeling like an eternity.

A knock on the door interrupted her thoughts. "Ma'am, breakfast is ready," a voice called. Though she had no appetite, she knew she needed to eat for the long journey ahead.

She walked to the kitchen and paused when she heard the women inside talking in hushed tones. She couldn't make out what they were saying, but the moment she stepped in, they fell silent.

Her breakfast was served, and she thanked them, then asked about Seth.

"He left early this morning," one of the women replied.

"Okay, thanks. Do you know when he will be back?" Gina asked, concern creeping into her voice. The women exchanged glances and shook their heads.

"We don't know, ma'am. It seemed like an emergency. He left in a hurry."

Gina nodded, lost in thought, and the women left her alone. She had wanted to ask about Rosa, but the question slipped her mind. Was she fired again? she wondered.

The hours dragged on. She wandered around the mansion, explored the garden, took some pictures, and even tried to nap. When she woke up, the mansion was eerily quiet. She checked her watch—8:43 p.m.

Worried, she rushed to the window and yanked open the curtain. A cold, airy night greeted her, the darkness heavy and oppressive. She stepped out from the room and laughter from the kitchen drew her attention, but before she could head there, she heard a car pulling up outside. She hurried down the stairs, ready to confront Seth for making her miss her flight.

She waited as the key turned in the lock, but when the door opened, no one walked in. A sudden sense of dread washed over her. She stepped forward and cautiously opened the door wider. The cold air rushed in, and there, lying on the floor, was Seth.

"Oh my God, Seth!" she gasped, rushing to him as the rain began to drizzle. She tried to lift his heavy body.

"F*ck!" she muttered, struggling to drag him inside. He reeked of alcohol. "What the fuck?" she grumbled, straining under his weight. One of the women from the kitchen appeared. "Oh no!"

"Help me out," Gina urged, and together they managed to haul Seth inside. "Be careful with his hand," she warned as they maneuvered him towards his room.

Seth muttered incoherently, and Gina wished she could understand what he was saying. As they tried to lay him on the bed, Seth threw up, some of it splattering onto Gina.

"F*ck!" she exclaimed, disgusted.

One of the women quickly fetched something to clean up the mess. Once they got Seth settled, Gina removed his shirt while another woman placed a damp towel on his forehead. As Gina prepared to clean herself up, she overheard one of the women mention that the baby was crying.

"Where is the baby?" she asked, her voice trembling with a mix of fear and hope.

The women hesitated.

"I'm his mother," Gina asserted, trying to steady her voice.

The women exchanged uneasy glances before one of them finally brought the baby to her. Gina took him into her arms, tears welling up in her eyes as she gently touched his cheek.

The baby screamed and kicked, but Gina held him close, rocking him gently. "Shhh…" she whispered, her tears falling freely as she smiled through them.

She laid him down on the couch, unhooked her bra, and fed him. The baby suckled eagerly, and Gina watched him, tears streaming down her face. She needed to see him clearly, but the tears wouldn't stop. She wondered how she would ever leave him after this.

When the baby finally fell asleep, Gina lay beside him, watching him intently. She touched his puffy cheeks, his silky hair, and his tiny hands, memorizing every detail. She stayed like that for nearly an hour until one of the women returned to take the towel and water.

"Ma'am, I need to take the baby now," the woman said softly.

"No, I'll sleep with him here," Gina whispered, not taking her eyes off the baby.

"I'm sorry, ma'am, but we were strictly ordered not to let anyone, especially you, see the baby."

Gina nodded slowly, her heart breaking as she handed the baby back. He let out a small cry before settling back to sleep in the woman's arms.

Gina watched them leave, then sat down on the couch for a few minutes, feeling the emptiness settle in. The smell of vomit reminded her of her own disheveled state, so she got up and went to the bathroom to shower.

She tied a towel around herself and stared at her reflection in the mirror. She looked different—worn, but also strong. She let the towel drop and studied her stomach, wondering if her mother would notice she had given birth.

"What are you doing here?" a voice startled her.

"Christ!" Gina gasped, quickly wrapping the towel around herself again.

Seth stood leaning in the doorway, looking weak but with a sharpness in his eyes that hadn't been there before.

"I took a shower after you vomited on me," Gina said, her voice trembling with both anger and something she couldn't quite name. "After you took off this morning and made me miss my flight."

She added and tried to storm past him, but he grabbed her arm, pulling her close. They stood face to face, the tension between them thick.

"What are you doing?" she asked, but Seth's response was a kiss. Gina didn't kiss him back; she pushed him away.

"Don't play with me," she warned, turning to leave, but he pulled her back again.

"I'm not playing with you," he said, his voice steady. She stared at him for a second,

"You're drunk."

"I'm fine."

Gina was taken aback. For a moment, she wondered if he had hit his head somewhere.

What is this? she thought. What's with the change of voice? Is he still drunk? Don't fall for it, Regina.

Seth touched her cheek softly, and she felt her resolve weaken. "Why do I keep thinking of you? I don't like it," he confessed.

"Then stay away from me."

"I can't," he said, his thumb brushing against her lips. "I don't think I can." His fingers traced the contours of her face. "I want you," he whispered, his voice husky. "I want all of you."

He kissed her again, and this time, Gina couldn't resist. The desire that had been simmering between them flared up, and she kissed him back, knowing she would regret it later. But in that moment, she wanted him too—she wanted all of him.

Seth's hands moved to untie her towel, and the touch of his strong chest against her made her moan softly. He broke the kiss to trail his lips down her neck, and Gina's body responded with a heat that surprised her. She helped him undo his belt, working around his injured hand, her mind screaming at her to stop, but her body refused to listen.

Seth gently carried her onto the bed, his lips and hands exploring every inch of her skin, leaving a trail of fire in their wake. He kissed her deeply, his hands roaming over her body as he moved over her. Their eyes locked as he slid into her, and they both moaned, bodies moving in sync.

The rain splattered against the window, the cold air outside a stark contrast to the heat they generated together. In that perfect moment, they unleashed all the desire they had been holding back for so long.

Gina woke up in the morning, Seth sleeping soundly beside her. Carefully, she slipped out of bed, picked up the towel from where it had fallen the night before, and wrapped it around herself. She hurried to her room, took a quick shower, grabbed her bag, and left the mansion without a word.

When Seth woke up, the space beside him was empty. His head pounded, and as he sat up, the memories of the previous night flooded back.

"F*ck," he muttered, rubbing his face in a mix of shame and something else—something that made him smile and bite his lip. He brushed his teeth, replaying the night in his mind, unable to shake the smile. After showering, he went to the baby's room, where the nanny was feeding him. Seth gently touched the baby's cheek before heading to the kitchen, deep in thought.

As he sat down for breakfast, he considered his next move regarding Gina and the contract. If she signed it, it would mean the end of whatever had sparked between them.

"Where is she?" he asked the cook.

"She left early, sir," she replied.

"What do you mean?" Seth's heart sank. "To where?"

"I'm not sure, sir. When I woke up, I saw her leaving with her suitcase."

"F*ck!" Seth exploded, storming out of the kitchen and rushing to Gina's room. It was empty, confirming his fears.

"Damn!" he yelled, kicking the door in frustration.

He pulled out his phone and dialed her number, but she didn't answer. He couldn't believe she actually left. What about the baby? What about... fuck! He thought and dialed Liam's number to confirm if Gina, perhaps, lodged back in the hotel.

———————————

Gina flagged down a taxi and climbed in her heart racing. She hadn't told anyone she was coming back home, and she could already imagine the look on her mother's face. Would she even let her in? When the taxi stopped, Gina stepped out and took a deep breath, soaking in the familiar sights of the neighbourhood. It had only been eleven months, but they felt like a lifetime. Last night's memories flickered through her mind, but she pushed them away and rang the doorbell.

She could hear her mom's favorite song playing inside, signaling that she was home. Moments later, footsteps approached the door. The door swung open, and Nora stood there, staring at her like she had seen a ghost.

"What? Did you see a ghost?" Gina teased.

"Mom! Regina is back!" Nora shouted without taking her eyes off Gina, as if trying to confirm what she was seeing.

Gina's heart skipped a beat.

"What are you doing here?" Nora asked, her tone sharp.

"What do you mean?" Gina replied, puzzled.

"Where have you been?"

"What do you mean 'where have you been?'"

"Well, you left and never called."

"I did call."

"Once?"

"Nora, can you at least move aside so I can come in or take the box?" Nora reluctantly moved aside, and Gina walked in.

The familiar smell of home enveloped her, bringing a sense of comfort she hadn't realized she missed. Home, she thought, is where you can always come back to refill your soul.

She saw her mom sitting in her usual chair, focused on her usual tasks. She didn't even glance up. Gina sat beside her. "Mom," she called softly but got no response. "Mom!" she repeated, taking the crochet from her mother's hands, earning an annoyed glare.

"Mom, you've not seen me for a long time," she said but got no response still. "I'm sorry I barely called or texted. My job was contractual and required a lot of privacy, which is why I didn't call often," she lied. "I missed you." She leaned in and hugged her mother.

"I was going to forget I had you as my daughter and I will if you don't explain to me where you got all that money Regina Rachel?" her mom asked, pulling away. Gina wasn't even angry, she just missed home.

"You heard me, young lady."

"I explained to you mom about the job before I left," "You did, I didn't say you didn't. I said I need to know how you made such money in few months"

Gina straightened up, trying to defend herself. "I am not supposed to talk about it"

She heard Nora snort.

Someone descended the stairs—it was Stephanie.

"Regina?" she called out, surprise and concern in her voice as she hurried down the stairs.

Gina's heart pounded. Could she have said anything?

"You're... back?" Stephanie said with a smile, though her eyes were searching. "What's going on?" she asked, sensing the tension in the room.

Their mom stood up and moved toward the kitchen, mumbling.

"Mom," Stephanie winked at Gina before following their mom to the kitchen, "I went to New York and saw her. She's actually a very busy person. She told me she wanted to resign, but I advised her not to. It's a good job."

"You told me you didn't see her," Nora interjected, skeptical.

"Well, I lied. But I didn't know you were coming home soon, sis," Stephanie said, smiling at Gina.

Gina rolled her eyes, deciding to play along. "I told you the job was tough, and I think I've saved enough to start my own business."

"See, Mom? Relax. You raised a good daughter. We should actually celebrate her comeback," Stephanie said, gently rubbing their mom's back.

"Whatever scheme you two are playing, you better play it well and don't let me find out," their mom warned before heading to her room. Nora shot a questioning look at her sisters before heading outside.

Once the coast was clear, Stephanie whispered, "So you really came back?"

"Don't talk to me," Gina snapped, grabbing her box and heading upstairs to her room.

CHAPTER TWENTY-SEVEN

"You mean she just left, just like that?" Liam asked, leaning back in his chair.

"Yeah," Seth replied, a hint of frustration in his voice.

"Well, I don't blame her," Liam said, catching Seth's surprised look. "I mean, you're making things hard for the two of you. you were blowing hot and cold. You like her, but you won't tell her. She's got a life too, you know."

"She acted like she wanted to stay, like she wanted to be with the baby and all and then she suddenly left. Without a word." Seth muttered defensively.

Liam raised an eyebrow and shook his head. "I wouldn't want you for her," he said bluntly.

"What do you mean?" Seth asked, narrowing his eyes.

"I mean she's too good for you. No offence, but you know that."

"Whose side are you on?" Seth's confusion deepened.

"Hers." He said laughing. "So, what are you going to do about the inheritance? It's almost a few months away," Liam changed the subject.

"I don't have to do anything. I just have to wait," Seth said, brushing off the topic.

"You're in a good position, I guess. Tricia is in prison, probably going to jail for murder, attempted murder, and kidnapping," Liam counted on his fingers. "Then there's Montserrat in the hospital, your Aunt Faith has a daughter, and even your Aunt Maria—it's all messed up, man."

"I don't care," Seth replied coldly.

"You never care," Liam sighed. "Can you get me the documents, hers?"

"Whose?" Liam asked, pausing mid-task.

"Gina's. Don't ask me why," Seth said, already heading for the door.

241

Liam grinned and followed him. "There's something you're not telling me."

"Something like what?" Seth said as they stepped into the elevator

"Should I guess?" Liam teased, but Seth ignored him as the elevator doors opened.

"You had sex with her," Liam blurted out, watching Seth's reaction. Seth stopped, his expression a mix of surprise and shame. Liam's mouth dropped open. "F*ck, man."

"I don't know what you're talking about," Seth retorted, starting toward the door.

"I know you, man. It's written all over your face," Liam said, joining him in the car.

"What are you doing?" Seth asked, annoyed.

"That's why she f*cking left. Man, you're doing this all wrong."

"What? Just get out," Seth snapped.

"Listen, she's a good catch."

"She's a dummy," Seth said dismissively.

"She's not, and you like her, Seth. I've never seen you like a woman before. Here's some friendly advice—she could be the one."

"Get out," Seth repeated, his patience wearing thin.

"Fine, just think about it before it's too late. Anyway, I'll get you the documents as soon as I can," Liam said, winking as he stepped out of the car.

"Drive," Seth instructed, and the driver started the engine.

Gina was in the backyard, pulling weeds from the flowerbed. The house looked different—Nora had been neglecting it, preferring to hang out with friends instead of cleaning. Just the other day, Gina had found a roll of marijuana and a condom in the house, under their roof. Nora had denied knowing how they got there, but it was obvious she was lying. Now, she was working at a restaurant not far from the church.

The church had even called Gina up last Sunday to announce her return, as if she'd been gone for years. Some people had come to the house to welcome her home. Gina had helped Stephanie with her debt, and after a week of staying with them, Stephanie had left, claiming she was on vacation. She mentioned she might be getting a divorce, but Gina decided it was best to let her handle it—Stephanie could take care of herself.

As Gina worked, her mind wandered. What could Seth be doing now? How was the baby? She sighed again.

"Do you need help?" a voice asked.

She looked up, squinting against the bright sun, and saw a man she didn't recognize. She sat up, taking off her gloves. "No, I'm fine, thank you." She said and went back to weeding.

"Nice to finally meet you," he said with a smile, getting ginas attention.

"You know me?" Gina asked, a little surprised, as she stood up.

"I'm Treyvon, but you can call me Trey or Devon, whichever you like. I live next door," he explained, extending his hand.

"You live next door? Mrs. Hench lives next door," Gina replied, shaking his hand.

"Oh… she passed away," Trey said, his tone softening.

"Oh my God, when? I'm so sorry," Gina said, genuinely shocked.

"Months ago," Trey replied.

"Oh no… are you related to her?" she asked.

"Grandson," he said.

"Oh…I didn't know she had another grandson, nice to meet you," Gina said, forcing a smile before excusing herself and heading inside.

In the kitchen, her mom was making toast for breakfast. "Take your bath and come down for breakfast," she instructed without turning around as Gina headed upstairs.

Her mom had been unusually nice since she returned. Gina knew it wouldn't last, but for now, she'd enjoy it.

After a quick shower, Gina slipped into one of her favorite free-flowing gowns. She checked her phone—Nicki had texted that she'd be back by tomorrow. Closing the message, Gina's wallpaper—a picture of the baby—appeared. She kissed the screen before heading downstairs.

Her mom was already sitting at the dining table. "Mrs. Hench is dead?" Gina asked, grabbing the jam from the fridge.

"Yes, she died months ago. Bring the jam," her mom replied.

"What happened?" Gina asked as she spread jam on her toast.

"I don't know. We all saw her the day before; she was fine. The next day, she didn't wake up."

"Oh my God… she was such a nice woman," Gina said, shaking her head.

"God rest her soul," her mom murmured.

"She has a grandson?" Gina asked, remembering Trey.

"Oh, you've met Trey? Such a good man," her mom said with a warm smile.

"Good indeed," Gina muttered, sitting down as someone walked into the kitchen carrying vegetables and a gallon of milk.

"Just drop it there by the fridge. Yes, there," her mom directed.

"Yes, ma'am," the man said.

Gina looked up, surprised to see Trey.

"Come and sit down and have breakfast with us," her mom offered, surprising Gina even more.

"Thank you, ma'am, but I have a lot of deliveries to do," Trey replied politely.

"Just a bite," her mom insisted.

Trey glanced at Gina and then back at her mom. "Okay," he agreed, taking a seat.

"I see you two have met. Bring another cup, Regina," her mom said.

"Oh… yes, ma'am. This morning," Trey confirmed, as Gina got up to fetch another cup.

"Nice," her mom said, and Gina noticed Trey watching her as she brought the cup. She gave him a polite smile.

"Regina, maybe tomorrow Trey can show you his garden. He's got wonderful herbs, and he's a good cook—makes the sweetest pie," her mom said, beaming.

Gina forced another smile, wondering what her mom was up to. She didn't like the idea of her mom playing matchmaker, especially with someone she barely knew.

"It's nothing, ma'am," Trey said, trying to downplay the compliment.

"Stop with the ma'am thing. I've told you to call me Geraldine," her mom insisted.

"Yes, Mrs. Geraldine," Trey replied with a chuckle.

Gina just watched the exchange, starting to piece together her mom's intentions. It wasn't like her to be so enthusiastic about someone new. Sure, Trey could cook, had a garden, was hardworking and God-fearing—but Gina didn't buy it. She didn't like him.

After breakfast, her mom left for a charity event, leaving Gina alone with Trey. As he started to help with the dishes, she stopped him.

"Let me do it," he offered.

"No, I thought you were busy," she said, a bit too quickly.

"Yeah," he said, turning to leave.

"Will you be free this weekend?" she asked, catching herself off guard.

"What?" he turned back to her, surprised.

"I'm having a little party, and I'll need some fresh vegetables to make dinner. It's just a small gathering," she explained, trying to sound casual.

"Uhmm… I'm not sure, but I'll try to be there," Trey replied, clearly unsure.

"Alright, see ya," he said, and left.

Gina stared at the door for a few seconds, feeling a mix of irritation and confusion. What was her mom up to? She finished the dishes and went upstairs, still unsettled by the whole encounter.

CHAPTER TWENTY-EIGHT

Gina sat in the cafe, staring outside. She watched the people passing by outside. She saw a woman carrying a baby about to cross the street, which reminded her of her first day in New York and her own baby. Shame washed over her.

"Snap out of it," she heard someone say. Nicki sat down and dropped two cups of cola on the table.

"You didn't even notice when I got in," Nicki said, pushing one cup towards Gina.

"You said you were coming back almost two weeks ago," Gina replied, taking a sip of the cola.

"Yeah, sorry, I didn't call back. I got a great deal. I would have included you, but you're still getting over just one," Nicki said, sipping her cola as her phone beeped. She glanced at it for a while before putting it down.

"What's wrong?" Gina asked.

"Just work."

"How's everything going?"

"I'm not here to talk about me. Fill me in, what happened?"

Gina took a sip of the cola. "Nothing; I just decided to come home."

"You just decided? I am glad you decided to, but why?"

"It felt like the right thing to do."

"It is the right thing to do and I heard you got kidnapped, again."

"Stephanie told you?"

"It doesn't matter who told me. You got kidnapped, the rich guy got shot, and the kinky girl got arrested. What happened next?"

"Nothing; I left after that."

"What about the deal?"

"It doesn't matter. The same deal put my life in danger many times."

"More reason you should have made him pay you more, because it wasn't in the deal."

"Nicki, this isn't just about money. It's... it's about my life and-" Nicki rolled her eyes and put her hand in front of Gina's face to stop her from talking.

"Enough. So what's up now? What's your plan?"

"I don't even know. Mom's been nice, surprisingly, and everything's been working out fine."

"So you're planning to stay at the house for how long?"

"I seriously don't know."

"I hope we're not back to square one."

"What am I supposed to do?"

"I know you're not lazy, but I'm sure you're feeling some sense of responsibility towards your mom."

"I don't know why you read me so well."

"Hey, girl—"

"My God!" Gina exclaimed as something poured on her.

"Are you okay?" Nicki asked.

"I'm so sorry." She heard and looked up to see Trey standing there,

"Trey?" Gina called, surprised to see him.

"Sorry," he said, trying to wipe the cold cola off her sleeve. "I spoilt your dress, I'm sorry."

"Its fine," she said, wiping her body. "What are you doing here?"

"Oh, I just came to get some yoghurt and cola."

"Okay," she said, nodding.

"Do you come here often?" he asked. It took her a moment to process the question.

"Yeah," she said, and Nicki stood up to introduce herself.

"Hi, I am Nicki, Gina's friend."

"Hi, nice to meet you. I'm Treyvon, Trey," he said, dropping the cola to shake Nicki's hand.

"Nice to meet you, Trey," she said, holding his hand for a few seconds before Gina pulled her hand away.

"Yeah, uhmm... you know it's tonight, right?"

"What's tonight?" Nicki asked.

"Yeah, I remember," Gina said, and he nodded.

"Alright, I hope to see you. Sorry again," he said, and Gina nodded. He smiled at Nicki and left.

"Who is he?" Nicki whispered, sitting down again.

"He's our new neighbour"

"And I've never heard about him? He's a hottie!"

"Hmhm," Gina said, rolling her eyes.

"Wait a minute, this hottie is your neighbour?"

"Don't start."

"If he were my neighbour, I would've done him a million times already. Do you think he would accept an offer?"

"Nicki!"

"What?! You know I like hotties."

"Well, my mom likes him."

"What?"

"I mean, like, she thinks he's a good guy, Nicki."

"Oh…" Nicki said, thinking.

"Yeah, she's invited him to eat with us several times."

"That's surprising. Mrs Geralding does't accept just anyone." she said sarcastically. "So what's he doing tonight?"

"A little party, he said."

"You're going, right?"

"No, why should I?" she asked, sipping her cola.

"I have a million reasons why."

"I don't feel good. And I've had enough people in this town asking me questions."

"Yeah, I get you."

"Yea,"

"Are you okay?" Nicki asked,

"I need to go home. I think I'm feeling nauseous, but I'm fine."

"Fine, I need to be somewhere too," Nicki said, finishing her cola.

…………………

Gina got home and laid down on the couch. Her body felt feverish, and she fell asleep immediately. When she woke up, she heard her mom's voice in the kitchen with Nora, getting things out of the refrigerator.

"What's happening?" Gina asked, stretching her body.

"The whole neighbourhood is going to the party, and we shouldn't go empty-handed," her mom said.

"Party? What party?" Gina asked, surprised.

"You don't need to know," Nora said.

"I thought he said he invited you. Treyvon is having a housewarming party, and we should be there as his neighbours. Now go wash up and join us," her mom said, leaving.

"You've met Trey?" Nora asked.

Gina stared at her. "You're going to the party dressed like this?"

"Why? It's a party," she said and left.

Gina went upstairs and sat on her bed, feeling tired. Laughter from outside drew her attention. She opened her curtains to see people trooping into Trey's house.

"He said it was going to be a little party, but he invited the whole town," she said, closing the curtain immediately as he looked up.

She undressed and went into the bathroom, nearly screaming when the cold water hit her. Her temperature was high; she hadn't been sick in a long time.

She opened her wardrobe, pulled out a yellow floral gown, and stared at it.
It is just a party next door.
She combed her hair, sprayed some perfume, and went downstairs. Her stomach rumbled but she doesn't have an appetite.

Ignoring it, she took the wrapped gift her mom left on the table and headed to the party.

Laughter greeted her as she approached the house. The door was open, so she walked in. She had been in the house before, often visiting as a child.

"You came," Trey said, standing behind her, tall and suddenly handsome, with his wide smile.

"Yeah," she said, handing him the gift.

"Thanks. Have you had dinner?"

"No—"

"Great, there's enough food here," he said, leading Gina to the food.

He started with the pie, which Gina found really great. She confessed this unconsciously. Then he introduced her to the chicken soup made with his fresh-scented herbs. He was explaining the dishes when a couple took him away.

Her stomach rumbled again, and her mouth was watering. She dished out some food and looked around but everywhere was filled. She took it outside and sat on the backyard step, starting with the heavenly-tasting chicken soup. She wanted more but felt embarrassed to go back in and out with another plate.

She wiped her mouth with a serviette, wondering what to do next. She stood up to leave and saw Trey talking with Nora and another girl. Looking through the window, she saw people coming and going.

Turning to leave, she saw his garden, which her mom talked about. She wanted to check it out but felt lazy and decided to go home and sleep more.

Walking through the backyard to the front of the house, her mom stepped out with Trey.

"Regina," she called out as Gina stopped. "Where are you going?"

"What?"

"I believe Trey will need help after the party."

"What?" Gina asked, surprised.

"No, Mrs. Geraldine, I can—" Trey started.

"Shhh... you would've done that without being asked."

"It's fine, I can do—"

"I insist. Regina, help him out. We just live next door. Good night, dear," her mom said, kissing him good night.

They watched her walk in and lock the house. Gina just stood there in disbelief. Trey smiled apologetically. "You don't have to—"

"It's fine," Gina said, walking in before him.

She lingered as he attended to the guests, finally seeing them off. Nora stayed with her friends and their boyfriends. Gina thought her mom wouldn't say anything about her, being the favourite daughter, it's fine for her to hang out with her friends and stay out late.

She sat on one of the couches, waiting until the guests were gone. She started stacking plates in the sink.

"I can help with the cleaning," someone said. She turned to see a girl she hadn't seen before. Trey looked at her, and she picked up another plate, heading to the kitchen.

She turned on the tap, wishing she had her phone to listen to music while washing the dishes.

Girls laughed outside after every word Trey said. She almost peeked to see what was going on but decided against it and continued washing the dishes.

When she finished, she cleaned the wash basins and table.

A lady walked in, dropped more plates, smiled at her, and left. Gina stared at the door for a few minutes before putting the gloves back on.

"Hey, I'm so sorry," Trey said when he walked in.

Gina turned and smiled weakly. "It's fine," she said, trying to hang the utensils.

"Let me do it," he said, taking them from her.

Gina looked around. There was nothing more to do in the kitchen.

"Do you need help with anything else?" she asked.

"No, thanks very much. I really appreciate it," he said, and Gina nodded.

"Do you care for some wine?"

"Hmm..." She checked the time. It was already 11:56 pm.

"Just a glass," he said, and Gina nodded.

He got two glasses, and they went outside by his garden.

"A lot has changed here," Gina said, sitting on the bench, which brought up a memory. She blinked it away and took the half-filled glass of wine.

"Thank you," she added.

"Yeah, I had to change some things when I moved in," he replied, sitting beside her.

"Thanks for tonight," he said.

"No, it's fine. The dishes are great."

"I took some classes."

"Really?" Gina asked, surprised.

"Yeah. I had the opportunity, so I took it."

"It's rare to find a guy who cares about cooking and gardening, same time."

"Thank you."

"You're welcome," she said, taking another sip.

"Your mom told me you had a job. What happened?" he asked. Gina looked at him for a few seconds.

"Uhmm, sorry. I run some errands for the neighbourhood, so I'm close with most of them and they tell me things," he said in defense. Gina nodded.

"Well, I had a job, but now I don't."

"What's the job?" He took a sip of his drink and realised he might be probing too deep. "If you don't mind."

"I don't like talking about it."

"Sorry," he said with a smile.

Gina finished her drink and stood up. "I need to go."

"Oh...sure," he said, standing up.

He walked her to her door and bade her goodnight.

Seth packed his bag for the one-week business trip. He zipped the bag and stared at the brown envelope on his desk. He had wanted to go see her. He didn't know if it was a wise decision, but he felt the urge. He took the envelope and shoved it into his bag.

"Just one week," he told himself and he went to the baby's room, where he saw Rosa feeding the baby. He turned and went to his study.

"Are you ready?" Liam asked as they headed to the car together.

As they tried to get into the car, another car pulled up. It was Katy.

"What is she doing here?" Seth asked.

"You don't know? She's going with us."

"Why?"

"Because we need her."

"We don't need her."

"Who doesn't need Katy, Seth?"

"Hello," she said, her red lips curling up in a smile. Seth almost rolled his eyes.

He ignored her and got into the car.

CHAPTER TWENTY-NINE

Gina turned and turned until something bubbled up in her mouth. She ran to her bathroom and threw up.

She sat there for a while, and when she tried to get up, her hand gave out, and she fell, hitting her elbow on the marble.

She felt sharp pain but no blood.

She sat there for a while, battling her thoughts and trying to ignore her instincts.

When she went down for breakfast, Nora was about to go grocery shopping, and her mom was giving her a list.

"I'll be late," Nora said, picking up her bag.

"Let me go," Gina offered, stopping Nora in her tracks.

"Why?" Nora asked, surprised.

"Are you okay?" Geraldine asked. Gina composed herself.

"Of course, I just want to get some things from the supermarket," she said, taking the list from Nora.

She went upstairs, changed into a dress, and came back down.

"You're not taking breakfast before leaving?" Geraldine asked.

"No, I'll be back soon," Gina said with a smile and turned to leave.

"Are you sure you're okay?"

Gina turned and nodded.

When she opened the door, Trey was about to knock.

"Hey."

"Hey," Gina said, surprised.

"Good morning, Mrs. Geraldine!" he shouted.

"Good morning, Trey. How was your night?"

"Fine, ma'am. How was yours?"

Gina rolled her eyes as they exchanged greetings.

Trey offered to take her to the store since he was heading there too.

Gina smiled at everything he said on their way, but after a while, he noticed she might not be fine.

"Are you okay?" he asked. Gina looked at him.

"Do I not look okay?" Her voice sounded mean, which was unintended.

"No... I mean... sorry."

"Sorry, I'm just... okay," she said, twisting her fingers, then looking away.

She tried to shove the thought forming in her head away because it was very scary. She prayed hard in her heart.

They stopped at the supermarket first. Gina got down and went in without waiting for him.

Could I be pregnant?

Oh God, please.

Please, no.

Please!

She went straight to get a dipstick. She saw Trey and changed lanes. She asked for the bathroom, but it was being cleaned, so she had to pick up toothpaste and body cream.

At the cashier, Trey was already there with just a can of beer. She dropped the cream and toothpaste. Trey offered to pay, but she insisted with a smile. He nodded and left. She dropped the dipstick and paid for everything.

She got into his car and thanked him, and he nodded. Gina noticed she might have embarrassed him, but she didn't care. She could be in deep trouble.

They entered the grocery store, and she told him to go ahead while she used the bathroom.

In the bathroom, she stared at herself in the mirror for two minutes.

God, please!

She entered the toilet and came out a minute later, standing at the mirror. She could hear her heartbeat. She dropped the dipstick on the wash basin, trying to gather confidence.

"Wow, congrats."

She looked at the woman beside her.

"Sorry?" she asked. The lady pointed to the dipstick and left.

Gina picked up the dipstick with shaking hands.

"Oh my God," her heart melted. She covered her mouth and cried.

No.
What am I going to do?

Oh my God! What-what happened?

What have I done?!

She wiped her tears and stepped out of the bathroom. Her head was swirling, and thoughts were running around in her head.

I am pregnant?

For Seth McGregor.

For Seth McGregor? No

Does it even make sense? It can't be.

She felt someone touch her. She turned, and the dipstick fell from her hand.

Trey stood in front of her. He looked at the floor to see what fell, and Gina rushed to pick it up.

"Are you okay? You don't look okay..." Trey said, his voice sounding deep.

"I'm fine," she said and took a few steps, feeling the world turn upside down.

Seth stared out at the beautiful night with a glass of champagne in his hand. He heard the door open and close but didn't care who it was because it was obvious.

She curled her hands around him from the back, and Seth stood stiff as ever.

"A man like you," she sighed, releasing her hands and pouring herself a drink.

"Who would believe I got rejected by a man?" she said, taking a sip. She looked at him.

"What are you thinking?" she asked. Seth left her to sit on the couch.

She smiled, took off her jacket, exposing her red, sexy lingerie, and sat on his legs. She took the glass from him and wrapped her arms around him.

"What should I do to make you mine?" she asked, snaking her finger over his face.

"I'll do everything," she said, bringing her lips to his, but Seth held her face.

"Get off me," he said, pushing her off and standing up.

"Is it because of her?" she asked. Seth stopped.

"I heard everything about the surrogate. Do you love her?" Seth turned and looked at her.

"It is none of your business," he said, turning to leave.

"You know I can help you get this inheritance even without your grandmother's will?"

"I don't need your help," he said. Her face turned red.

"I thought you had a little bit of sense," he said.

"What?"

"You should know when to stop. It's becoming embarrassing," he said. She slapped him across the face and stormed out of the room. Liam walked in, unsurprised.

"You've done it again, haven't you?"

"Do you have the document?" Liam sighed and handed him an envelope.

"I guess it's going to be hard to convince them, and I pray we haven't lost our opportunity due to your attitude towards her. I told you we needed her."

"How long is this going to drag?"

"Seeing the way things are, I bet we need another week or two."

When Gina woke up, she saw a nurse looking over her.

"Ma'am?"

"Where am I?" she asked, sitting up.

"You are in the hospital," the nurse replied. Gina looked around. She saw Trey and a doctor talking. Trey was just standing there, rubbing his lips. He turned and looked at her, and she felt her heart drop. He smiled at the doctor, who walked away.

Minutes later, she was discharged. They didn't talk to each other on their way back. They were just quiet. Gina knew he had found out, and it scared her. Immediately, they turned into their neighbourhood, and her heart skipped again.

He stopped the car in front of their house. Her mom was cutting the wildflowers.

Gina had forgotten about the groceries. She thought about excuses, but her mind was still in chaos.

"What happened?" Geraldine asked when she noticed Gina had bought nothing.

"I, uhmm..."

"Something came up, so I couldn't get us to the grocery store. It's my fault," Trey said.

"No, no... it's fine," Geraldine said with a smile. "Is everything alright, though?"

"Yes, Mrs. Geraldine," Trey said, glancing at Gina for just a second before hopping back into his truck and driving off.

"Is everything okay?" Geraldine asked, more concerned about Trey than her. Gina nodded and went inside.

Gina opened her curtain and looked at Trey's house. Everything seemed calm. She twisted her fingers, wondering what to do. She checked the time and walked downstairs.

"Where are you going this late?"

"Jesus!" she screamed and turned to find her mom standing by the kitchen door.

"Well..."

"I just want to get some air," she said. Her mom looked at her and went to her room.

Gina held her heart and took a deep breath. She opened the door and crossed over to Trey's house. She knocked on the front door but got no reply. She waited and knocked one last time, then went around the house and found him in his garden.

When he saw her, he stood up and stared at her, surprised.

"Hey," she said.

"Hey," he replied, surprised.

"I see you're busy."

"No, no, I just, um... changed the water pipe."

"Oh."

"Uhmm... is everything okay?"

"Yes," she said, and a minute of silence passed.

"Please come in," he said, removing his gloves.

Gina followed him in through the back door.

"Coffee, tea, water?"

"I'm fine."

"Then I'll get water," he said, opening the fridge and pouring some.

"About yesterday..." Gina began. He gave her the water and told her to sit down.

"Thank you," she said, sitting down. She dropped the glass and began again, "About the other day..."

"The other day?" he asked, pouring himself a glass of water.

"At the mall and the hospital..." She rubbed her neck, thinking of how to ask the question.

"I won't tell," he said. Gina looked at him. She wished he hadn't found out. She drank the water and held the glass, touching the tip.

"Thank you," she said.

"Dad?" Gina turned and saw a little boy standing on the stairs.

"Hey, Tyler," he said, walking past Gina to the little boy. "Did you have a bad dream?" he asked. The boy nodded.

Gina watched them in awe. Trey carried the little boy in his arms, and they went upstairs. Gina stood there, wondering what was actually happening.

He has a son?

He's married?

She sat down there for a while, wondering whether to leave or wait for him. She tapped her nails on the table, waited a bit, and decided to go.

"Gina," he called, jogging down the stairs. Gina sat back down.

"Sorry, it's actually hard to put him back to bed," Trey explained, and Gina nodded. She disliked intruding on other people's business, though some preferred it. She never knew when to ask or when to stay silent. And now, she doesn't know whether to ask or not.

"Uhmm... I think I should..."

"I made soup earlier today. Would you like to try it?" he asked, heading to the fridge.

"No, you don't have to," she said, standing up. "It's late, and I just came to..."

"Believe me, you don't want to miss this," he interrupted. "It's just soup. Mrs. Geraldine told me you like soups with a bit of vegetables and lots of meat." He said that, and Gina was amazed and shocked.

"What else did she tell you about me?" Gina asked, sitting back down.

"Hmm... she mentioned you used to like planting things and painting but stopped. Why?"

"Nothing; I guess I got busy. What else?"

"She showed me your pictures."

"Oh my God, when did all this happen? How did you get close to her?"

"Well... I am good-looking," he said with a smirk.

"Ugh!" Gina said, and they laughed.

"She said you're hard-working and the best among her daughters."

"My mom told you that?"

"Mm-hmm," he confirmed, bringing out two soup plates. "I guess she missed you while you were gone."

"Nah... she'll get tired of me soon."

He looked at her and smiled. She watched him, reminded of how Seth used to prepare food for her when she was pregnant. Her heart skipped a beat.

"So, do you have any plans to go back to work?" he asked, his back facing her.

She stayed silent for a while. He turned and saw her staring at the table.

"Sorry, I didn't mean to pry." Gina looked up and smiled.

"Can I trust you?" she asked, and he stopped what he was doing.

"Of course."

Gina stared at him for a while and took a deep breath. She felt comfortable with him, even though she didn't know why. But most importantly, she needs someone to advise her on what to do. A single dad would understand.

"Actually... I didn't get a job in New York, not the kind of job you're thinking of," she said, trying to see if he's judging her already, but he was just looking at her. She told him everything that had happened.

"I fell in love with him," she licked her lips, "and I left my baby with him." She wiped away a tear. "And I'm currently pregnant with his child," she added, tears flowing uncontrollably. She cried, unable to stop, especially when she felt his hands on her shoulders.

A few minutes later, a hot bowl of soup was in front of her.

He didn't say a word. She felt embarrassed for spilling everything to a man she barely knew. She felt like a fool even more, as he's not saying anything.

"Go ahead before it gets cold. It tastes better when it's hot," he said, and Gina picked up her spoon and started eating.

After they finished, he took the dishes, and Gina went to the bathroom. When she came out, she saw pictures hanging on the wall. She stood there, staring at them, and Trey joined her. They seemed close.

"That's my grandma and grandpa." He said pointing to the pictures.

"Yes, I know Mrs. Hench."

"Then that's my mom," he said, pointing to a picture of a woman with two teens wearing graduation gowns, "with me and my sister."

"She's cute. What about her?" she asked, pointing to the woman laughing widely beside him.

"Uhmm..." he hesitated. Gina saw his face change. "I'm sorry, I didn't mean to..."

"No, it's fine," he said, taking the picture off the wall and wiping dust off it.

"She died giving birth to Tyler."

Gina looked at him, seeing the love in his eyes as he stared at the picture. Then she felt guilty and more ashamed. She read him all wrong in all ways.

"I'm so sorry."

"We weren't married. I met her during one of my tours. She was a chef," he said, still gazing at the picture. "She had the best smile," he added, and Gina nodded, seeing the smile in the picture too.

Gina listened as he described the lady and how they met. He brought out an album, and they sat on the couch, sharing their stories and experiences.

When Gina woke up, she was lying on the couch with a duvet over her. She tried to recall where she was, and it all came back to her. She checked the time; it was 10:05 a.m. She sat up immediately, walked to the window, and looked over at her house. She saw a car drive off and wondered if they had looked for her.

"Good morning," Trey said, holding a cup.

"Oh my God, I slept here. I'm so sorry," she said, walking towards him.

"It's fine," he said, putting down the cup. "Have some tea. It's good for your body and the weather."

"No, I have to go. Thanks."

"Don't worry, they know you're here."

"What?"

"Your mom came earlier. She said I should let you know she'd be back late."

"She knows?" Gina asked, surprised, and he nodded.

She sat back down and took the cup. "Is that snow?" she asked, taking a sip.

"Yeah."

"Wow, it came late, though," she said, taking a long sip.

"Yeah, but not too late for Christmas," he said, watching her finish the tea.

"Do you like it?"

"Yeah, it's... it's great. I like the flavour," she said, sitting up.

"Thanks."

"I have to go."

"Yeah," he nodded, opening the door for her.

She smiled and walked to her house, leaving footprints in the snow.

Gina stared at her stomach in the mirror. It was beginning to show a little. It was almost two months, and she still hadn't told her mom. Besides Trey, she hadn't told anyone, not even Nicki.

She tried to avoid her mom most of the time, struggling with her feelings. Last week had been the worst. She told her mom she was sick and stayed mostly in her room. She thanked God that Nora was not always around. Trey came almost every day to check on her, and she had become addicted to his chicken soup and mint flavoured tea.

She was lost in thought and didn't hear footsteps. Her room door opened, and Stephanie walked in.

"Hey, sis!" Gina turned in shock. They stared at each other for a while. Gina pulled down her top, covering her stomach.

"What are you doing here?" she asked, but Stephanie stood there, her mouth open.

"What are you staring at?" Gina asked, trying to pretend. Stephanie walked to her, and they sat down on her bed.

"Regina Rachel, tell me the truth."

"What do you mean?" Gina asked, taking her hands from hers.

"Are you pregnant?" Stephanie asked. Gina covered her mouth with her hand, then removed it, her eyes wide open.

"Oh my God, Regina, who's responsible?" She whispered, but Gina stayed quiet.

"Wait a minute, how many months old is this?" Gina couldn't speak.

"Don't tell me..."
"Lower your voice." She said and Stephanie nodded,
"Is he…"

"He's the one," Gina said, and Steph's mouth fell open.

"What the f*ck! How did this happen?" They heard footsteps and stayed quiet. The door opened, and Nora walked in.

"Mom said—" she stopped when she saw Stephanie. "When did you come back?"

"Just now," Stephanie replied.

Nora looked at the two of them. "Anyway, breakfast is ready. She wants to know if you want to eat in your room or downstairs."

"In my room," Gina replied.

"No, we're coming downstairs," Stephanie said, and Gina looked at her.

"Whatever," Nora said and left.

"I'm not ready to tell her yet."

"Are you going to rot in your room then?"

"What are you doing here anyway? It's Christmas."

"I divorced."

"What?" Gina's mouth fell open.

"Since I know your secret, keep mine. I don't want Mom to know yet."

"I know lots of your secrets."

"And I know yours too. Come down, let's eat," Stephanie said and left.

Gina sat there for a while, changed into a loose dress, and went downstairs.

She saw Stephanie hugging their mom and knew she had already worked her charm.

"You look fine to me," Geraldine said to Gina.

"I'm okay now," she replied.

"She has been fine," Nora said, pouring some cereal into her mouth. Everyone ignored her.

"Trey must be making breakfast now. Take this wrapped pie to him. He shared his recipe with me, and I want him to know how I did," Geraldine said.

"Who's Trey?" Stephanie asked.

"A good fellow," Geraldine replied.

"A good fellow? Who?" Stephanie asked again. Gina took the pie, and Stephanie offered to go with her to see who the good fellow was.

They knocked, and Trey opened the door.

"Hey," he said with a big smile, hugging Gina.

"Hey," Gina replied.

"Oh wow, such a good fellow," Stephanie said, enchanted.

"This is my sister, Stephanie."

"Hi," Stephanie said with a big smile.

"Nice to meet you, Stephanie."

"Me too."

Gina gave him the pie. "From Mom."

"Wow... I am making breakfast, though. Would you..."

"No, we're about to have ours."

"Oh..."

"What are you making? Can I come in?" Stephanie asked.

"Stephanie"

"What?"

"We'll see you later, Trey. Our breakfast is probably getting cold," Gina said, dragging Stephanie out. Trey smiled.

CHAPTER THIRTY

"It ended sooner than I thought," Liam said, collapsing on the sofa.

"It should've ended two weeks ago," Seth replied, loosening his tie.

"Kate left earlier. You really did her wrong."

"She wasn't of any use after all," Seth said, walking into the room.

"You lie freely. Don't you think you're being too hard on women? Loosen up, bro!" Liam shouted but Seth ignored him and walked into the bathroom.

Minutes later, he came out, all dressed up. "Where are you going?" Liam asked.

"I need to go somewhere. Go on without me," Seth said, leaving. Liam sat there, wondering where Seth could be going that was so urgent.

The snow was getting heavier each day.

The sound of laughter woke Gina up. She heard Trey's voice but couldn't get herself out of bed.

When she finally got up around eleven, the sun was up, but the weather was still cold. She went downstairs and immediately noticed a big tree. She knew Trey must have brought it. It had been a long time since they last celebrated Christmas with a tree. She went and touched it.

Hearing someone's voice, she looked out the window and saw Trey talking with their neighbour. She opened the door, pretending she was going to the backyard.

"Hey, Gina!" Trey called, but she pretended not to hear him.

"Gina?!" he called again, now closer.

"Yes. Hey," Gina answered, turning around. She walked towards his house.

"Good morning," she said.

"Blessed morning. We want to shop for Christmas gifts; come with us," he said, smoke puffing out of his mouth from the cold

"Sure," she said. He extended his hand towards her, and she took it. They hopped into his truck, where his son was waiting.

"Tyler, have you seen Gina today?" Trey said, buckling his seatbelt.

"Good morning," Tyler said.

"Good morning, little man," Gina responded, rubbing his head.

They went to the mall first and then to the town centre, which was filled with people. Christmas songs were playing loudly, restaurants were bustling with activity, people smiled, and children were playing around. They found a space in a restaurant to eat, then went to a gift shop and a chocolate shop before deciding to go home.

When Gina got back, her mom and Stephanie were in the kitchen. She joined them for a while before going upstairs.

She took out a small package Trey had given her and wondered what could be inside. Sitting on her bed, she untied the ribbon. A necklace glimmered in the light. She smiled, feeling her heart flutter. She removed the necklace she was wearing and put the new one on.

Standing up, she admired herself in the mirror. It reminded her of when Seth had given her a necklace. She got lost in the memory for a second, but the sound of the telephone downstairs brought her back. She heard her mom's voice and decided to go down and see what was happening.

She saw her mom sitting emotionlessly in her chair, tapping her feet, while Stephanie was on the phone. Gina waited for her to end the call.

"What's it?" Gina asked.

"Nora was arrested."

"What? For what?"

"I don't know yet," Steph said, grabbing her jacket and leaving.

Gina sat quietly beside her mom, and they waited.

One hour later, Gina called Steph, who told her they were on their way home.

Gina sat up immediately after the door opened. Nora walked in, looking messed up. Her mascara had run down her face and it had already dried up. Her hair was looking messy.

"Honora, what is all this?" Gina asked but Nora ignored her and went straight to the fridge and poured herself a glass of water.

"I'm asking you a question, Nora!"

"What? I got arrested and now I'm free; that's what happened!" Nora asked and their mom sprang up and smacked her across the face, surprising everybody.

"how dare you?", Geraldine asked but Nora still held her face, surprised,

"I carried you for ten whole months and I raised you the best I could!", their mom screamed,

Nora giggled and tried to walk away, "don't you dare walk away when am talking to you, young lady!",

Nora stopped and turned, "you know what, f*ck all of you. I am tired of this f*cking family!",

"Mind your words!" their mom warned.

"Mind my words? As if I were a kid. To hell with everybody in this family!",

Geraldine grabbed a broom stick and Stephanie had to hold her back.

"What did you say?", Geraldine asked, trying to get to her

"I'm not scared of you, ma!" Nora screamed.

"Nora, go to your room now!" Stephanie ordered.

"And who are you to tell me what to f*cking do?" Geraldine felt her leg wobble and Steph had to help her sit down.

"I am still your older sister! And you will listen to me and do exactly as I say,"

"since when?", she asked, giggling again,

"I am so disappointed in you", Geraldine said, "I raised you-",

"Enough mom! Nobody f*cking raised me; I did it myself and nobody cared. Everyone thought they had it worse but none of you knew what I went through. I was raped by your f*cking husband when I was just thirteen!" She said that, and everywhere went quiet for a while.

"yes, I was raped by that b*stard. I didn't tell anyone because everybody was busy with their own lives. But everybody kept judging me. "

"What do you mean?" Gina asked,

"What do I mean?", Nora asked sarcastically.

"You should've told someone." Stephanie said,

"Who? You? When you were busy hanging out with friends, Gina was busy with her boyfriend and whatever the hell happened then, mom was all lovey dovey with the b*stard and I made it my secret. Talking about secrets, I mean, who doesn't have secrets in this house? But everyone in.this.house blames me for every wrong turn I make."

"Why didn't you tell me?" Geraldine asked, still shocked,

"No, Mom, this is not time to get all emotional; I'm done with that part a long time ago, alone. Actually, this is a great moment. I went to college and I met friends who noticed me, who made me feel like I existed and I did some things that I don't still regret. I did drugs, I

274

party with friends, I drink alcohol and etcetra, but I am still on the bright side," she said, looking at their mom.

Gina felt her heart sinking.

"Mom, I am still on the bright side. I did all those but I am better than those two," she said, pointing at Gina and Stephanie.

They looked at each other.

Gina looked at her mom; her face was filled with tears, maybe of regret, but it's emotionless. She tried to remember where she was when Nora was raped but she couldn't get her mind to think.

"Nora, that's enough; let's go to your room first", Gina said.

"Why? Are you afraid I might spill your secret?" she said and Gina felt her heart jug a bit.

"Don't look at me like that. Mom, I am not the bad daughter here," she said, turning to Gina and staring her down. Gina gave a warning look.

"Regina is pregnant and her, she's divorced. Boom!" she said, raising her hand.

"What?", Geraldine said, shocked.

Gina looked at her mother and she was sure she had never seen that face before.

How did she find out?

"What are you talking about?" Gina asked.

"Are you out of your mind?" Stephanie asked.

"No need to pretend; we're family after all, right? We shouldn't keep secrets. I mean, Gina, you are pregnant. I knew something was fishy about the job you got, all the way to New York and then the money. Wow."

"Shut your f*cking mouth!",

"And my dear elder sister, who got divorced, I wasn't surprised; you are way too selfish and stup-", Stephanie smacked her face and she fell to the ground,

"How dare you lay your filthy hands on me!", Nora stood up and launched at Stephanie. Dragging her by the hair, she pushed her down to the floor.

"What the hell, stop-", Gina tried to separate the two but Stephanie pushed Gina and she fell on the couch. She tried to get up but then she saw their mom already on the floor.

"Mom?" She sat up and ran to where she lay on the floor. "Mom? Oh my God! Mom please answer me! Mom!!!", she screamed and shook her body. Nora and Stephanie stopped fighting and rushed to their mom.

"Call the hospital!" Stephanie said and Nora rushed and dialed 911. They came later and she was taken to the hospital.

Nora and Stephanie sat quietly on the bench while Gina paced up and down. She saw Trey walk in. He walked to her and hugged her as she began to cry.

"She's gonna be fine," he said, patting her hair.

Minutes later, the doctor came and told them that their mom had high blood pressure, which caused fatigue and a change in the heartbeat cycle.

They stayed for another few minutes. Gina felt pain below her stomach and strength left her leg. She almost slumped but Trey caught her.

"you need to rest. She'll be fine", he said but Gina shook her head,

"I can't", she said, feeling the pain again.

"at least let the doctors look at you",

"I am fine",

276

"I'll come back and stay here; you and your sisters need to go home and wash up, okay?",

Gina nodded and watched as he went and convinced her sisters.

Nora and Stephanie got off the truck first. Trey got down and helped Gina down.

"Are you sure you're okay? he asked and she nodded.

"Gina?" Stephanie called Gina,

"Hm", she answered, looking at her. Stephanie pointed at something. Gina followed her hand to the direction she was looking and almost peed on herself.

In the prison, Tracy sat by the edge of the prison, thinking of what to do next. She can't just give up like that.

"Hey!", She turned to know what's going on and felt someone's hand slap her across the cheek. She tasted blood. She looked back at the huge woman staring back at her.

"What was that for?", She asked. The women gave her a crooked laugh.

"What do you think you were doing sitting around and letting us do the chores for you?" One of them asked,

"Excuse me?" She asked and they laughed again.

"Excuse you", the woman said, throwing the mob at her. She stared at it for a while, then threw it back at her.

"I'll pay you if you do it for me," she said with a smirk. The woman stared at the mob for a while and picked it up. She broke it and ordered one of the women to beat Tricia with it.

"What?! wait! I'll pay you doubl-", she was saying when the stick landed on her, they beat her till she had blood all over her. That's when the wardens came and took her.

After the incident, which repeated again, she vowed to get out of prison.

One morning while cleaning, the woman tried to pick on her again and she drank a cleaning detergent and fainted after some minutes of pain.

She was taken to the hospital outside the prison.

Two weeks later, she was discharged.

On their way back to prison, she tried to escape; she fought the police with her and managed to shoot one of them; their car tumbled and in defence of being shot, the other police shot her twice.

CHAPTER THIRTY-ONE

Stephanie placed two cups of coffee in front of them and smiled at Seth before winking at Gina.

Gina stared at the table, unable to believe who was sitting before her. She twisted her fingers, waiting for him to speak first, her heart slamming against her chest. She glanced towards her mom's room and saw Steph and Nora peeking out. Steph was signaling something to her, but she didn't care to know what.

Seth picked up his cup and tried to take a sip. "What are you doing here?" Gina asked, causing him to drop the cup.

He looked at her, but she wouldn't even spare him a glance. He wanted to start by asking about the guy he saw holding her, if she was sick, or why she ran away.
"Uhmm..." he said, looking around the house.

"What do you want?" Gina asked again, still not looking at him.

"You left," he said, and she glanced at him for just two seconds.

"So?"

"We didn't get to close the deal—"

Gina stood up, cutting him off. From the corner of her eye, she saw Steph and Nora close the curtain. "Please leave."

"What?"

"Get out."

"What?"

"I said get out. And don't come back again," she said, her eyes wide open as she went to open the door.

After a few seconds, Seth stood up and walked to the door. Gina felt the urge to ask him about the baby, but then she remembered he just came to close a f*cking deal and realised she was pregnant with this monster's child. She covered her belly and waited for him to walk out.

"I'll see you later," he said.

"You won't."

"We need to talk."

"We have nothing to talk about," she said, closing the door. She waited a while and looked out the window, seeing him drive off. She closed the curtain and took a deep breath. She was shaking terribly. Steph and Nora walked out of their mom's room.

"Is he the one responsible for the pregnancy?" Nora asked, and Gina looked at Steph.

"She wanted to know," Steph said.

"And you told her?!"

"So y'all weren't going to tell me? Well, I'm not surprised."

"You always run your mouth! Look at us!" Gina said.

"Everyone kept judging me, and you two always knew how to do things without me!"

"Don't play the victim here!" Gina snapped.

"Enough, you two!" Steph said, and both stopped talking. Gina sat down, and Nora stood with her arms folded against her chest.

"Our mom is already in the hospital because of us!" Steph held the chair but didn't sit down. "See, I know I did a lot of things wrong and failed in my duty as the first daughter, and I sincerely apologise for that. We all made mistakes, but we're grown-ups now. We should learn from them and try to mend things, right? I'm not against anyone living their life the way they want, but let's try and stick together, okay? At least for Mom," she stopped and looked at the two. "First, let's eat, then change and go to the hospital before Mom wakes up, alright?" Gina got up and went to her room, then Nora left to hers.

They sat around the table for breakfast. After a while, Steph asked, "So, what does the rude guy want?" Gina took a slice of bread and spread a spoonful of butter on it.

"He wants to close the deal."

"Damn," Steph said, dropping her cup. "He came all the way here to close a f*cking deal?"

"Did you tell him about your pregnancy?" Nora asked.

"Of course not."

"Why?" Nora asked, and Steph scoffed.

"I wonder what sh*t he'll do."

"I need to get something first," Nora said, downing her tea. "So this rich dude paid you to be his surrogate, and then you got kidnapped twice in the process. Then what happened? You got pregnant?"

"Let me tell you the real story here," Steph said. "In the middle of all this, your sister fell in love with that dude who is rich and rude to the core, and she got attached to the baby and stuff. She almost refused to come home. They had sex, and she ran away, later finding out she was pregnant. And now, that rich, rude dude came knocking at her door because he wanted to close the surrogacy deal. I don't think I missed anything," she finished, looking at Gina, who just stared at the table, taking deep breaths.

"So, what do you want to do?" Nora asked.

"What am I supposed to do?" Gina asked, still not looking up.

"Well, I would've told you to go for the money first. I mean, extract more money from him, close the f*cking deal, relax, and raise your kid without him. But damn, this is serious," Steph said.

"What do you want to do?" Nora asked Gina.

"I don't know."

"Do you still love him?"

"I-I don't know."

"Do you think he loves you?"

"I doubt it."

"What if he does love you?" Nora asked, and Gina looked at her, feeling her chest tighten.

"I mean, he came all the way down here just to close a f*cking deal?"

"You don't know him."

"That could be true," Steph said. "You had sex with him. What if that woke something up in him? He's not a rock; he's a man."

"That's it; he's a man," Gina said, and they went silent.

"Look, sis," Steph began. "Hey, you need to release yourself now. Forget about the past and Mom's experience with men. Not all men are bad."

Gina raised her eyebrows. "Seriously?"

"Well..." Nora said, packing the cups into the sink.

"Yes, men are animals, and I'm not even in the state to say this, but I mean it. Men will always be men, but some are better than most."

"Your point?"

"My point is, maybe you should give him a chance. Give a man a chance."

"You know what? Let's just stop and go to the hospital first, before Mom wakes up and we're not there," Gina said, getting up.

Seth stood by the hotel window, staring into the dark night. Shame washed over him as he covered his face with his hand and took a deep breath. He recalled the face of the man he had seen holding Gina and a hundred thoughts rushed in.

Did she get married? What if she did?
Why am I here, and why does my chest hurt so much?
F*ck! Her face... the way she stared at me—damn! She has another man! She left for just two f*cking months and already had a man? Or maybe she lied. The way she looked at me, she asked me to get out. Me? Damn, she still looks beautiful.

He touched his chest, which ached again. He wants her.
That night.
He couldn't deny he still wanted her—he really wanted her for himself, alone. He downed his glass of whisky and walked out of the room.

They all got out of Trey's truck. He and Stephanie helped get Geraldine to her room. She asked to be left alone, and they closed the door behind them. Gina left with Trey.

"Hey, thanks for everything," she said as they walked to the front of his house.

"Don't even mention it," he said, smiling at her, and she smiled back.

"You shouldn't dress so lightly; the weather is too cold," he said, adjusting Gina's scarf. She chuckled.

"Thank you."

"Anything for you," he said, and the air went stiff for a moment.

"You should go in."

"Yes."

"It's Christmas Eve tomorrow. Do you want anything?"

"Not really," she said with a smile.

"Alright, good night," he said, pecking her. She turned and went back inside.

Stephanie and Nora sat quietly at the dining table. Gina joined them, and they sat there for a while without speaking.

"What do we do?" Nora asked.

"Shouldn't we just sleep tonight and then talk to her in the morning?" Steph suggested.

"That sounds better. Let's let her rest," Gina agreed. Nora stood up.

"Coffee, anyone?" They both raised their hands.

"So, you got something going on between you and Trey?" Nora asked.

"Me? Trey? No! Why?"

"I mean, the two of you seem to have something going on."

"Nothing is going on," Gina said, glancing at Steph.

"It doesn't look like it's nothing."

"It's obvious," Nora said.

"What is obvious?" Gina asked.

"It's very obvious he likes you."

"The way he looks at you, damn."

"Stop," she said, taking her coffee from Nora. "Good night."

"Are you running?" Steph asked.

284

"No...why would I run?" she said, climbing the stairs.

"Girl, you're messed up," Steph said, and they laughed.

Seth sat in his car and saw Gina stepping out. He opened his door to go and talk to her but saw the same guy again behind her. He went back in and watched. He watched them stop walking; the guy touched her hair and adjusted her scarf. She laughed at what he said, and he pecked her before she went back in.

He lives next door.

His hand hurt, and he loosened his grip on the steering wheel. He stayed there for a while. He sat in his car, just looking at the house, wondering whether he should go and knock or not. He saw Gina open her window and sit on it, drinking something. He watched her until she closed the window and turned off the light.

He drove back to the hotel. As soon as he opened the door, his phone rang.

"Yes," he answered.

"Where have you been?" Liam's voice came through.

"What's up?"

"Your sister was shot."

"What?"

"Yes, she was shot on their way back to the prison from the hospital. I guess she tried to escape," Liam said, and the line went silent.

"You there?"

"Yes," Seth said, taking a deep breath. "I'll be back by the weekend."

"Where are you, anyway?" Liam asked, but Seth cut the call and poured himself a glass of whisky.

Gina walked out of her room, still stretching, when she heard someone in the kitchen. She walked down the stairs to find their mom making breakfast.

"Mom?" Gina said, surprised.

"Wake your sisters up," she said without looking up. Gina was still standing there when Stephanie and Nora walked down, surprised and ashamed, not knowing what to do.

"Sit down, all of you," Geraldine commanded. They all sat down. Their mom said grace and began eating. The sisters exchanged glances, unsure of what to do. They had planned to apologise to their mom for their misbehaviour in the morning, but... what was happening? This was so unlike their mom.

After eating, Nora packed the mugs, and Steph and Gina got up, trying to avoid staying at the table with their mom.

"Sit down, all of you," Geraldine commanded, and they all sat down.

Gina and Nora tried to urge Steph to speak for them, but their mom spoke first.

"All of you know why I called y'all." She paused and continued. "I married at the age of 17 to y'all's dad. I had you," she said, referring to Stephanie, "at the age of 20, and you, Regina, at 24, and Honora at 29, before y'all's dad died. I might have made some mistakes after, but all I wanted was for this family to be complete. Stephanie got married and divorced. Regina, you got pregnant out of wedlock, and you got raped? How did all of this happen?" She wiped away a tear. "I wondered if it was my mistakes that caused all of this," she said, wiping another tear and turning to Nora. "I am sorry for not being a good mom to you, to all of you," she said, drying her nose.

Gina wiped the tears rolling down her cheeks. She didn't look up to see if her sisters were crying or not, but this was way too emotional for her.

"But maybe before I die, I'll make this family good again. But before that, there should be no more secrets," she said, looking at the three of them. "If there is more I need to know, spill it now," she said, and the room went quiet.

"Who's responsible for the pregnancy, Gina?" Geraldine asked. Gina felt her heart melt into her stomach. Should she tell her about the surrogacy?

"I...I did...I did surrogacy," she said, hearing her blood pumping hard and her heart beating to the rhythm.

"What do you mean?" their mom asked. Stephanie looked at Gina as if she had made a mistake.

"I had a baby for a man through surrogacy."

"You...had?"

"That was the job I got... then," she said, twisting her fingers, tears rolling down her cheeks as she wiped them away.

Geraldine covered her face for a few minutes. Gina's heart was beating so hard she thought it might kill her.

"Is he responsible for this one too?" Geraldine asked, uncovering her face. Gina nodded.

"Anyone else?" she asked, and the room was silent for a while.

"I dropped out of college," Nora said. "I didn't graduate."

"So you faked your results and certificates?" Nora looked down, and Geraldine nodded.

"Anything else? Stephanie?"

"I was divorced. I...cheated on my husband."

"It was a mistake," Steph said and she just stopped. They sat there in silence for minutes.

"If there are any more secrets that I didn't hear now, I won't forgive them," she said, waiting for a minute.

"I put the house on collateral, but it's all settled now." She said and they all just looked at her.

Geraldine nodded and stood up. "Get ready for church," she said, and she entered her room.

Just like that.

The sisters stared at each other, then got up and went to get ready for church.

It's Christmas.

CHAPTER THIRTY-TWO

After church, everyone gathered outside. There was plenty of food and many people to greet—grandsons, aunts, city folks, classmates, and friends. Everyone was exchanging Christmas wishes, but Stephanie, Regina, and Nora weren't in the mood. The morning had been rough, and although their mom wasn't exactly acting out of character, she was acting strangely. She went around wishing everyone a Merry Christmas, as if nothing had happened, which unsettled them.

Trey walked up to Gina, and they exchanged pleasantries.

"Not heading home yet?" Trey asked.

"Uhmm... not really doing anything," Gina said, fiddling with her jacket.

"Would you mind helping me out then? I'll have a lot of guests today," he said with a wink. Gina laughed.

"You won't even let me do anything."

"Your presence is enough."

"Just go already," Steph said, but Gina looked at their mom, who was approaching.

"Uhmm... I don't know," Gina hesitated.

"What's wrong?" Geraldine asked.

"Merry Christmas, Mrs. Geraldine," Gina said.

"Wish you the best, darling," Geraldine replied, hugging her. "I want to have a little Christmas party, so I was wondering if I could borrow her, just for a while."

"Of course, dear... I have extra hands," Geraldine said, pointing to Steph and Nora.

"Alright then. Shall we?" Trey said, calling Tyler from where he was playing with other kids. They climbed into the truck.

They cooked and played around until Gina got tired. People from the church came by, but most left to celebrate elsewhere. It was a tradition in their small town.

Stephanie, Nora, and their mom visited another neighbour's home. When they returned in the evening, their own gathering was sparsely attended. Gina went back to Trey's place to help with a little cleanup since only a few guests came.

Trey put Tyler to bed and came downstairs to the kitchen, where Gina waited.

"Tea?" Trey asked.

"You wouldn't give me coffee if I asked."

"Tea is better," he said, handing her a cup.

"I have a present for you," Gina said, digging into her pocket.

"Really?"

"Yes, guess."

"Guess?"

"Yeah, guess," she said with a laugh.

"Hmm... a tie?"

"Hmm, no, you're not a tie person."

"Thank God, you know. Hmm... I can't... I don't know," Trey said, laughing and placing his hand on his head. Gina laughed and pushed the gift towards him, bending over the table with her hands on her chin.

"Open it."

He unwrapped it, exposing a necklace made of carved wood.

"I thought it might fit your country-boy look," she said, giggling.

"Country boy, huh?"

"Yeah."

He put it on and touched it. "Do you like it?" Gina asked.

"I... I don't like it," he said, and Gina sat up straight, surprised.

"Yo... you don't?"

Trey walked around and stood between her legs, staring up at her. He slid his hands beside her, gripping the stool and making Gina's legs tighten around his body, her already bulging stomach touching him.

"I love it," he whispered, bringing his lips closer to hers. Gina felt her heart pounding and her lips aching for his. Their lips touched and his lips softly and tenderly took hers in a kiss. She felt his muscles against her as he kissed her more passionately. He moved closer as her legs wrapped around his waist. She felt the intensity of his touch but also a nagging sense that something was wrong or that someone was watching them.

When his hand moved up her body, she broke the kiss, looking away and avoiding his gaze.

"Hey," he said, lifting her face gently with his finger.

"I... I'm s-sorry," she stammered, climbing down from the stool and walking out straight to her house.

She closed the door quietly. Stephanie and Nora were putting the remaining food in the fridge.

"Look who's back," Nora said.

"Are you okay?" Steph asked.

"Yeah, I'm just tired," Gina said, heading for the stairs.

"Something happened, right? You don't look good," Steph said.

"I'm fine. What about Mom?"

"She went to bed a few minutes ago," Nora said.

"Alright."

"We're planning to go to the supermarket tomorrow morning. Are you coming with us?"

"I'm not sure," Gina said, heading up to her room.

In her room, Gina stood in front of the mirror, touching her lips and feeling a deep ache for someone's touch. She wondered why she was thinking of Seth at that moment.

She walked away from the mirror and opened the window, still thinking of Seth. She had told him to leave and never come back, and he did. He had come all the way down just to close a deal. She closed her eyes, trying to push him out of her mind. When she opened them, she saw Trey coming out of his house, carrying something. He looked up, and Gina quickly closed her window and climbed into bed.

The next morning, Gina woke up feeling unwell. Her belly felt heavier, and she couldn't feel her feet on the floor. It felt like something was pulling at her abdomen.

After taking a warm bath, she managed to make her way downstairs. Her sisters were already in the kitchen.

"Good morning," Nora said.

"Morning," Gina replied, sitting down carefully.

"Are you okay?" Stephanie asked.

"Yes, just...," she winced as the discomfort hit her again, "a little pain, not pain exactly, I don't know."

"When last did you go for antenatal care?" their mom asked, stepping out of her room.

"Just last week"

"Then get ready. After breakfast, we'll have Trey take us," Geraldine said, sitting down.

"We don't have to do that."

"Don't make me start this morning. If you take on a responsibility, you should see it through," she said firmly, and everyone fell silent.

"What's today?" she asked.

"Friday," Steph answered, and they fell silent again.

Nora called Trey, who arrived later. Gina was sitting on the sofa, ready to go. Her heart pounded when Nora came back with Trey. She avoided looking at him as he greeted her mom.

"Hey, how are you doing?" he asked softly.

"Fine," she shrugged.

Geraldine came out. "Let's go."

Gina tried to stand, and Trey helped her up from behind.

"Thanks," she said. They got into the truck and headed for the hospital.

Two hours later, on the way back, Geraldine stopped, leaving only Trey and Gina in the truck.

After a few moments of silence, Trey spoke up.

"Did you make this yourself?" he asked, touching the necklace.

"Yes," Gina said, looking at him.

"Tyler likes it. Can you make another one for him?"

"Sure," she said with a smile.

Another silence followed.

"About last night... I'm sorry if I made you uncomfortable," Trey said.

"It's not about being uncomfortable, I...," she started, then stopped, "I just..."

"The guy I saw the other day, is he the one?" Trey asked, looking at her.

Gina looked at him for a moment, then turned away. Trey nodded, touched his lips, and continued driving.

When they got home, Trey helped her out of the truck and led her to the door.

"Hey," he said, turning to her, "we're cool?"

"Yeah," Gina smiled, and he smiled back. "Thank you," she added, just as a car pulled up.

They watched as Seth got out of the car, his gaze fixed on them as he walked over. Gina's heart raced.
What is doing here again?

She glanced at Trey, wishing she could sink into the ground.

Seth stopped in front of them, removing his sunglasses and focusing intently on Gina.

"Hey," he said.

"Hi, I'm Trey," Trey introduced himself. Seth acknowledged him with a brief smile before turning his attention back to Gina. She instinctively pulled her jacket tighter around her belly.

"Alright, I'll see you later," Trey said, giving Gina a quick peck on the cheek before heading off.

Gina walked inside, with Seth following her. Trey glanced back at the house before driving away. Gina paused and turned.

"What are you doing here?" Gina asked, but Seth just stared at her, noticing how different she looked.

"You're pregnant" he said. Gina wrapped her jacket tighter around her stomach.

"What are you talking about?" she said, looking him in the eye.

"You're pregnant," he said again, stepping closer. He reached out and forcefully opened her jacket, revealing her noticeably growing belly.

"Stay away from me," she said, stepping back and covering her stomach once more.

"How can you... Who's responsible?" Seth demanded.

"What do you care?" Gina shot back.

"When? How many months along are you? Am I the father?" Seth pressed.

Gina looked at him, struggling with her emotions.

"Get out, please; just go," she said, her voice trembling. The last thing she wants is her mom seeing Seth.

"Stop telling me to leave. Answer my question!" Seth insisted, moving closer.

"You need to leave before my mom comes back. Just go and leave me alone!" she urged.

"Am I the father?" Seth asked again, grabbing her shoulders.

"Yes! You are!" Gina screamed, tears streaming down her face.

"What?" Seth was stunned.

"Yes, you're responsible for this, so what?!" she yelled through her tears. "You want to make a deal out of it?!"

"Why didn't you tell me?" Seth demanded.

"Why? Why didn't I-" Gina retorted.
"You were planning not to tell me, weren't you?"

295

"Yes. Of course. Because you would take her away from me! Again!"

Seth was left reeling, his strength drained.

"You should've told me," he said weakly.

"This has nothing to do with you, okay. Just go back to the city and leave us alone," Gina said, holding her stomach.

"I—" Seth started, but Gina turned away.

"This weather is something else," Gina heard her mom say as she walked towards the house.
"f*ck," she said wishing the ground could swallow Seth. Geraldine stopped when she saw Seth and Gina.

"We have a guest?" Geraldine asked.

"Uh, no... he was just about to leave," Gina said, trying to push Seth away.

"To leave...?" Geraldine echoed.

"Yes, Mom," Gina said sensing something off.

"Good day," Seth said.

"Is he the one?" Geraldine asked, her gaze piercing. Gina's hand trembled as she shook her head.

"He should have some tea before leaving," Geraldine said, removing her gloves. She opened the door and ushered Seth in. She gave Gina a piercing look before walking in.
"Sit down, gentleman," she instructed, taking a seat herself.

Seth, perplexed, sat down, as told.

"Regina, make us some tea, will you?" Geraldine said, her eyes never leaving Seth.

Nora and Steph arrived, shocked by the scene.

They went to Gina in the kitchen after greeting their mom.

"What's going on?" Steph whispered. Gina, sweating and distressed, couldn't explain. She set two cups of tea down and sat with them.

"Leave the table," Geraldine commanded.

"Hm?" Gina said.

"I said leave the table," Geraldine repeated. Gina gently sat up. She looked at Seth, who looked rigid as ever. She and her sisters went upstairs.

"What are your intentions towards my daughter?" they heard their mom ask. The rest of the conversation was muffled.

Gina sat on Steph's bed, anxiously wondering what her mom would say and how Seth would respond.

"He's leaving," Nora said, tapping Steph. Gina's heart raced again. *Leaving?*

They went downstairs, and their mom seemed perfectly normal, not mentioning Seth at all. They didn't dare to ask.

Seth sat in his car, staring at the hotel. His mind was a whirlwind of thoughts: Gina's pregnancy, the guy next door, and her mom's reaction. He sighed, running a hand through his hair.

He needed to return to the city by tomorrow. Another sigh escaped him as he bit his hand, struggling to decide what to do. He wondered why making decisions about her was always so difficult.

CHAPTER THIRTY-THREE

By midnight, Gina still couldn't sleep. Her mind was consumed with thoughts of what her mom and Seth had discussed. She decided to get out of bed and went downstairs.

In the dining room, she saw her mom sitting at the table with her Bible, a jar, and a glass of water.

Gina walked in quietly. Geraldine glanced at her over her glasses.

"Couldn't sleep? It happens," she said, closing her Bible. Gina took a seat and poured herself a glass of water.

"When I was pregnant with Nora, I couldn't sleep either. I'd be up at all hours, either crocheting or craving strange foods. Your dad would get frustrated but he kept it to himself," Geraldine reminisced with a soft laugh. Gina smiled at the memory.

"He was such a gentleman, whatever happened to him after." She said, looking at the light.

Gina decided to ask her question. "What did you tell him?"

"Who?" Geraldine asked, seeming to snap back to the present.

"Seth. The one responsible…"

"Oh, the gentleman who came earlier," Geraldine said, setting her glasses aside. "What do you think I told him?"

Gina looked at her mother, unsure of how to react.

"I told him what any mother would say in this situation," Geraldine said, closing the jar and packing up her Bible.

"I told him to leave and never come back if he wasn't going to marry you."

Gina was conflicted, feeling a mix of anger and relief. The Seth she knew would never settle for someone like her. It was a bitter truth she had to accept—he was a manipulative man who believed he could get whatever he wanted.

"And he left," Geraldine continued. "What's done is done. There's no use dwelling on regrets. I want to believe you learn from it and move forward." She took Gina's hand. "That man may have second thoughts about you, but there's someone else who's ready to work hard for your well-being. Choose wisely."

With that, Geraldine left the kitchen, leaving Gina deep in thought.

Seth stood by the wall as people arrived. The room was dark, with Tricia supposedly lying in the closed casket.
After the service and burial, everyone returned to the mansion. Seth frequently checked on the baby.

Montserrat, looking thinner and more rigid than before, sat with her mother and husband. Faith came with her husband and a girl Seth didn't recognise. Maria arrived with her fiancé and daughter. Seth couldn't help but think that the inheritance had grown with one less heir.

Later in the evening, Liam arrived.

"Your grandma must be disappointed," Liam said. "She wanted to bring the family together, but now people are dying. What a shame."

Seth didn't respond.

"Oh, look who's here," Liam said, pointing. Seth moved quickly to greet the lawyer.

As expected, the lawyer scheduled a meeting for the following day.

The next day, everyone gathered in the room. The only one missing was the deceased. The great-grandchildren were present as well. The lawyer began promptly at ten.

"Good morning, everyone," he said. "I'm deeply sorry for your loss. Mrs. McGregor wouldn't have wanted this." He opened his case and continued, "We were supposed to meet in a few weeks, but due to Miss Tricia's passing, we're having it now. According to the will, the properties will go to the great-grandchildren," he said, looking around.

Everyone remained silent.

"I'm sure you have questions, the biggest being What happens to Miss Tricia's property?" He adjusted his glasses. "We are still going according to Mrs. McGregor, your mother, grandmother's will."

"What do you mean?" Theresa asked.

"Well, Mrs. McGregor was aware of everyone's secrets. Maria, she knew about your daughter and her son. Theresa, she expected more from you, but…" The lawyer shrugged. "Miss Tricia had her own secret." He pulled out pictures of Maria's daughter and her son, handing them to Maria; then Theresa's picture with a boy, and handed it to Theresa; followed by Faith's picture, and gave it to her. He dropped Tricia's picture on the table.

"I believe you all received private letters from your grandmother. She knew everything. Maria, she knew of your past. Theresa, you had a son whom you tried to hide. Faith, she always knew about your situation. Tricia, as well, has a son who will inherit her property, but Seth," he said, turning to Seth. "While writing the will, Mrs. McGregor wondered about you. She knew you well but couldn't predict your actions."

The lawyer returned to his seat. "We'll stick to our schedule, as Mrs. McGregor intended."

The room fell silent.

Seth tapped his fingers on the desk, loosened his tie, and left the room first.

Liam cracked his neck and downed a glass of whisky.
"Okay, let me get this straight," he said. "Tricia has a son? And Aunt Theresa actually has a son too? This is mind-blowing—no, it's brain-wrecking!" He poured another glass and took a long drink. Seth stood beside him, matching his pace with the alcohol.

"Tricia had a son? How is that even possible? Since when?" Liam said, taking another swig.

"I went to see her," Seth said, finishing another glass.

"Who?" Liam asked, pouring himself more.

"Gina."

"You went to see Gina?" Liam's eyes widened. "I knew it!"

"She looked different," Seth said, his voice almost wistful.
Liam nodded, looking at his friend.

"She was with a man and she's pregnant." Liam choked on his drink, "what? wait! She's married already?"

Seth took another glass, almost gagging on it.
"He's her neighbour. She said the baby is mine."

"Damn, Seth…" Liam whispered, astonished.

Seth laughed dryly, his throat hoarse.
"This is funny to you?"

"She asked me to get out of her life. I even met her mom."

Liam stared at him, processing the information. "She asked me to leave her and her baby alone. She looked at me like I was a monster." He said that and gulped another glass.
"Her mom said I should either marry her or leave her alone forever." He said as Liam nodded.

301

"Man, you're in deep sh*t," Liam said, resting his hands on his back. "But I'll give you some advice. First, do you love her?"

Seth looked at him, conflicted. "I don't know. I think I do, but I don't know."

"You should know," Liam said. "Do you think about her all the time? Does your heart race when you see or think about her? Do you get jealous when she's with another guy? That's your answer. If you saw her with someone else, they might be hitting it off right now. Think fast."

Seth sat in silence, deep in thought.

Montserrat stepped out of the car and walked stiffly into the house. She went straight to the living room and waited for her mother. When Theresa walked in, Montserrat turned to her.

"Who was that in the picture?" she demanded, but Theresa walked past her to the kitchen. Montserrat followed, slapping the glass of water from her mother's hand and shattering it on the floor.

"Tell me why you adopted me in the first place!" she screamed. "Who is he? Is he alive? Do I know him?"

Theresa looked startled. "Control yourself, woman!"

Montserrat dragged her mother back, pushing her against the wall and drawing a knife from the stand.

"What are you doing?" Theresa cried.

"Why did you make me suffer all these years? Are you protecting him?" Montserrat's voice trembled with anger.

"You ungrateful child! Have you forgotten what I did for you?" Theresa shouted back.

"What did you do? You made me endure abuse and criticism from your family! I can't take it anymore!" Montserrat yelled, tears streaming down her face. Theresa tried to push her away, but Montserrat kicked her leg. Theresa fell onto the broken glass, which cut her hand, making her scream.

Hector rushed in, running to Theresa's side, shocked by the scene. "Help me! She's lost her mind!" Theresa cried.

"What are you doing?" Hector asked, but Montserrat ignored him, continuing her rage. Hector managed to grab the knife from her, trying to calm her down.

"Don't do this!" Hector pleaded.

"She has a biological son, Hector!" Montserrat sobbed. "I'm just an object to her."

Hector dropped the knife and went back to Theresa, helping her up. Montserrat wiped her tears and saw Hector applying ice to Theresa's bleeding hand.

"What are you doing?" Montserrat asked, approaching them. She snatched the ice from him, threw it away, and pushed Theresa back down. She felt Hector drag her up and she felt a sharp pain on her cheek. She looked up at Hector in shock.

"What did you just—?" She saw Theresa sitting up. She picked up the ice and tossed it at her. "You might need this, pumpkin," Theresa said coldly before walking out.

Montserrat stood there, confused and hurt. "What is happening? Hector?" She looked at him, stunned.

"You? You a...you're her son?" She asked, struggling to comprehend. Hector reached out to help her, but Montserrat pushed away the ice pack, still in disbelief.

Her world felt like it was crumbling. "My life has been a lie," she thought. "What does this mean?"

Hector left the kitchen, leaving Montserrat to grapple with the overwhelming revelations.

Gina opened the door to Nicki, who stepped inside with a playful grin. "Hope this is safe for me?" she asked, dropping her bag. "Last thing I want is to be nagged by Mrs. Geraldine."

Nora came downstairs to join them, followed by Stephanie.

"Wait a minute, is this is true?" Nicki asked, referring to Gina's pregnancy. "Damn, Regina, you're full of surprises. Your mom knows about everything?"

"Yes, she does," Gina confirmed.

"And you're still living under her roof?" Nicki said, glancing at Nora and Steph. "A miracle indeed!"

They talked about recent events, but Gina chose not to go further, so the conversation shifted to lighter topics.

"So, when will you be leaving?" Nicki asked Nora.

"Soon, next week or so," Nora replied.

"You could work for me instead," Nicki suggested. "It would pay better than going back to college." Gina looked at her curiously.

"I'm just saying," Nicki added with a grin.

After chatting for a while, Nicki decided to share her news. "So, girls," she said, raising her hand to show off a sparkling ring, "I'm getting married!"

"Excuse me?" Gina said, taken aback.

"You mean?" Steph asked in disbelief.

"Yes, I'm getting married," Nicki said proudly.

"Are you being serious?" Gina asked.

"What? You don't believe me?" Nicki said, feigning hurt.

"Are you joking, cause I personally don't, unless it's one of your deals," Gina said skeptically.

"What? Hey, I'm a human too, with a heart!" Nicki protested.

"We know, but..." Nora said, tilting her head.

"Are you serious right now?" Gina asked, still in shock.

"Hell yeah, I am!" Nicki insisted.

"Are you sure about this?" Gina pressed.

"Very sure," Nicki said confidently. Gina exchanged glances with Steph.

"Then let's celebrate! A girls' night out: Nora's farewell party and my engagement party. Let's go!"

CHAPTER THIRTY-FOUR

"Why does it feel like I'm doing all the dirty work for you?" Liam said, slapping a file down on Seth's desk before taking a seat.

"Did you find out?" Seth asked, flipping through the documents.

"Of course. What do you take me for? I have the best people," Liam said, hands raised in mock offense. He sat up and began to outline the findings.

"Okay, so," he said, pulling out one document, "your cousin Tricia had a son—he's thirteen and deformed. That might explain why she kept him hidden. She took him to a convent, and he's been there ever since."

"Deformed?" Seth asked, surprised.

"Yeah. Nobody knew she was pregnant, and she was never off the screen. Whatever she did must have affected the baby," Liam explained.

"Does the boy know her?"

"I think so. CCTV footage from the convent shows she visited once every three months and captured her with the boy in his wheelchair," Liam said. Seth nodded.

"What about Theresa?"

"Oh, this is a shocker," Liam said, settling in to deliver the news. "Theresa had a son before she married her Mexican esposo. Five years after their marriage, she adopted your cousin, who was thirteen at the time. Her son was sixteen."

"Why not just bring her son into the family?" Seth asked, puzzled.

"Exactly. But they're a family of ruthless politicians. I'm guessing she was protecting her own son. Her husband died, leaving nothing to Montserrat or her but to their son-in-law and grandson. Probably thought women shouldn't inherit property. Your aunt figured this out, so she arranged for her son to marry your cousin, securing both sets of properties."

"Wait, Montserrat's husband is Theresa's son?"

"Exactly," Liam confirmed, leaning back. "So, did he get the property?"

"Not likely. The family was probably against your aunt's marriage to their son. Despite their son's will, they didn't accept Montserrat," Liam said.

"And Montserrat lost her baby," Seth noted. "Does she know about this?"

"She should by now," Liam said. "Honestly, I don't like your family at all. They're a mess. Your grandmother, though…damn her," he said, twirling in his chair.

"Has Nora called in yet?" Geraldine asked as she headed for the door.

"No, but she said she'd call once she arrived," Steph replied. Geraldine stepped out.

"Where are you going?" Gina asked as Steph rummaged through their mother's crochet box.

"I have an interview," Steph said, searching for a pin.

"An interview? You didn't mention it."

"Well, I'm mentioning it now," Steph said, pinning her hair up. "How do I look?"

"Fantastic," Gina said with a smile.

"See you later," Steph said, heading for the door.

"Good luck!" Gina called after her.

"Hi, Trey," Gina heard Steph say from outside. She stood up immediately.

"Hey," Trey said, peeking in.

"Hi," Gina replied, and Tyler walked in with Trey.

"Hey, little man," Gina said, picking up Tyler, who touched her cheeks and smiled, showing his incomplete teeth.

"Good morning, little man!" Gina said, feeling his cheeks and forehead.

"Yeah, sorry, but can he stay with you? I would have sent him to his grandma, but—"

"It's fine, of course," Gina said, touching Tyler's cheeks.

"Alright," Trey said, pecking Tyler on the cheek. He lingered close to Gina, causing her heart to skip a beat. "Daddy will be back soon, okay?" Trey said to Tyler before leaving.

"So, what are we going to do today, little man?" Gina asked as she set Tyler down.

"What's that?" Gina asked, taking the paper Tyler was offering her as they walked upstairs.

Tyler began drawing on the white paper. "Daddy," he said, focused on his work. Gina watched him, her thoughts drifting to the baby she was expecting with Seth. He had left without a second thought, never intending to be a part of their lives.

Maybe it was time for her to move on. He was no match for her anyway.

"I need to pee," Tyler said, tugging at her.

"Okay, let's go," Gina said, taking his hand.

"Do you want cookies after?" Gina asked and Tyler nodded eagerly.

A month later

Seth sat in his car, scrolling through the headlines on his tablet. The top story was about Theresa's secret, and Montserrat had held a public interview announcing her divorce from Hector. Seth had met Montserrat earlier in his office, where she'd submitted her CV, hoping to work for his company. He hadn't given her a response yet.

He watched as a car pulled up, and Theresa and her son stepped out, heading into the building. Seth watched them for a moment before making his way inside.

He entered the room, pushing a baby's cradle in front of him. The room was filled with family members, all eyes on him. Rosa waited outside, as only family was allowed in. They had all anticipated this day for 18 months, now that all the secrets had been revealed and the inheritance was at stake.

Seth took a seat, and the lawyer began to speak.

"Good day, everyone," the lawyer said, adjusting his glasses. "We've finally reached the end of a long journey. I'll begin."

Seth glanced at the large portrait of his grandmother hanging on the wall. Her wild smile seemed to watch him as the lawyer continued.

"I'll get straight to the point," the lawyer said, pulling out a document.

Faith sat to the lawyer's left, with her daughter. Maria sat with her daughter and grandson. Theresa and her son were seated separately at the end of the table. To the lawyer's right sat Seth, with the baby's cradle beside him, and Tricia's son.

"To my granddaughters and great-grandchildren," the lawyer began, "it has indeed been a difficult journey. Your mother, grandmother, and great grandmother was sick; she wanted to say a lot, but she thought she didn't have enough time. God rest her soul."

He paused, then continued, "I will read her will as she wrote it."

"To my children—David, Joseph, Maria, Theresa, and Faith—they will each receive 5 percent of my properties. To my grandchildren—Seth, Patricia, Montserrat, Hector, Maryglory, and Anna—they will each receive 10 percent. The remainder of my properties will be equally divided among the great-grandchildren, and the Wally-Tons properties will be shared, partly, as well. The rest of my estate is to be allocated to orphanages, care homes, and the families who supported my granddaughters and great-grandchildren. The mansion must remain intact; it belongs to the entire family and cannot be sold or rented. Should my will be contested, the properties will be donated to the government. Anyone who disputes this will be stripped of their inheritance.

"To my family, whether you have learnt the importance of truth or not, remember that my wish was for us to be truthful and to value family above all. Jealousy, envy, lies, and secrets only destroy. Let's build our family, because it's the strongest bond ever. I wish I could be with all of you now, but as life has it...farewell, my dear family."

As the lawyer finished, the room fell silent. The baby began to whimper, and Seth gently shook the cradle to soothe him, but the crying grew louder.

Maria stood up and approached the cradle. "Can I take him?" she asked.

"No," Seth replied firmly.

"He's adorable," said Tricia's son.

"Grandma, he looks like me," said Peter, Maria's grandson, from behind her.

The baby continued crying, and Maria picked him up, not minding Seth, and began to rock him, calming him down.

"He's so cute," Faith said from behind Maria.

"I think he's hungry."

"Shouldn't you call his mom?" Faith asked, touching the baby's cheek.

"This isn't fair!" Theresa suddenly shouted, slamming her hand on the table, which startled everyone and made the baby cry again.

"Jesus, Tessa!" Maria exclaimed, still rocking the baby. "Why are we only getting a small share? Just because I don't have a grandchild? This doesn't make sense. The lawyer could have faked it!"

"You saw and confirmed it yourself on the first day, Tessa," Faith said.

"This is unacceptable! Montserrat isn't my daughter. How can she get a larger share than me?" Theresa shouted.

"Can you hear yourself, Tessa? You adopted her and now you're denying her? It's shameless," Maria retorted.

"Shameless? You sloth!" Theresa shot back.

"Enough!" the lawyer commanded, silencing the room. "Remember, I have the authority to revoke inheritance if anyone opposes the will. So, does anyone object?"

The room was silent.

"Good. Any questions?" the lawyer asked.

"What about the properties my father inherited?" Seth inquired.

"You can do whatever you want with it. The will was designed this way intentionally. Distribution may take time, possibly months," the lawyer explained, closing his case.

"Finally, since Miss Patricia has passed, may her son remain in the mansion under your care, Mr. Seth?"

"What?" Seth asked, surprised.

"Given that he can't return to the orphanage, and since you'll be his guardian, you'll manage his inheritance under legal supervision until he comes of age. Do you agree?" the lawyer asked.

"Fine," Seth said, glancing at the boy, who was smiling.

"Excellent. I'll start processing everything immediately. Thank you for your trust," the lawyer said, bowing.

Theresa and Hector left first. Maria returned the baby to his cradle and left with her family, followed by Faith and her family. Seth remained with his son, who was now sucking his thumb, and Tricia's son.

"Hi, I'm Joseph Junior. My mom told me I was named after my grandfather, and she told me about everyone. You're my uncle. Nice to meet you. Will I be living with you now?" the boy asked.

Seth looked at him, noting how much he talked like his mother. Ignoring him, Seth stood up as Rosa entered and took the baby. Seth then turned to the boy and asked, "Can you drive yourself?"

"Yes!" the boy replied, maneuvering his chair towards Seth.

"My nanny used to push me around because my hands were paralysed. Sometimes they freeze, but most of the time they don't. The doctors said I might walk again, though they're not optimistic. I believe in miracles. Do you, Uncle Seth?"

Seth glanced at him and replied, "No. Now be quiet." They walked out to the garage, where Joseph's guardian was waiting to take him back until everything was processed. Joseph insisted on staying, which annoyed Seth.

A child under his care? He had no choice, noticing the lawyer watching and smiling. Seth helped the boy into the car, and they drove back to the mansion.

He had gained the inheritance he wanted and a surprising bonus. Maybe even a triple bonus. F*ck!

CHAPTER THIRTY-FIVE

Three months later

Gina sat at the kitchen table, watching Tyler eat while Trey gathered his belongings. Around her, everyone seemed to be living their best lives. Nora was in college with a boyfriend, Stephanie was working and in a serious relationship, though she hadn't met the guy, and Trey was traveling with no clear return date. Even Nicki had gotten married—how did that happen?

Her mother was absorbed in church activities and socialising with friends. And Gina was left, big belly and all, feeling like the unlucky one.

Two months ago, Trey had confessed his feelings for her, and she had turned him down. She regretted it but didn't, in some ways. His heartbreak led to a period of silence between them, but lately, things have warmed up again between them, thanks to Tyler.

Weeks ago, Trey had informed her that he was moving out for a while; Tyler's grandmother wanted him to stay with her. Trey had offered to stay if Gina accepted him, but she had coldly rejected him. Now, she felt bad about that decision.

Gina touched Tyler's hair. "Do you want more?" she asked, wiping cereal from his lips.

"No, I'm full," he said, smiling and lifting his shirt to show off his round stomach.

"Wow, it's really big," Gina said, and Tyler nodded, still grinning.

"Did the baby move again?" he asked, placing his tiny hands on her belly.

"Do you want to see it?" she asked.

"Yes!" Tyler replied.

Gina opened her shirt and they waited until the baby kicked. Tyler giggled loudly, making Gina laugh.

"I see you two are having fun without me," Trey said, coming into the kitchen and removing his boots.

"Daddy, he moved again!" Tyler exclaimed.

"Oh really?" Trey said, walking over.

"Yes, come and see!" Tyler urged. The baby kicked again, and Trey marveled, "Wow."

"Are you ready, little man?" Trey asked, lifting Tyler into his arms. Tyler giggled.

"Yes!" Tyler responded enthusiastically.

"Alright, go get your bag upstairs," Trey said, setting Tyler down. Tyler scampered up the stairs to fetch his bag.

The kitchen fell quiet for a moment. "It's sad we won't be here for the baby's birth," Trey said.

"Oh, yeah," Gina replied, touching her belly.

"I see you're not changing your mind," Trey observed, noting Gina's sombre expression.

"Hey, I'm not trying to make you uncomfortable. I just hope he's worth the wait, which I doubt," Trey said, forcing a smile.

Tyler came bounding down the stairs with his bag, and they all walked outside.

"You don't need to worry about the garden. I can start over. You're not in a good condition to handle it," Trey said.

"I've told you, I can manage. I don't have much to do anyway. The house is safe," Gina replied.

"I wish we could stay. You need support now more than ever," Trey said, pointing to her belly.

"My mom's here, the neighbors are supportive, and I'm fine," Gina said. Trey gave her a hug and a quick kiss.

"I'll call you," he said, checking that everything was okay before getting into his car.

"I'll see you soon, Tyler," Gina said, kissing his hair.

"You're not coming with us?" Tyler asked, his face reddening as he looked at Trey.

"No," Gina said. Tyler looked at Trey with tears in his eyes.

"Hey, don't cry. I'll see you soon, and I'll bring the baby with me, okay?" Gina said, trying to reassure him.

"Promise?" Tyler asked, his voice cracking.

"I promise," Gina said, and Trey drove off. Gina waved as Tyler watched, tears rolling down his cheeks.

Gina stood there for a while, feeling the weight of loneliness settle in. No Tyler, no Trey—just her. She went back inside and made herself a cup of tea.

Seth was buried in paperwork when Joseph entered the room unnoticed. The boy continued talking, but Seth barely registered his presence. When Seth finally noticed him, he poured himself a glass of whisky, realising it was already dark outside.

"What are you doing here?" Seth asked, seeing Joseph engrossed in a book.

"Wow, you've been working for fifteen hours straight," Joseph said.

Seth checked his watch and felt his muscles ache from the long hours. "What are you doing up so late? You should be in bed."

"I was just wondering about my mom," Joseph said, following Seth to his room. "Is she a bad person?"

Seth paused, surprised by the question. "Yes, she is," he said, heading to his bathroom.

When Seth returned, he found Joseph still in his room. "You should really go to bed now," Seth said, pointing to the door.

"Okay, but can I borrow this?" Joseph asked, lifting a sweater—a gift from Gina.

"Give me that!" Seth said, snatching it from him and almost pulling him from his wheelchair.

"Sorry," Joseph said, wheeling out of the room. Seth felt a pang of guilt as he watched him leave.

Liam stared at Seth, his feet propped up on the desk and hands on his cheeks. "So, you brought the boy to the mansion because the lawyer suggested it, and you actually did?"

"What was I supposed to do? I couldn't leave him there," Seth replied.

"You could have. Do you even realise what you're doing? This could be chaotic. His mother died because of this inheritance mess, and now you're a target," Liam warned.

"What do you mean?" Seth asked.

"I mean, he could be trying to get close to you to gain an advantage. He seems bright, even though he's just a child," Liam explained.

"I understand your concern, but I know what I'm doing, and yes, he's still a child." Seth insisted.

"If you say so?" Liam said, pouring himself a glass of whisky.

"Yes, I have a plan," Seth said.

"You do?" Liam asked, raising an eyebrow.

"I'm going on a vacation," Seth said.

"A vacation? Where?" Liam inquired.

"Just for a week or so. It depends," Seth replied.

"Depends on what?" Liam pressed.

"I'm leaving early tomorrow morning," Seth said.

"Tomorrow? What about the kids?" Liam asked.

"Rosa can take care of them," Seth said.

"Where exactly are you going?" Liam asked.

"Just keep an eye on them until I get back," Seth said, leaving the study. Liam followed him.

"Are you hiding something from me?" Liam asked.

"What do you mean?" Seth replied.

"You're not really going on vacation, are you?" Liam asked.

Seth stopped and looked at him. "I want to bring her back," he admitted, feeling almost embarrassed.

"Wait a minute, are you talking about Gina?" Liam asked, incredulous.

"Who else?" Seth replied.

"Oh my god, you're finally growing up. I thought you'd forgotten about her. Looks like you've been thinking about her all along. Damn, man, you're in love," Liam said.

"You're making me feel like a kid," Seth said, walking into his room. Liam followed.

"Well, you act like one. So you actually love Gina? Why did you hold back?" Liam asked.

Seth didn't answer immediately, lost in thought. "What if..." he began but trailed off.

"What if she rejects you or is with someone else?" Liam finished.

Seth looked at him, conflicted. "I'm afraid she might not feel the same way."

"Advice, my friend. If she's with someone, let her be. You left her once, and she's moved on. But if she's single, go for it," Liam advised.

"What if her mother doesn't accept me? She's been critical of me," Seth said.

"I can't guess. But you got her into a tough spot, so it's understandable she might not like you," Liam said.

"I'll leave early tomorrow morning," Seth repeated.

"Leaving?" Joseph's voice came from the door. "Dinner is ready," he said, and then left.

"You should be easier on him," Liam suggested.

"I am," Seth replied.

"Where's our little boy? I need some positive energy right now," Liam said, leaving to find him.

Seth sat at the edge of his bed, deep in thought. He hadn't pursued anyone in a long time, and the thought of Gina's eyes on him made his heart race.
What if she rejected him? What if his mother didn't accept him? What if Gina was with someone else? What if she didn't feel the same way?

He rubbed his face and took a deep breath.

Gina slowly walked down the hospital stairs and hailed a taxi, feeling drowsy on the way home. Once she arrived, the phone rang—Trey was calling. They had a long conversation about life, her cravings for his pies, and updates on Tyler.

As they spoke, Gina heard her mother come in. She signaled her to wait a moment and ended the call. Stepping into the living room, she saw her aunt and mother sitting together on the couch. Gina was surprised to see her aunt, who lived far away and whom she hadn't seen in a long time.

"Aunt Sarah?" Gina said, her voice filled with surprise.

"Oh my Lord, it's true!" Sarah exclaimed, standing up to hug Gina. "Look at you—when did you grow up so much?"

"When did you get back, Aunt Sarah?" Gina asked, laughing.

They spent hours catching up on their lives, discussing her pregnancy, Stephanie, Nora, and more. Gina was relieved to have someone to talk to who could offer her advice and support.

Sarah was the youngest of Gina's mother's four siblings: the eldest was her mom, followed by Florence, Josephine, and then Sarah. Florence and her mom had never been close, while Josephine was more business-minded and distant from the family. Sarah, however, cared deeply about family but had distanced herself because of the family's issues.

Sarah mentioned she would only be staying for two weeks due to work commitments. During the first week, Gina enjoyed Sarah's company; she was funny and easygoing. Stephanie and Nora would have loved to be home to see her, but they couldn't make it.

By the second week, however, Gina felt that Sarah was becoming more probing. They had a deep conversation while over at Trey's house, where Sarah questioned her choices and motivations. Sarah presented Gina with three options: stay with Trey, wait for someone who might never come back, or remain single and raise her child alone. Gina felt overwhelmed by Sarah's scrutiny and questioned her own choices, including why she had rejected Trey.

On a sunny afternoon, after her mother and Sarah returned from an unannounced shopping trip for baby supplies, they settled in Gina's room to sort through their purchases. Sarah excused herself to get a glass of water. When the doorbell rang, Gina volunteered to answer it.

"Tell Sarah to get me a glass too," her mother called out.

"Okay, Mom," Gina replied, heading towards the door. Sarah quickly grabbed her hand and whispered urgently, "He's here."

"Who?" Gina whispered back.

"Seth!" Sarah replied, her eyes wide.

Gina's heart skipped a beat. "What?" she whispered, incredulous.

"Shhh… Just go on," Sarah urged.

Gina stood there, stunned, unsure if this was a prank. "I got you," Sarah said with a grin and returned to getting her water.

Gina walked into the living room, her heart pounding. She opened the door slowly, holding her breath. There he was—Seth, standing right outside. Their eyes locked, and in that moment, Gina felt a whirlwind of emotions: happiness, sadness, overwhelm, and hesitation.

What could he possibly want this time? She wondered, her heart racing uncontrollably.

CHAPTER THIRTY-SIX

Gina stared at Seth in disbelief for several moments.

"Hi," he said, jolting her back to reality.

"H-hi," she stammered.

"How have you been?" he asked.

Gina looked at him, noting the unfamiliar expression on his face. "What did you come for?" she demanded, trying to regain her composure.

"Can I... come in?" Seth asked tentatively.

"No!" Gina said firmly, stepping outside and locking the door behind her. "What do you want?"

"Hey, we need to—"

"You want to finalise the deal?" she interrupted, holding out her hand.

"No—"

"Fine, I'll sign it," she said, spreading her arms.

"I didn't come for that."

"You didn't? Then what?"

"I want you," he said, his eyes intense and filled with desire.

"What?"

"Yes."

"I don't understand."

"I want you," he repeated boldly.·

322

"Well, Seth McGregor, I'm not an object or property to be claimed just because you want it," she said, turning and going back inside. She locked the door behind her.

Back in the room, her aunt and mother were still sorting through baby clothes.

"What did he want?" her mother asked.

"What?" Gina replied, glancing at her aunt.

"I told him we'd call him if we had anything to sell," her aunt explained.

"Oh, I told him the same thing."

"So, what took you so long?" her mother asked.

"I just went to the garden to check something," Gina said.

"Come here," her aunt said, holding up a piece of clothing. "You wore this when you were little," she added, but Gina was distracted, her thoughts still on Seth.

He said he didn't come for the deal. So what did he come for? Gina wondered, her heart racing.

"Are you okay, honey?" her aunt asked, noticing her distress.

"Do you want to get some sleep?" her mother offered.

"Let's just finish packing this up. We can continue later," they moved the clothes to the corner and left the room.

Gina looked out the window but saw no sign of Seth.

"So you told her you wanted her?" Liam asked.

"That's what I said," Seth replied.

"Is she a property or something? You should have told her about your feelings. That's what she needs to hear."

323

"What do I say to her?" Seth asked.

"Were you even listening to me? How do you feel about her? Do you love her?"

"I do."

"Then tell her you love her and mean it. If she shuts the door, knock again. Show her you love her—kiss her, get her flowers, do something."

Seth ended the call, looking out the window, his mind racing with thoughts.

"Good morning, sweetheart," Sarah said, pecking Gina on the cheek.

"Good morning, Aunt," Gina replied, sitting up.

"Breakfast is ready. Do you want it in bed?" Sarah offered.

"No," Gina said.

"Alright then, I'll leave you to get ready," she said, leaving the room.
Gina sighed and got off the bed.

It had all been a dream, she thought. In the dream, Seth was romantic, they had children, and everyone was happy—her mom, her aunt, Stephanie, Nora, and even Cate.

She buttoned up a dress her mom had said she wore when pregnant with her.

She wasn't actually hungry and wasn't listening to her aunt and mother's conversation. Her mind was focused on Seth, who had come back for her and whom she had turned away.

"Are you not hungry?" her mother asked.

"Do you feel any pain? Do you want to see a doctor?" her mother added.

Gina appreciated the attention but yearned for something more—love from a man and from her child. She burst into tears.

"What's wrong, dear?" her aunt asked.

"Does anything hurt?" her mother asked again, as they both hugged her to comfort her.

After a while, she calmed down. They all sat on the couch, and her mother made her a special tea.

Once she was composed, her mother asked if anything had happened. Gina tried to hold back but ended up telling them about Seth.

"He came here, and none of you told me?" her mother demanded.

"That's not the problem right now," Sarah said.

"It is. He left my daughter. He doesn't deserve her!"

"Is that what she wants?" Sarah asked, looking at Gina.

"Do you still love him?" her mother asked. Gina looked down into her tea.

A knock came at the door. Sarah answered, and Geraldine followed her. Seth stood there, holding a bouquet and a small box.

"What are you doing here?" Gina's mother asked, and Gina walked to the door.

"Mom," she said, touching her shoulder, but her mother pushed her away. "Just go inside," her mother instructed.

Sarah nodded for Gina to comply. Gina slowly retreated, not looking back at Seth.

Geraldine stared at Seth. "What are you doing here?"

"I came to see Gina."

"For what?"

"Because... because I love her," Seth said, holding tightly to the bouquet.

"Since when? You chose to leave the first time we met."

"I had things I needed to resolve."

"More important than my daughter?"

Seth hesitated. Geraldine shook her head. "I see."

"No—I mean—"

"Goodbye, young man. You don't deserve my daughter," she said, closing the door.

Sarah smiled sympathetically at Seth. "I'll make sure she gets these," she said, taking the bouquet and small box from him.

Seth stood there for a moment before walking away.

Sarah entered Gina's room with the bouquet and gift.

"Has he left?" Gina asked, glancing up.

"Yes. This is for you," Sarah said, placing the items down before leaving.

Gina picked up the bouquet and smelt it. Though she didn't like the scent, she appreciated the gesture. She opened the gift to find a butterfly hairpin. She laughed at the thought of Seth choosing it.

Her smile faded as she overheard her mother and aunt talking. She went to the door to listen.

"They have a child together, and she's with another one," Sarah said.

"So?" Geraldine replied.

"They aren't children anymore; they can make their own decisions."

"Have you forgotten that this happened to me?" her mother asked.

"I know, but this is different. Regina is old enough to care for herself. And he loves her."

"How do you know that?"

Sarah exhaled. "He came back for her."

"Well, Robert came back many times as much as he left."

"He's different. I can see that. Just give them a chance."

"I don't have a good feeling about this."

"Believe me, their love is real," Sarah said, hugging her sister from behind. "Please, just give them a chance."

"It depends on him," her mother said, getting up and walking into her room.

"Hey, man, how's it going over there?" Liam asked.

"Not well. What's up?"

"I'm sorry, but you need to know this. Your aunts are staying at the mansion for a while."

"What?"

"Rosa called me, and it's true. I can't tell them to leave."

Seth exhaled deeply. "When are you coming back?"

"I don't know," Seth said, rubbing his hair.

"So, what do I do?"

"Just keep an eye on them for me," Seth instructed.

"Alright, man. Keep it together," Liam said before hanging up.

Seth stared out the window, lost in thought.

Should he buy gifts for them? Should he propose in front of her family? His mind was racing with possibilities.

———————————— -

"Are you sure you're okay alone?" Sarah asked Gina.

"Of course," Gina replied.

"Stay inside and don't do anything. We'll be back soon," her mother said.

"Call us if you need anything," Sarah added.

Gina closed the door and went to the kitchen to retrieve a slice of pie. She heard a knock and wondered if they'd forgotten something. She took a bite of the pie and went to open the door.

To her surprise, Seth was there, carrying several bags and boxes.

"What—" Gina began.

"Can I... come in?" Seth asked.

Gina stepped aside to let him in. He set everything down on the couch.

"What's all this?" Gina asked, eyeing the bags.

"They're baby clothes, feeding supplies, lotions, baths, and—" Seth began.

Gina broke out laughing. She laughed so hard tears came out. "What's... funny?" Seth asked, still catching his breath from carrying everything.

"You are," Gina said, managing to stop laughing.

Seth took a few steps towards her. "I wish I could make it up to you."

"This doesn't seem like you, Seth."

"I don't care."

"You don't?"

"I love you."

"You look too cute."

"Very much."

They stood facing each other, their eyes locked. Seth's gaze fell to her lips just as a sudden sensation made Gina's breathing quicken.

"Oh my God... it's happening," Gina gasped as she saw water dripping down her legs.

"What?" Seth asked, panicking.

"It's coming," Gina said, struggling with the pain. Seth's eyes widened in realisation.

"Shit!" he exclaimed. He supported her as they rushed out of the house. They met a neighbor who was also a church member, and she helped them.

"Breathe, breathe," she instructed.

"My mom... my mom... it's... coming..." Gina continued to breathe heavily, the urge to push growing stronger.

At the hospital, Gina was taken to the labour room. Seth was reluctant but was ushered in as well. He found it horrifying to watch—Gina was sweating and veins were visible, and her screams broke his heart.

When the baby's cry filled the room, Gina collapsed back onto the bed. Seth's heart ached as he touched her.

"Sir," a nurse said, handing him the baby. "Congratulations! You have a baby girl."

Seth looked at the tiny, wiggling baby. "My baby," Gina murmured weakly.

"Yes, she's here," Seth said, bringing the baby closer so Gina could touch her.

Just then, Gina's mother and aunt rushed in.

"Oh my baby!" Geraldine cried, touching Gina's hair. Sarah held Gina's hand, both of them tearful.

"I have a baby, Mom," Gina said.

"Yes, sweetheart, you do," Geraldine said. Gina touched her baby before her hand fell limply, and the machine began beeping.

"Gina?" Seth called; panic was rising. "Gina!"

"Oh my God, Regina!"

"Please leave the room, ma'am," a nurse instructed.

"Call the doctor, fast!" another nurse demanded.

"Get the oxygen!"

"Please leave!" they insisted.

They were ushered out, watching from the hallway as the doctor worked on Gina, pressing against her chest. Seth, who was holding the baby, wept as the situation unfolded.

CHAPTER THIRTY-SEVEN

Seth slumped in the corner of his bed, nursing his seventh glass of whisky. His nose was running, and he wiped it with his hand, barely noticing. The room was a blur, filled with muffled voices that he couldn't quite make out.

The door creaked open, and Liam walked in. He took a long look at Seth, clearly dismayed. "Man...I don't like what I'm seeing," he said, sitting beside Seth and grabbing the glass from his hand. "Enough. What the hell happened down there to make you like this?"

Seth rubbed his face, feeling numb all over.

"It's been almost two weeks. Did something happen? I know she rejected you, but I've seen you bounce back before. So what's going on?" Liam pressed.

Seth remained silent, as if Liam wasn't even there.

"Okay, I'm done with this. Do you even know what's happening out there? Your business is in jeopardy, and you've got a family to think about—"

"I lost her," Seth said finally, his voice barely above a whisper.

"What?"

"I lost her... That's what happened," Seth said, sitting up.

"Wait a minute... You lost her, as in, lost her?"

"I don't know."

"Wait, I don't get it. You lost her and now you don't know?"

Seth stood by the window, staring blankly. Liam stood there for a moment before leaving the room, frustrated.

A new presence walked in, but Seth didn't care who it was. His mind was foggy, unable to focus on anything other than the weight of his thoughts.

A hand rested on his shoulder. Seth turned to see his aunt Maria standing behind him. She frowned at the smell of alcohol and began opening the windows.

"What the heck is going on in here? It reeks of alcohol," she said, dusting off her clothes.

"What are you doing here?" Seth asked, still not engaging.

"We both know you shouldn't be asking that," Maria replied. Seth returned to his distant stare out the window.

Maria sat on his bed. "Has it been twenty-five years since we were like this together?" she mused, not expecting a response. "You know, my brother wouldn't have wanted you to turn out like this— so rigid and unhappy. You were so bright when you were little."

She smiled, then continued, "I thought maybe you had lost it all— your feelings and everything—but then, you fell in love."

Seth turned to look at her.

"I'm sorry for interfering, but I was worried and I had to make him talk to me," she said defensively. "Love isn't something you just leave to work out on its own. Sometimes there's something more you need to do."

"What do you know?" Seth snapped.

"I might not know everything, but I'm just—"

"Leave," Seth said firmly.

Maria sat silently for a moment before getting up and heading for the door. "At least think about the kids. They need you," she said before leaving.

Seth stared at the door, a thought forming in his mind. He stepped out and went to the kitchen, where his baby was crying in Rosa's arms and Joe was trying to comfort him.

"Shhhh... don't cry," Joe said.

Liam was sipping coffee and rolling his eyes when he saw Seth standing there. He was clearly fed up.

Seth took the baby from Rosa, holding him gently. "Get ready. We're going somewhere," he told Rosa.

"Where are you going?" Liam asked, but Seth left with the baby in his arms, ignoring the question.

Gina stood by the hospital window, staring out at the busy street. Her baby slept peacefully in the cradle. Her aunt had filled her in on the aftermath of the birth—how her mother had blamed Seth and almost threatened him. Since she woke up, Gina hadn't been able to face her mother. She felt she had ruined her chance to be with Seth.

She had begged her aunt to stay a while because she couldn't bear being alone with her mother.

The door opened, and her mom walked in with Sarah.

"We can go home now, dear," her mom said, but Gina remained frozen.

Sarah took the baby from the cradle. "I told Stephanie to make you some soup at home instead of coming here," she said, but Gina remained silent.

They left the hospital, and when they got home, Stephanie greeted Gina with a hug.

"Hey, sis! Heard we almost lost you," she said, holding the baby. "She's so cute! We're definitely having a baby party, right?"

Gina smiled faintly, but her mind was elsewhere.

"What about Nora?" Sarah asked.

"She has exams. We'll video call her later," Stephanie replied. "She smells so good. She's tiny."

"Come have some soup," Geraldine said as they all moved to the dining area.

They chatted and joked, but Gina remained detached, her mind preoccupied. She barely touched her soup.

"What's wrong?" Geraldine asked, concerned. "Are you feeling sick?"

"Are you okay?" Sarah asked.

Gina dropped her spoon and stood up. "Where are you going?" her mom called.

"What do you care?" Gina screamed.

"Oh my God," Stephanie said, alarmed.

"What's wrong?" Sarah asked.

Gina slammed the door and went over to Trey's, seeking solace. She sat on a high stool, wanting to be alone.

"I always knew he was kind," Stephanie said, joining her. "I mean, he gave you his house key even though you kicked him in the butt." She sat beside Gina. "Talk to me, sis."

Gina poured out her feelings to Stephanie.

"So you really love him, huh?" Stephanie asked.

Gina wiped her tears and nodded.

"Hey, I know you love him, but if it's meant to be, it will be. From what you told me, even though it's hard to believe, he probably loves you too. If he does, he'll come back. But if not, someone else might be waiting for you," Stephanie said, nudging Gina.

"I don't want Mom making decisions for me," Gina said.

"I'll talk to her," Stephanie promised.

"If she'll listen."

"I'll convince her," Stephanie said as they headed back to the house. it, and
"Do you love him that much?" Geraldine asked as they entered.

"She does, Mom. It's obvious," Stephanie replied.

"If you love him, then go ahead," Geraldine said, and she walked into her room.

Gina looked at Stephanie and her aunt, who winked at her.

....

Gina heard the doorbell ring, but Stephanie offered to check it out. She took the baby and rocked her gently in her lap, making her giggle and wiggle.

"Who's that?" Gina asked when Stephanie came back in.

"Just our neighbour," Stephanie replied. "I want to go somewhere."

"Where?" Gina asked.

"I'll be back soon. Do you need anything?"

"Hmmm, not really," Gina said.

"Alright, I'll be back soon," Stephanie said and left.

Gina smiled, wondering if Stephanie was going to see her boyfriend. She laid the baby back in the cradle and her phone rang—it was Trey.

They talked for a long time, and Gina also spoke with Tyler, who reminded her of her promise.

Gina woke up to her baby's cries. It was already dark. She got up and went to the cradle, but the baby was missing. She heard the crying again and walked downstairs.

"Mom?" she called out, but the house was silent except for the baby's wailing.

"Stephanie?" she called again, but the crying stopped.

Gina felt as though she were dreaming or hallucinating.

"Rosa?" she called, blinking rapidly.

Rosa appeared, rocking the baby in her arms and patting his back. Gina's heart raced, and tears stung her eyes.

"Is that you, Rosa? Is that... is that..." she walked towards Rosa, who handed the baby to her.

Gina took a deep breath as she cradled her child. "He's grown so much," she said, kissing his cheeks as tears streamed down her face. "What are you doing here? Oh my God, he's grown so big."

Seth emerged from the shadows, and Rosa stepped aside.

Gina wiped her tears to clear her vision. Seth stood right before her, and she wondered if she was dreaming.

"Hey," Seth said softly.

"Hey," Gina replied, her voice trembling.

Seth moved closer. "Firstly, I want to apologise for everything. For everything I put you through. Honestly, I've never been so scared in my life. I thought I had lost you. I've never felt this way about anyone before. You make me feel things I've never felt. At first, I was scared and vulnerable because you made me act differently. My heart yearned for you, and my mind couldn't rest. I couldn't get you off my mind. You are the best thing that has ever happened to me. I love you, Gina. I don't think I can live without you. I don't know how it happened, but you caught me. I want to spend my life with you. I want to have my children with you. I want you in my arms always. I'm crazy for you," he said, his breath mingling with hers. He gently lifted her chin. "Please be mine," he whispered, his nose touching hers.

Rosa took the baby from Gina, who chuckled through her tears.

"I will," Gina said, and Seth kissed her.

They broke the kiss when the lights came on and everyone started clapping.

Gina felt shy and buried her face in Seth's chest. Stephanie was there with her baby.

Gina looked around—Liam was there with a little boy on wheels, Rosa with her son, Stephanie, and her aunt and mom. Her mom smiled emotionlessly. Seth's hand slid a cold, thick ring onto her finger.

"Spend the rest of your life with me, please," Seth said, kissing her hand.

"I will," Gina replied, and they embraced.

They walked into Gina's room. Gina felt a bit uneasy; her room was nothing compared to his expansive one.

"This is my room," she said.

"It's beautiful," Seth replied.

"Thank you," she said. They sat on the bed, and Seth began to express his regret about leaving her in the hospital. Gina listened attentively.

They lay back on the bed, and she questioned him about various things, including the inheritance. They stayed awake through the night, sharing stories.

Despite the awkwardness, their connection felt different—a kindling fire that would never burn out.

The next day, Liam left, but Seth, Rosa, and the kids stayed a few more days. Sarah returned to the city, and Stephanie went back to work. Geraldine struggled to accept Seth but pushed them forward for the sake of the children.

Gina marveled at how her life had unfolded. In just under three years, everything had changed. She had never imagined she would have two children and be on the brink of marriage. It was surreal to think of herself as a bride-to-be.

BONUS CHAPTER

Gina waited while Seth finished his meetings.

He kept glancing through the glass wall of his office to check if she was still there, and she smiled back every time.

When he finally walked into the office, he took her into his arms. "Sorry, I made you wait," he said, pulling her into a kiss.

"Hm hm," someone cleared their throat, interrupting them. They pulled apart to see Liam standing by the door, with Montserrat behind him.

"Sorry to interrupt yourrr romantic moment," Liam said with a smirk.

"The gown and suit are ready," Montserrat announced.

Seth signaled for Gina to go first, and he followed behind her. Liam rolled his eyes slightly. To him it's an eyesore seeing Seth being romantic.

At the boutique, Gina was taken to a room where she could try on her wedding gown. After she found the perfect dress, they took pre-wedding pictures, and then Seth and Gina went out for their first date.

Gina could hardly believe everything that was happening; it all felt surreal. But the reality hit her hard when Seth stared deeply into her eyes, slid the ring onto her finger, and declared their fate together. As he gently pulled down her sleeve and held her close, she wanted to savor the moment forever. He was hers through thick and thin, in sickness and in health, until death do them part.

She closed her eyes as Seth buried his face in her neck, his touch sending shivers down her spine. She let herself get lost in the moment, feeling her whole body crave him. Seth knew exactly how to satisfy her, and she responded eagerly, letting herself fall apart as he embraced her.

Gina arrived at the VIP room, where her friends were waiting.

"What took you so long, girl?" Nicki asked.

"I had to put the kids to sleep," Gina replied.

"Oh, right... the kids," Nicki said.

"So, how about the guy?" Stephanie asked.

"The guy?" Gina echoed, and Nora laughed.

"We're here to have fun!" Nicki exclaimed.

"Yes!" Nora added.

"Look who's here!" Stephanie said, downing a glass of whisky.

"Lucy!" Nicki called out.

"Why are you calling her?" Stephanie asked, pulling Nicki's hand back.

"Oh... she's with someone," Nora said.

"Wait... Is that Liam?" Gina asked, surprised.

"You know him?" Nora asked.

"He's my husband's friend, I'm not sure. I thought Lucy was engaged," Gina said.

"It's Lucy, girl," Stephanie said, flipping her hand.

"But wait..." Nora said, "What did you say?"

"Me?" Gina asked.

"My husband?" Nora repeated.

"You heard that right!" Nicki said, laughing.

"I was thinking the same thing!" Nicki added, still laughing.

The girls joined in the laughter, while Gina sat shaking her head. "Can y'all stop?"

"Cheers, please," Nicki said, raising her glass.

"Gina?"

"No, I don't drink... anymore," she said, and the others exchanged glances before bursting into laughter again.

"Alright, that's cool, that's cool," Stephanie said, and they drank up.

"Guess you'll have to go home early too?" Nora asked.

"Yeah," Gina replied.

"Shit, I was joking," Nora said.

"I have kids at home," Gina explained.

"Kids, you've already put to sleep," Stephanie said.

"Yes, Janina wakes up often at night," Gina said.

"Shit... God knows I can't handle that," Nicki said.

"Be careful what you say," Gina said.

"Ugh, those tiny humans can be annoying," Nicki said.

"They're cute and adorable," Gina countered.

"Duh," Nicki said.

"Hey, look at that," Nicki pointed out to a guy.

"Ooohhh," Nora said.

"Hotty," Nicki added.

"Should I remind you, Nicki, that you're married, Stephanie, you're engaged, and Nora, you have a boyfriend?" Gina said.

"Pff... so we can't drool over a hottie?" Nicki said.

"Is it my eyes, or is he coming over here?" Nora asked.

"Oh my God," Nicki said, adjusting her outfit as the guy approached them.

341

"Hey ladies," he greeted.

"Hey, handsome," they chorused as Gina rolled her eyes.

"Can I get y'all more drinks?" he asked.

"Sure," they replied.

Gina felt embarrassed and took a sip of her water.

"Hey, beautiful," he said to Gina, making her nearly choke.

"Sorry," he said, rubbing her back. Gina shrugged it off.

"Wait," he said, using his handkerchief to wipe some water from her lips, their faces uncomfortably close.

Suddenly, a hand grabbed the guy and yanked him away from Gina.

"Shit!" Nora screamed.

"F*ck!" Nicki shouted simultaneously, and Gina screamed.

The guy took a series of blows to the face, with Seth delivering each hit.

"Seth. Stop!" Gina screamed, but Seth continued to hit the guy.

"Seth! Stop!" Gina shouted again. Seth halted and turned to her, only to receive a blow to the face himself. Gina jumped in between them, staring at Seth with desperation. She walked out of the room, with Seth chasing after her.

They drove home in silence. Gina wiped her tears away until they arrived. She walked in first and went straight to their room, sitting on the bed. Seth entered slowly, standing by the door, pulling at his collar.

"Why did you do that?" Gina finally asked.

"He was touching you and trying to kiss you," Seth said.

"He wasn't trying to kiss me; he was just wiping some water off my face," Gina explained.

"Did you see the way he was looking at you? He was watching you the whole time!" Seth asked.

"The whole time?" Gina replied.

"I was watching him!" Seth admitted.

"You followed me?" Gina asked, standing up and pointing at herself.

"No, I... it was late," Seth stammered.

"You don't trust me," Gina said.

"Of course I do," Seth insisted. Gina sighed.

"You know what? I don't want to do this," Gina said, walking out of the room.

Seth sat on the bed, feeling dejected. Gina returned later with an aid kit. She placed it on the bed and began tending to his wounds.

"You shouldn't be so overprotective of me. I can take care of myself," Gina said.

"I know... I just can't stand seeing anyone around you," Seth replied.

Gina chuckled softly. "Are you laughing?" He asked,

"Just... smiling," she said, cupping his face in her hands.

"I love you and no one else," she said, kissing him.

"I love you crazy," Seth said, wrapping his arms around her waist and drawing her close. She wrapped her arms around his neck. Seth laid her on the bed, and they shared a passionate kiss as lightning struck and rain began to fall, creating the perfect moment.

BEING HIS WIFE

Foreword

It all started with the desire to leave home and get a good job and most importantly, to avoid her mom's nagging and prove to her that she is better and to the world that she can survive if she keeps on following her principle.

But life never gives it to us the way we want. It's the same for Gina.

She's a young Christian girl raised by a born-again, devout Christian mother. But living under the same roof after university with her mother wasn't easy.

When her best friend Nicki, a popular chain bar manager, offered her a deal on surrogacy, Gina knew that it wasn't possible but then surrogacy was a much better option than her messed-up family. There's her elder sister, who's busy messing up marriages because of greed and a younger sister, who's living a wayward life behind their mothers backs.

She thought of how messed up her life might turn out to be under her mother, made up her mind, lied to her her family and went to become a surrogate for a man she never knew.

But it wasn't what or how she thought it would be.

"What! For goodness sake, Gina, all you have to do is get that shit inside of you, get pregnant, give him the baby and get paid millions! Billions! What's wrong with you?!" Nicki had said.

But it wasn't that easy; it wasn't easy dealing with a man like Seth and his goddamn rules.

°°°••°°°

For Seth, it has always been money, ever since he lost his parents. so far as

He puts his mind to it. He commands, not obeys.

He is someone who believes that once you have money, you can do anything and control anyone. Just like someone he adored most, his grandmother.

But when it came to Gina, his mind was always blank; she made him vulnerable and weird, and he barely recognised himself in front of her. And he hated that effect so he guarded.

He just wanted to use her to get the inheritance his late grandmother left for the family, which he is sure he is most eligible to get. Once she gives him the baby, he'll end the contract, and she'll leave for wherever she came from. He never wanted to fall into her trap but it happened anyway.

He lost himself to love. Funny how selfless and vulnerable love makes one.

When the contract was over, Mighty Seth fell in love and made love with Gina and she got pregnant again!

Unbelievable, Gina thought.

Scared and knowing she'd messed up upon the already existing mess, she ran home.

When in chaos, we always end up choosing the already existing solution look alike, no matter how uncomfortable it might be. We choose it, and then we take our time to figure things out.

But it felt real when Seth came knocking at her door. Unbelievable!

But she was left to choose between the kind and sexy single father living in their neighbourhood and the mean, rich, and annoying Seth.

But then, love has a very funny and manipulative way of making things happen the way it wants.

Gina thought having two children for him was enough to make him choose him, but that was an excuse.

Clearly, both of them don't know what hit them. Seth barely knew how to love, but when it came to Gina, he could barely get her out of his mind; his heart changed rhythm and this weird desire came up. He just knew he wanted her and she's his and no one can have her but him.

Gina, on the other hand, has seen it all around, from her dad to stepdad's to her mom and sisters and she's been in one relationship herself. If she had followed her principle, she wouldn't have fallen for Seth, but there's nothing she could do. She couldn't stop the feeling; she liked it.

What she doesn't know very well is what she got herself into by choosing the annoying and arrogant Seth.

Trying to get comfortable with Seth, making him understand that she's his and no one else's, and dealing with his family. Of the many things she had to deal with, just like before, life never gives it to us the way we want.

All in all, having a woman who's willing and able to stand beside her man through thick and thin—that is Gina.

Seth is one lucky man.

About The Author

A.P. Harriet

Harriet is an intelligence analyst, an artist, a chef, a singer, and a writer. She is a multi-talented lady passionate about creating a simple life for as many people as possible.

Books In This Series

Being His Wife

They thought it was over, but it was just getting started.

Seth and Gina got married, and with their two children, they made a family.

The inheritance was shared, but not everybody was happy about it.

The fight is not over until it's over.

There's a lot at risk, and there's a lot no one expected.

Enemies, revenge, claims, love, money, and power!

All in one!

The Surrogate Proposal 2!

Being His Wife

The Surrogate Proposal

Made in the USA
Columbia, SC
05 October 2024